THE RED HOOK

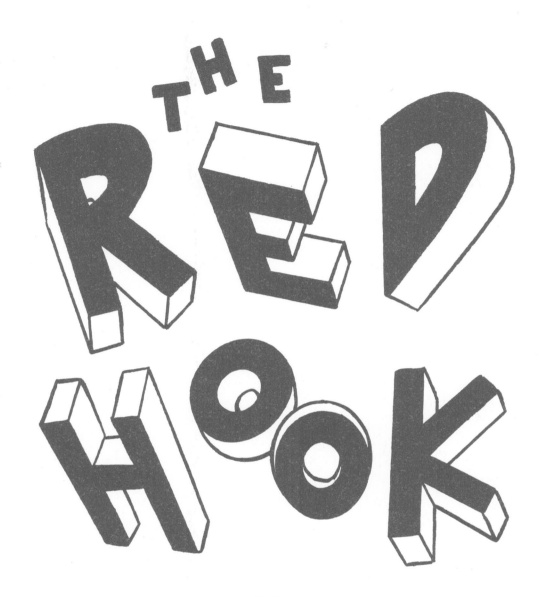

BY
DEAN HASPIEL

GRAPHIC
Red Hook
v1

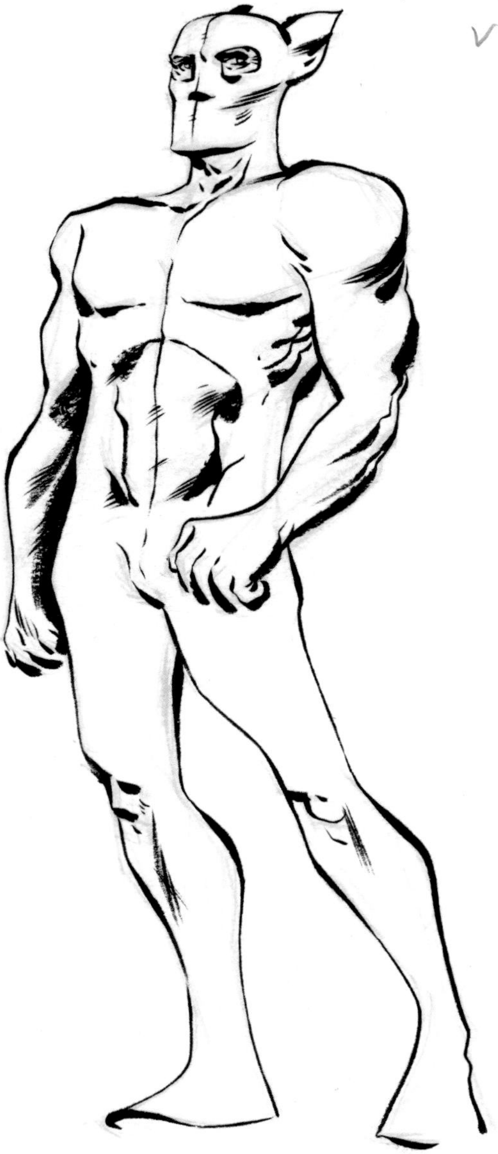

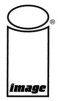

"New Brooklyn" is dedicated to the late/great Seth Kushner.

Thanks to Tom Akel, LINE Webtoon, Eric Stephenson, Drew Gill, the Image Comics crew, Vito Delsante, Christa Cassano, Jen Ferguson, Hang Dai Studios, Ricardo Venâncio, The Atlantic Center for the Arts, and Yaddo.

Inspired by the works of Jack Kirby, Joe Blair, Irwin Hasen, Alex Toth, Will Eisner, Steve Ditko, Bill Parker, C. C. Beck, Stan Lee, Gerry Conway, Al Milgrom, Ben Oda, and Frank Miller. Thank you!

"New Brooklyn" first appeared as *The Red Hook season one* at LINE Webtoon and won a Ringo Award for Best Webcomic of 2017. "Emotional Ebola" first appeared as a 3-part story in *Dark Horse Presents #29–31*. "Hooking The Red Hook" first appeared in Dean Haspiel's *Psychotronic Comics #1*, and later in Erik Larsen's *Savage Dragon #216*.

Production and design for this collection by Drew Gill with Dean Haspiel.

IMAGE COMICS, INC. • Robert Kirkman: Chief Operating Officer • Erik Larsen: Chief Financial Officer • Todd McFarlane: President • Marc Silvestri: Chief Executive Officer • Jim Valentino: Vice President • Eric Stephenson: Publisher / Chief Creative Officer • Corey Hart: Director of Sales • Jeff Boison: Director of Publishing Planning & Book Trade Sales • Chris Ross: Director of Digital Sales • Jeff Stang: Director of Specialty Sales • Kat Salazar: Director of PR & Marketing • Drew Gill: Art Director • Heather Doornink: Production Director • Nicole Lapalme: Controller • IMAGECOMICS.COM

INTRODUCTION BY DEAN HASPIEL

On the brink of the 21st century, Brooklyn confirmed herself to be a haven for many Manhattan refugees, including myself, fleeing the "Big Apple" to sustain a freelance lifestyle in NYC. But, over the years, she, too, has become outrageously expensive and a brutal challenge to maintain a good quality of life, as fellow artists and entrepreneurs make their exodus upstate or to other, more affordable destinations in America. NYC is no longer interested in underwriting the avant garde and cultivating soothsayers. It got bamboozled by real estate developers more concerned with leasing empty spaces that hemorrhage money and often stay empty. An evil shell game of dog-eat-dog, while local bodegas and art spaces vacate and resurrect into a deluge of banks and all-purpose pharmacies, where cultural and culinary institutions of the past vex us with their historical significance like ghosts.

After I conceived a short *Red Hook* story in 2012, a "what would happen if Jack Kirby and Alex Toth co-created a superhero" experiment as a creative palette cleanser my first night on retreat at Yaddo (the legendary artists/writers colony in Saratoga Springs, NY), my then studiomate and great friend, the late Seth Kushner, created *The Brooklynite*. He was an amazing photographer who loved comic books and wanted to produce them, too. He'd been writing a comix memoir illustrated by an array of artists called "Schmuck," done in the spirit of Harvey Pekar's *American Splendor*. Seth was in search of a collaborator for *The Brooklynite* which he eventually found in Shamus Beyale. But, back then, we'd threatened to produce a two-man Brooklyn comics anthology done in the spirit of the 1960s Marvel Comics *Tales To Astonish* series, where I'd draw my *Red Hook* stories and Seth would write *The Brooklynite*. But, paying gigs got in the way and, tragically, Seth got cancer and passed away. When editor Tom Akel approached me at a New York comic convention in 2015, and asked me to pitch something for the LINE Webtoon App, I thought about *The Red Hook,* yet wanted to honor Seth's posthumous superhero. I needed a spectacular hook to give our independent characters a common theme to tether them.

When the white flags replaced the American flags on the Brooklyn Bridge for one week in 2014, a stunt perpetrated by German artists, I thought about a way to give Brooklyn a good science-fiction/John Carpenter-inspired twist. And, so, Brooklyn reveals herself to be sentient; whose heart was broken by the apathy and indifference of the world, and she physically secedes from NYC, ergo, America, to spark a "New Brooklyn" where art can be bartered for food and services. Where technology is scrutinized and property is intellectual. And, the day-to-day operating system becomes a grass roots commitment towards community and culture for a better quality of life while inadvertently causing a pandemic of new heroes and villains. Which also meant she needed an avatar, a cosmic guardian to speak for Brooklyn's heart and protect it. So, I also co-created *The Purple Heart* with writer Vito Delsante and artist Ricardo Venâncio. I pitched the idea of a *New Brooklyn Universe* to Tom Akel and he loved it. He asked for one comic and got three (with a fourth concept brewing called *Aquaria*, written by Adam McGovern and illustrated by Paolo Leandri, in our back pocket)!

I think what makes Brooklyn a force for consistently manifesting superheroes comes from the fact that blue collar workers and war veterans like Jack Kirby and Will Eisner, and a slew of other progenitors of the comix form, hailed from Kings County. Kinda like Neil Armstrong planting the American flag on the moon, they got there first and Brooklyn is where the genesis of many famous cartoonists created extraordinary characters to deal with extremely tough times dating as far back as Captain America punching out Adolf Hitler during World War II. Lots of heroes and stories are spawned from war and economic strife. And, as a creator, I think it's important for writers and artists to express what they want the future to be. It helps us make sense of the world and, hopefully, makes it better.

"New Brooklyn" is dedicated to Brooklynite Seth Kushner. Schmuck. Mensch. Superhero.

Dean Haspiel
April, 2018

Emmy and Ringo award winner Dean Haspiel created *Billy Dogma*, and The Red Hook. He illustrated for HBO's *Bored To Death*, is a Yaddo fellow, a playwright, and helped pioneer personal webcomics. Dino has written, drawn and collaborated on many superheroes (including *The Fox*, *Spider-Man*, *Wonder Woman*, *Deadpool*, *X-Men*, *Batman*, *The Fantastic Four*, *Godzilla*, and *Mars Attacks*), and literary graphic novels (including *The Quitter*, and *American Splendor* with Harvey Pekar, and *The Alcoholic* with Jonathan Ames) for DC/Vertigo, Marvel, Archie, IDW, Dark Horse, Heavy Metal, and LINE Webtoon.

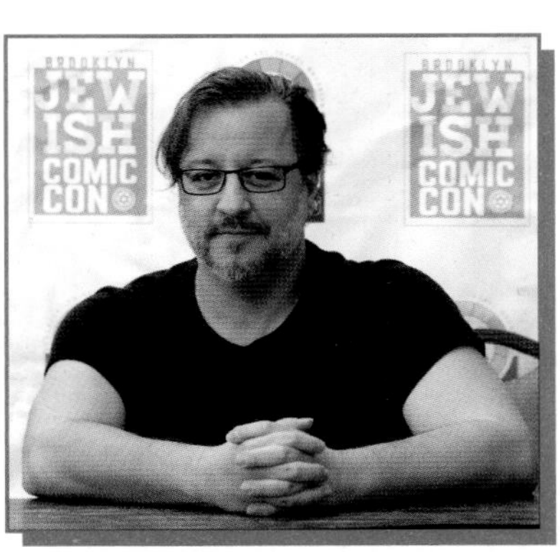
JEWISH COMIC CON
JEWISH COMIC CON

Photo by Julian Voloj.

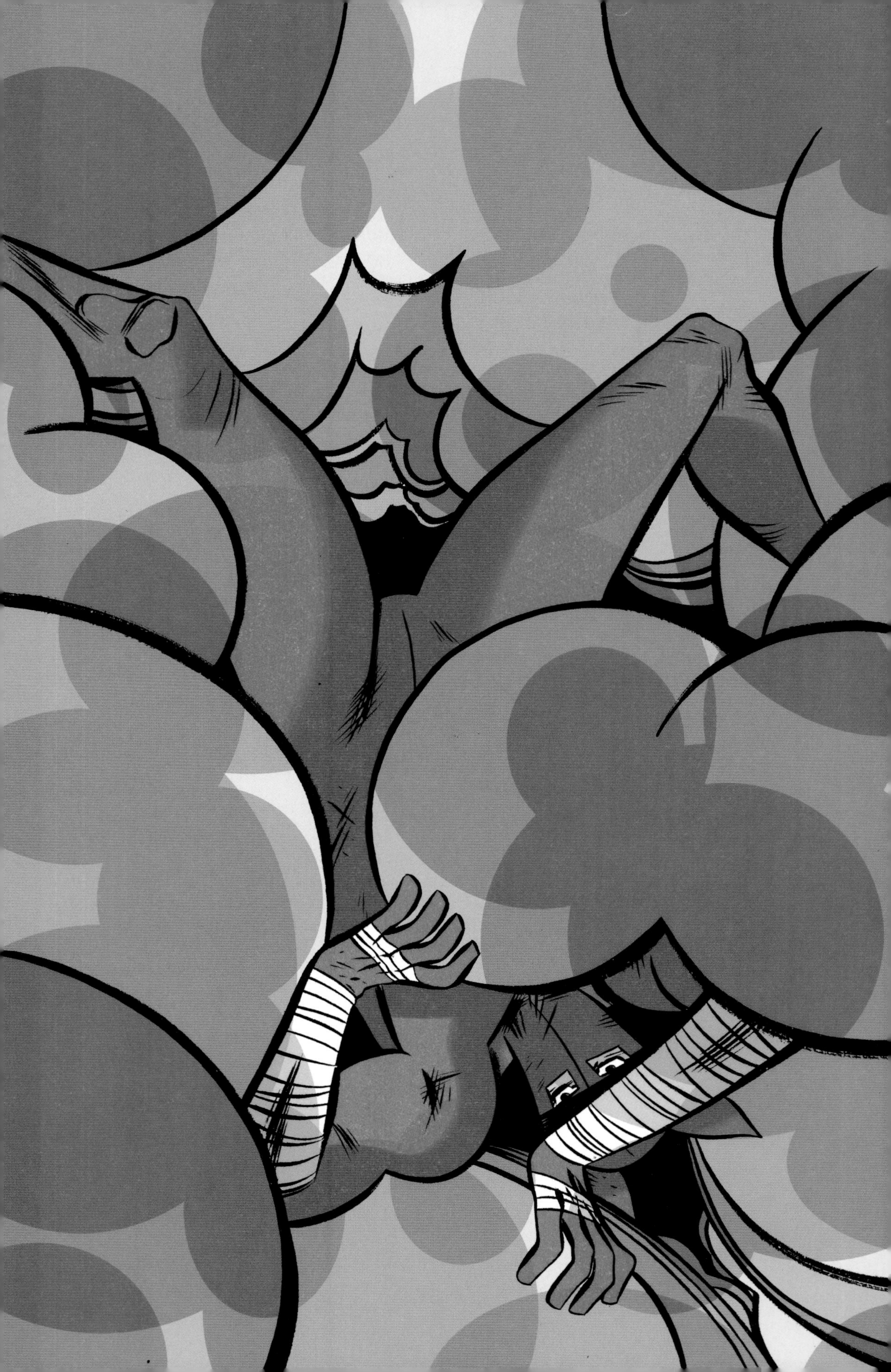

WHILE MY BETTER HALF, THE POSSUM, IS BUSY SEEDING A DOUBLE-CROSS WITH MAFIA KINGPIN BENSON HURST--

THE RED HOOK IN
"EMOTIONAL EBOLA" PART ONE
BY DEAN HASPIEL

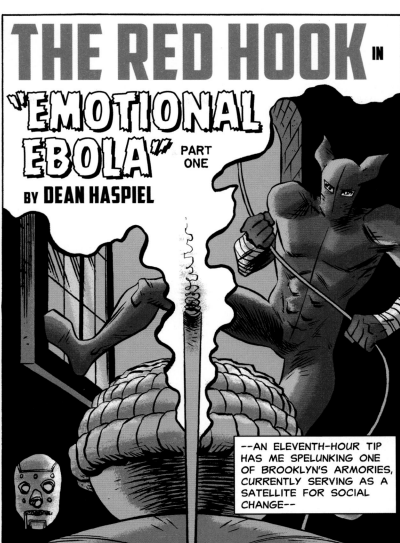

--AN ELEVENTH-HOUR TIP HAS ME SPELUNKING ONE OF BROOKLYN'S ARMORIES, CURRENTLY SERVING AS A SATELLITE FOR SOCIAL CHANGE--

--WHILE CONCEALING A PENTHOUSE HOSTING THE VENUS OF BEDFORD-STUYVESANT, READY FOR FETCHING!

A PLATINUM-PLATED PEACE OFFERING MEANT TO REPLACE YE OLDE "BED-STUY, DO OR DIE" SLOGAN WITH--

SLAM

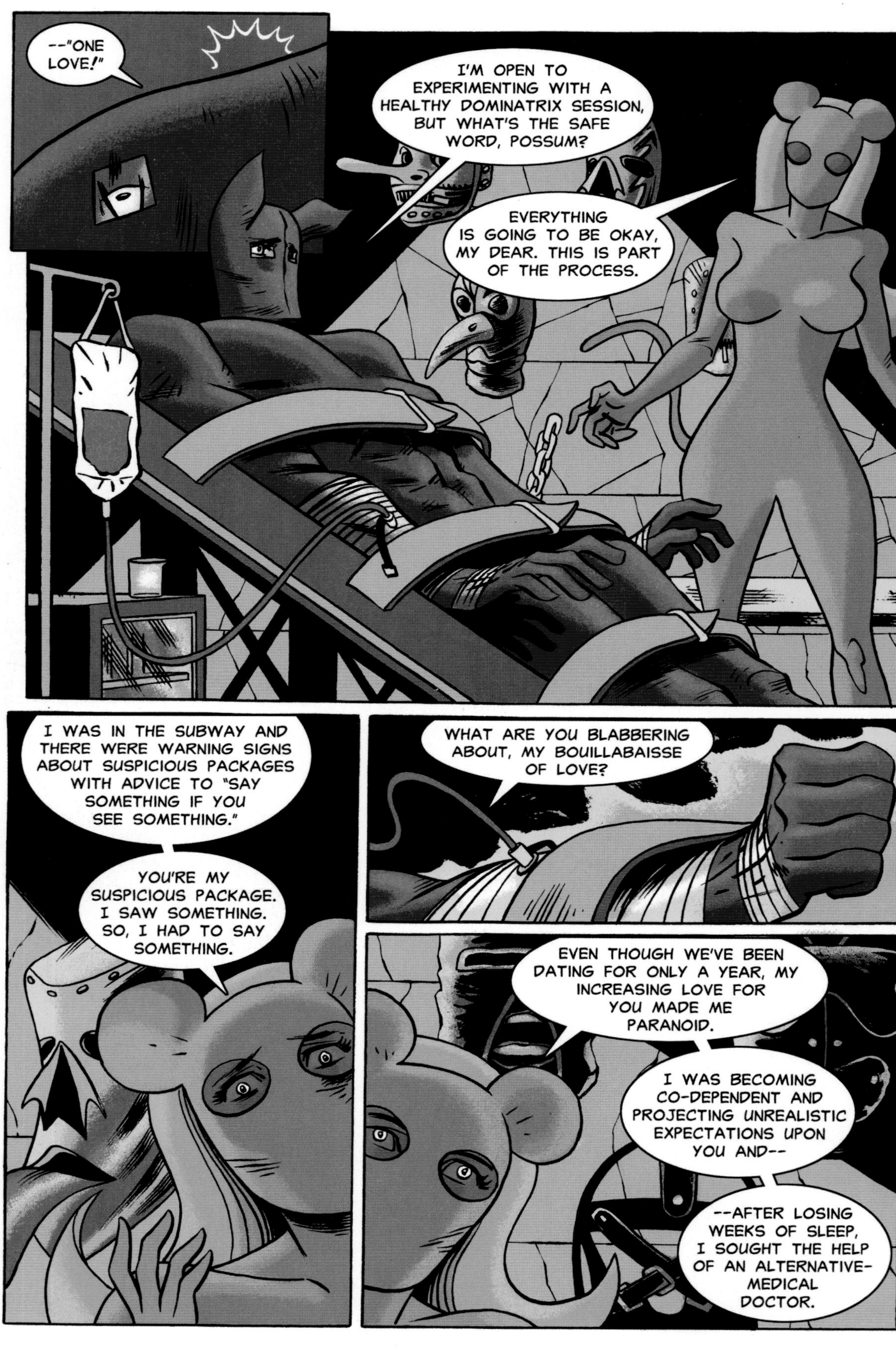
--"ONE LOVE!"
I'M OPEN TO EXPERIMENTING WITH A HEALTHY DOMINATRIX SESSION, BUT WHAT'S THE SAFE WORD, POSSUM?
EVERYTHING IS GOING TO BE OKAY, MY DEAR. THIS IS PART OF THE PROCESS.
I WAS IN THE SUBWAY AND THERE WERE WARNING SIGNS ABOUT SUSPICIOUS PACKAGES WITH ADVICE TO "SAY SOMETHING IF YOU SEE SOMETHING."
YOU'RE MY SUSPICIOUS PACKAGE. I SAW SOMETHING. SO, I HAD TO SAY SOMETHING.
WHAT ARE YOU BLABBERING ABOUT, MY BOUILLABAISSE OF LOVE?
EVEN THOUGH WE'VE BEEN DATING FOR ONLY A YEAR, MY INCREASING LOVE FOR YOU MADE ME PARANOID.
I WAS BECOMING CO-DEPENDENT AND PROJECTING UNREALISTIC EXPECTATIONS UPON YOU AND--
--AFTER LOSING WEEKS OF SLEEP, I SOUGHT THE HELP OF AN ALTERNATIVE-MEDICAL DOCTOR.

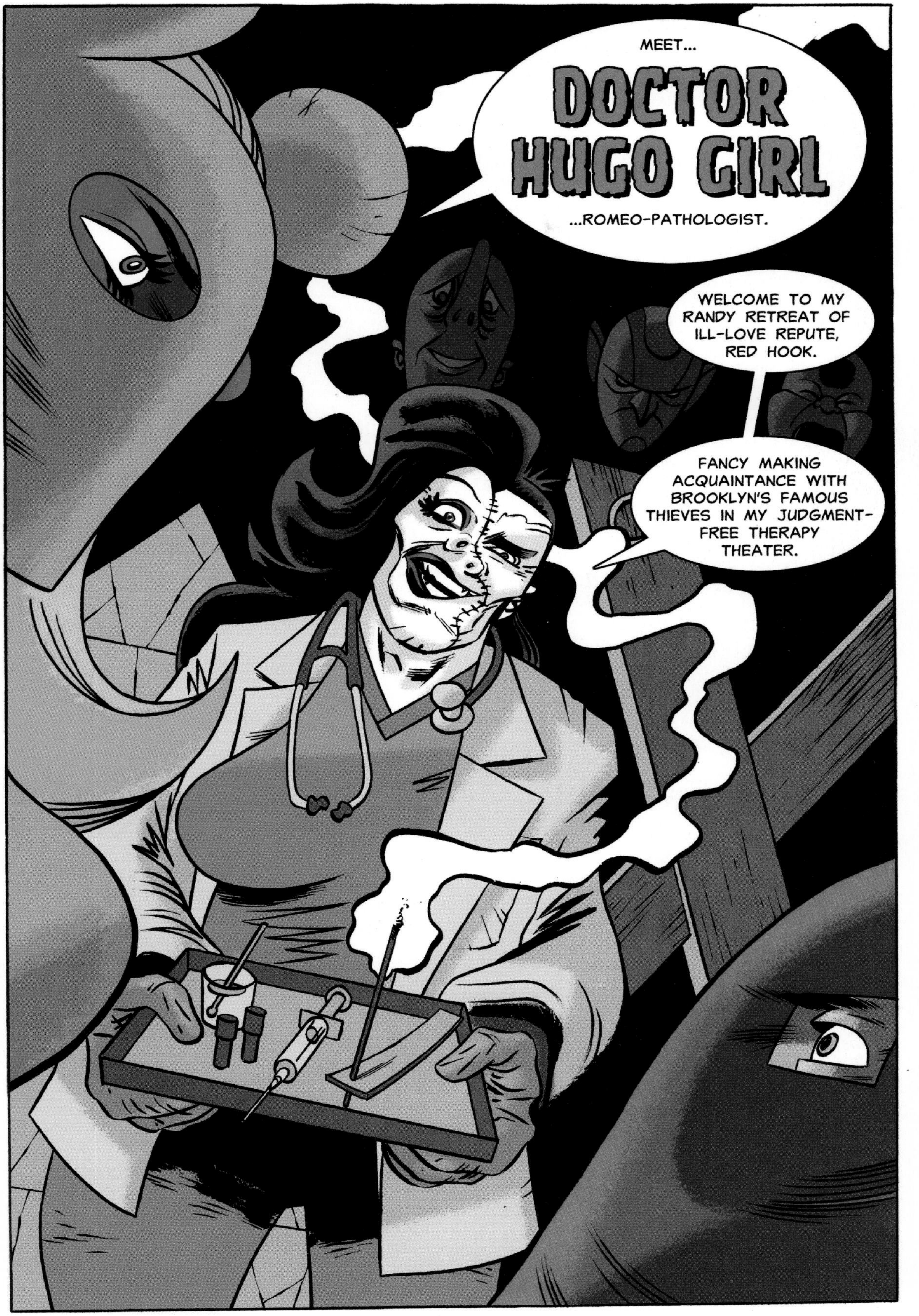
MEET... DOCTOR HUGO GIRL ...ROMEO-PATHOLOGIST.
WELCOME TO MY RANDY RETREAT OF ILL-LOVE REPUTE, RED HOOK.
FANCY MAKING ACQUAINTANCE WITH BROOKLYN'S FAMOUS THIEVES IN MY JUDGMENT-FREE THERAPY THEATER.

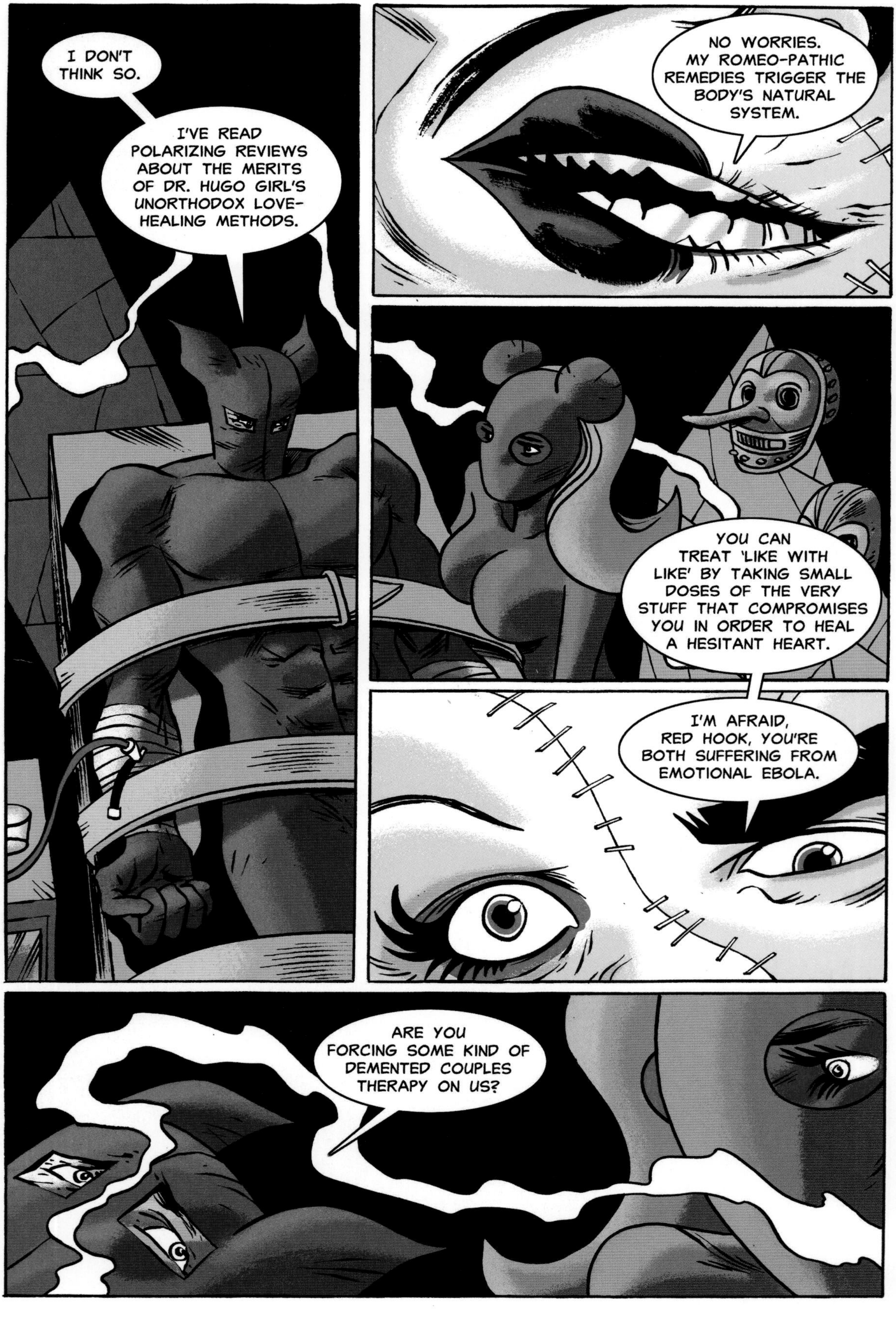
I DON'T THINK SO.
I'VE READ POLARIZING REVIEWS ABOUT THE MERITS OF DR. HUGO GIRL'S UNORTHODOX LOVE-HEALING METHODS.
NO WORRIES. MY ROMEO-PATHIC REMEDIES TRIGGER THE BODY'S NATURAL SYSTEM.
YOU CAN TREAT 'LIKE WITH LIKE' BY TAKING SMALL DOSES OF THE VERY STUFF THAT COMPROMISES YOU IN ORDER TO HEAL A HESITANT HEART.
I'M AFRAID, RED HOOK, YOU'RE BOTH SUFFERING FROM EMOTIONAL EBOLA.
ARE YOU FORCING SOME KIND OF DEMENTED COUPLES THERAPY ON US?

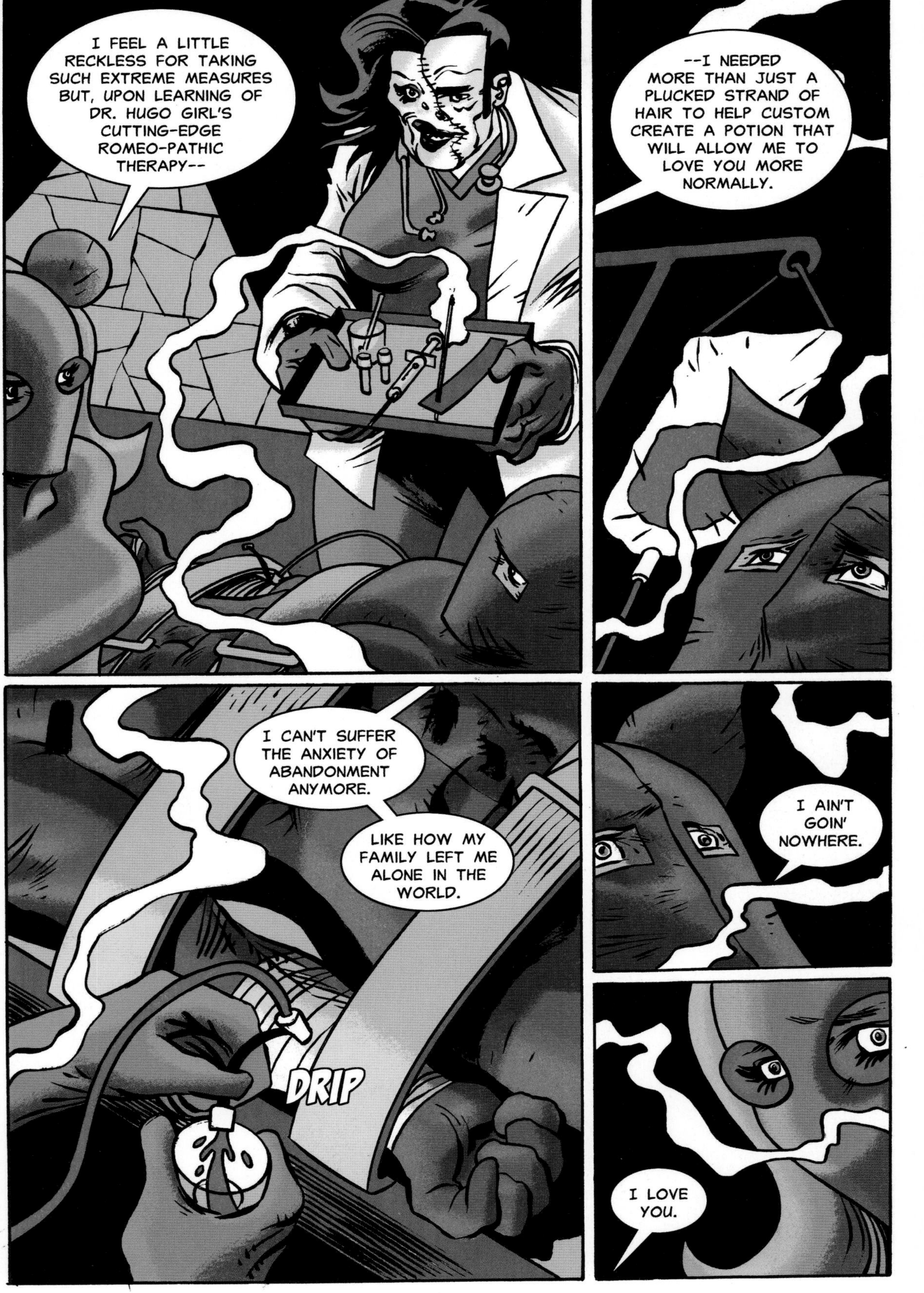
I FEEL A LITTLE RECKLESS FOR TAKING SUCH EXTREME MEASURES BUT, UPON LEARNING OF DR. HUGO GIRL'S CUTTING-EDGE ROMEO-PATHIC THERAPY--
--I NEEDED MORE THAN JUST A PLUCKED STRAND OF HAIR TO HELP CUSTOM CREATE A POTION THAT WILL ALLOW ME TO LOVE YOU MORE NORMALLY.
I CAN'T SUFFER THE ANXIETY OF ABANDONMENT ANYMORE.
LIKE HOW MY FAMILY LEFT ME ALONE IN THE WORLD.
DRIP
I AIN'T GOIN' NOWHERE.
I LOVE YOU.

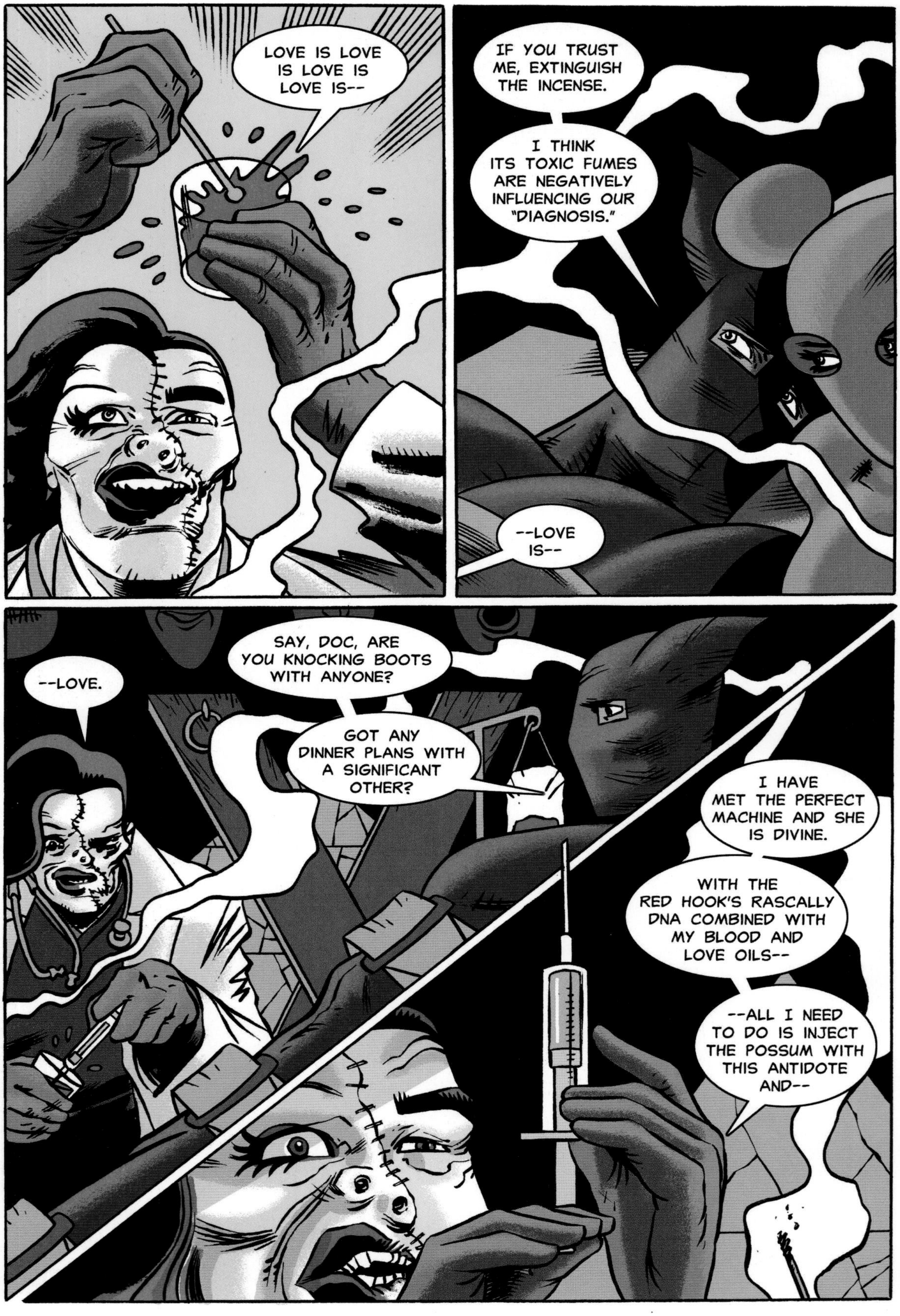
LOVE IS LOVE IS LOVE IS LOVE IS--
IF YOU TRUST ME, EXTINGUISH THE INCENSE.
I THINK ITS TOXIC FUMES ARE NEGATIVELY INFLUENCING OUR "DIAGNOSIS."
--LOVE IS--
--LOVE.
SAY, DOC, ARE YOU KNOCKING BOOTS WITH ANYONE?
GOT ANY DINNER PLANS WITH A SIGNIFICANT OTHER?
I HAVE MET THE PERFECT MACHINE AND SHE IS DIVINE.
WITH THE RED HOOK'S RASCALLY DNA COMBINED WITH MY BLOOD AND LOVE OILS--
--ALL I NEED TO DO IS INJECT THE POSSUM WITH THIS ANTIDOTE AND--

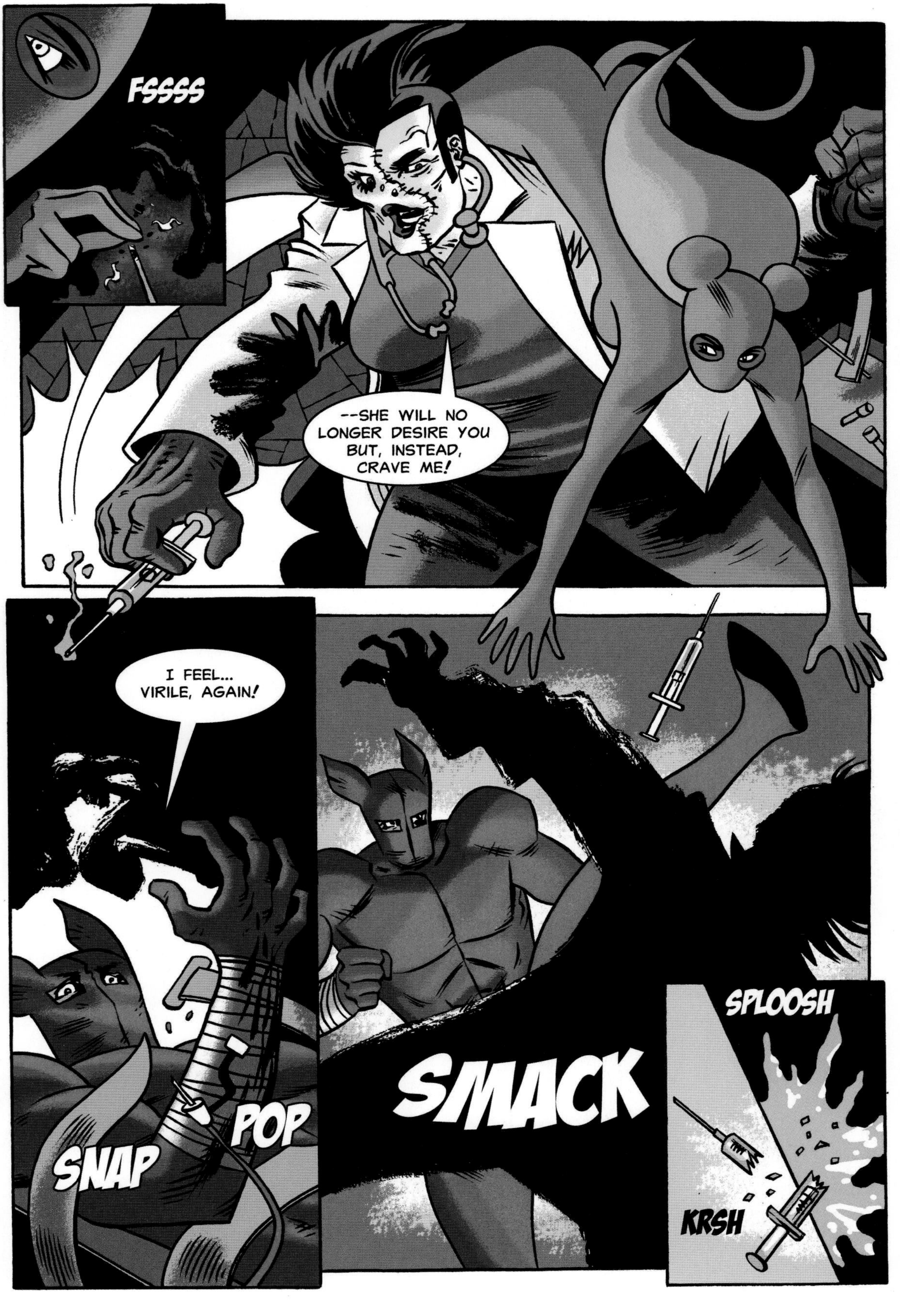
FSSSS
--SHE WILL NO LONGER DESIRE YOU BUT, INSTEAD, CRAVE ME!
I FEEL... VIRILE, AGAIN!
SNAP
POP
SMACK
SPLOOSH
KRSH

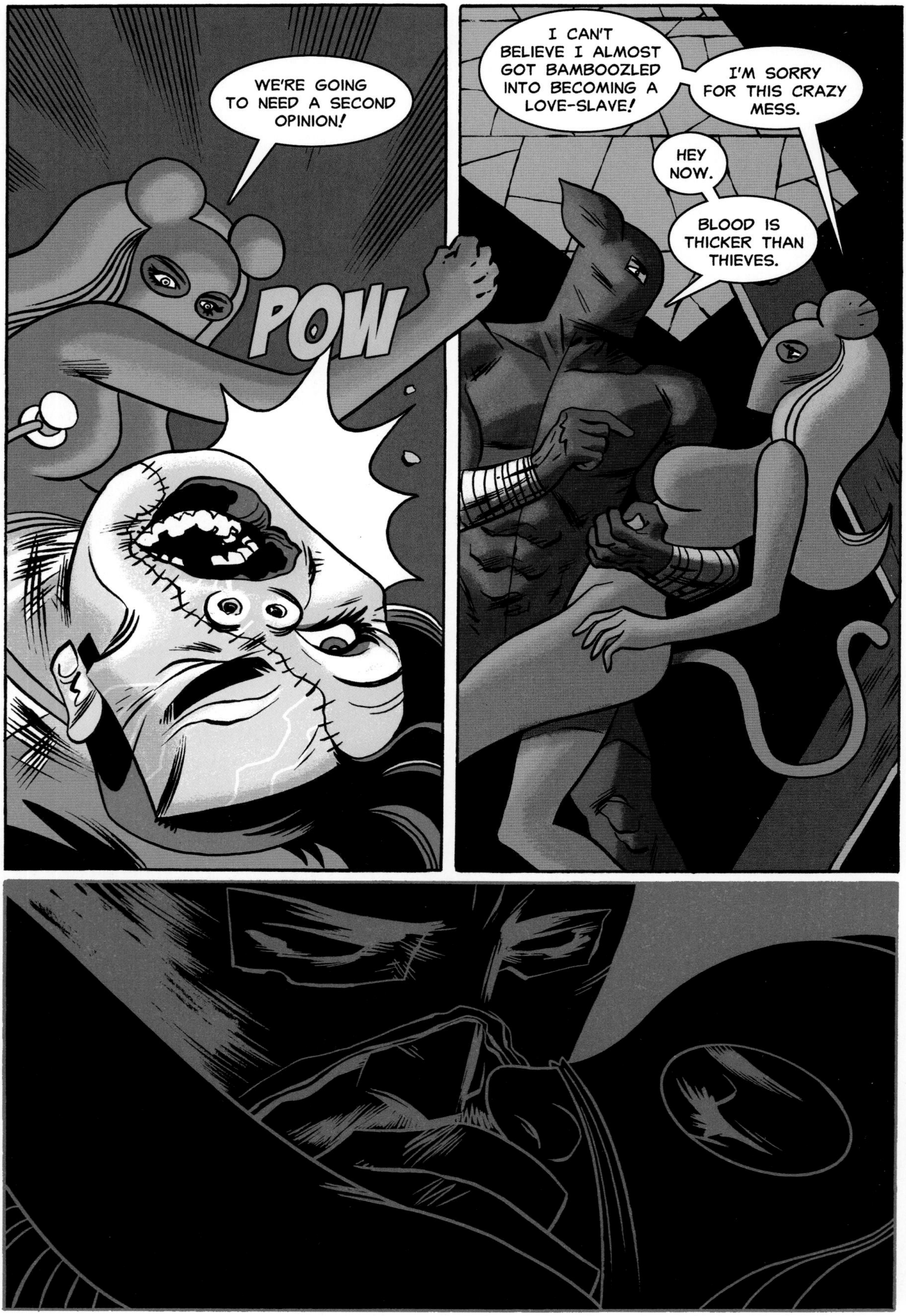
WE'RE GOING TO NEED A SECOND OPINION!
POW
I CAN'T BELIEVE I ALMOST GOT BAMBOOZLED INTO BECOMING A LOVE-SLAVE!
I'M SORRY FOR THIS CRAZY MESS.
HEY NOW.
BLOOD IS THICKER THAN THIEVES.

THE RED HOOK IN "EMOTIONAL EBOLA"

PART TWO

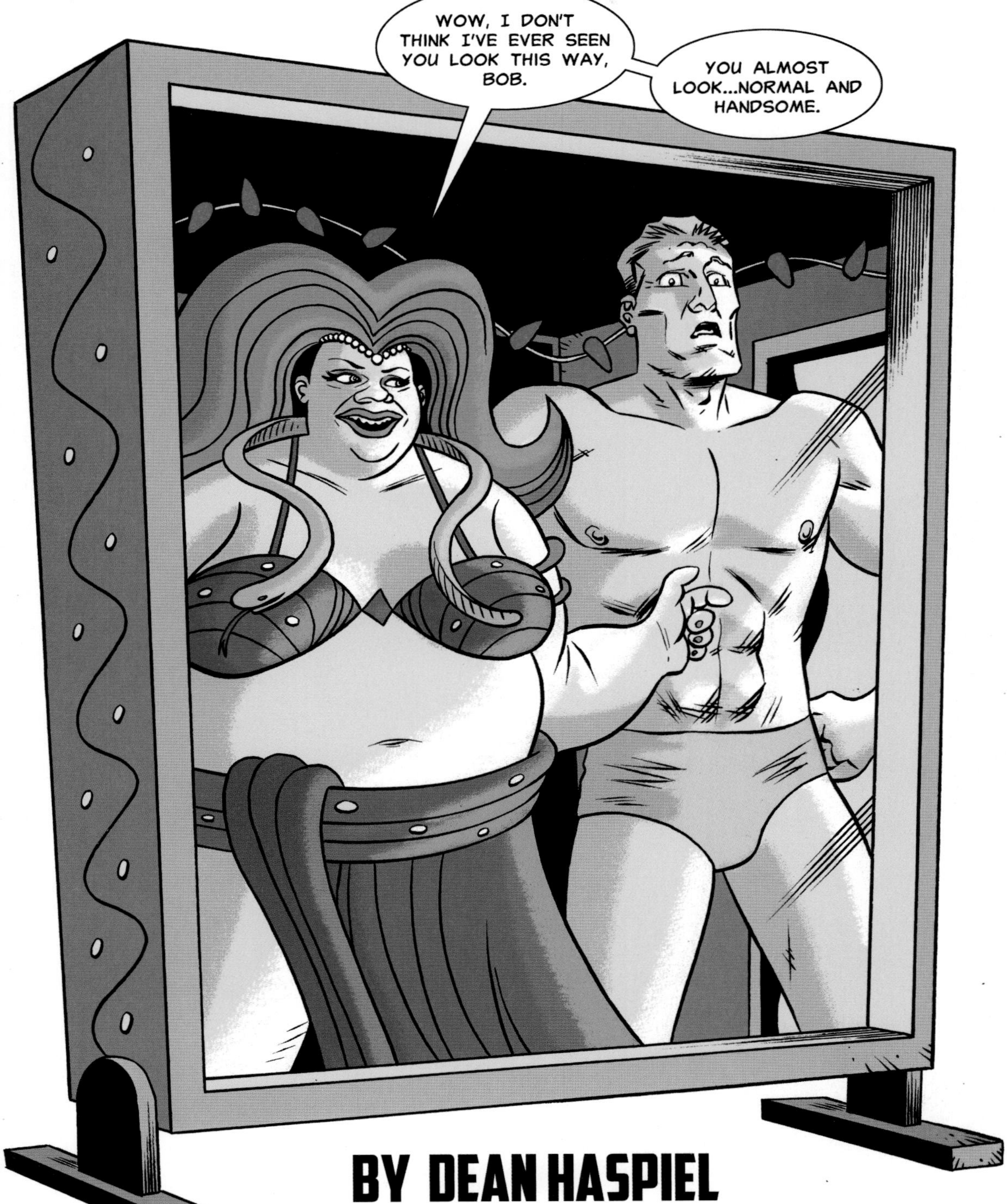
WOW, I DON'T THINK I'VE EVER SEEN YOU LOOK THIS WAY, BOB.
YOU ALMOST LOOK...NORMAL AND HANDSOME.

BY DEAN HASPIEL

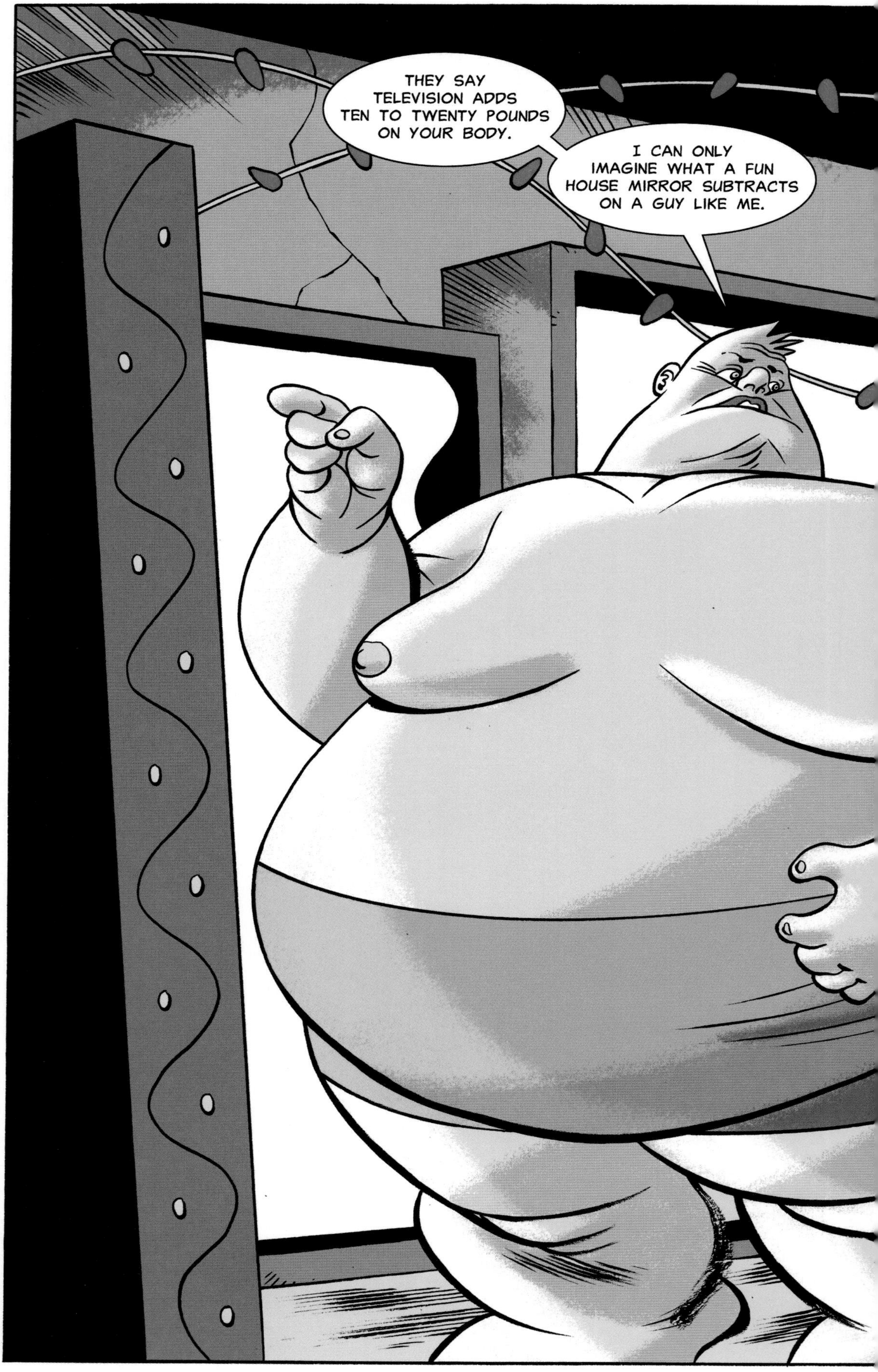
THEY SAY TELEVISION ADDS TEN TO TWENTY POUNDS ON YOUR BODY.
I CAN ONLY IMAGINE WHAT A FUN HOUSE MIRROR SUBTRACTS ON A GUY LIKE ME.

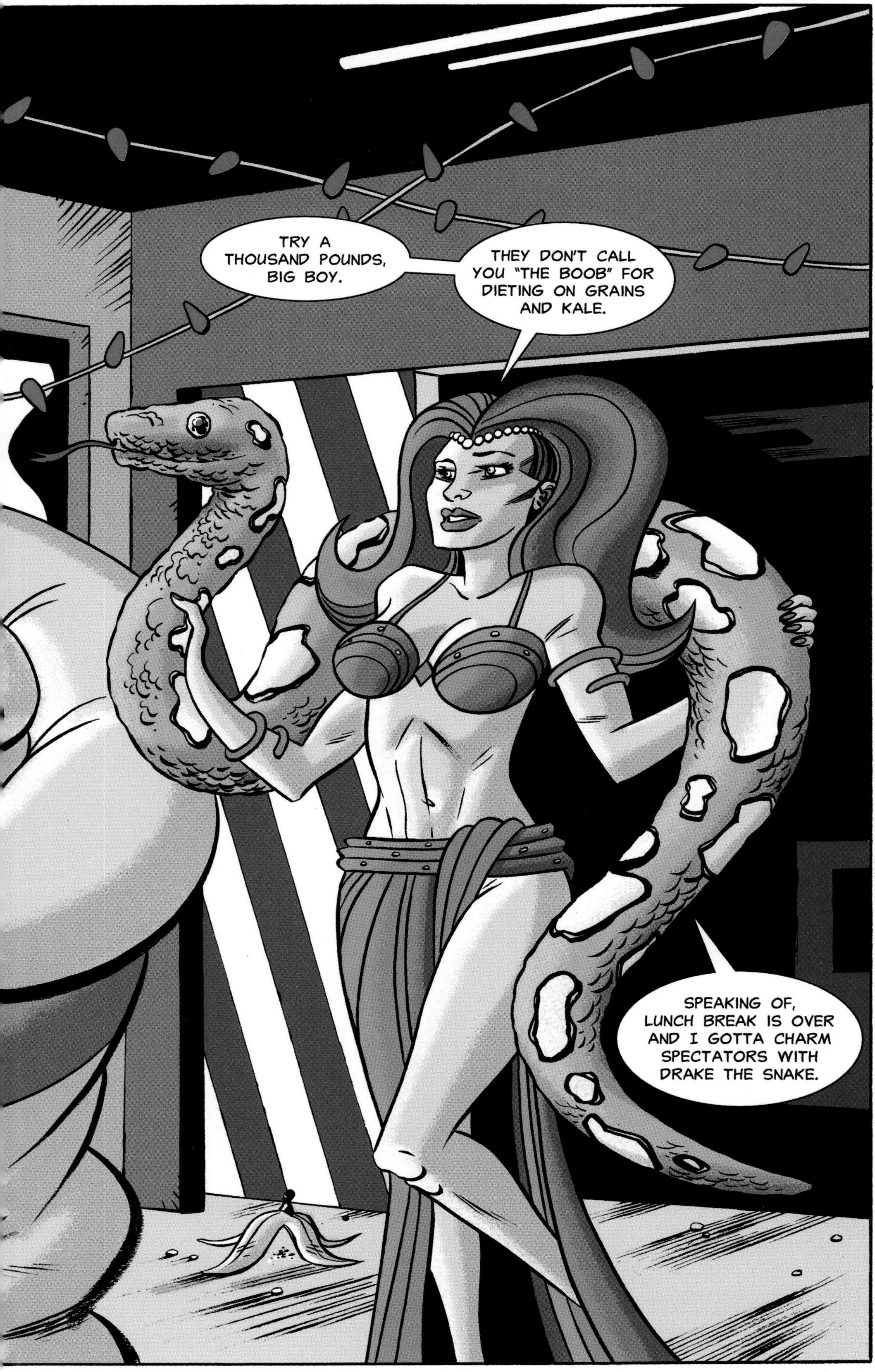
TRY A THOUSAND POUNDS, BIG BOY.
THEY DON'T CALL YOU "THE BOOB" FOR DIETING ON GRAINS AND KALE.
SPEAKING OF, LUNCH BREAK IS OVER AND I GOTTA CHARM SPECTATORS WITH DRAKE THE SNAKE.

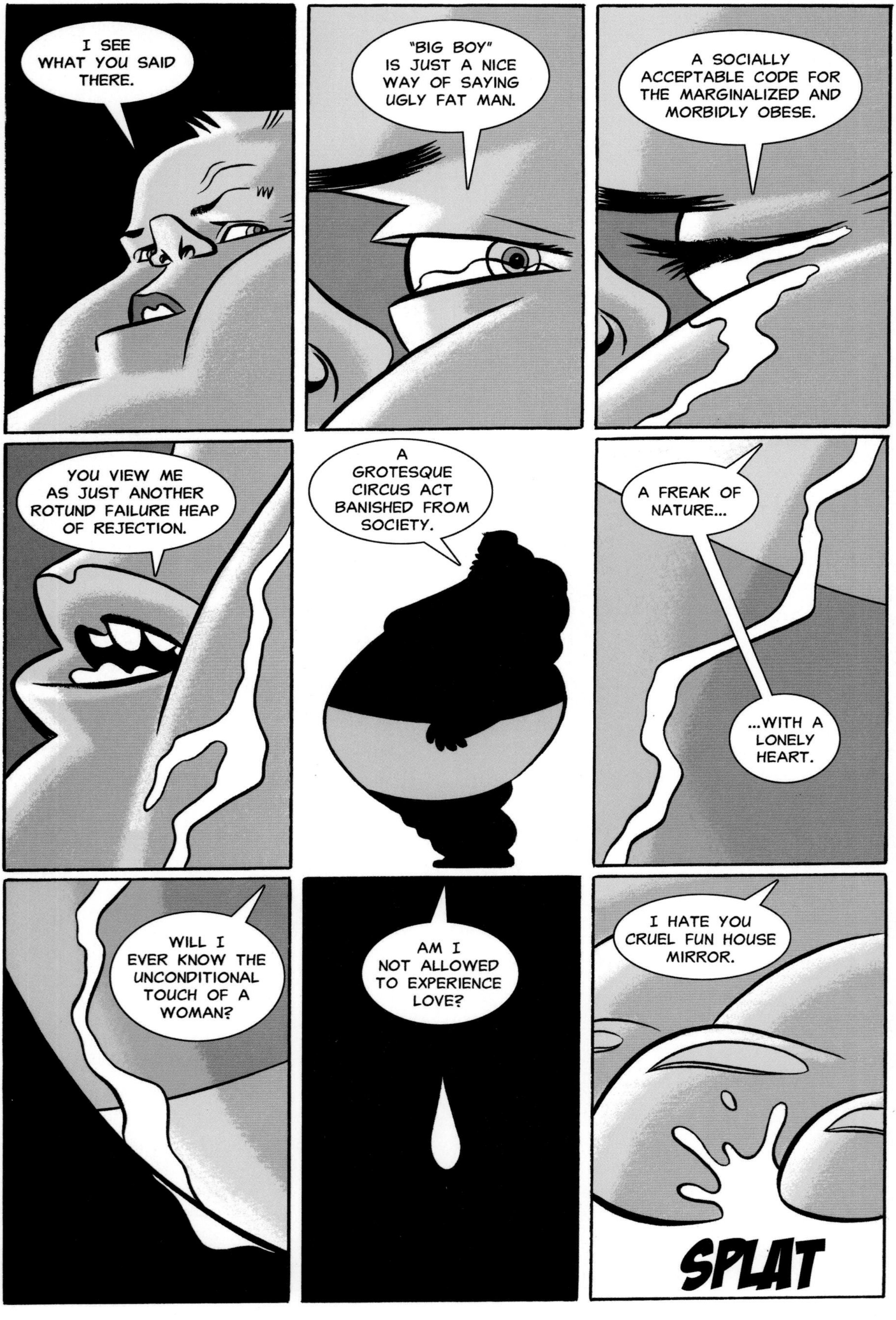
I SEE WHAT YOU SAID THERE.
"BIG BOY" IS JUST A NICE WAY OF SAYING UGLY FAT MAN.
A SOCIALLY ACCEPTABLE CODE FOR THE MARGINALIZED AND MORBIDLY OBESE.
YOU VIEW ME AS JUST ANOTHER ROTUND FAILURE HEAP OF REJECTION.
A GROTESQUE CIRCUS ACT BANISHED FROM SOCIETY.
A FREAK OF NATURE...
...WITH A LONELY HEART.
WILL I EVER KNOW THE UNCONDITIONAL TOUCH OF A WOMAN?
AM I NOT ALLOWED TO EXPERIENCE LOVE?
I HATE YOU CRUEL FUN HOUSE MIRROR.
SPLAT

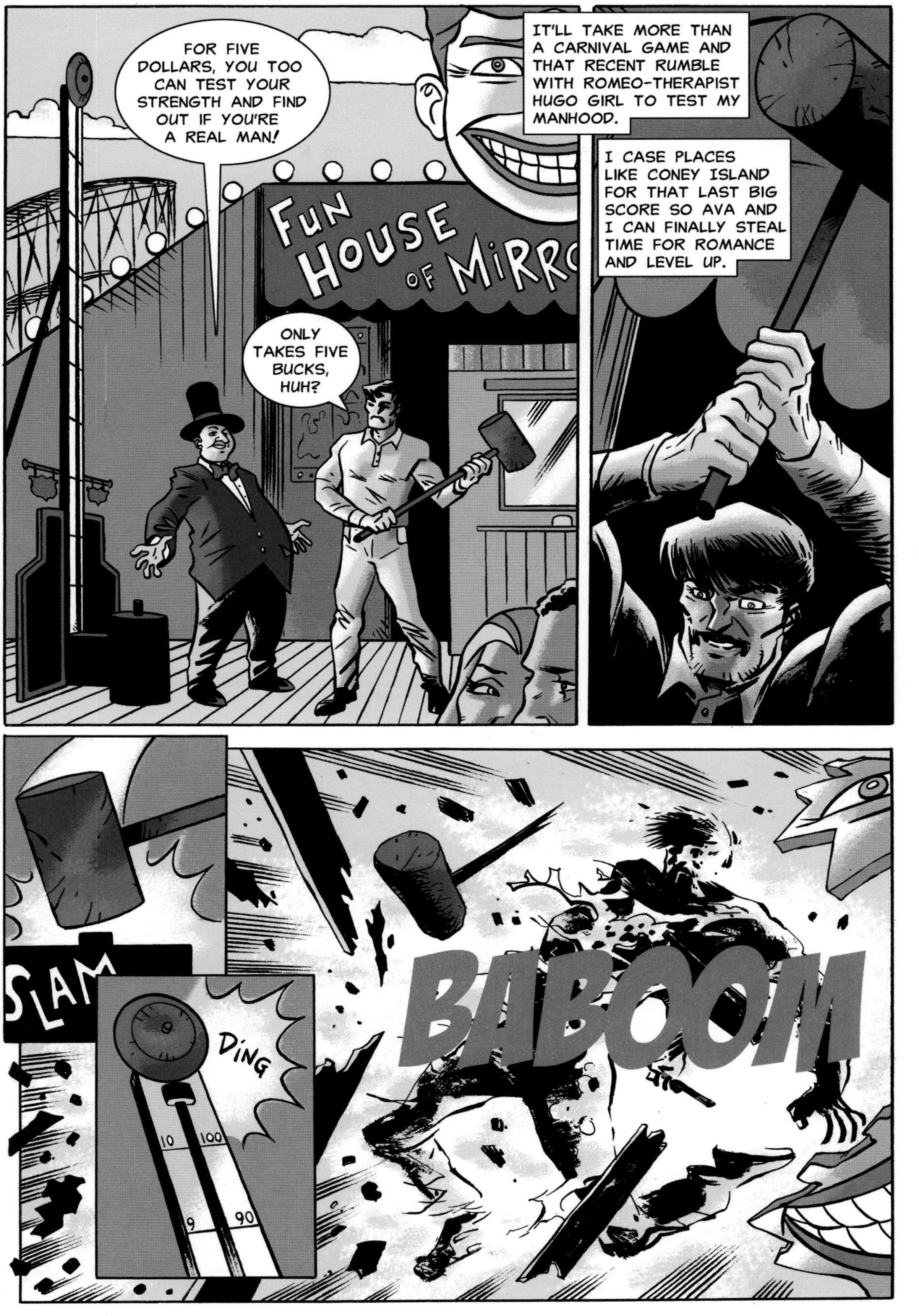
FOR FIVE DOLLARS, YOU TOO CAN TEST YOUR STRENGTH AND FIND OUT IF YOU'RE A REAL MAN!
FUN HOUSE OF MIRRO
ONLY TAKES FIVE BUCKS, HUH?
IT'LL TAKE MORE THAN A CARNIVAL GAME AND THAT RECENT RUMBLE WITH ROMEO-THERAPIST HUGO GIRL TO TEST MY MANHOOD.
I CASE PLACES LIKE CONEY ISLAND FOR THAT LAST BIG SCORE SO AVA AND I CAN FINALLY STEAL TIME FOR ROMANCE AND LEVEL UP.
SLAM
DING
10
100
9
90
BABOOM

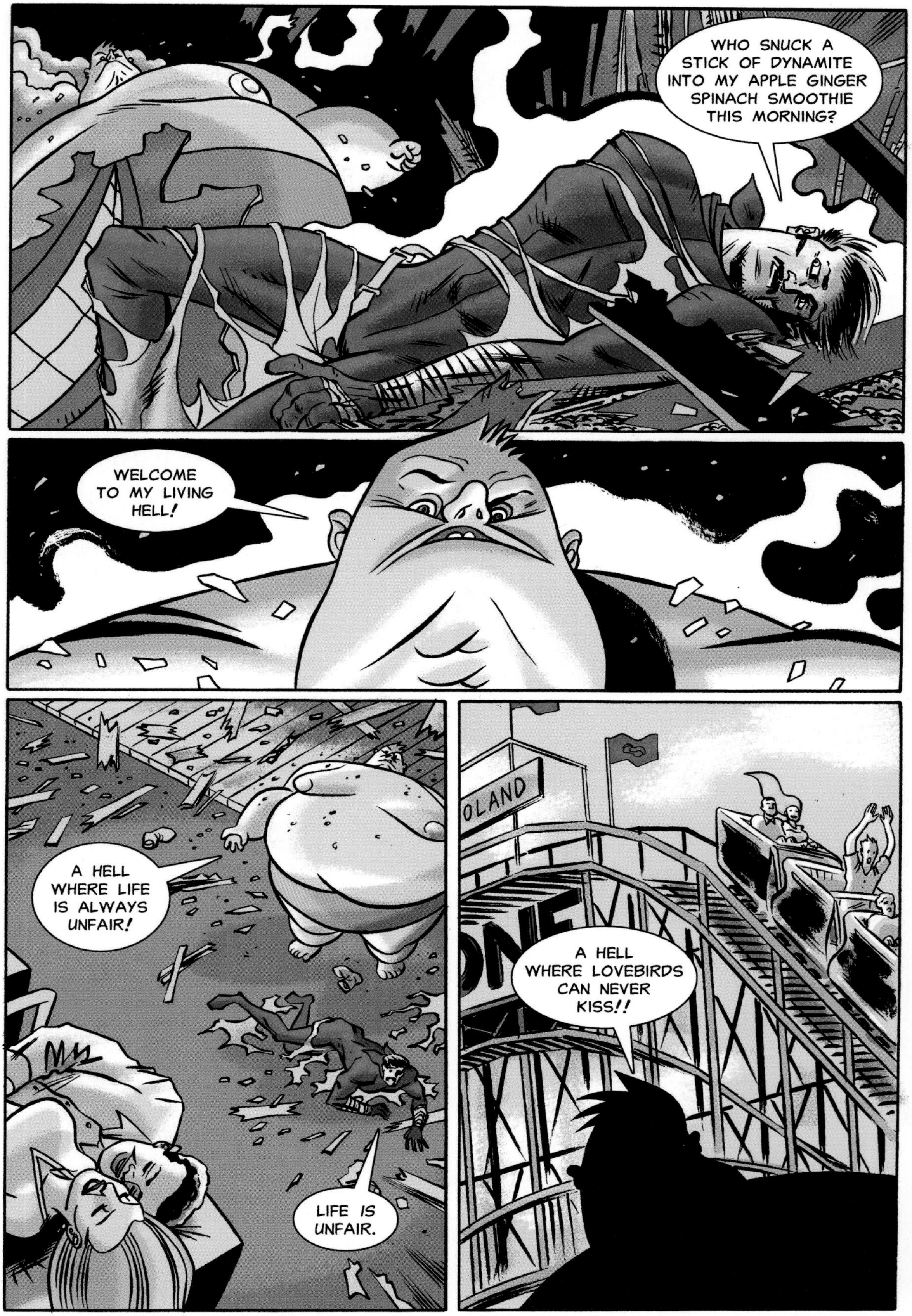
WHO SNUCK A STICK OF DYNAMITE INTO MY APPLE GINGER SPINACH SMOOTHIE THIS MORNING?
WELCOME TO MY LIVING HELL!
A HELL WHERE LIFE IS ALWAYS UNFAIR!
LIFE IS UNFAIR.
A HELL WHERE LOVEBIRDS CAN NEVER KISS!!

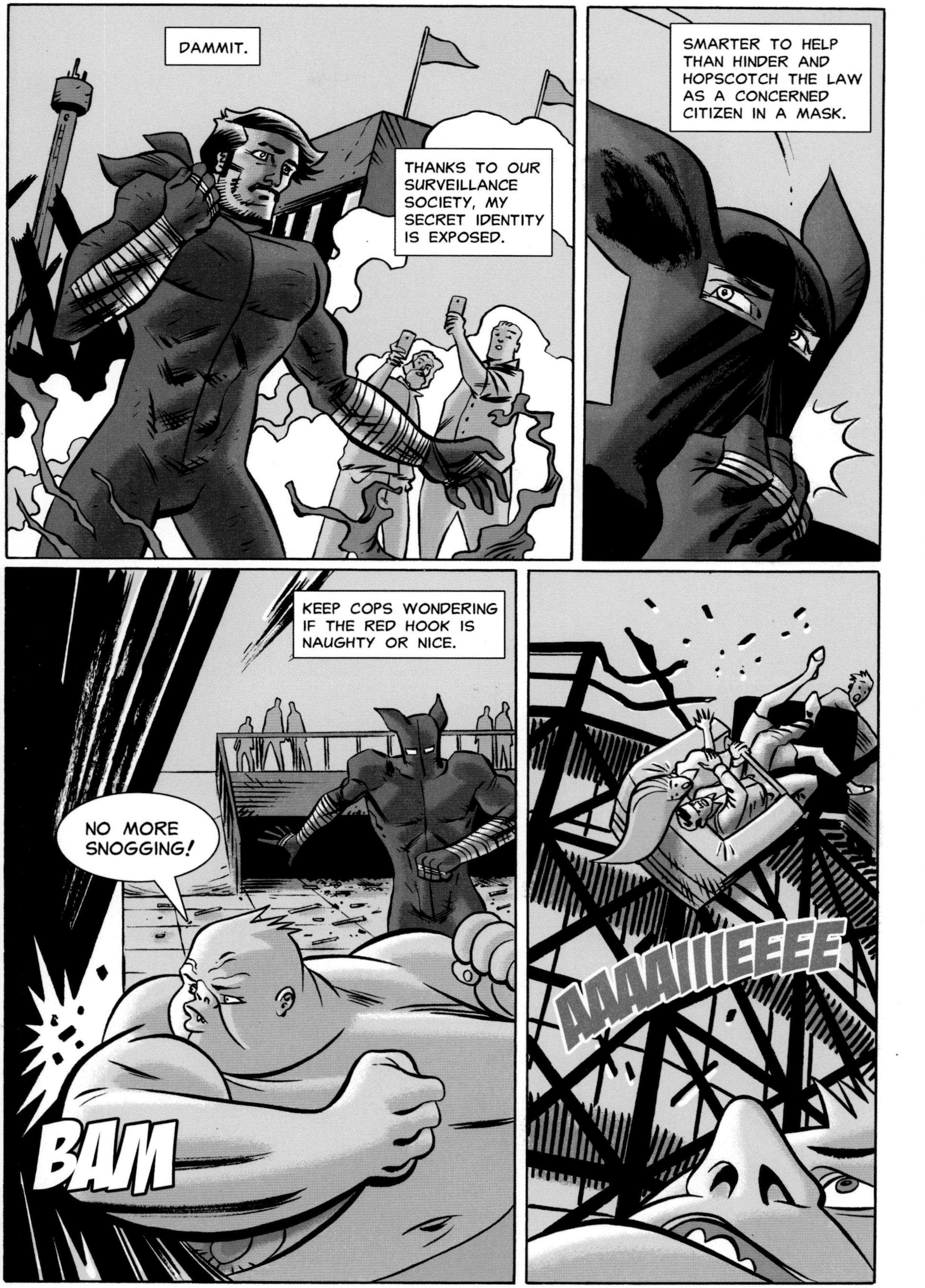
DAMMIT.
THANKS TO OUR SURVEILLANCE SOCIETY, MY SECRET IDENTITY IS EXPOSED.
SMARTER TO HELP THAN HINDER AND HOPSCOTCH THE LAW AS A CONCERNED CITIZEN IN A MASK.
KEEP COPS WONDERING IF THE RED HOOK IS NAUGHTY OR NICE.
NO MORE SNOGGING!
BAM
AAAAIIIEEEE

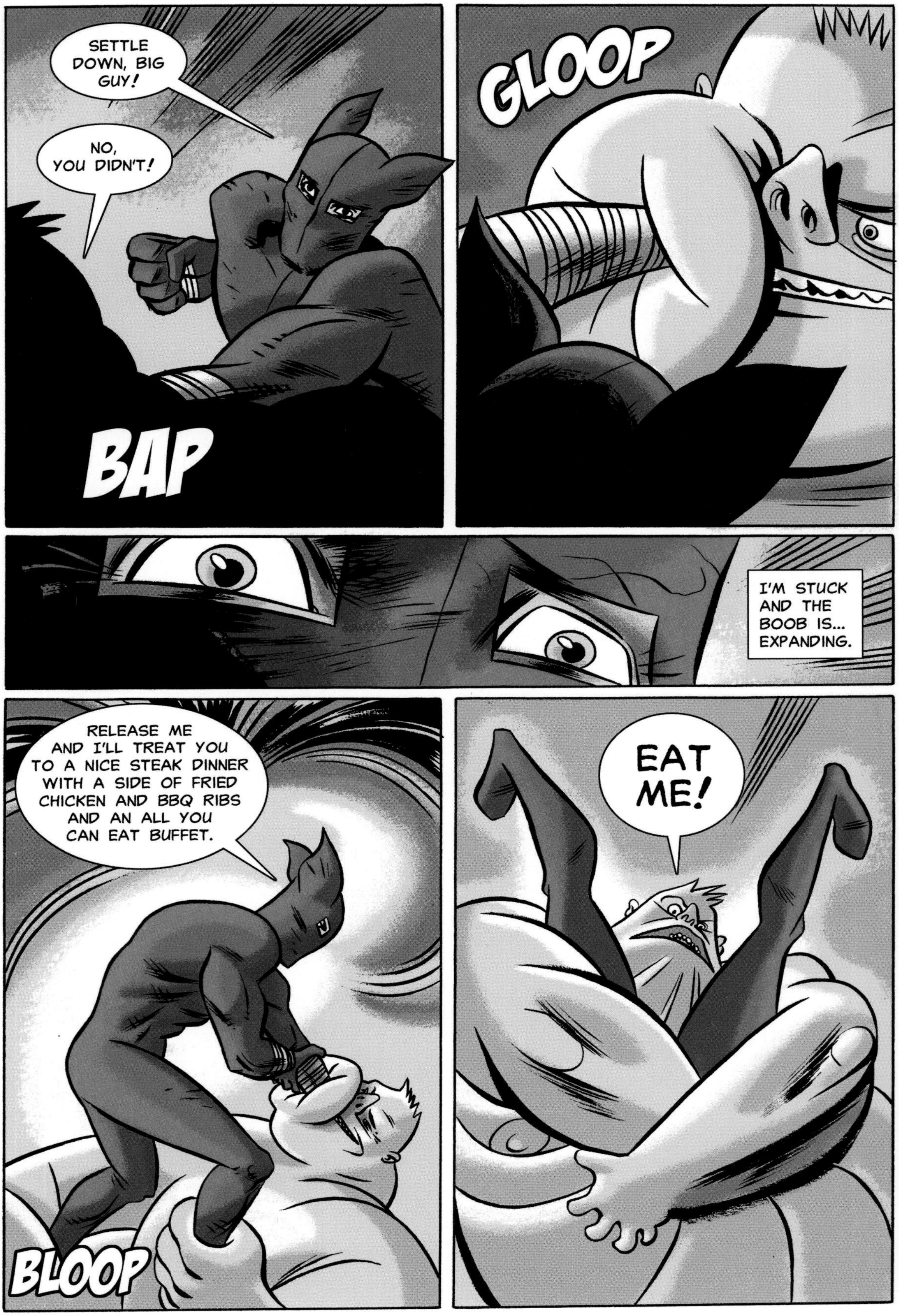
SETTLE DOWN, BIG GUY!
NO, YOU DIDN'T!
BAP
GLOOP
I'M STUCK AND THE BOOB IS... EXPANDING.
RELEASE ME AND I'LL TREAT YOU TO A NICE STEAK DINNER WITH A SIDE OF FRIED CHICKEN AND BBQ RIBS AND AN ALL YOU CAN EAT BUFFET.
BLOOP
EAT ME!

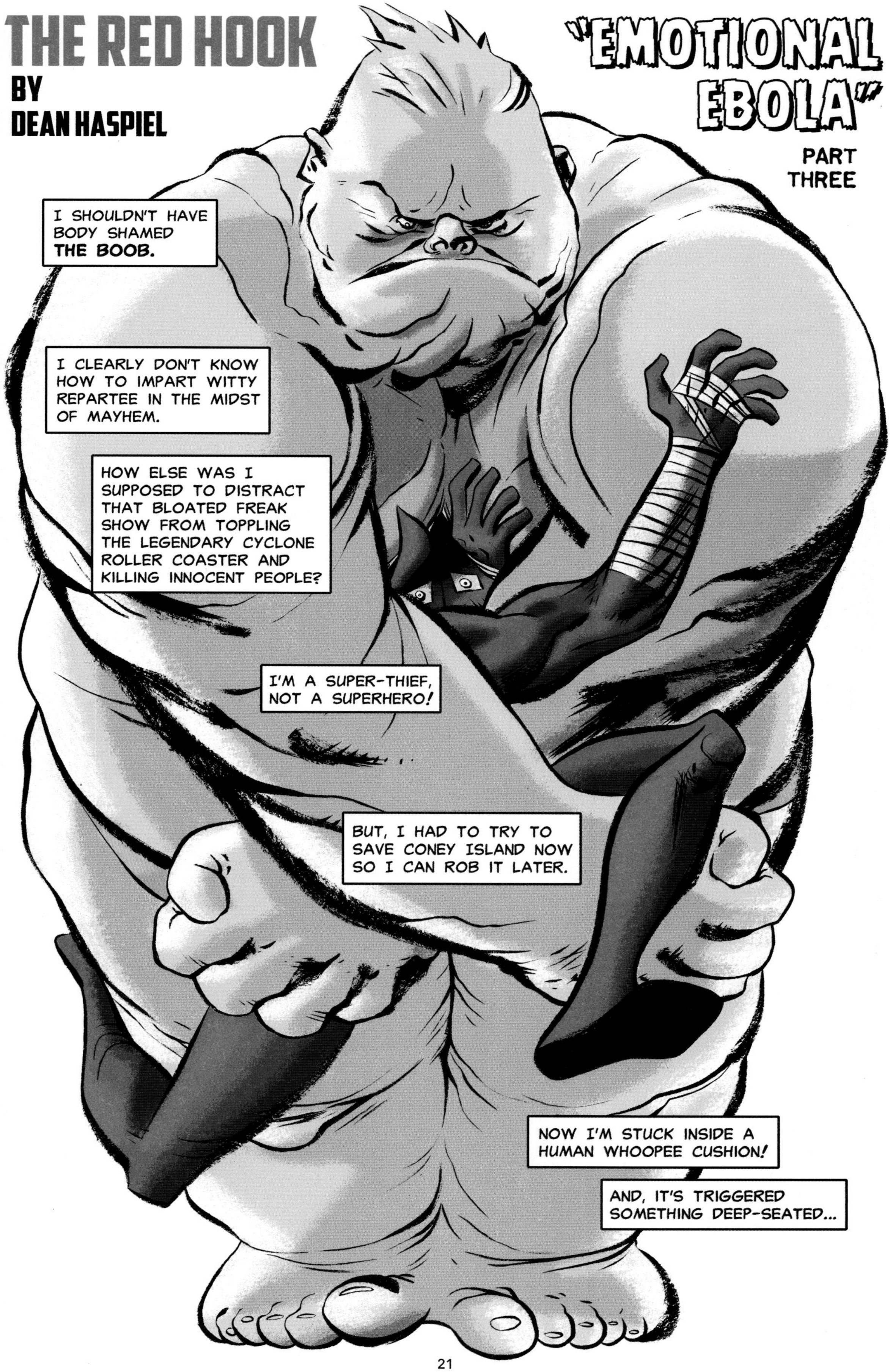

THE RED HOOK
BY
DEAN HASPIEL
"EMOTIONAL EBOLA"
PART THREE
I SHOULDN'T HAVE BODY SHAMED **THE BOOB.**
I CLEARLY DON'T KNOW HOW TO IMPART WITTY REPARTEE IN THE MIDST OF MAYHEM.
HOW ELSE WAS I SUPPOSED TO DISTRACT THAT BLOATED FREAK SHOW FROM TOPPLING THE LEGENDARY CYCLONE ROLLER COASTER AND KILLING INNOCENT PEOPLE?
I'M A SUPER-THIEF, NOT A SUPERHERO!
BUT, I HAD TO TRY TO SAVE CONEY ISLAND NOW SO I CAN ROB IT LATER.
NOW I'M STUCK INSIDE A HUMAN WHOOPEE CUSHION!
AND, IT'S TRIGGERED SOMETHING DEEP-SEATED...

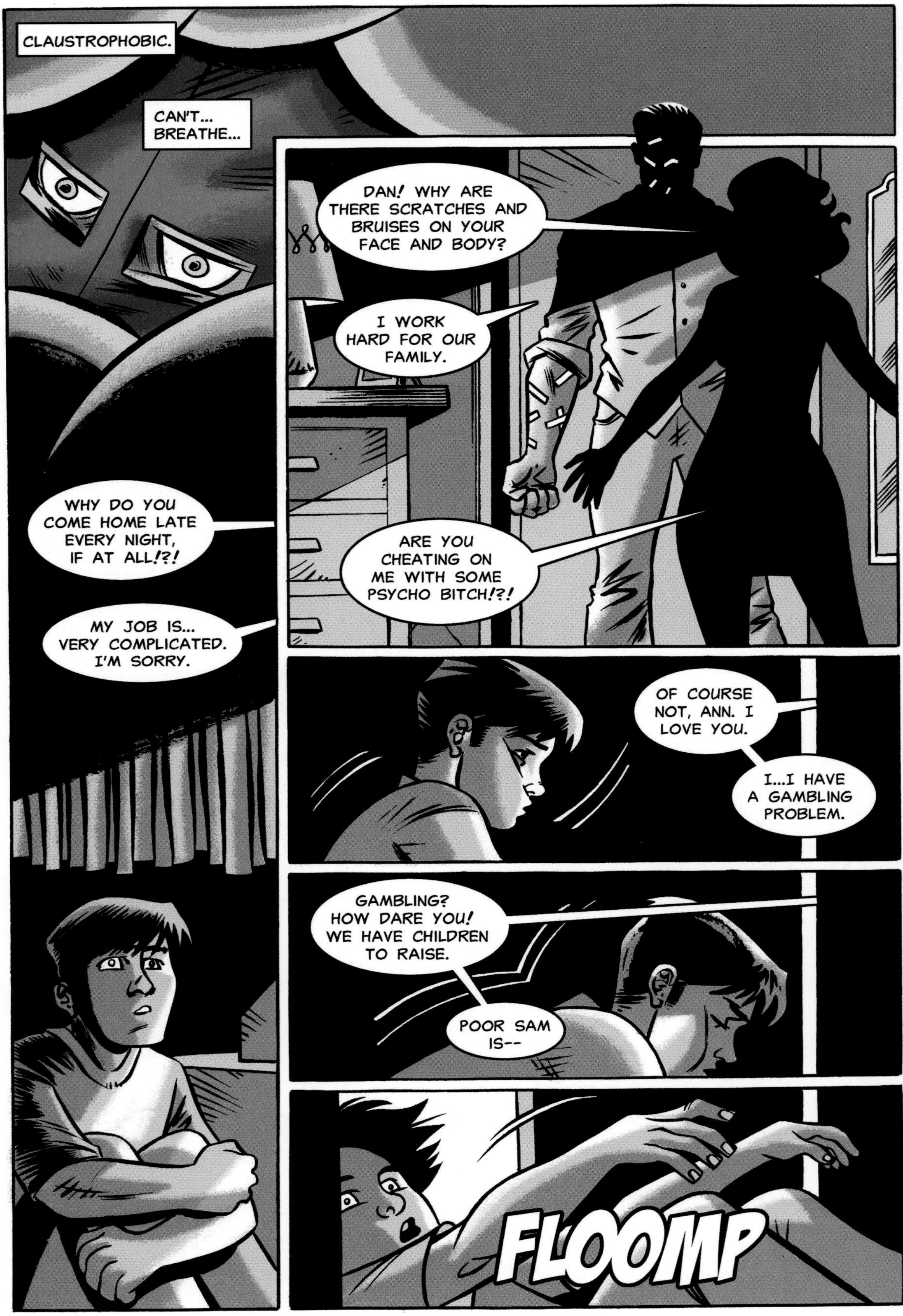
CLAUSTROPHOBIC.
CAN'T... BREATHE...
DAN! WHY ARE THERE SCRATCHES AND BRUISES ON YOUR FACE AND BODY?
I WORK HARD FOR OUR FAMILY.
WHY DO YOU COME HOME LATE EVERY NIGHT, IF AT ALL!?!
ARE YOU CHEATING ON ME WITH SOME PSYCHO BITCH!?!
MY JOB IS... VERY COMPLICATED. I'M SORRY.
OF COURSE NOT, ANN. I LOVE YOU.
I...I HAVE A GAMBLING PROBLEM.
GAMBLING? HOW DARE YOU! WE HAVE CHILDREN TO RAISE.
POOR SAM IS--
FLOOMP

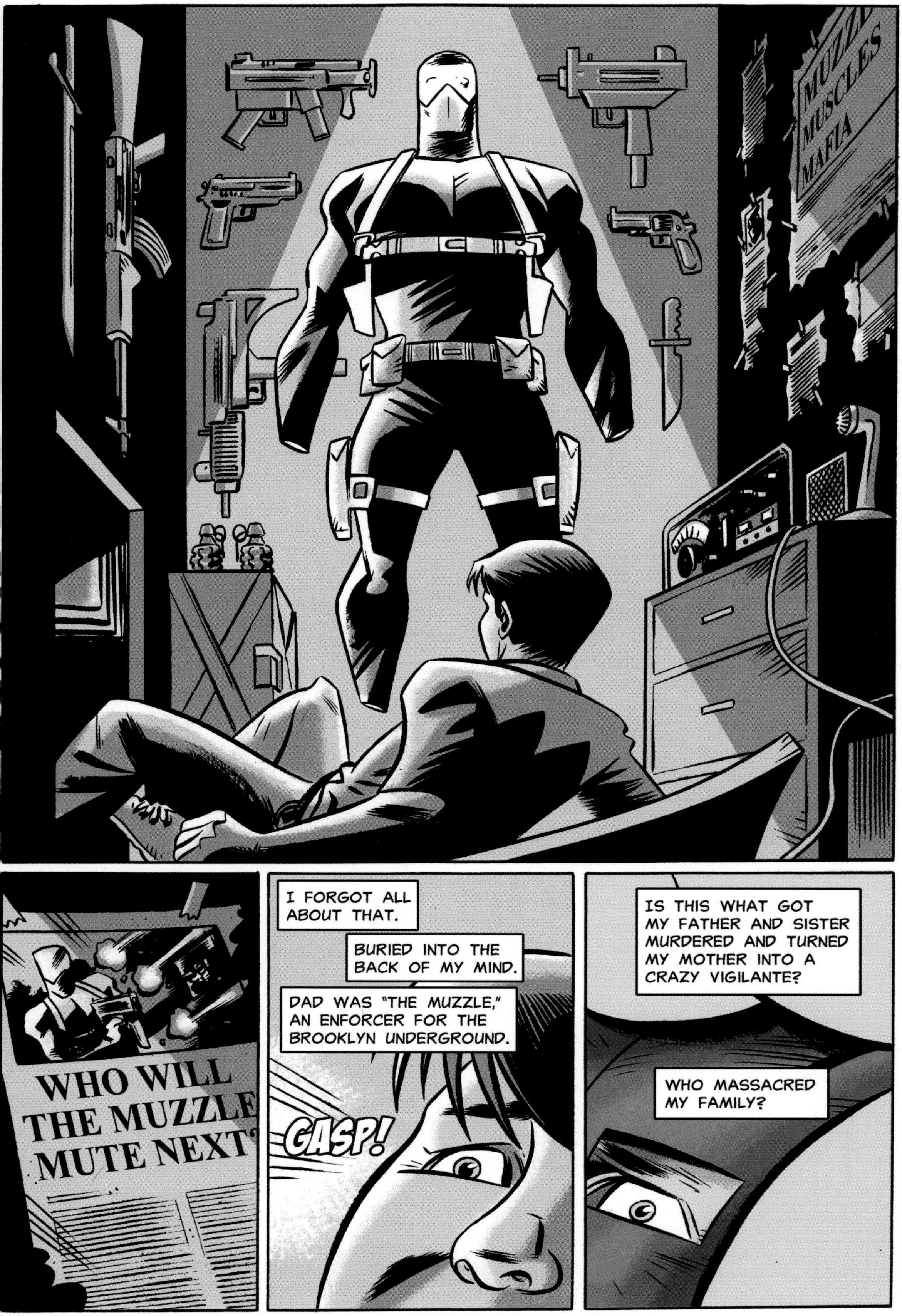
MUSCLES
MAFIA
WHO WILL THE MUZZLE MUTE NEXT
I FORGOT ALL ABOUT THAT.
BURIED INTO THE BACK OF MY MIND.
DAD WAS "THE MUZZLE," AN ENFORCER FOR THE BROOKLYN UNDERGROUND.
GASP!
IS THIS WHAT GOT MY FATHER AND SISTER MURDERED AND TURNED MY MOTHER INTO A CRAZY VIGILANTE?
WHO MASSACRED MY FAMILY?

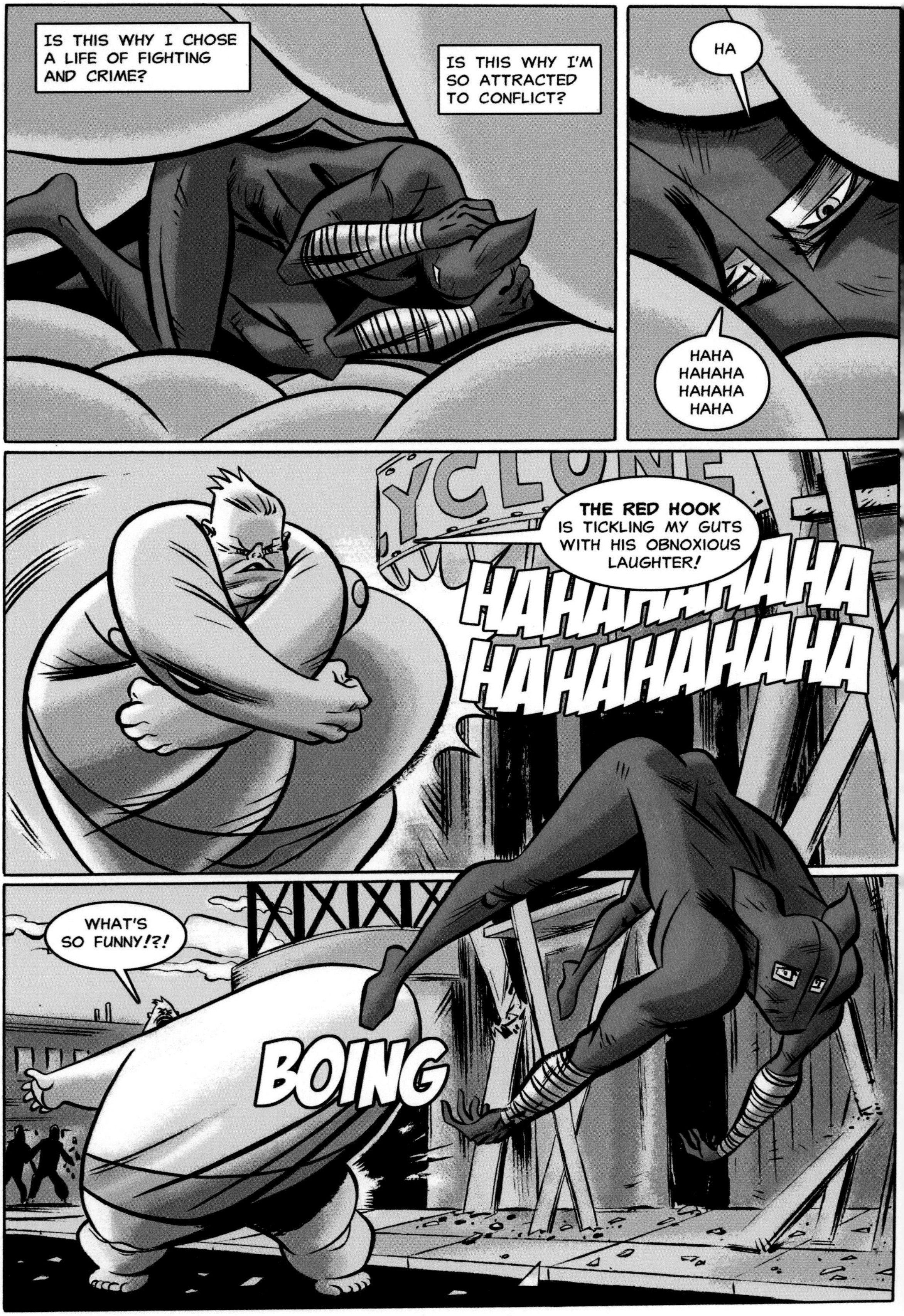

IS THIS WHY I CHOSE A LIFE OF FIGHTING AND CRIME?
IS THIS WHY I'M SO ATTRACTED TO CONFLICT?
HA
HAHA HAHAHA HAHAHA HAHA
YCLONE
THE RED HOOK IS TICKLING MY GUTS WITH HIS OBNOXIOUS LAUGHTER!
HAHAHAHAHAHA HAHAHAHAHAHA
WHAT'S SO FUNNY!?!
BOING

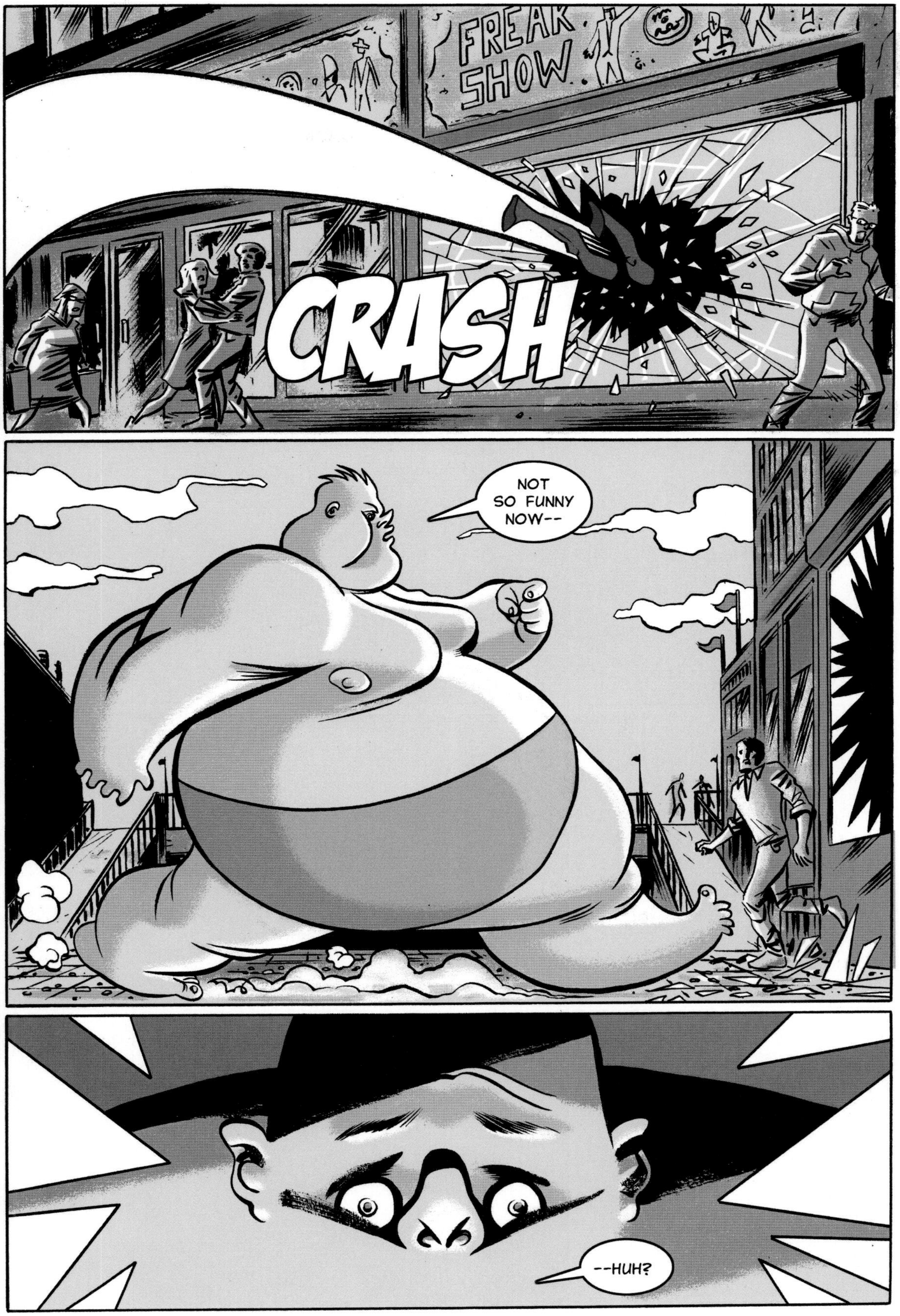
FREAK SHOW
CRASH
NOT SO FUNNY NOW--
--HUH?

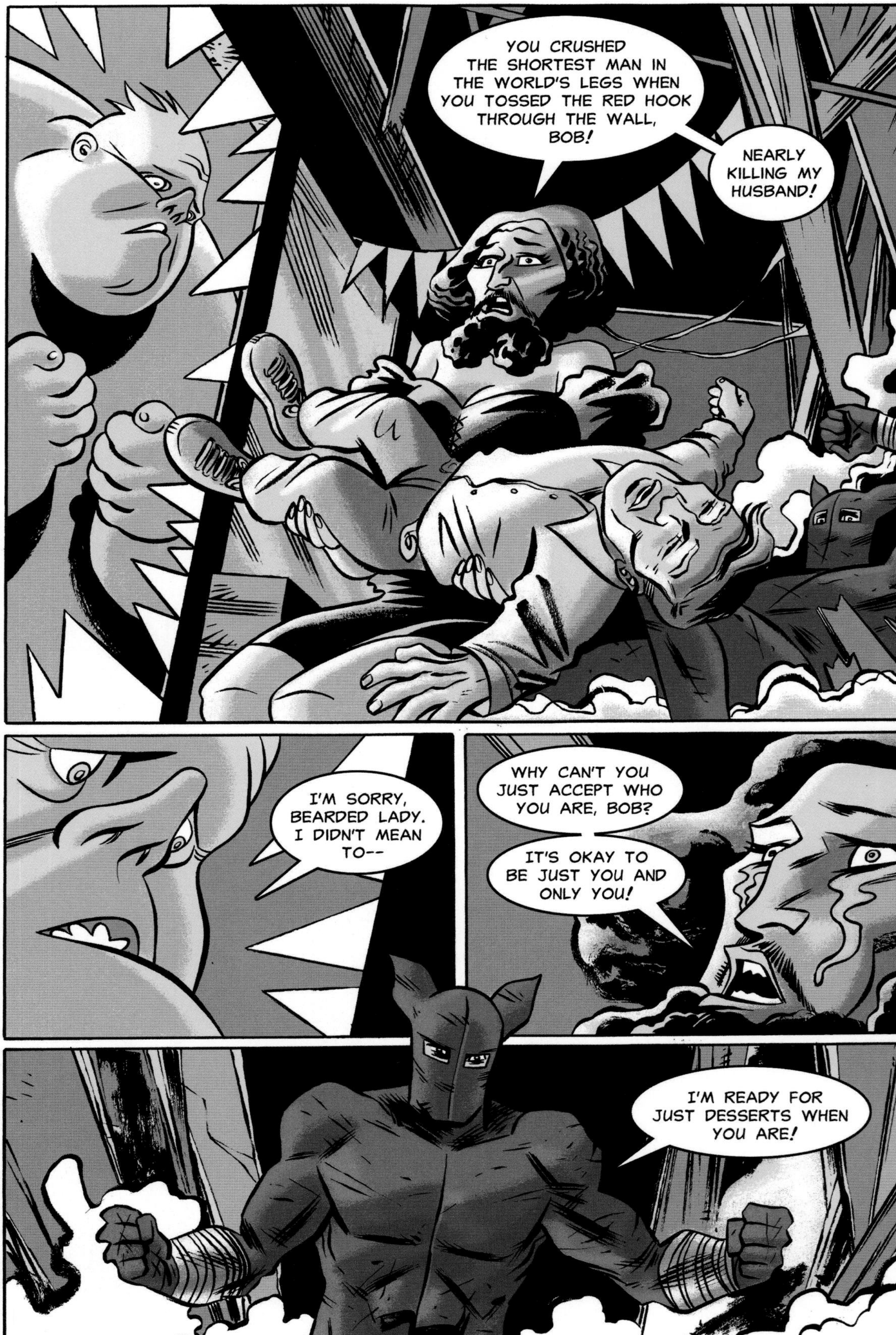
YOU CRUSHED THE SHORTEST MAN IN THE WORLD'S LEGS WHEN YOU TOSSED THE RED HOOK THROUGH THE WALL, BOB!
NEARLY KILLING MY HUSBAND!
I'M SORRY, BEARDED LADY. I DIDN'T MEAN TO--
WHY CAN'T YOU JUST ACCEPT WHO YOU ARE, BOB?
IT'S OKAY TO BE JUST YOU AND ONLY YOU!
I'M READY FOR JUST DESSERTS WHEN YOU ARE!

I'M SO VERY SORRY.

I'VE WITNESSED THE WONDER AND POWER OF TRUE LOVE AND IT LEAVES ME HUMBLED.

ASHAMED.

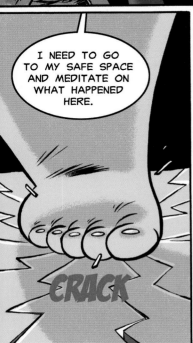

I NEED TO GO TO MY SAFE SPACE AND MEDITATE ON WHAT HAPPENED HERE.

CRACK

CRASH

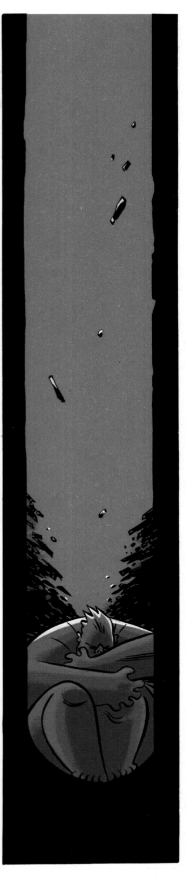

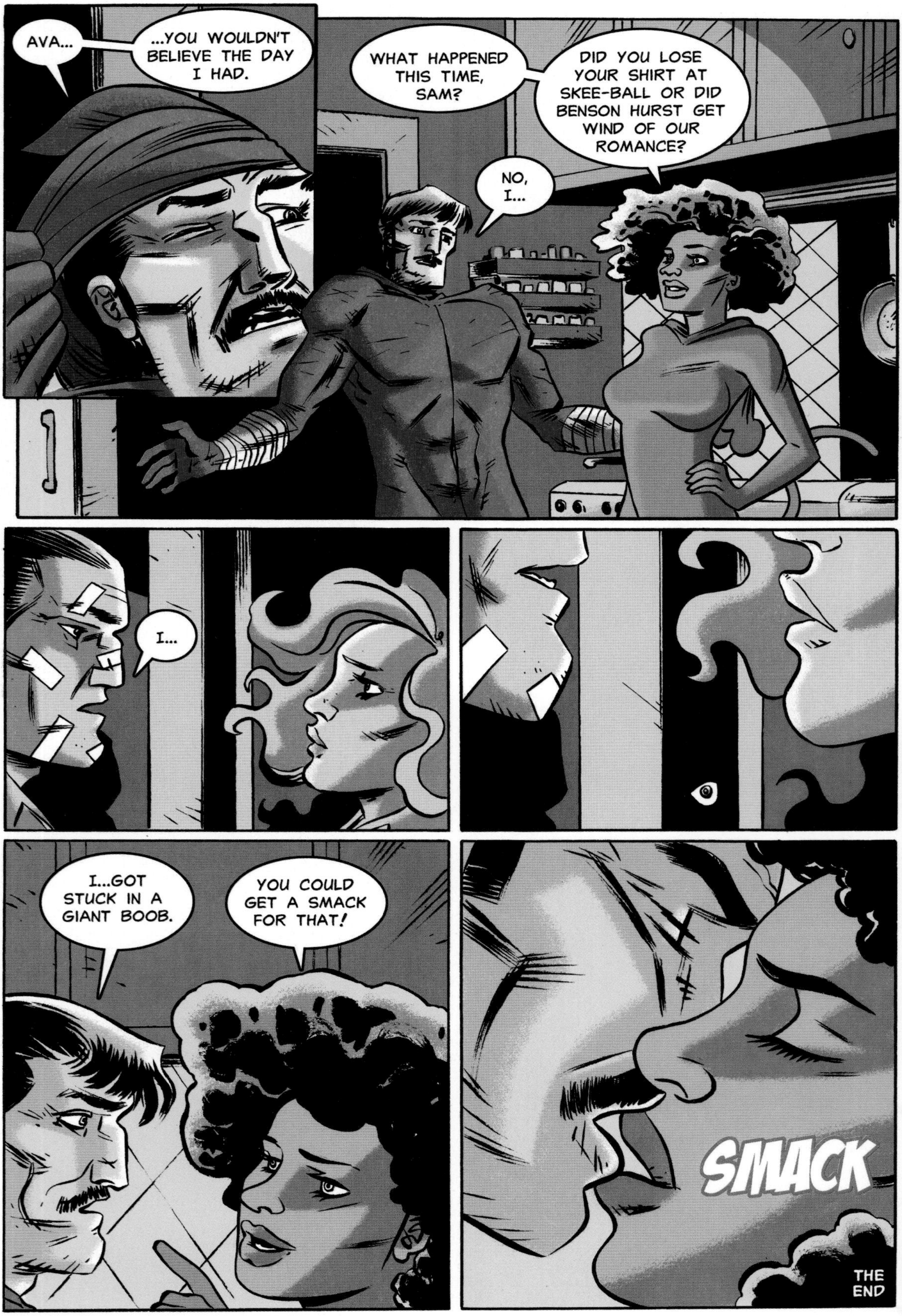
AVA...
...YOU WOULDN'T BELIEVE THE DAY I HAD.
WHAT HAPPENED THIS TIME, SAM?
DID YOU LOSE YOUR SHIRT AT SKEE-BALL OR DID BENSON HURST GET WIND OF OUR ROMANCE?
NO, I...
I...
I...GOT STUCK IN A GIANT BOOB.
YOU COULD GET A SMACK FOR THAT!
SMACK
THE END

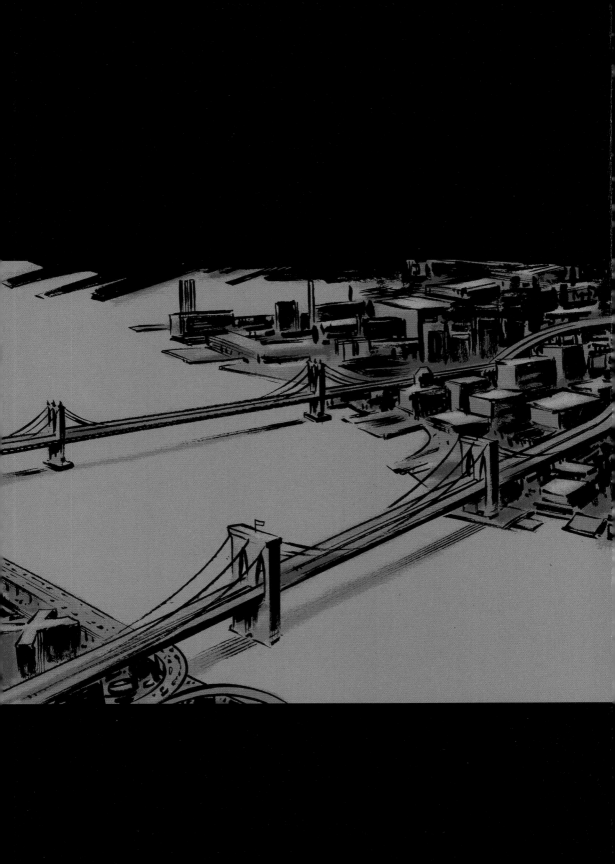

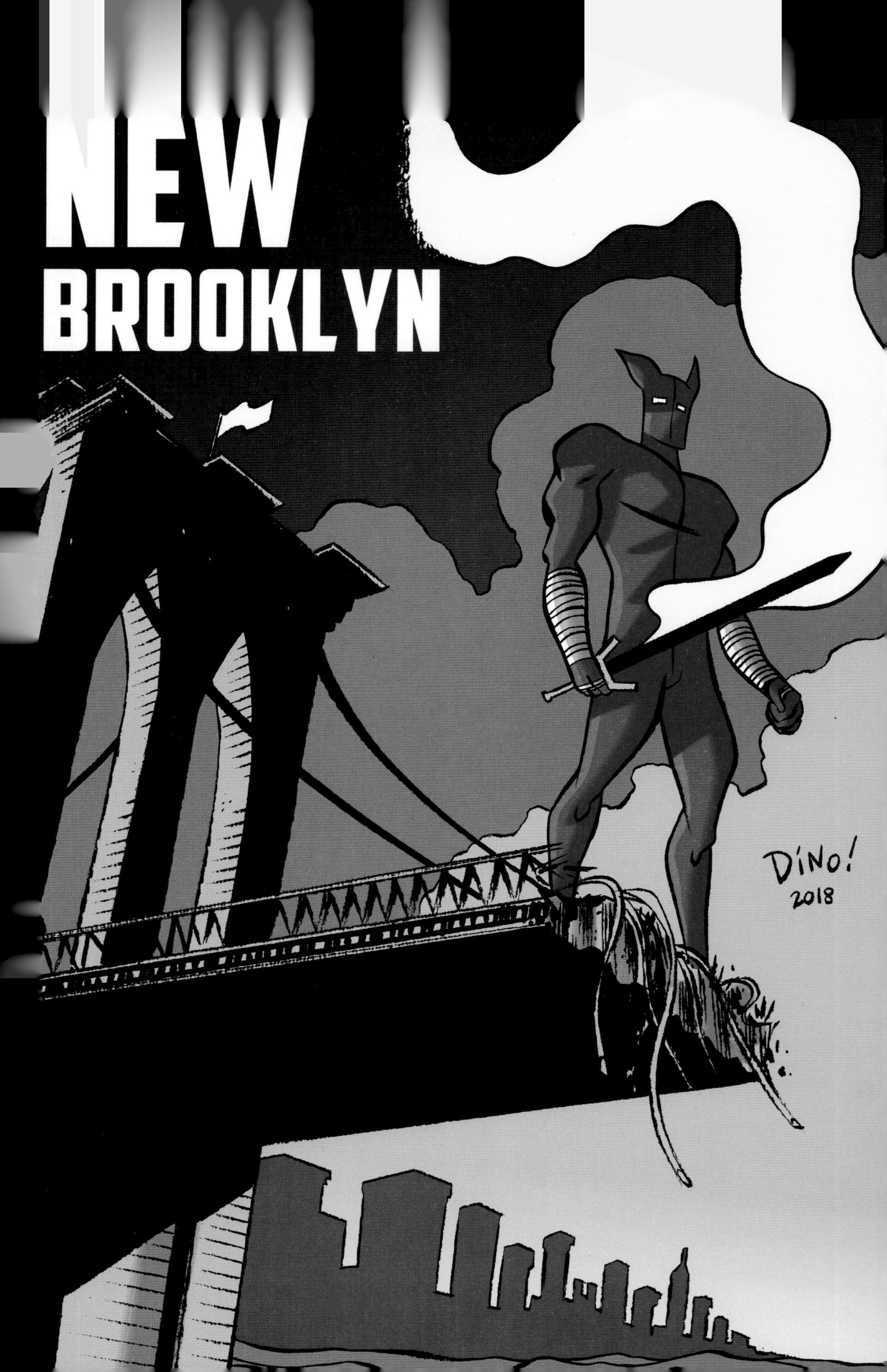
NEW
BROOKLYN
DINO!
2018

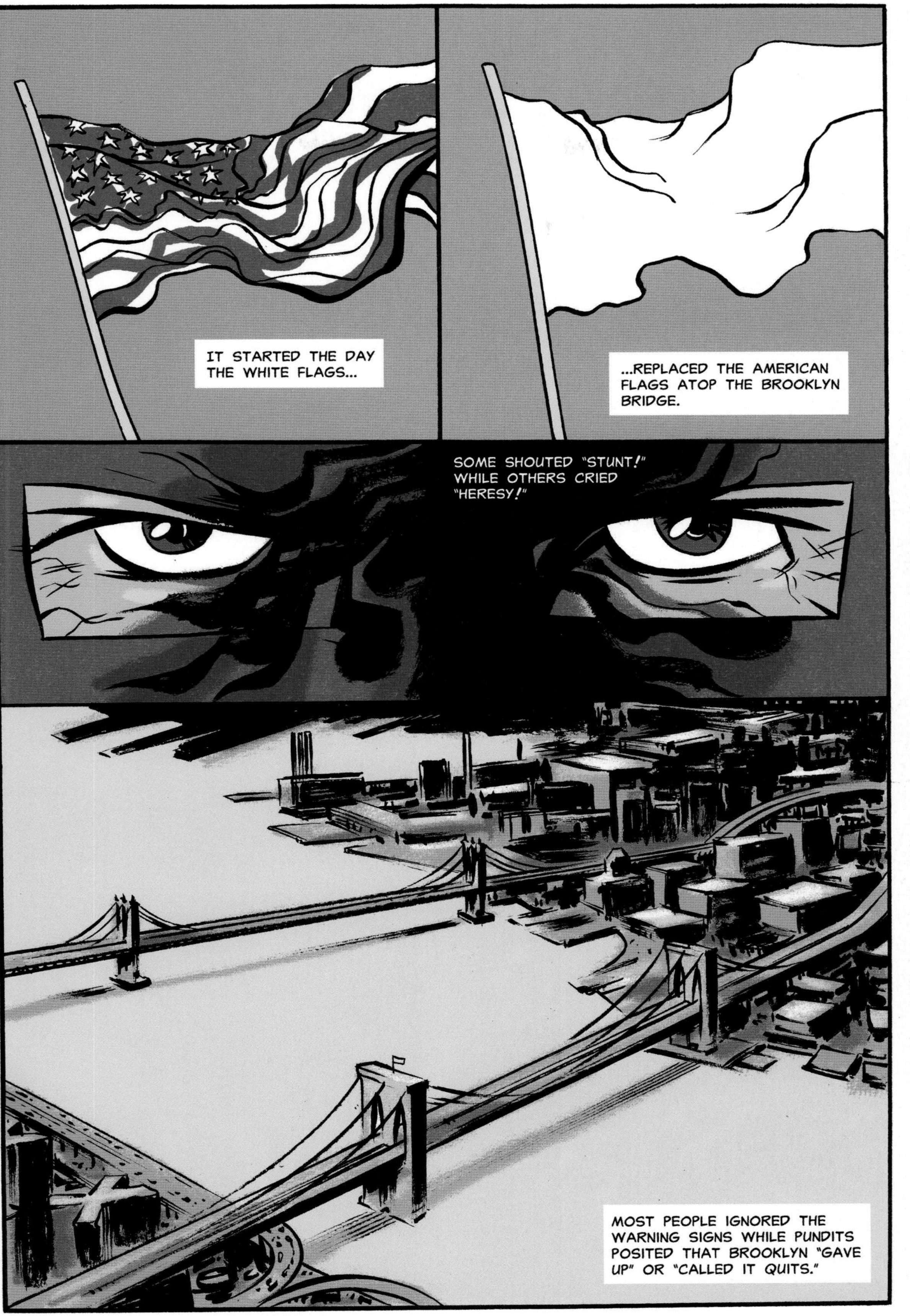
IT STARTED THE DAY THE WHITE FLAGS...
...REPLACED THE AMERICAN FLAGS ATOP THE BROOKLYN BRIDGE.
SOME SHOUTED "STUNT!" WHILE OTHERS CRIED "HERESY!"
MOST PEOPLE IGNORED THE WARNING SIGNS WHILE PUNDITS POSITED THAT BROOKLYN "GAVE UP" OR "CALLED IT QUITS."

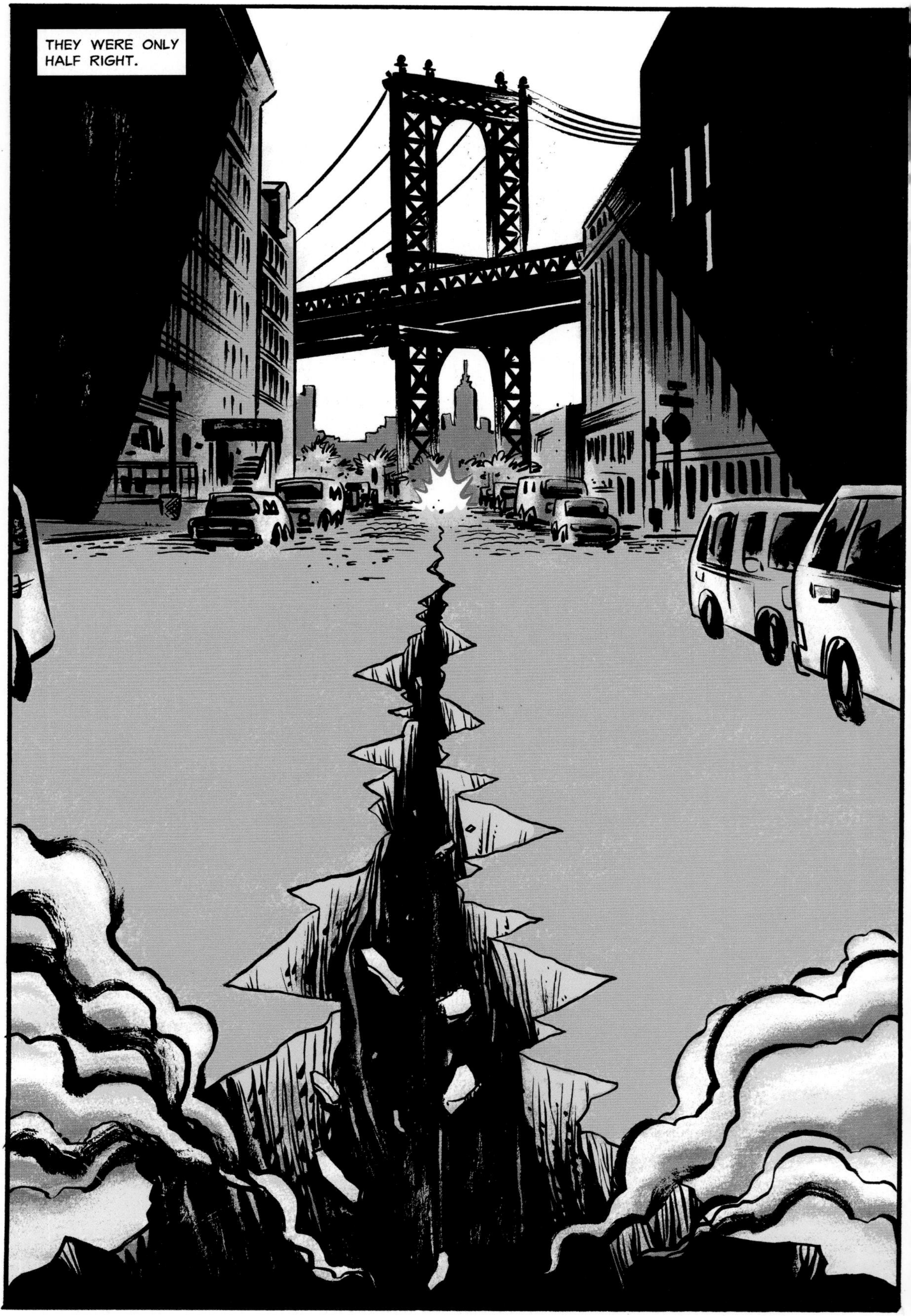
THEY WERE ONLY
HALF RIGHT.

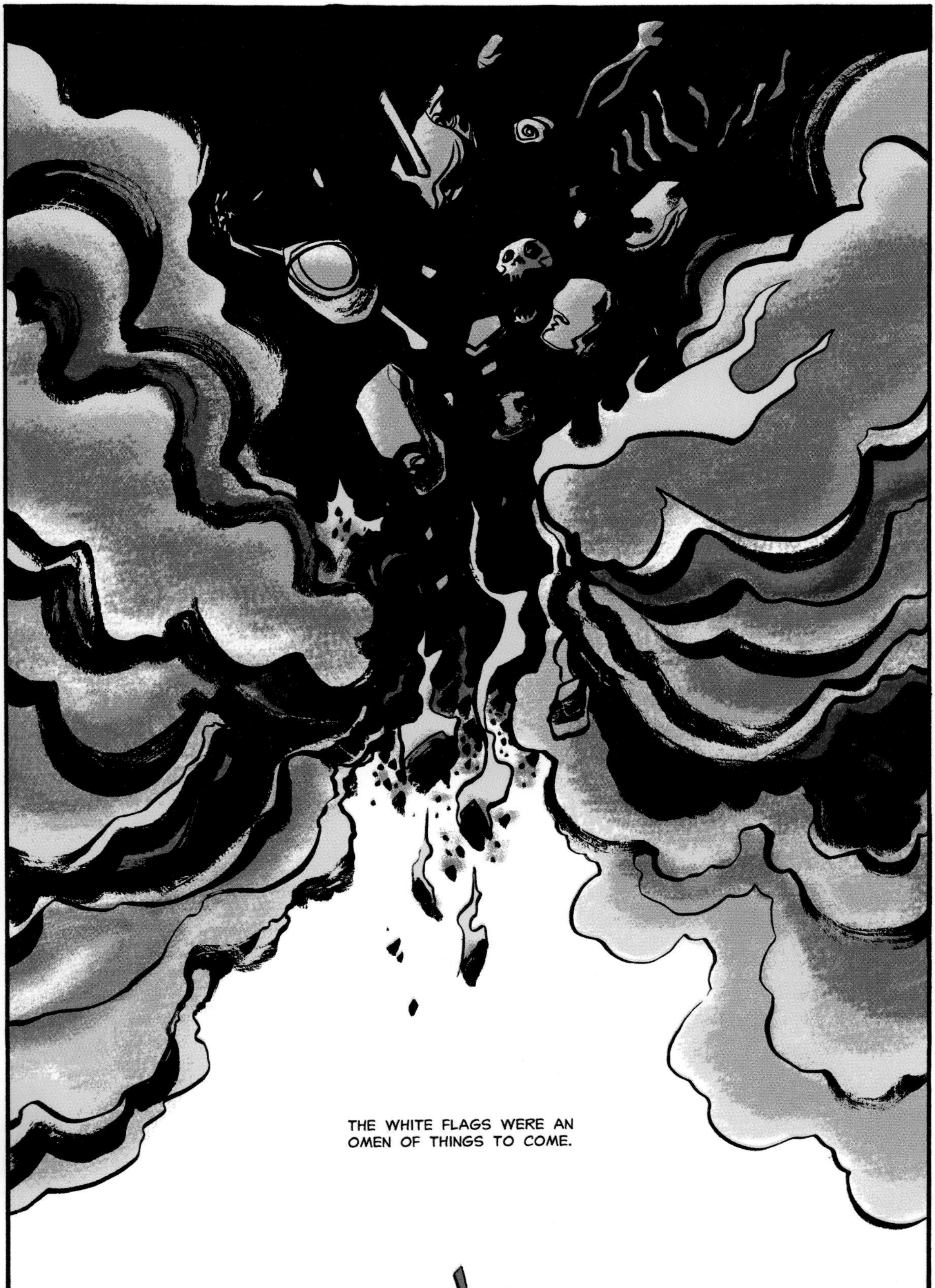
THE WHITE FLAGS WERE AN
OMEN OF THINGS TO COME.

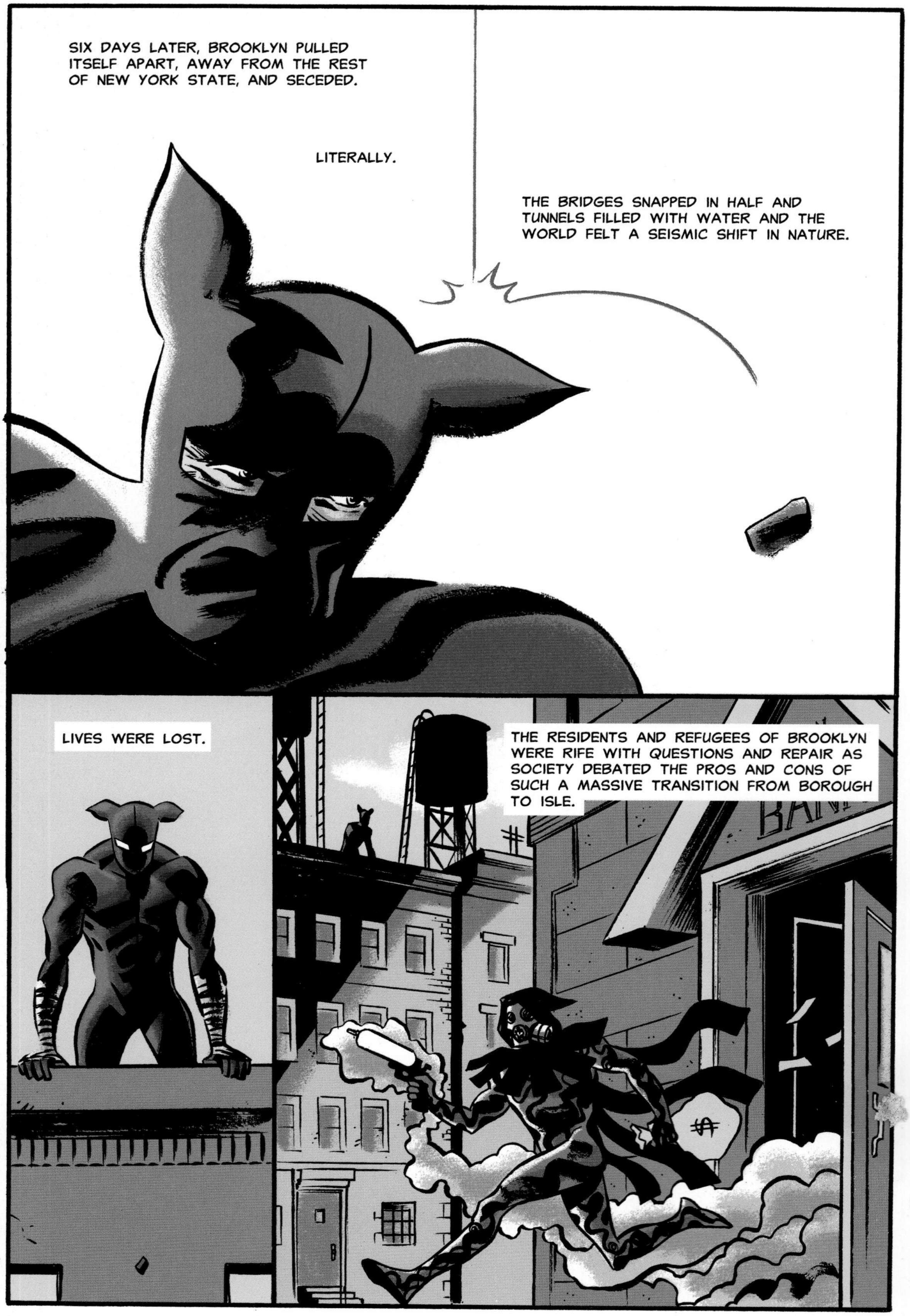
SIX DAYS LATER, BROOKLYN PULLED ITSELF APART, AWAY FROM THE REST OF NEW YORK STATE, AND SECEDED.
LITERALLY.
THE BRIDGES SNAPPED IN HALF AND TUNNELS FILLED WITH WATER AND THE WORLD FELT A SEISMIC SHIFT IN NATURE.
LIVES WERE LOST.
THE RESIDENTS AND REFUGEES OF BROOKLYN WERE RIFE WITH QUESTIONS AND REPAIR AS SOCIETY DEBATED THE PROS AND CONS OF SUCH A MASSIVE TRANSITION FROM BOROUGH TO ISLE.

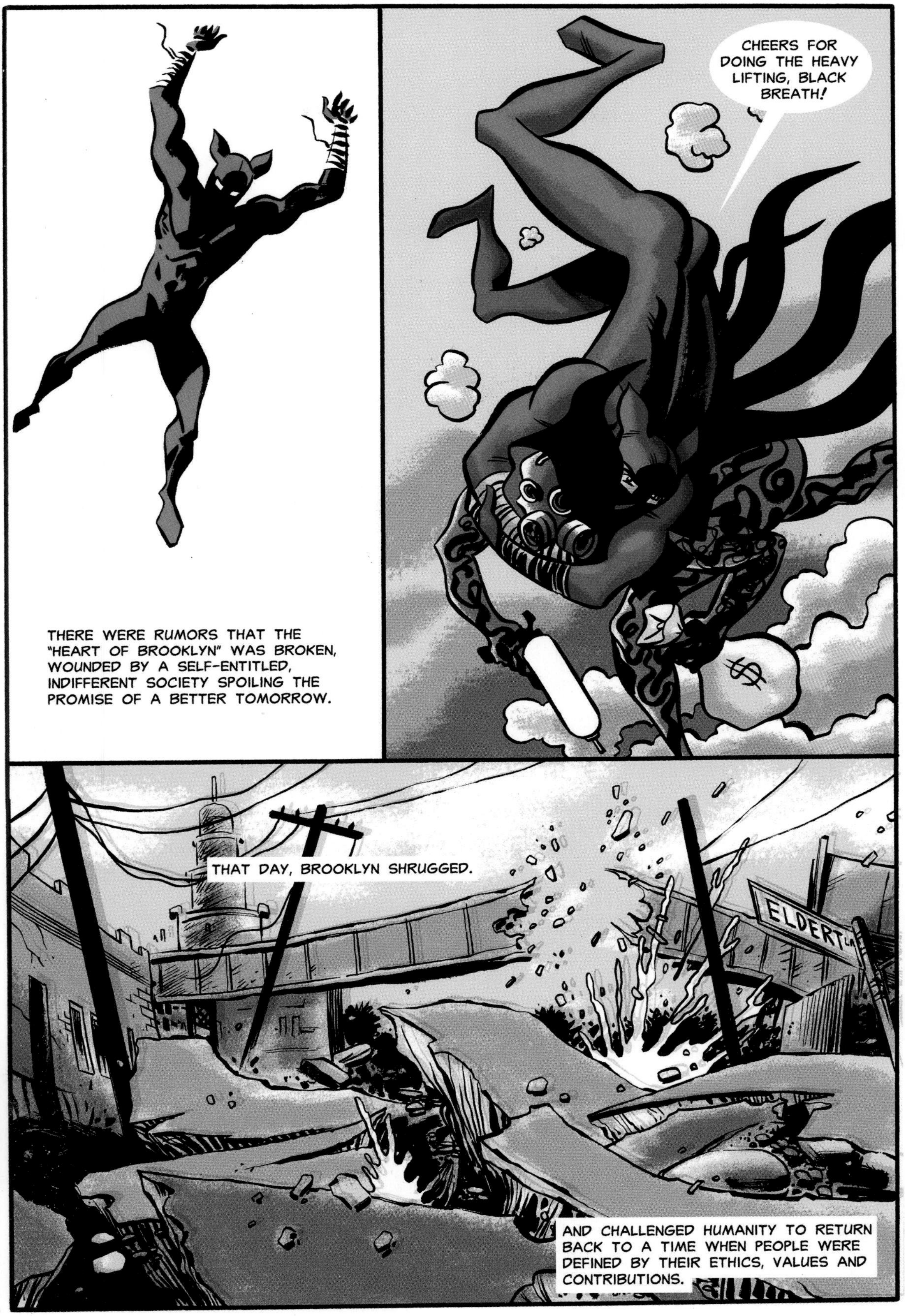
THERE WERE RUMORS THAT THE "HEART OF BROOKLYN" WAS BROKEN, WOUNDED BY A SELF-ENTITLED, INDIFFERENT SOCIETY SPOILING THE PROMISE OF A BETTER TOMORROW.
CHEERS FOR DOING THE HEAVY LIFTING, BLACK BREATH!
THAT DAY, BROOKLYN SHRUGGED.
ELDERT
AND CHALLENGED HUMANITY TO RETURN BACK TO A TIME WHEN PEOPLE WERE DEFINED BY THEIR ETHICS, VALUES AND CONTRIBUTIONS.

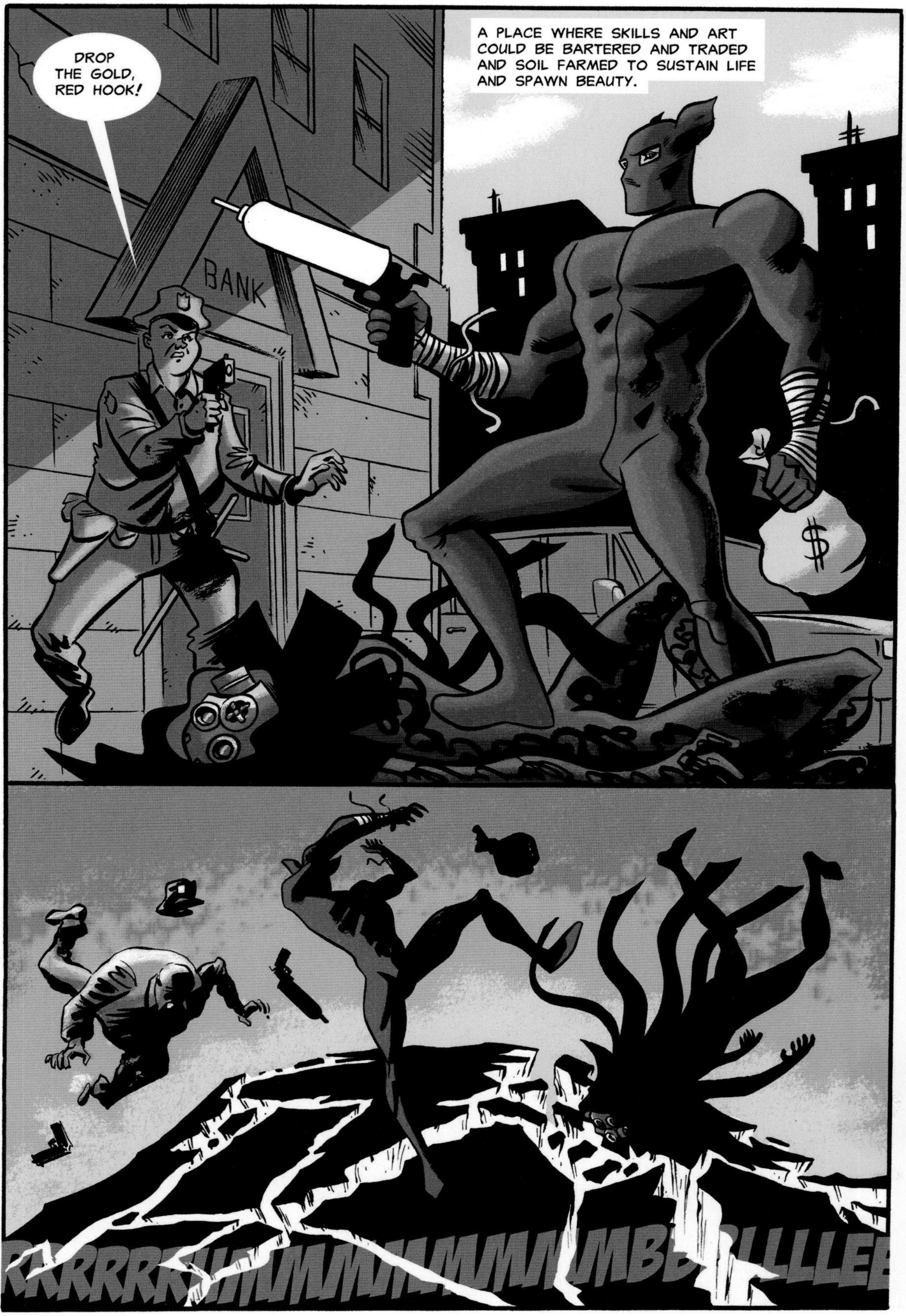
DROP THE GOLD, RED HOOK!
A PLACE WHERE SKILLS AND ART COULD BE BARTERED AND TRADED AND SOIL FARMED TO SUSTAIN LIFE AND SPAWN BEAUTY.
BANK

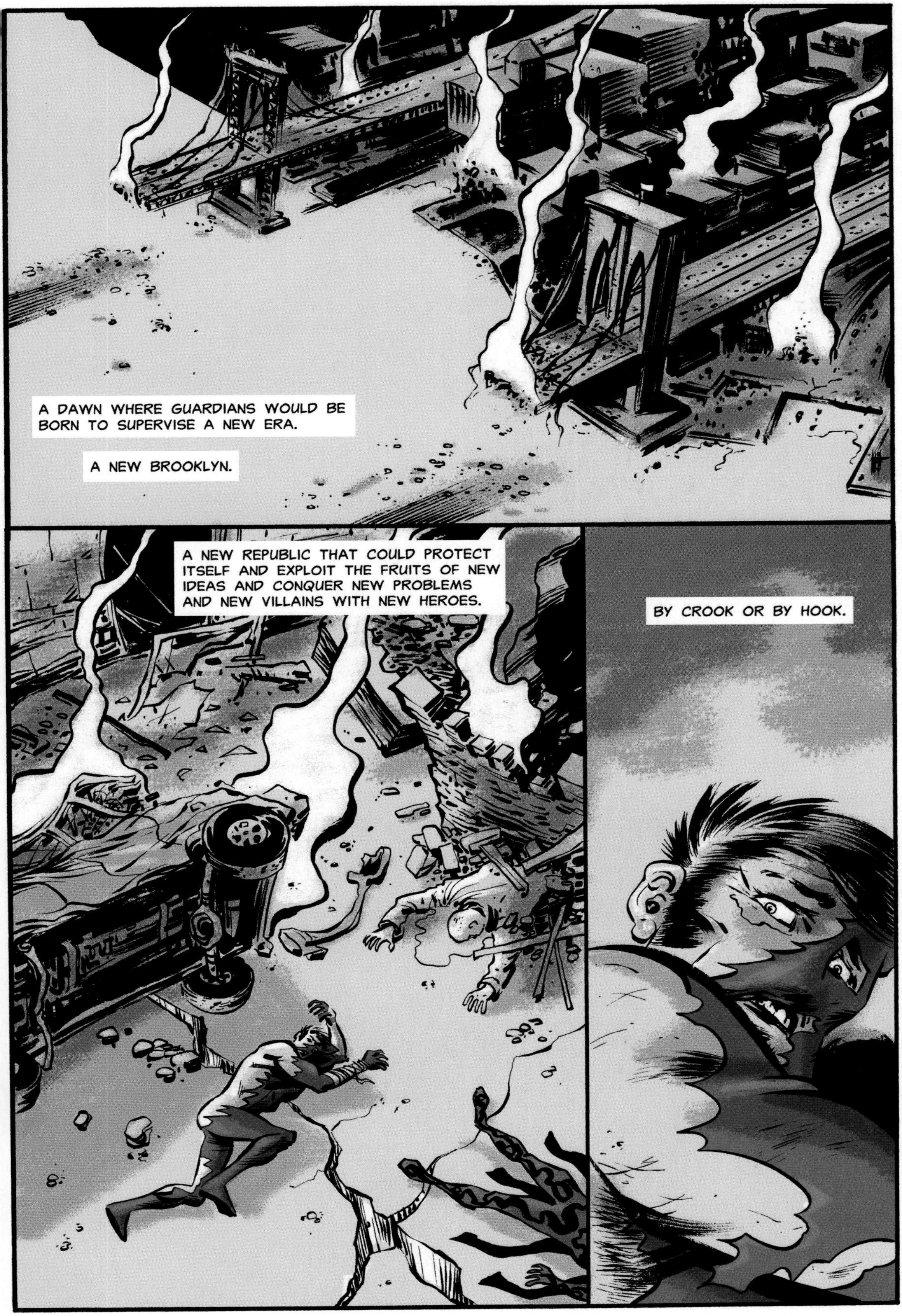
A DAWN WHERE GUARDIANS WOULD BE BORN TO SUPERVISE A NEW ERA.
A NEW BROOKLYN.
A NEW REPUBLIC THAT COULD PROTECT ITSELF AND EXPLOIT THE FRUITS OF NEW IDEAS AND CONQUER NEW PROBLEMS AND NEW VILLAINS WITH NEW HEROES.
BY CROOK OR BY HOOK.

ONE YEAR LATER...

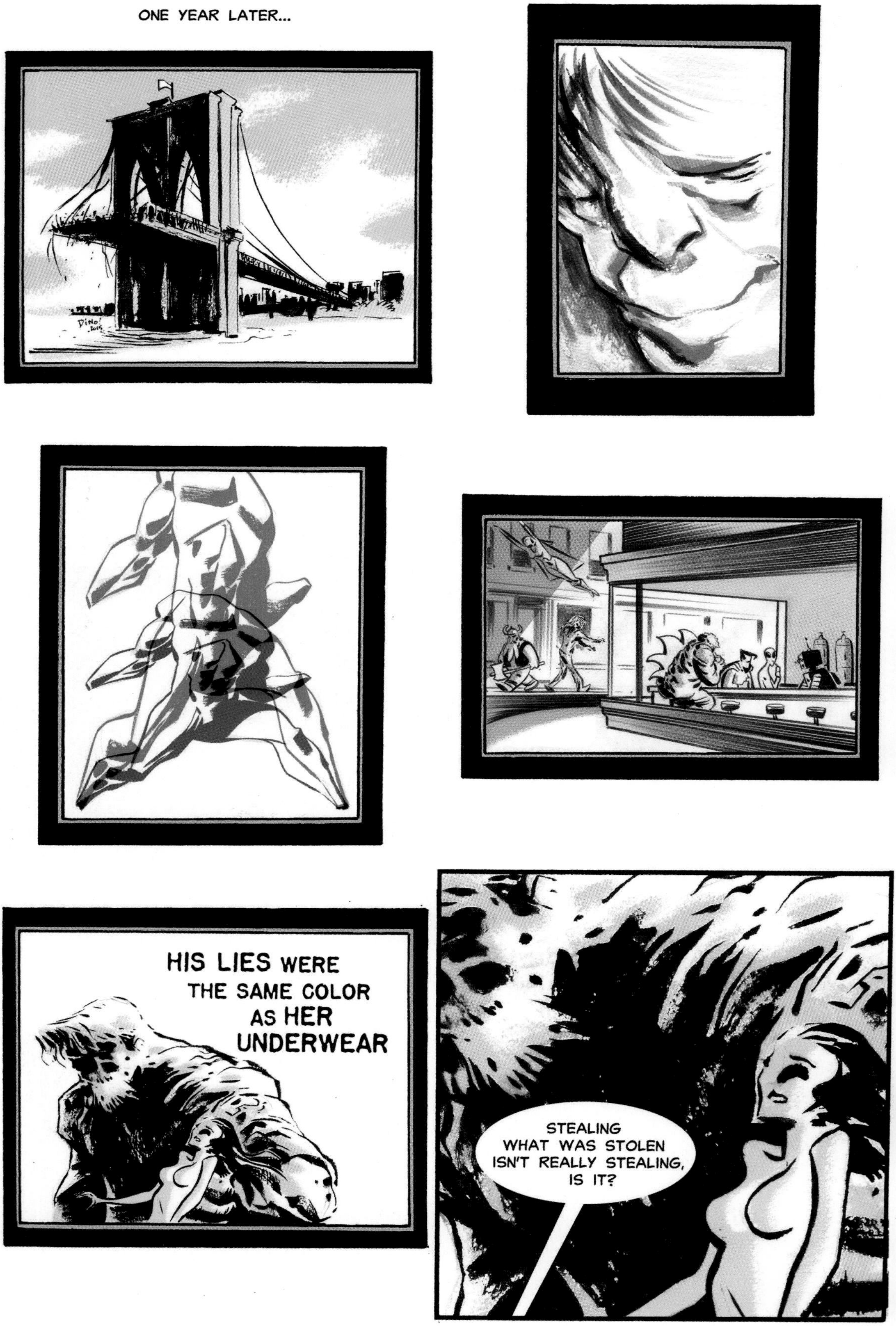
HIS LIES WERE THE SAME COLOR AS HER UNDERWEAR
STEALING WHAT WAS STOLEN ISN'T REALLY STEALING, IS IT?

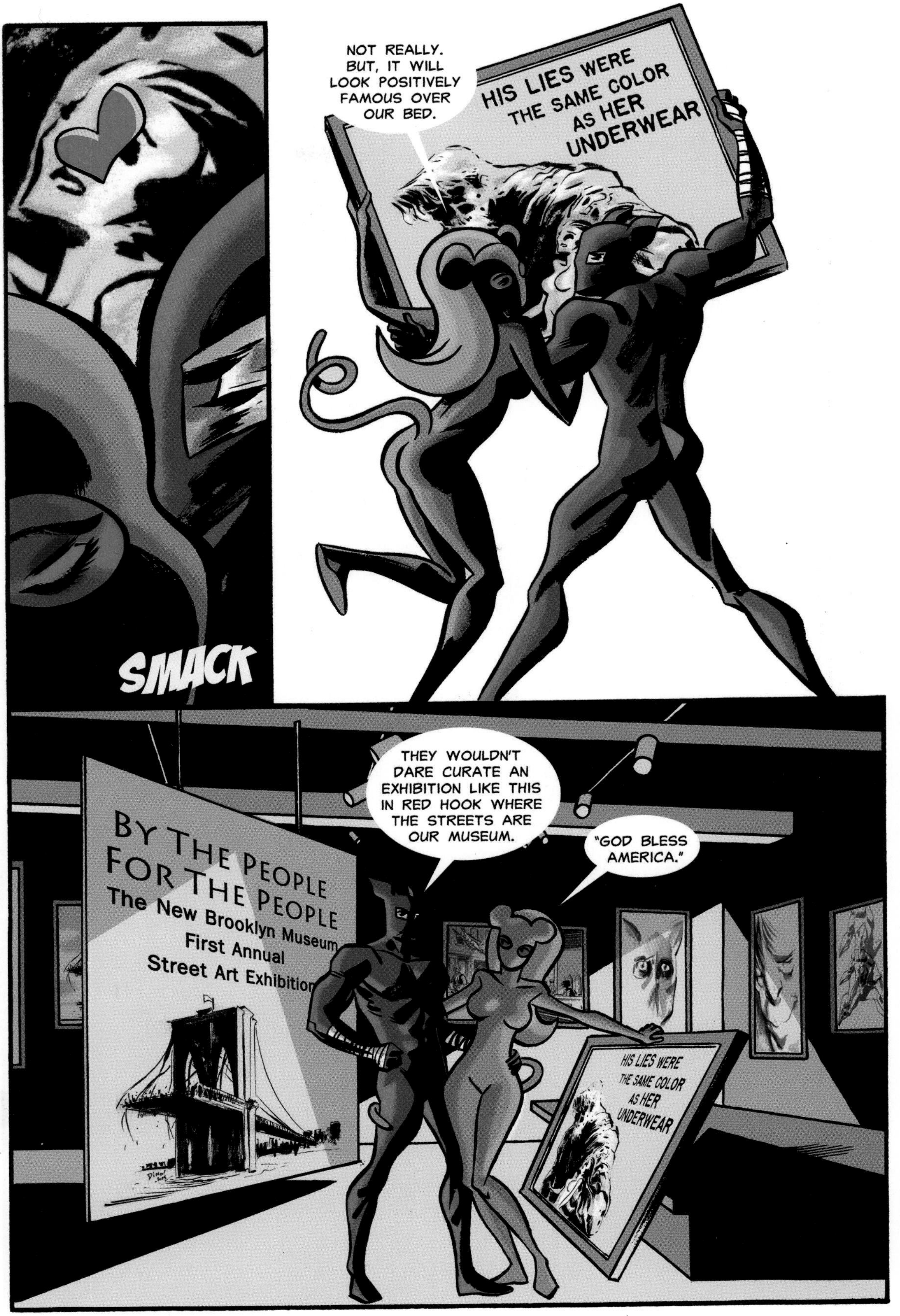
SMACK
NOT REALLY. BUT, IT WILL LOOK POSITIVELY FAMOUS OVER OUR BED.
HIS LIES WERE THE SAME COLOR AS HER UNDERWEAR
BY THE PEOPLE FOR THE PEOPLE
The New Brooklyn Museum
First Annual
Street Art Exhibition
THEY WOULDN'T DARE CURATE AN EXHIBITION LIKE THIS IN RED HOOK WHERE THE STREETS ARE OUR MUSEUM.
"GOD BLESS AMERICA."
HIS LIES WERE THE SAME COLOR AS HER UNDERWEAR

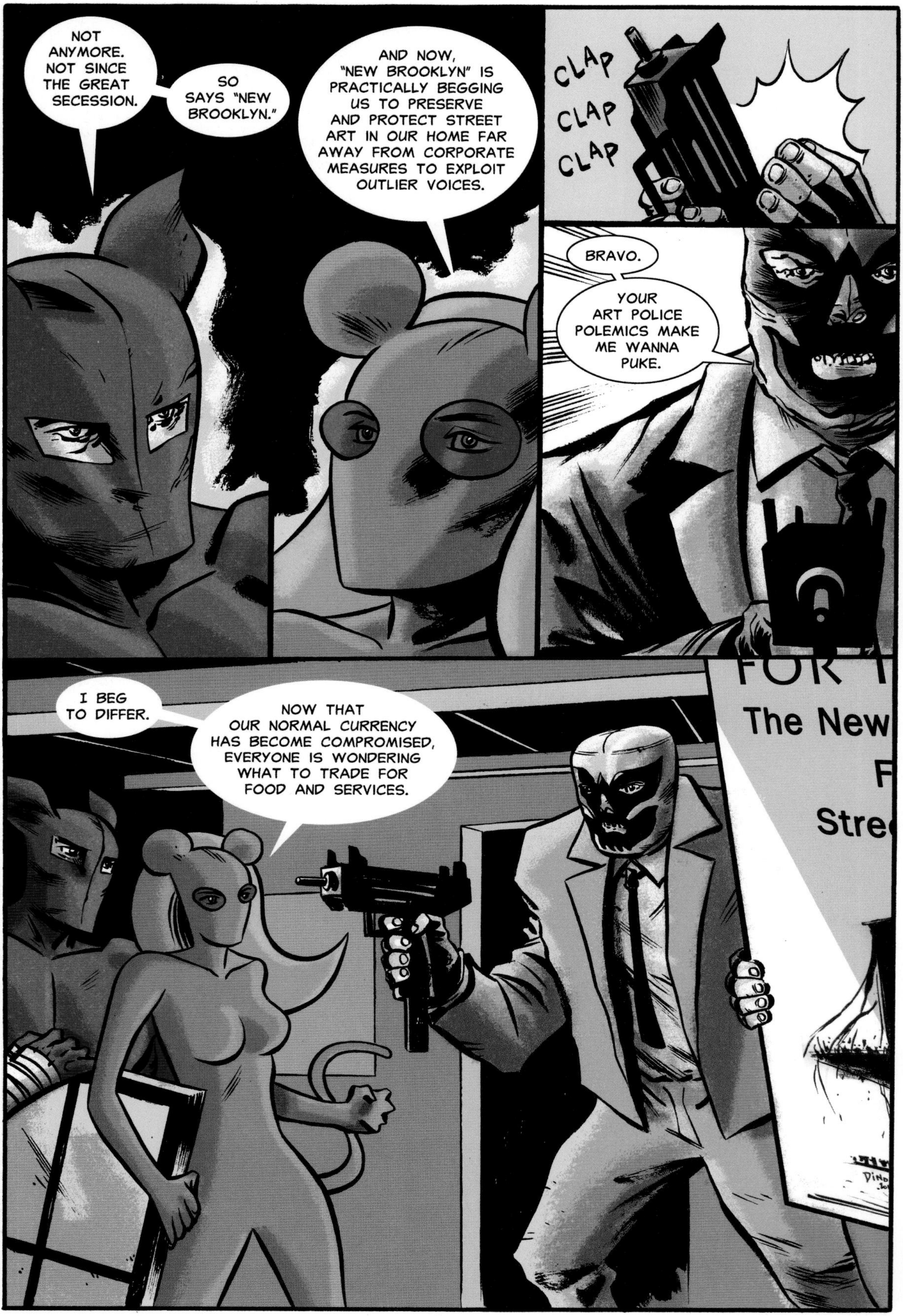
NOT ANYMORE. NOT SINCE THE GREAT SECESSION.
SO SAYS "NEW BROOKLYN."
AND NOW, "NEW BROOKLYN" IS PRACTICALLY BEGGING US TO PRESERVE AND PROTECT STREET ART IN OUR HOME FAR AWAY FROM CORPORATE MEASURES TO EXPLOIT OUTLIER VOICES.
CLAP CLAP CLAP
BRAVO.
YOUR ART POLICE POLEMICS MAKE ME WANNA PUKE.
I BEG TO DIFFER.
NOW THAT OUR NORMAL CURRENCY HAS BECOME COMPROMISED, EVERYONE IS WONDERING WHAT TO TRADE FOR FOOD AND SERVICES.
FOR
The New
F
Stre

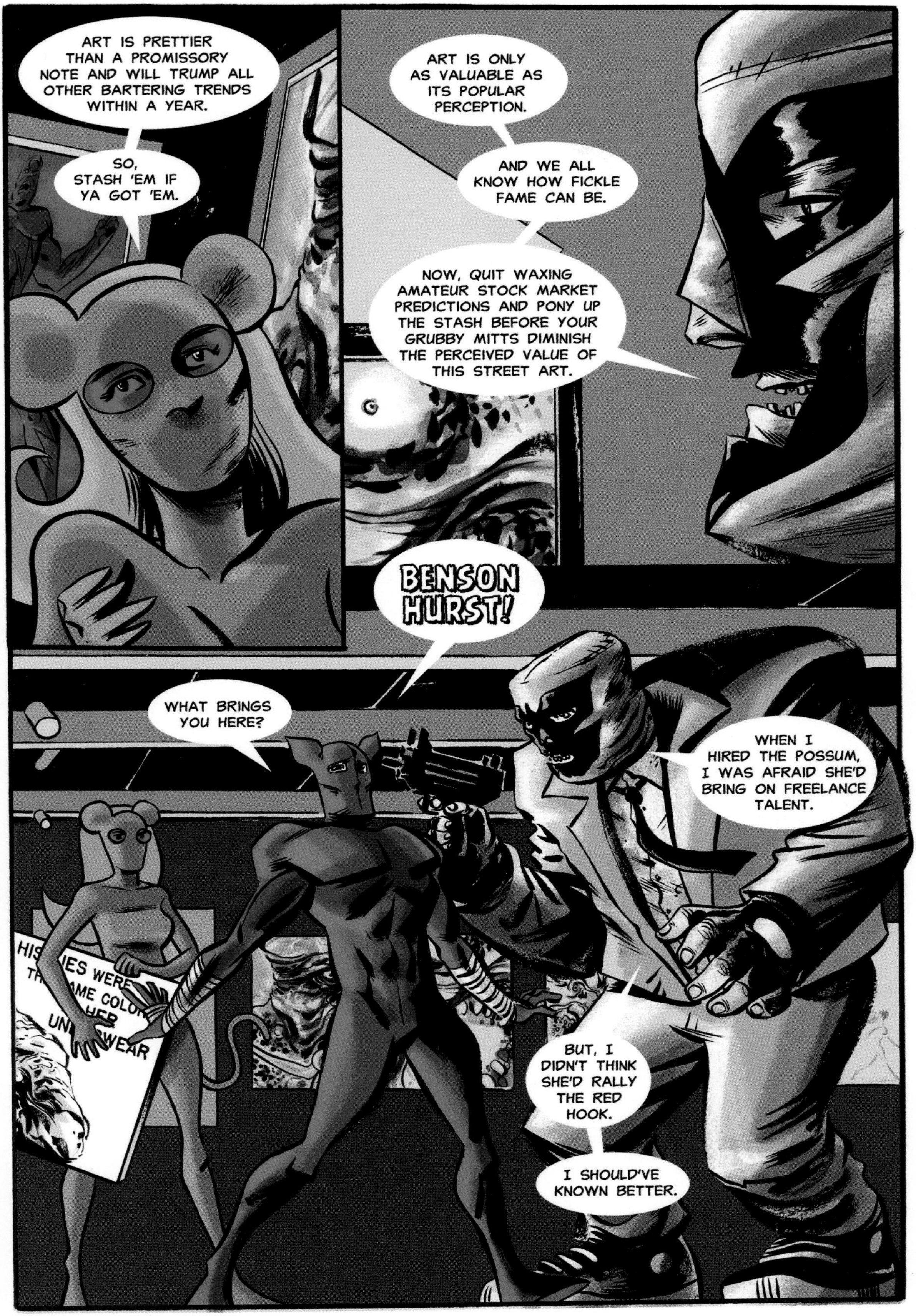
ART IS PRETTIER THAN A PROMISSORY NOTE AND WILL TRUMP ALL OTHER BARTERING TRENDS WITHIN A YEAR.
SO, STASH 'EM IF YA GOT 'EM.
ART IS ONLY AS VALUABLE AS ITS POPULAR PERCEPTION.
AND WE ALL KNOW HOW FICKLE FAME CAN BE.
NOW, QUIT WAXING AMATEUR STOCK MARKET PREDICTIONS AND PONY UP THE STASH BEFORE YOUR GRUBBY MITTS DIMINISH THE PERCEIVED VALUE OF THIS STREET ART.
BENSON HURST!
WHAT BRINGS YOU HERE?
WHEN I HIRED THE POSSUM, I WAS AFRAID SHE'D BRING ON FREELANCE TALENT.
BUT, I DIDN'T THINK SHE'D RALLY THE RED HOOK.
I SHOULD'VE KNOWN BETTER.

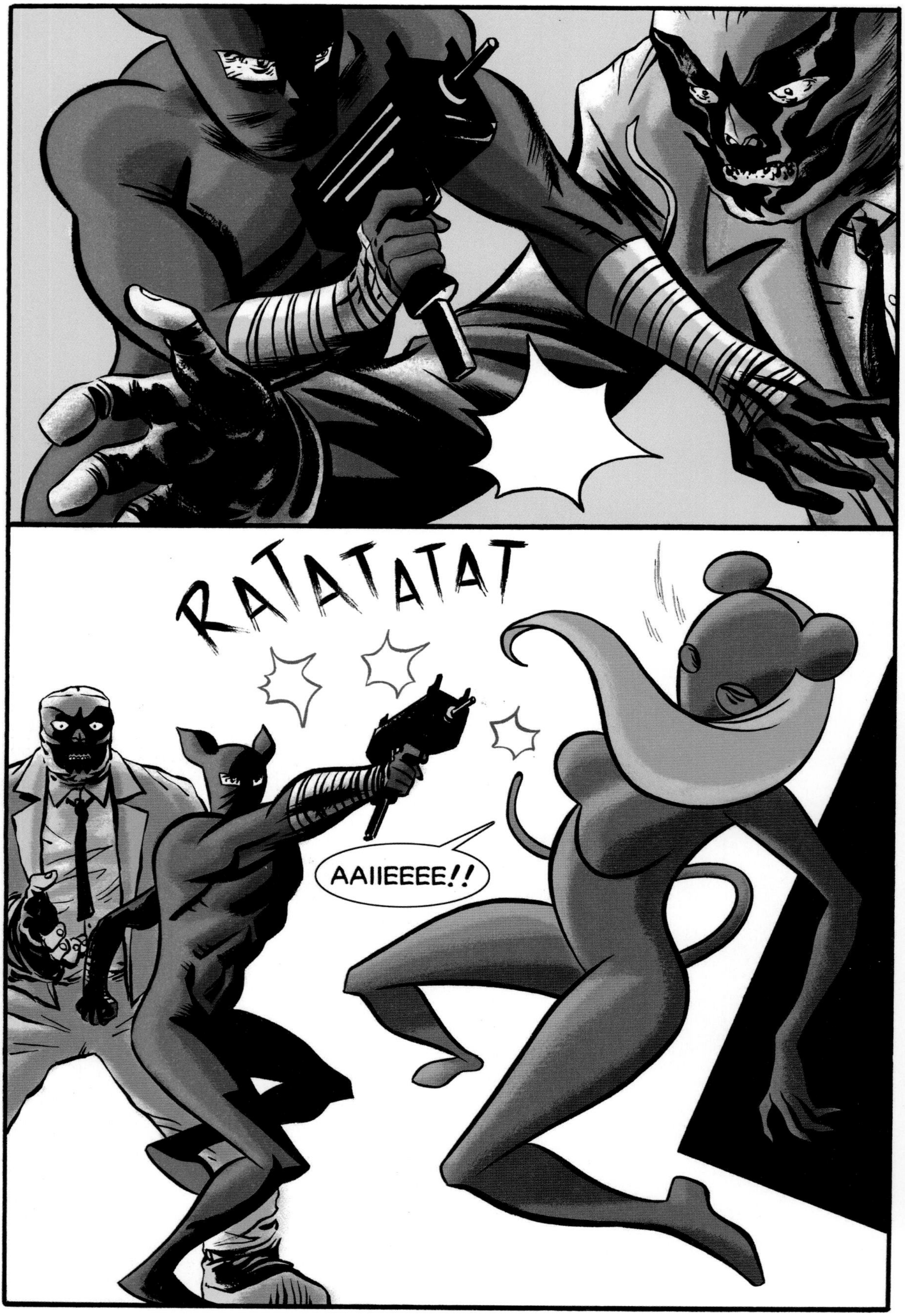
RATATATAT
AAIIEEEE!!

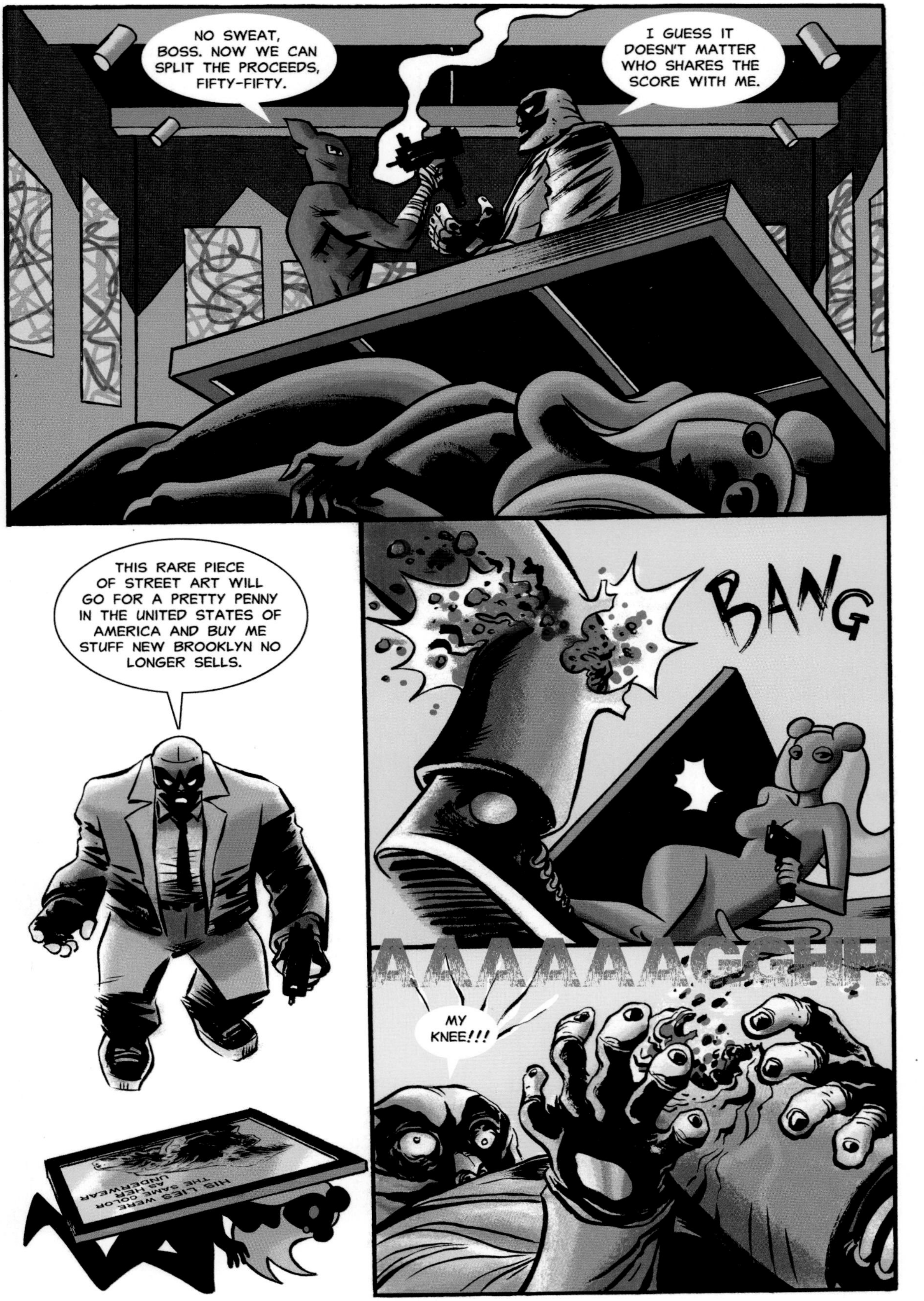
NO SWEAT, BOSS. NOW WE CAN SPLIT THE PROCEEDS, FIFTY-FIFTY.
I GUESS IT DOESN'T MATTER WHO SHARES THE SCORE WITH ME.
THIS RARE PIECE OF STREET ART WILL GO FOR A PRETTY PENNY IN THE UNITED STATES OF AMERICA AND BUY ME STUFF NEW BROOKLYN NO LONGER SELLS.
HIS LIES WERE THE SAME COLOR AS HER UNDERWEAR
BANG
AAAAAAGGHH
MY KNEE!!!

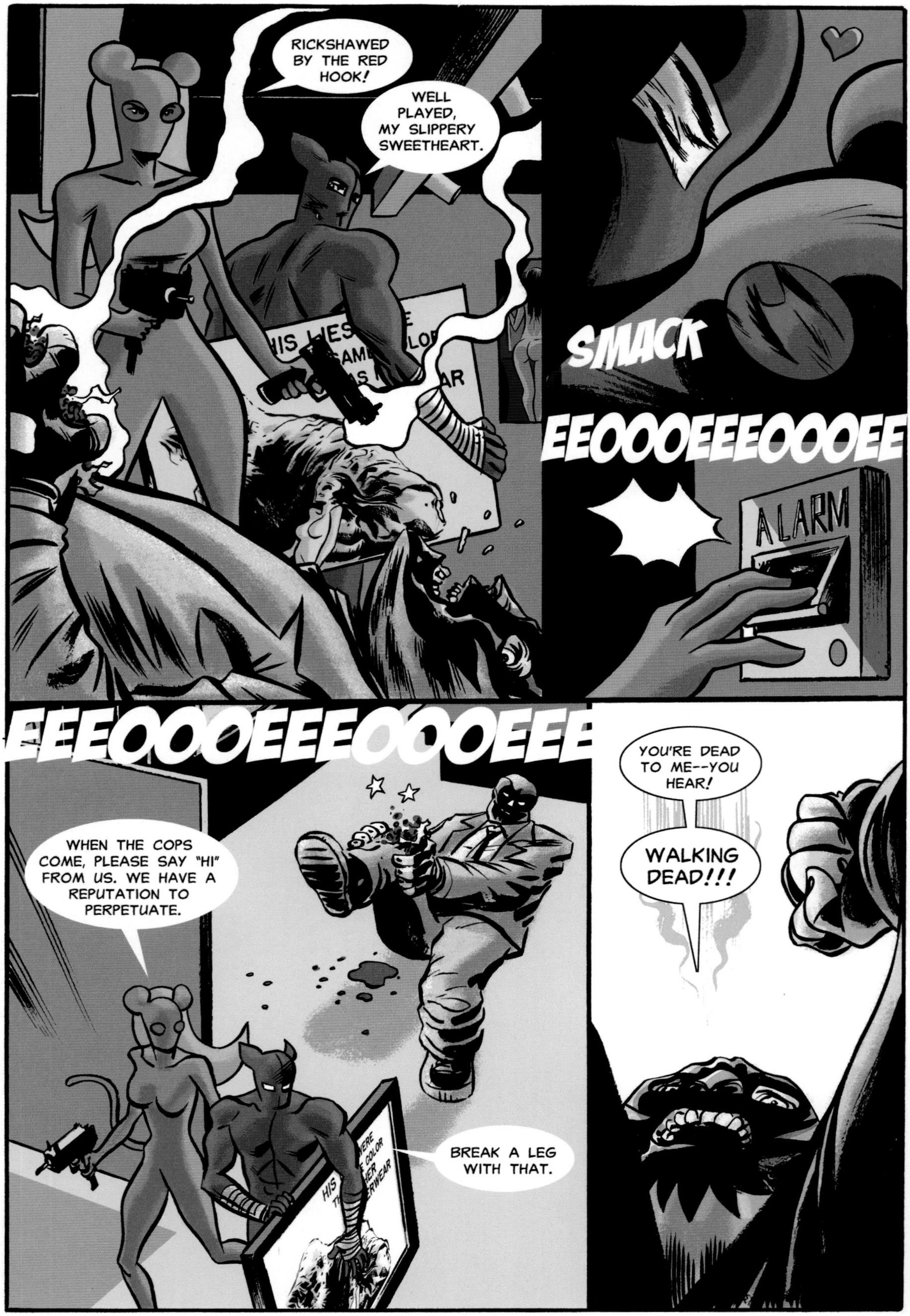
RICKSHAWED BY THE RED HOOK!
WELL PLAYED, MY SLIPPERY SWEETHEART.
SMACK
EEOOOEEEOOOEE
ALARM
EEEOOOEEEOOOEEE
WHEN THE COPS COME, PLEASE SAY "HI" FROM US. WE HAVE A REPUTATION TO PERPETUATE.
BREAK A LEG WITH THAT.
YOU'RE DEAD TO ME--YOU HEAR!
WALKING DEAD!!!

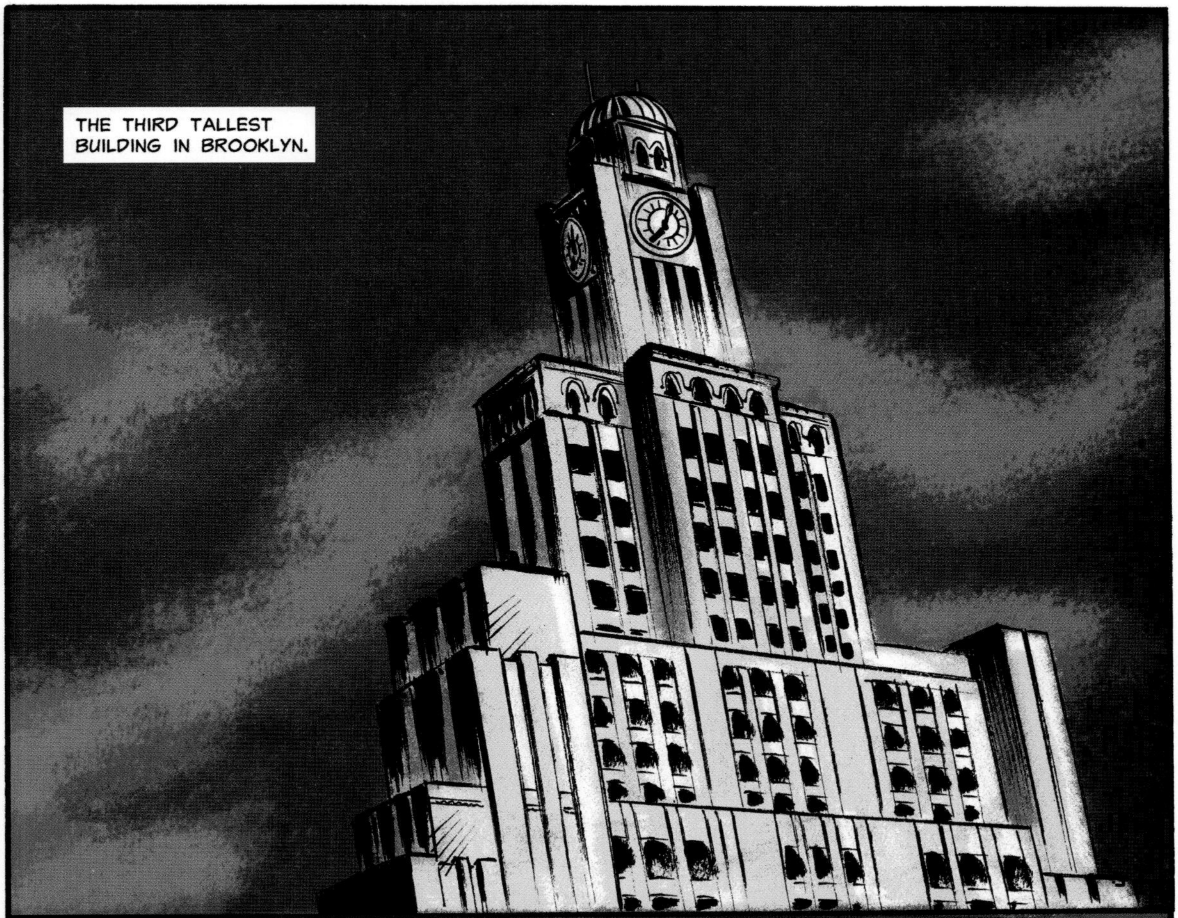
THE THIRD TALLEST
BUILDING IN BROOKLYN.

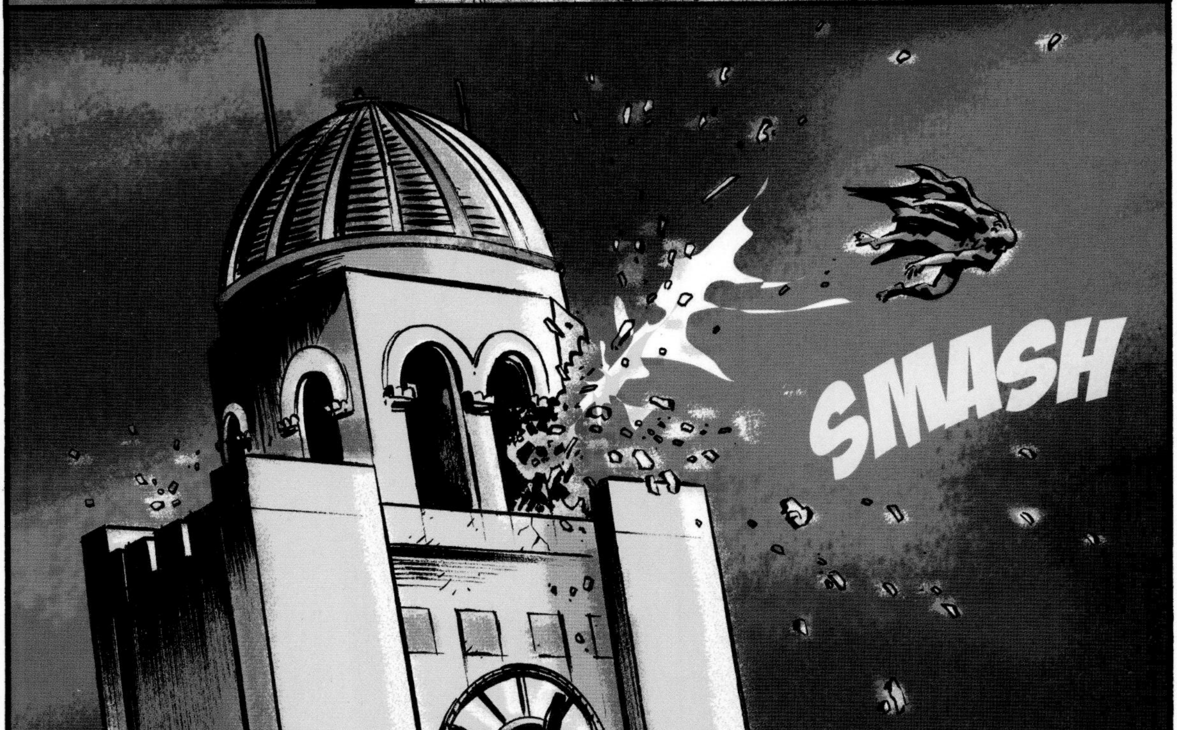
SMASH

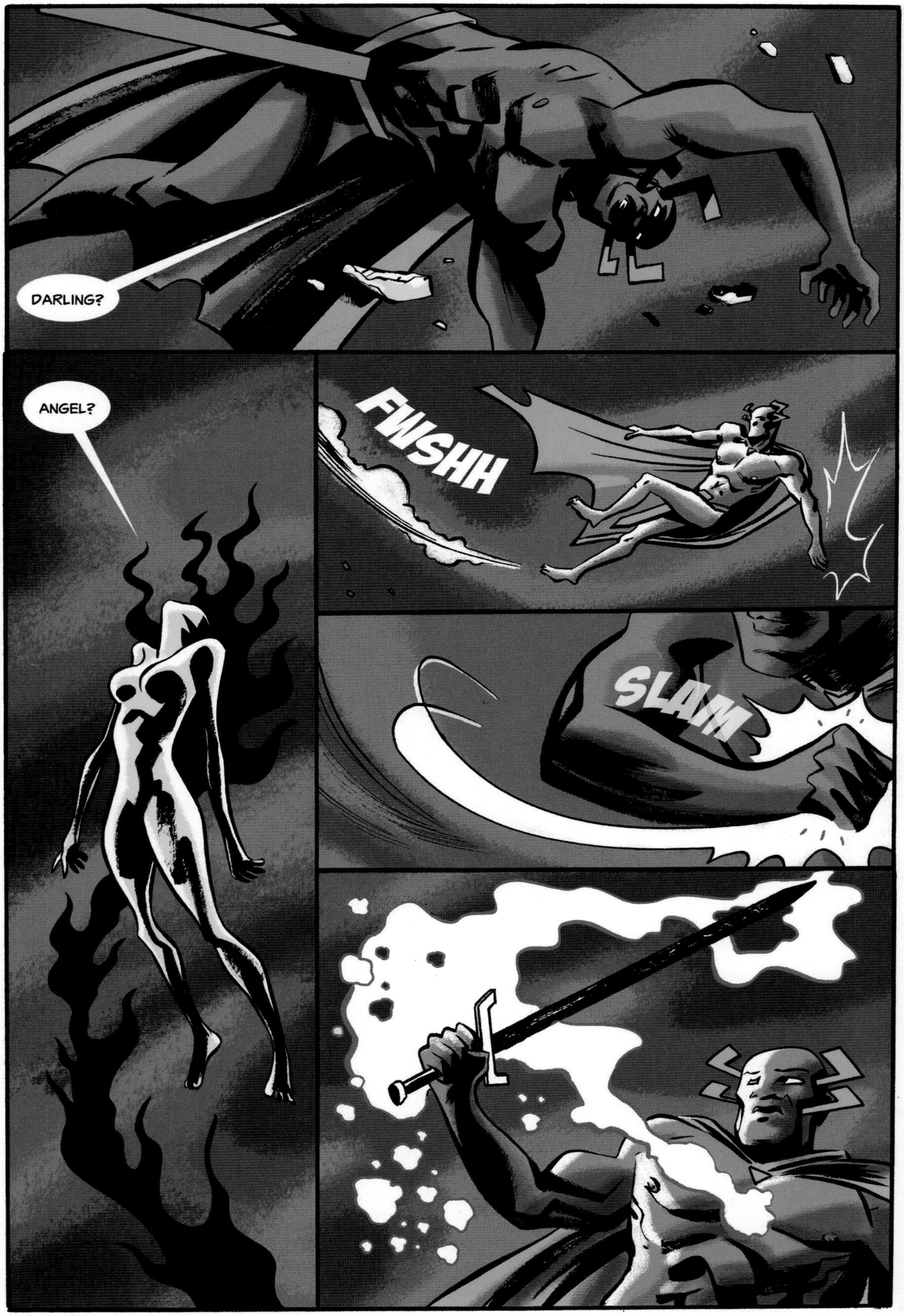

DARLING?
ANGEL?
FWSHH
SLAM

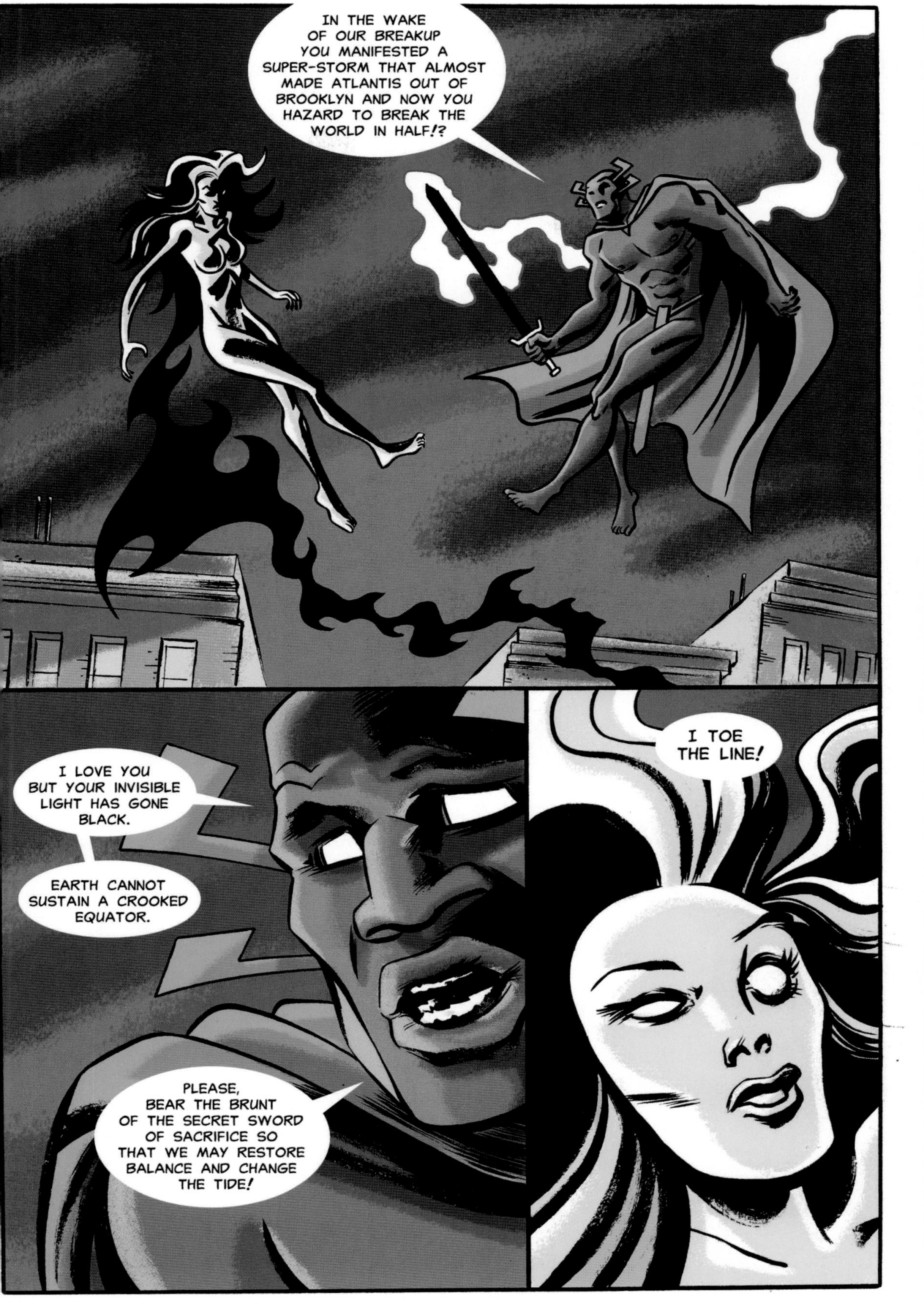
IN THE WAKE OF OUR BREAKUP YOU MANIFESTED A SUPER-STORM THAT ALMOST MADE ATLANTIS OUT OF BROOKLYN AND NOW YOU HAZARD TO BREAK THE WORLD IN HALF!?
I LOVE YOU BUT YOUR INVISIBLE LIGHT HAS GONE BLACK.
EARTH CANNOT SUSTAIN A CROOKED EQUATOR.
PLEASE, BEAR THE BRUNT OF THE SECRET SWORD OF SACRIFICE SO THAT WE MAY RESTORE BALANCE AND CHANGE THE TIDE!
I TOE THE LINE!

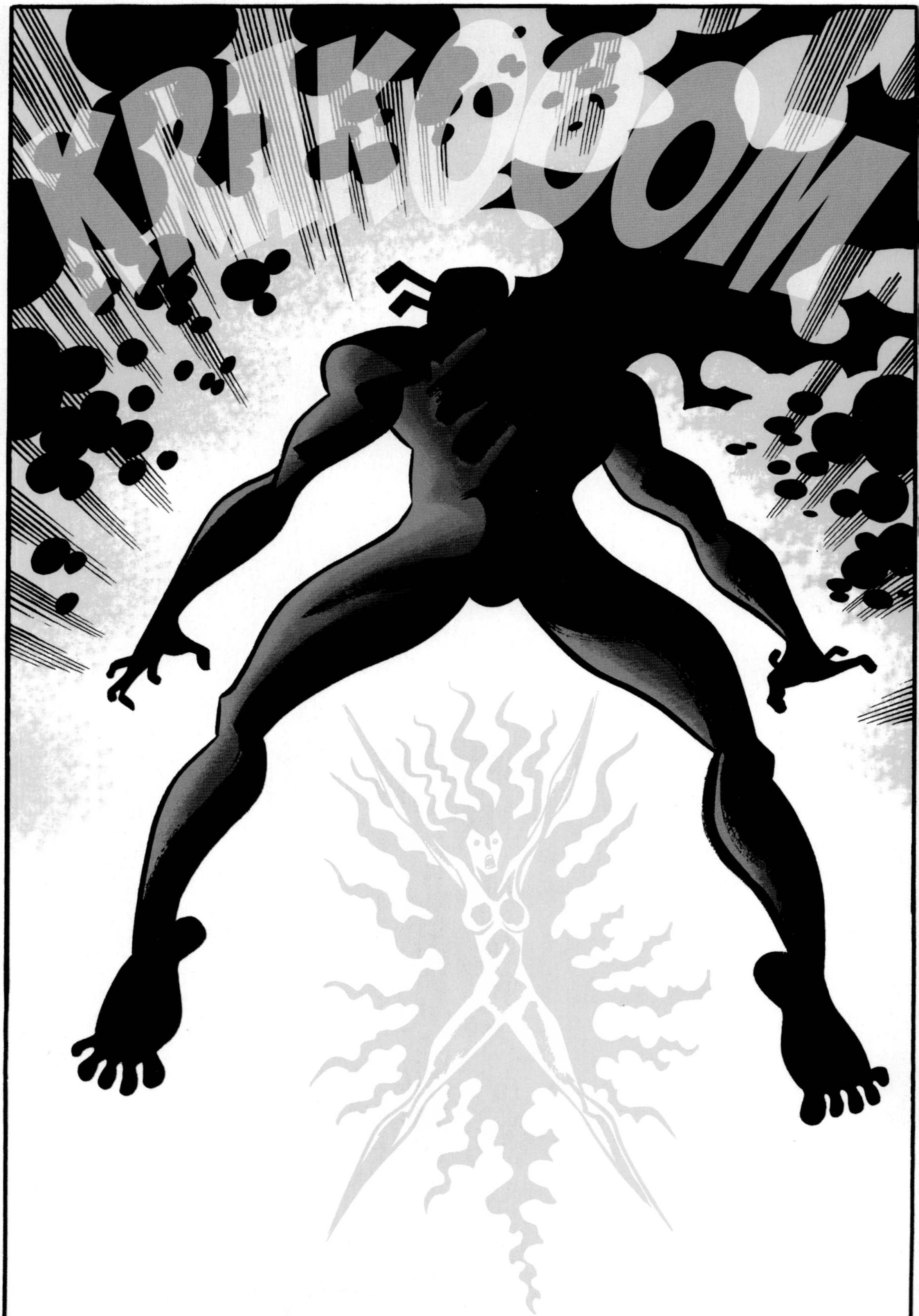
KRAKOOOM

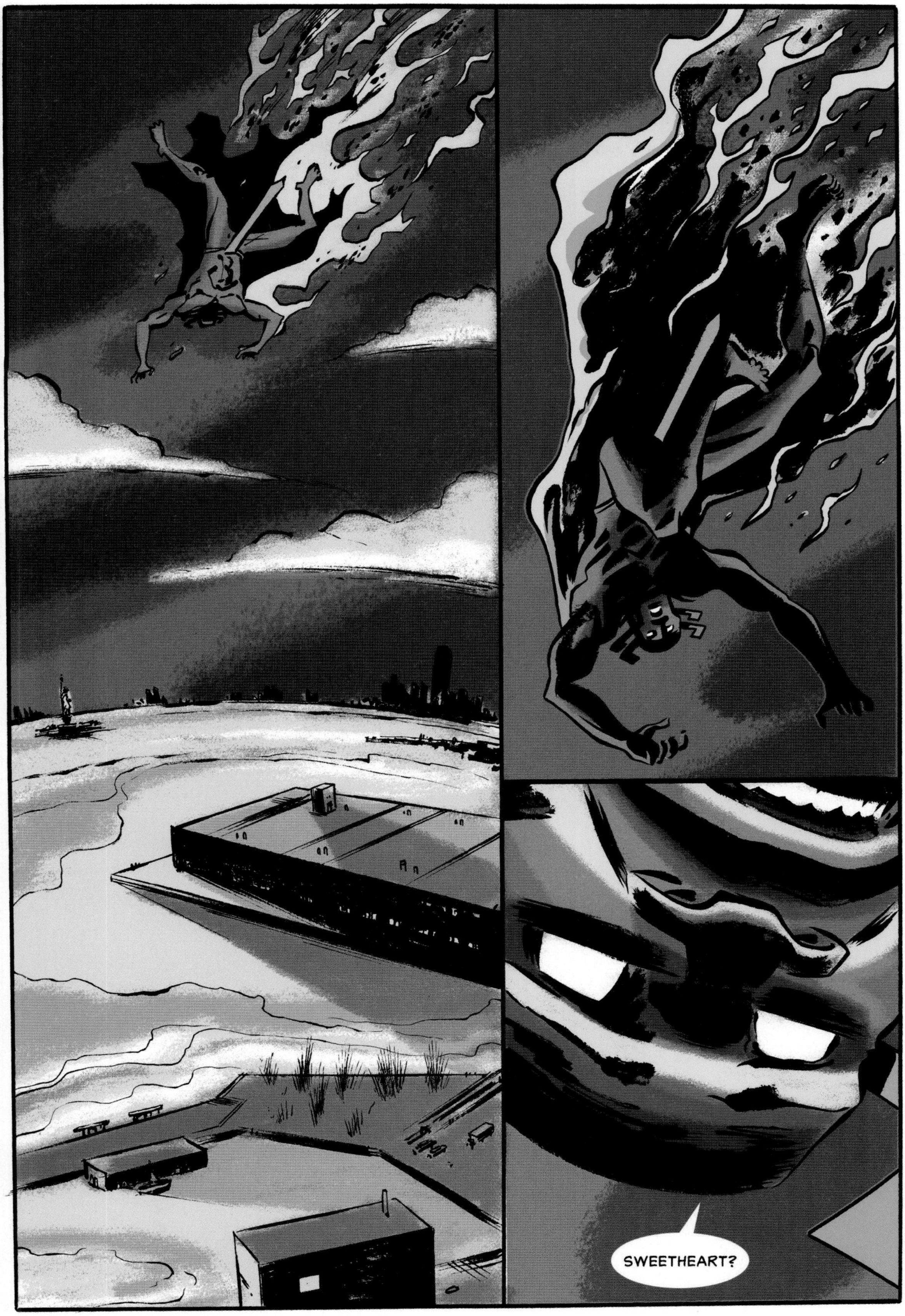
SWEETHEART?

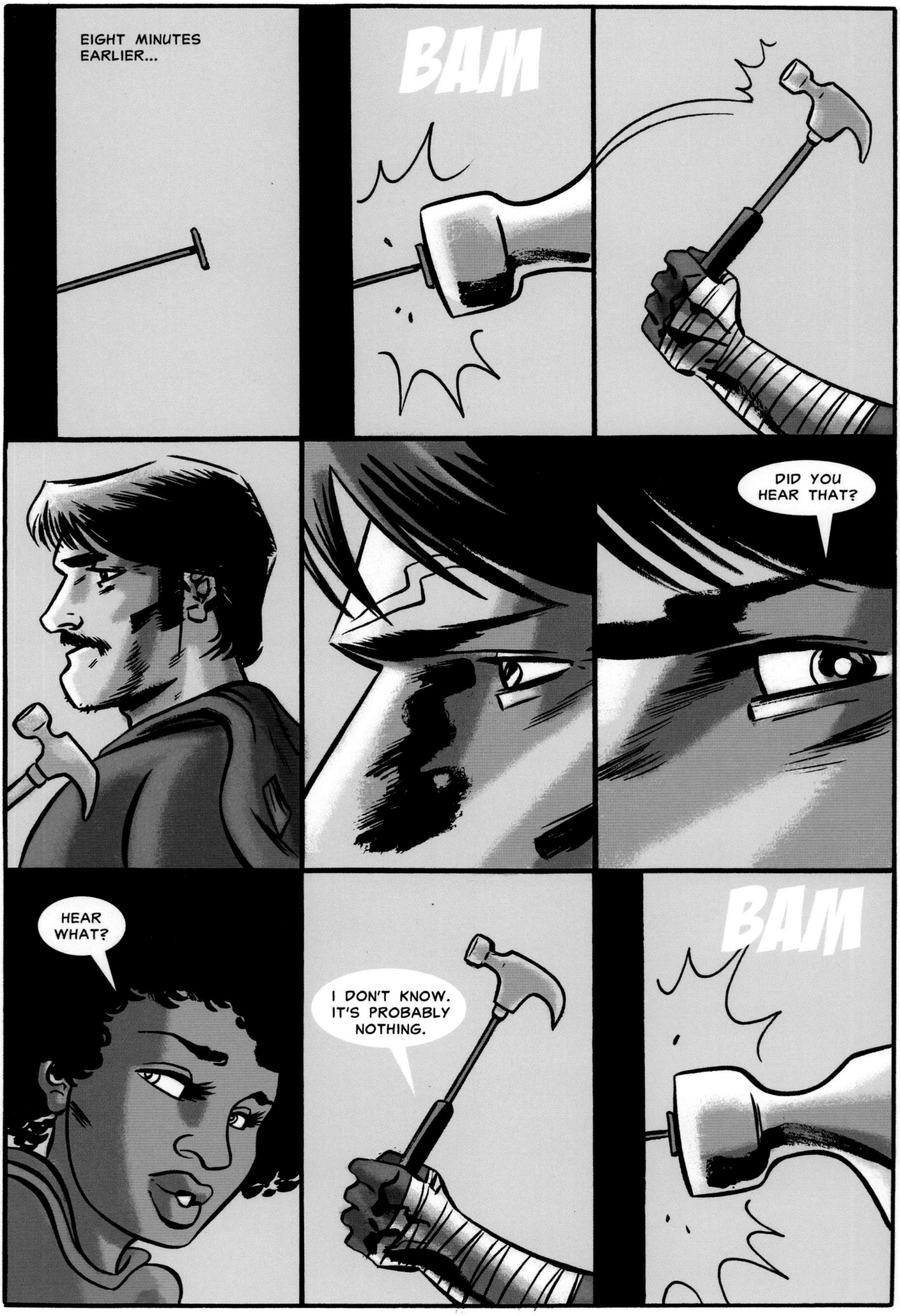

EIGHT MINUTES EARLIER...
BAM
DID YOU HEAR THAT?
HEAR WHAT?
I DON'T KNOW. IT'S PROBABLY NOTHING.
BAM

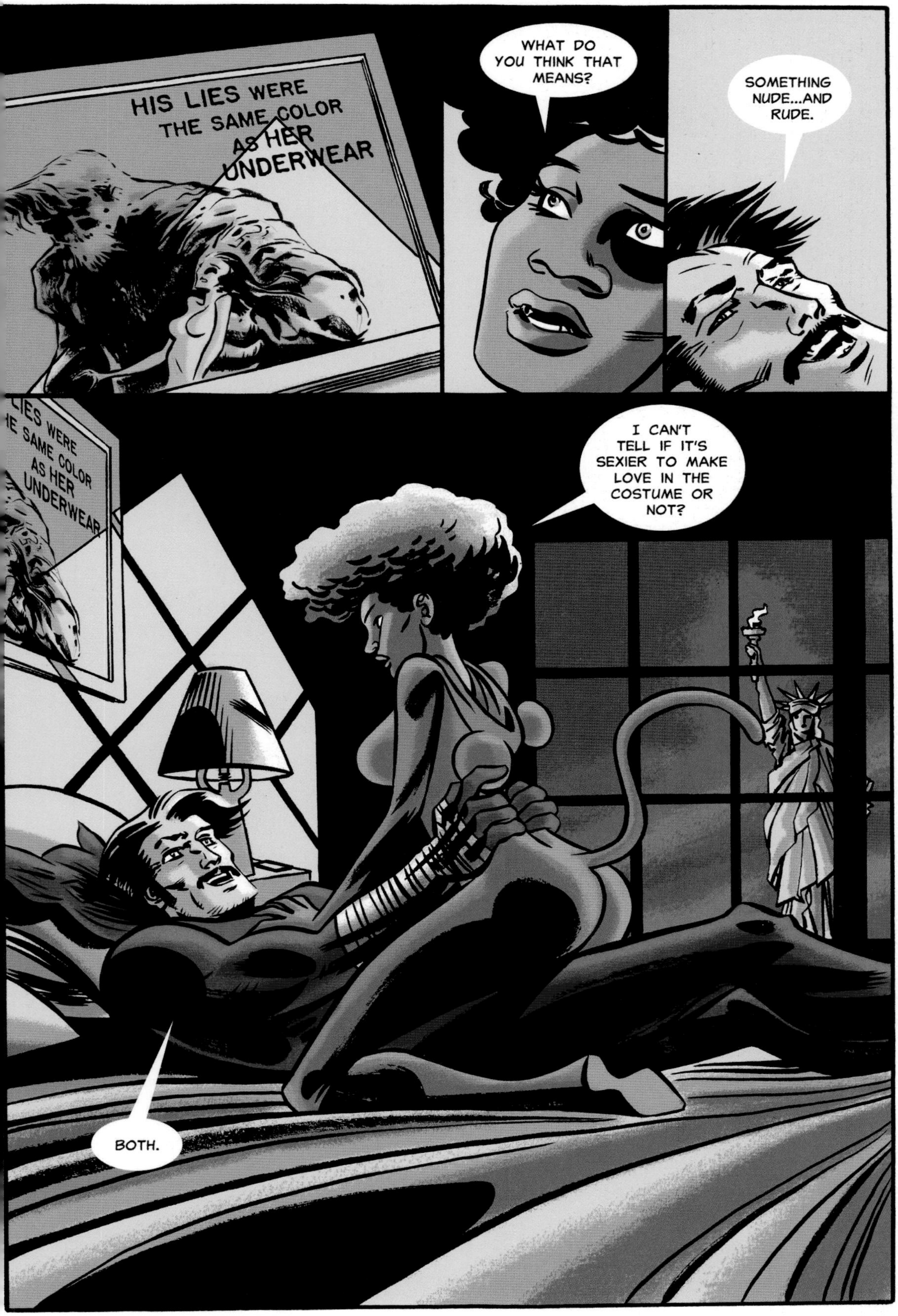
HIS LIES WERE THE SAME COLOR AS HER UNDERWEAR
WHAT DO YOU THINK THAT MEANS?
SOMETHING NUDE...AND RUDE.
LIES WERE THE SAME COLOR AS HER UNDERWEAR
I CAN'T TELL IF IT'S SEXIER TO MAKE LOVE IN THE COSTUME OR NOT?
BOTH.

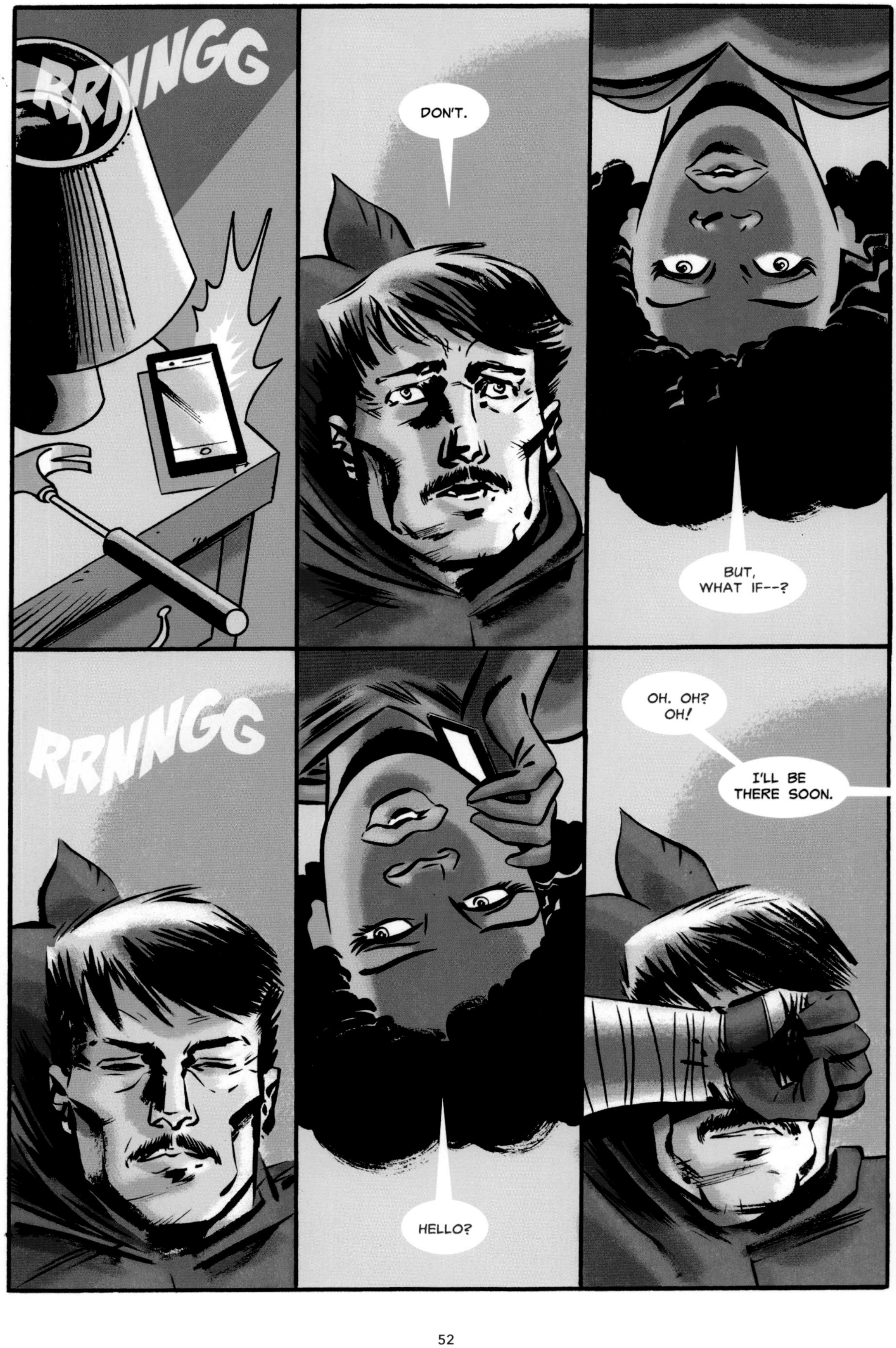
RRNNGG
DON'T.
BUT, WHAT IF--?
RRNNGG
HELLO?
OH. OH? OH!
I'LL BE THERE SOON.

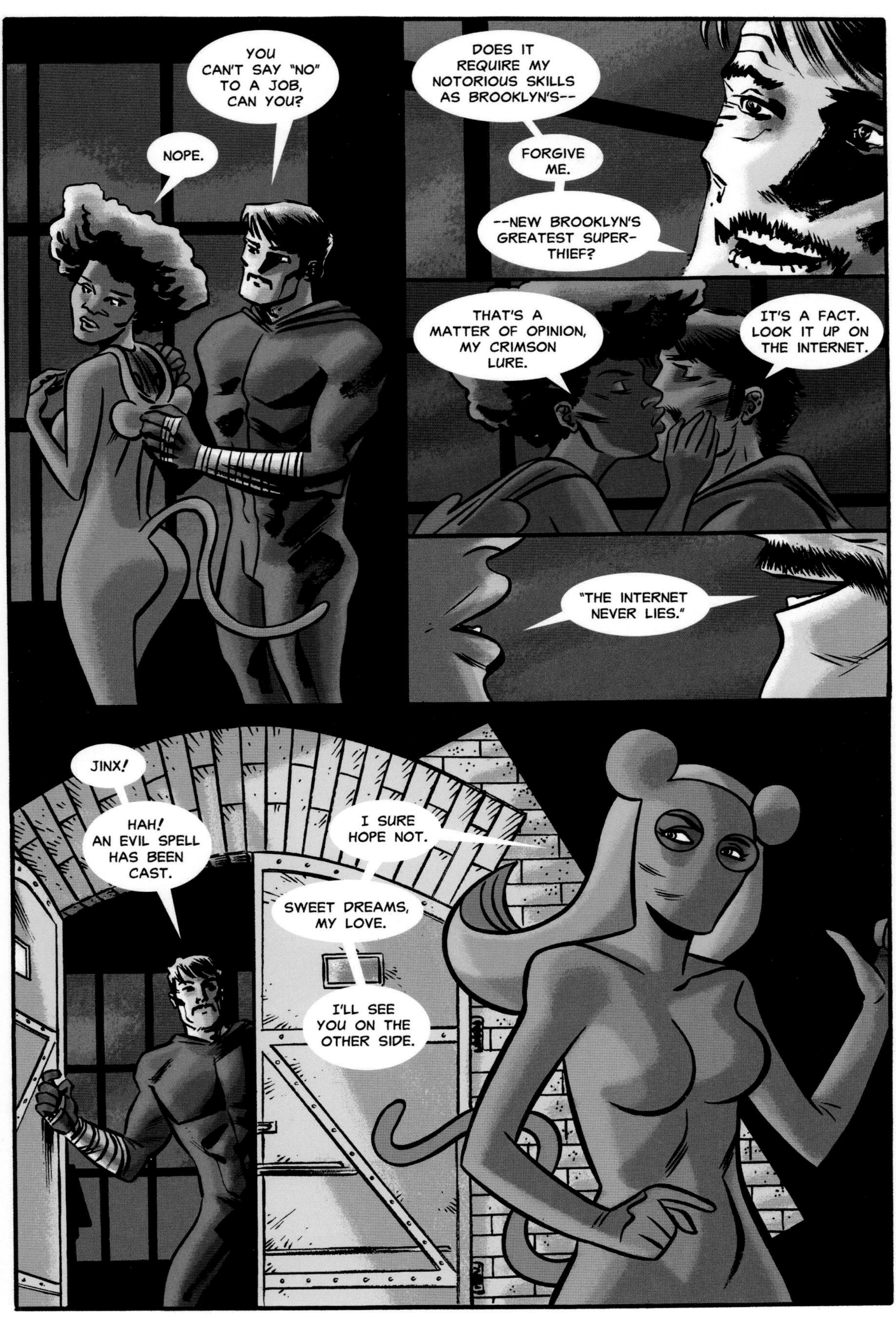
YOU CAN'T SAY "NO" TO A JOB, CAN YOU?
NOPE.
DOES IT REQUIRE MY NOTORIOUS SKILLS AS BROOKLYN'S--
FORGIVE ME.
--NEW BROOKLYN'S GREATEST SUPER-THIEF?
THAT'S A MATTER OF OPINION, MY CRIMSON LURE.
IT'S A FACT. LOOK IT UP ON THE INTERNET.
"THE INTERNET NEVER LIES."
JINX!
HAH! AN EVIL SPELL HAS BEEN CAST.
I SURE HOPE NOT.
SWEET DREAMS, MY LOVE.
I'LL SEE YOU ON THE OTHER SIDE.

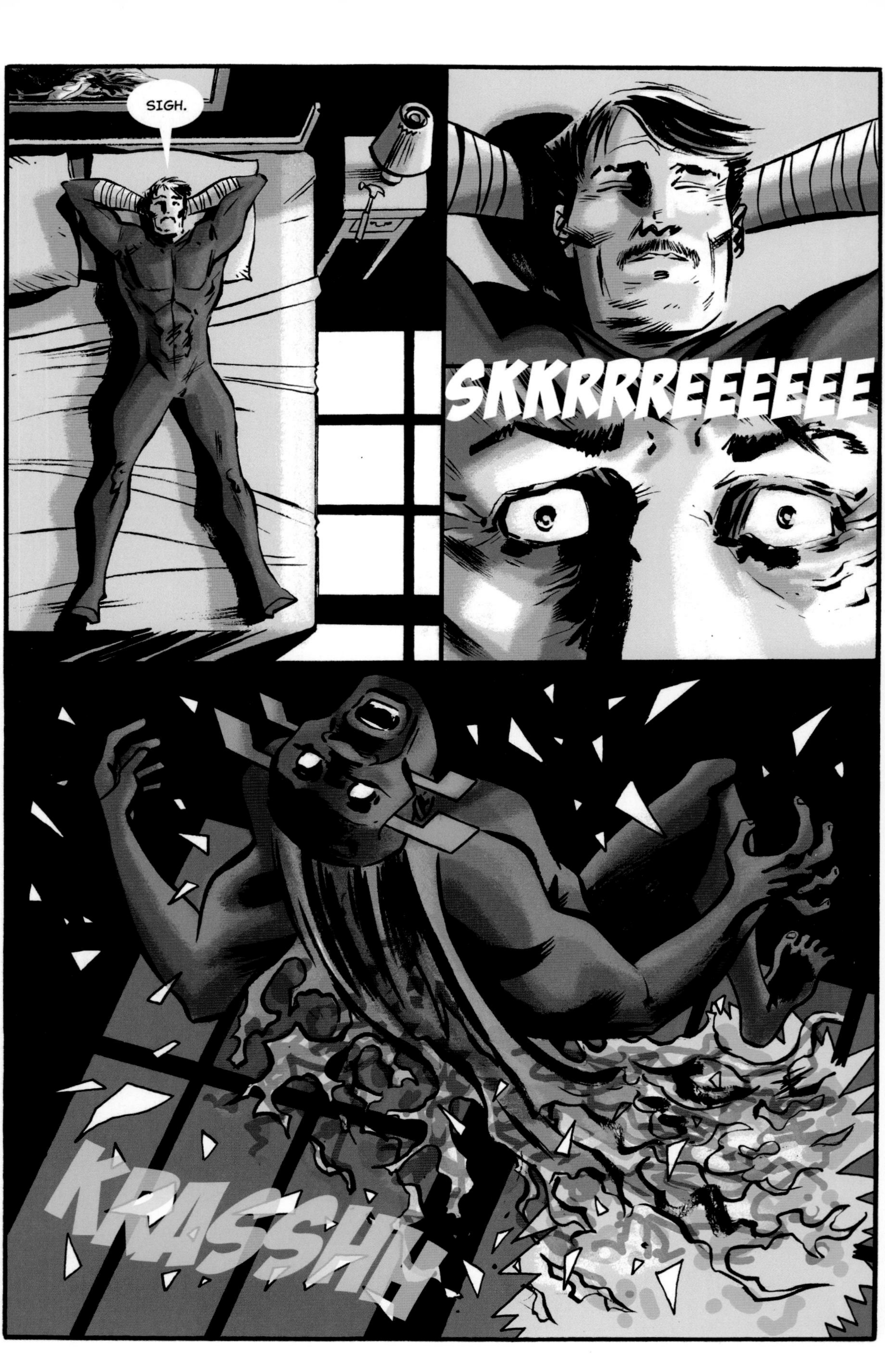
SIGH.
SKKRRRREEEEEE
KRASSH!!

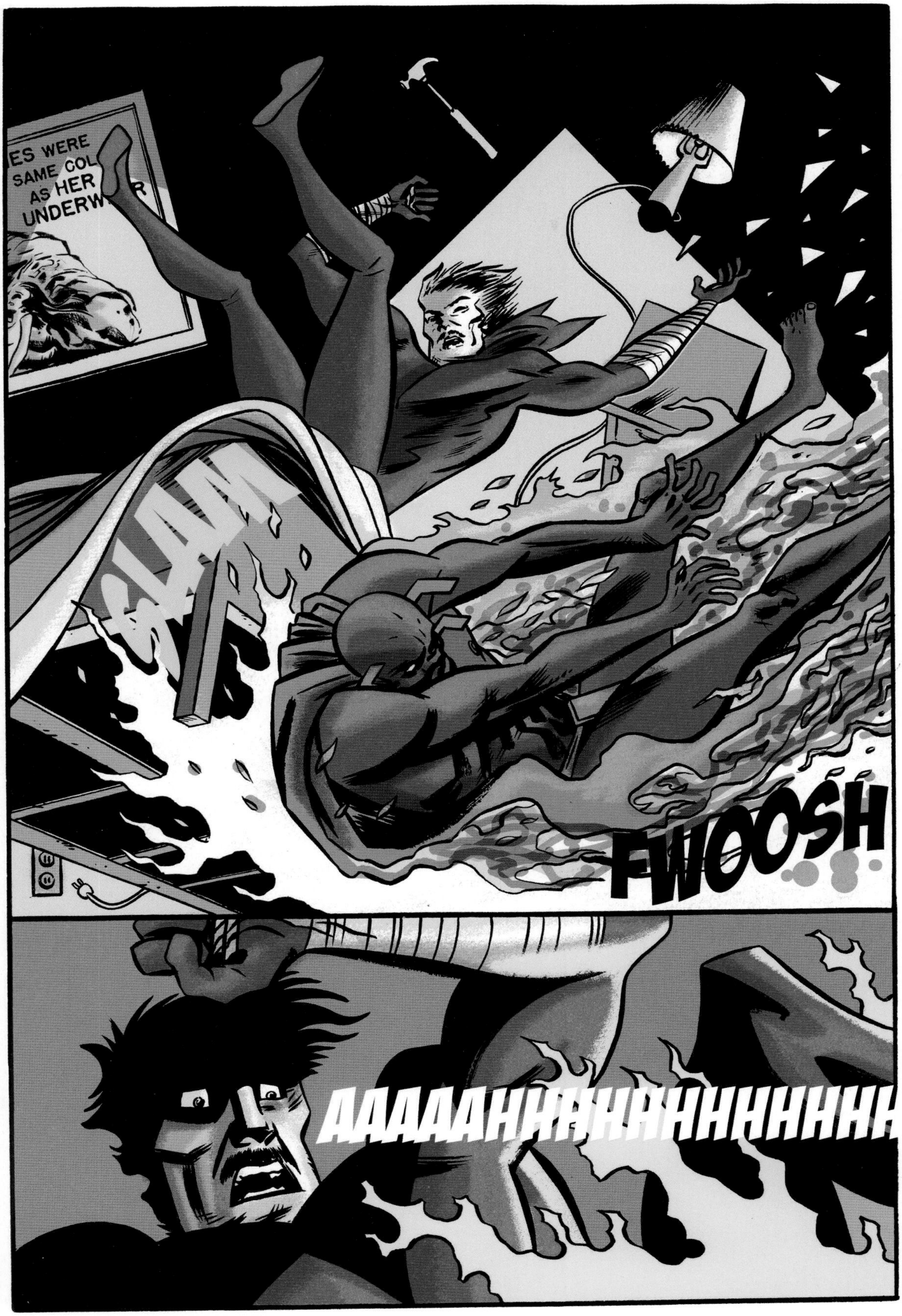

ES WERE
SAME COL
AS HER
UNDERW
SLAM
FWOOSH
AAAAAHHHHHHHHHHHH

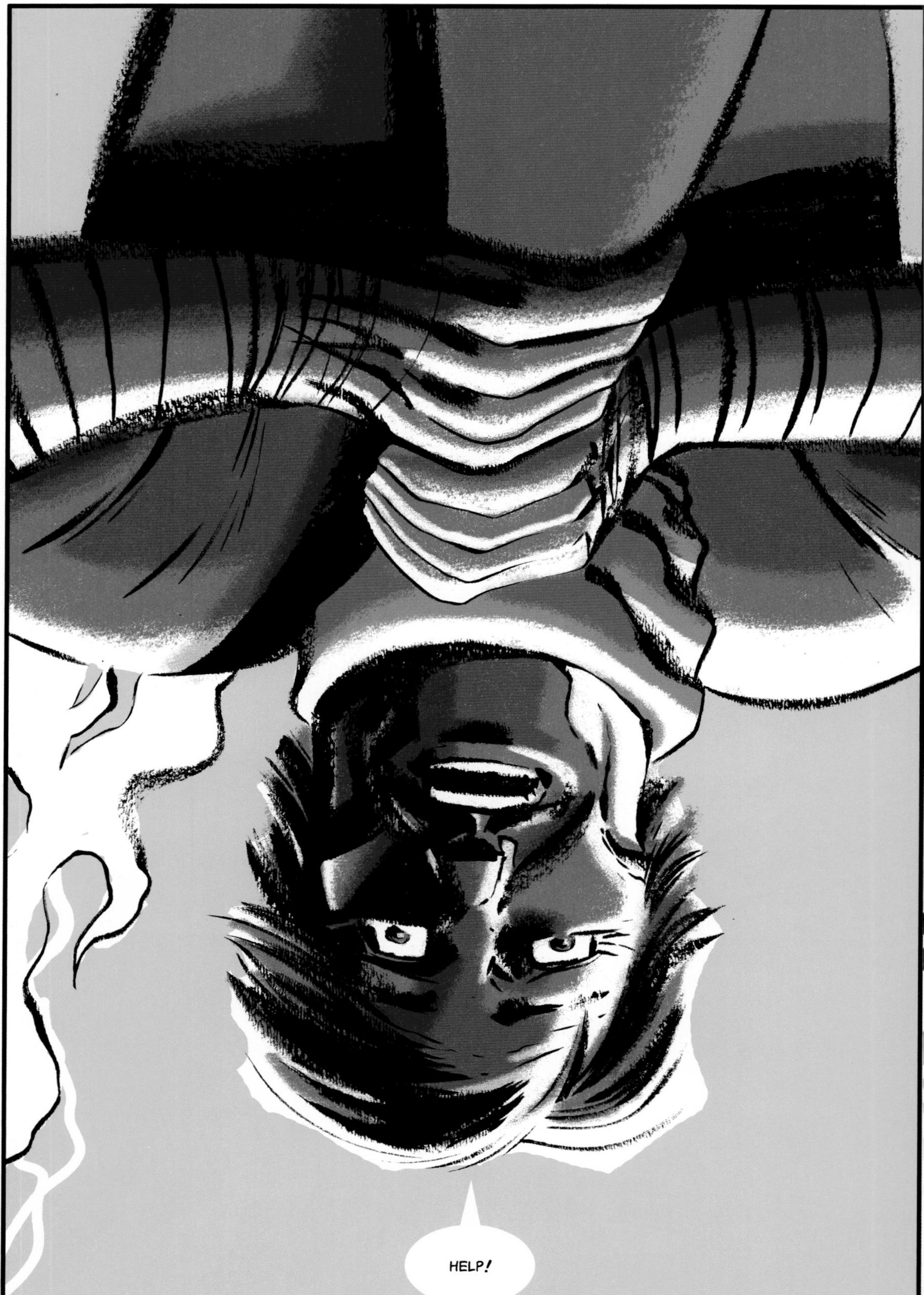
HELP!

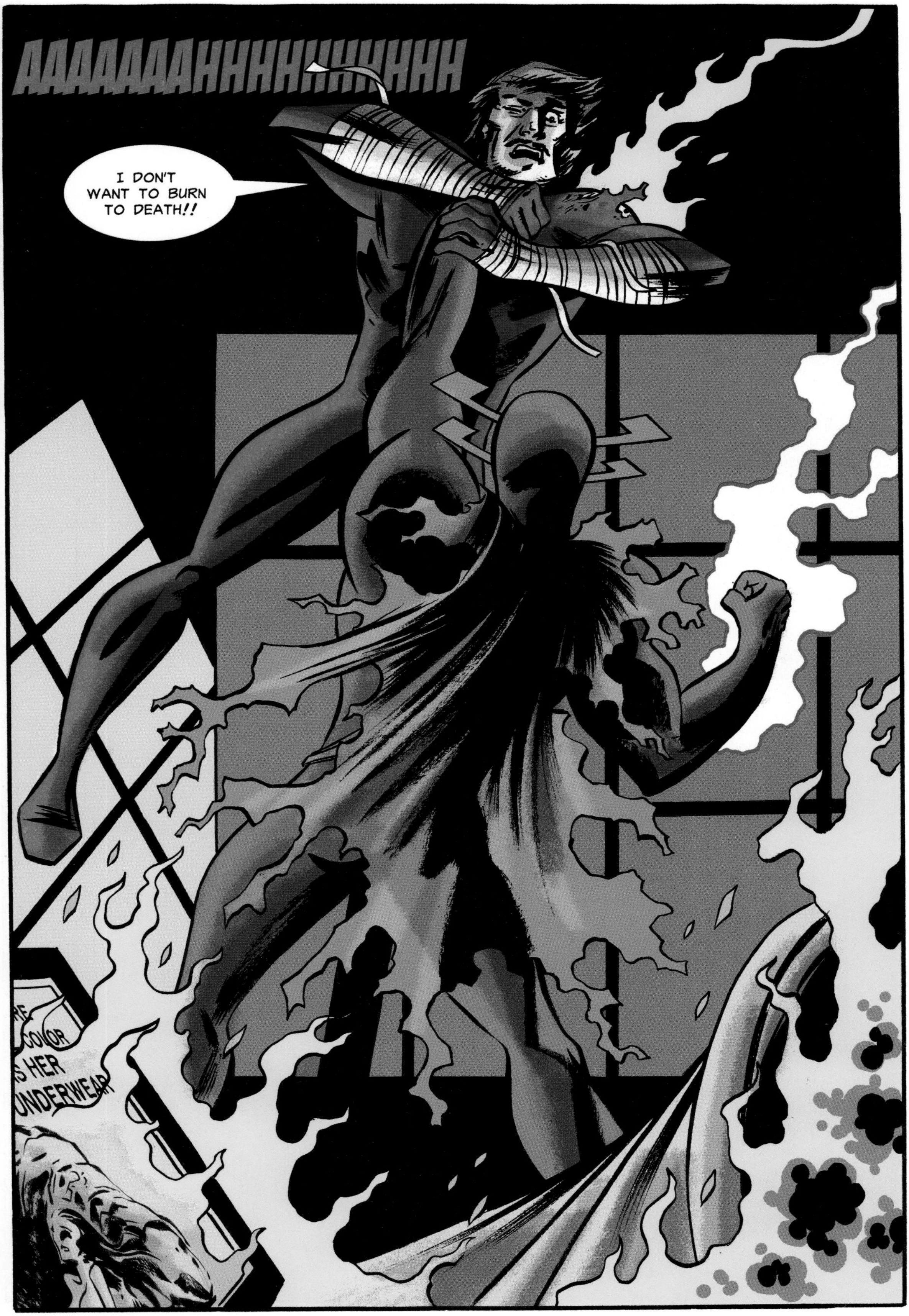
AAAAAAAHHHHHHHHHH
I DON'T WANT TO BURN TO DEATH!!
COLOR
HER
UNDERWEAR

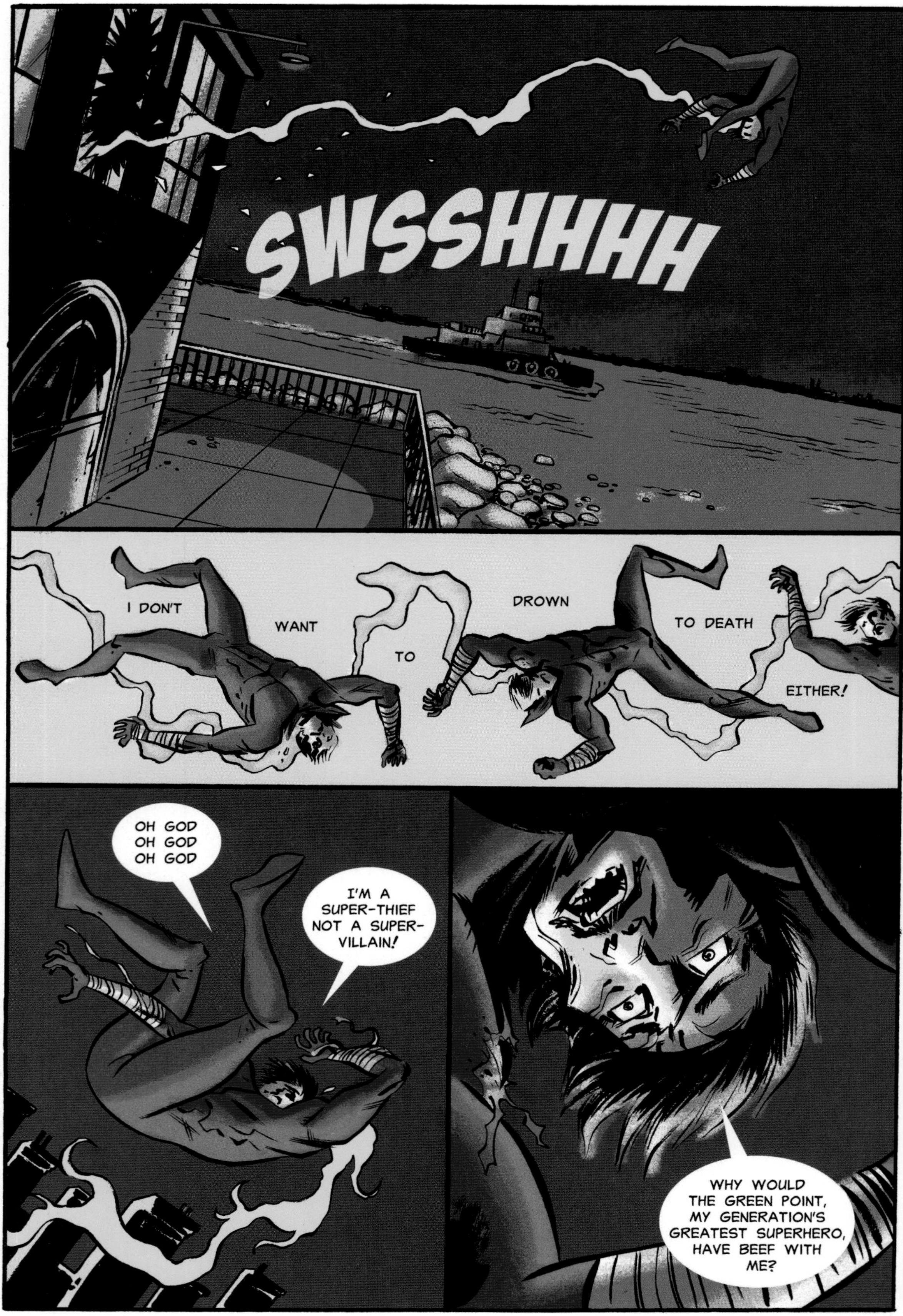
SWSSHHHH
I DON'T
WANT
TO
DROWN
TO DEATH
EITHER!
OH GOD
OH GOD
OH GOD
I'M A
SUPER-THIEF
NOT A SUPER-
VILLAIN!
WHY WOULD
THE GREEN POINT,
MY GENERATION'S
GREATEST SUPERHERO,
HAVE BEEF WITH
ME?

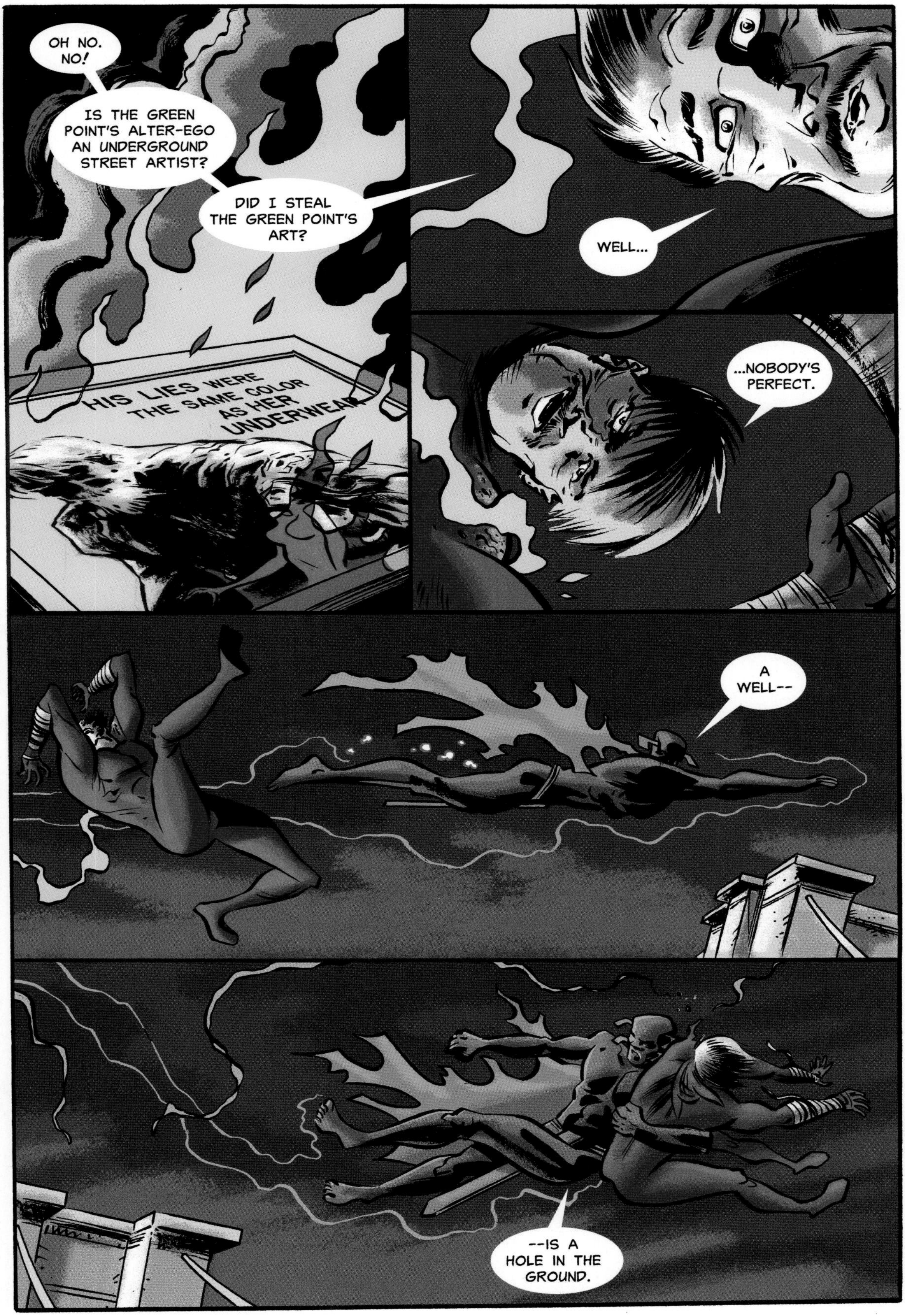
OH NO. NO!
IS THE GREEN POINT'S ALTER-EGO AN UNDERGROUND STREET ARTIST?
DID I STEAL THE GREEN POINT'S ART?
HIS LIES WERE THE SAME COLOR AS HER UNDERWEAR
WELL...
...NOBODY'S PERFECT.
A WELL--
--IS A HOLE IN THE GROUND.

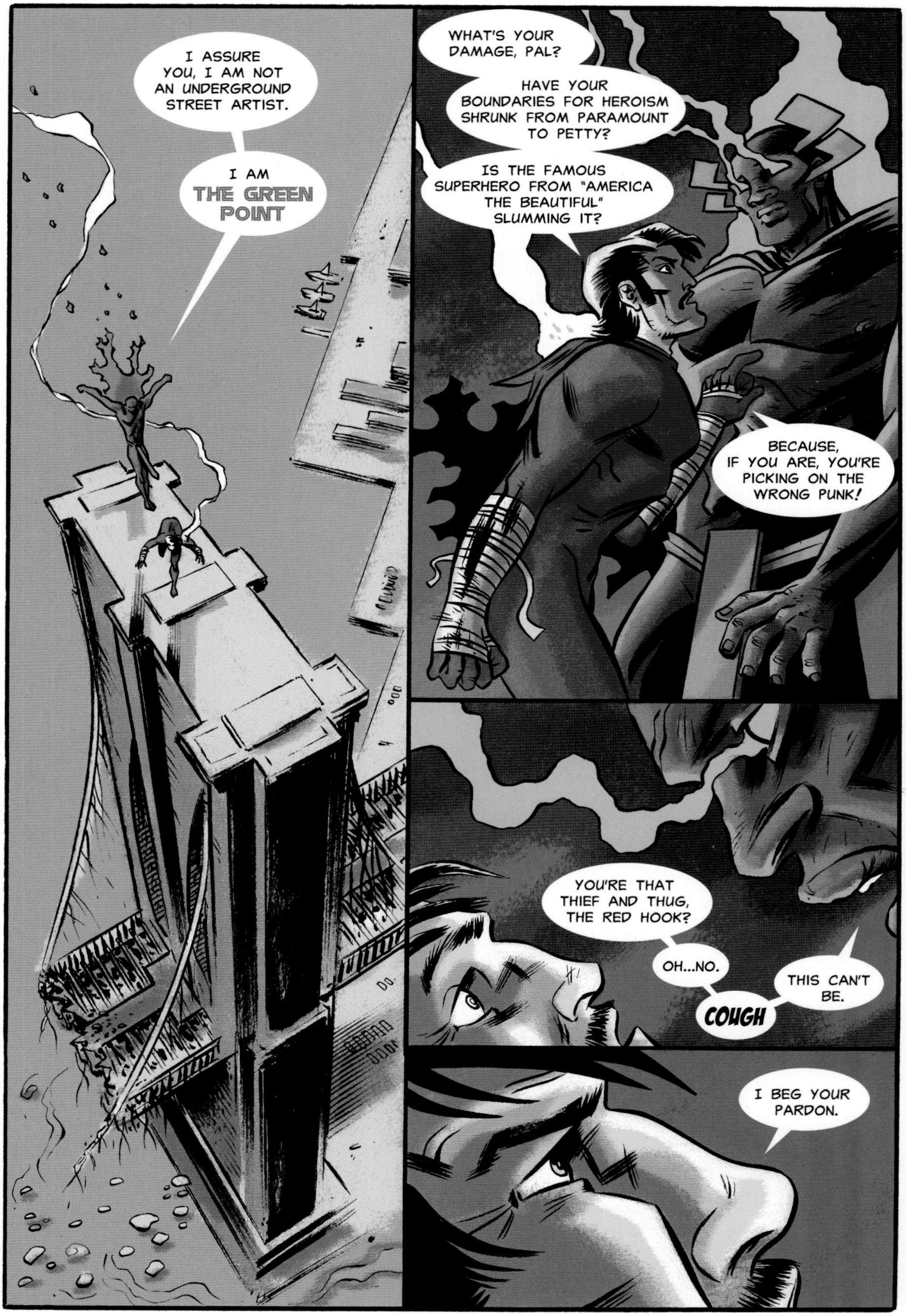
I ASSURE YOU, I AM NOT AN UNDERGROUND STREET ARTIST.
I AM THE GREEN POINT
WHAT'S YOUR DAMAGE, PAL?
HAVE YOUR BOUNDARIES FOR HEROISM SHRUNK FROM PARAMOUNT TO PETTY?
IS THE FAMOUS SUPERHERO FROM "AMERICA THE BEAUTIFUL" SLUMMING IT?
BECAUSE, IF YOU ARE, YOU'RE PICKING ON THE WRONG PUNK!
YOU'RE THAT THIEF AND THUG, THE RED HOOK?
OH...NO.
COUGH
THIS CAN'T BE.
I BEG YOUR PARDON.

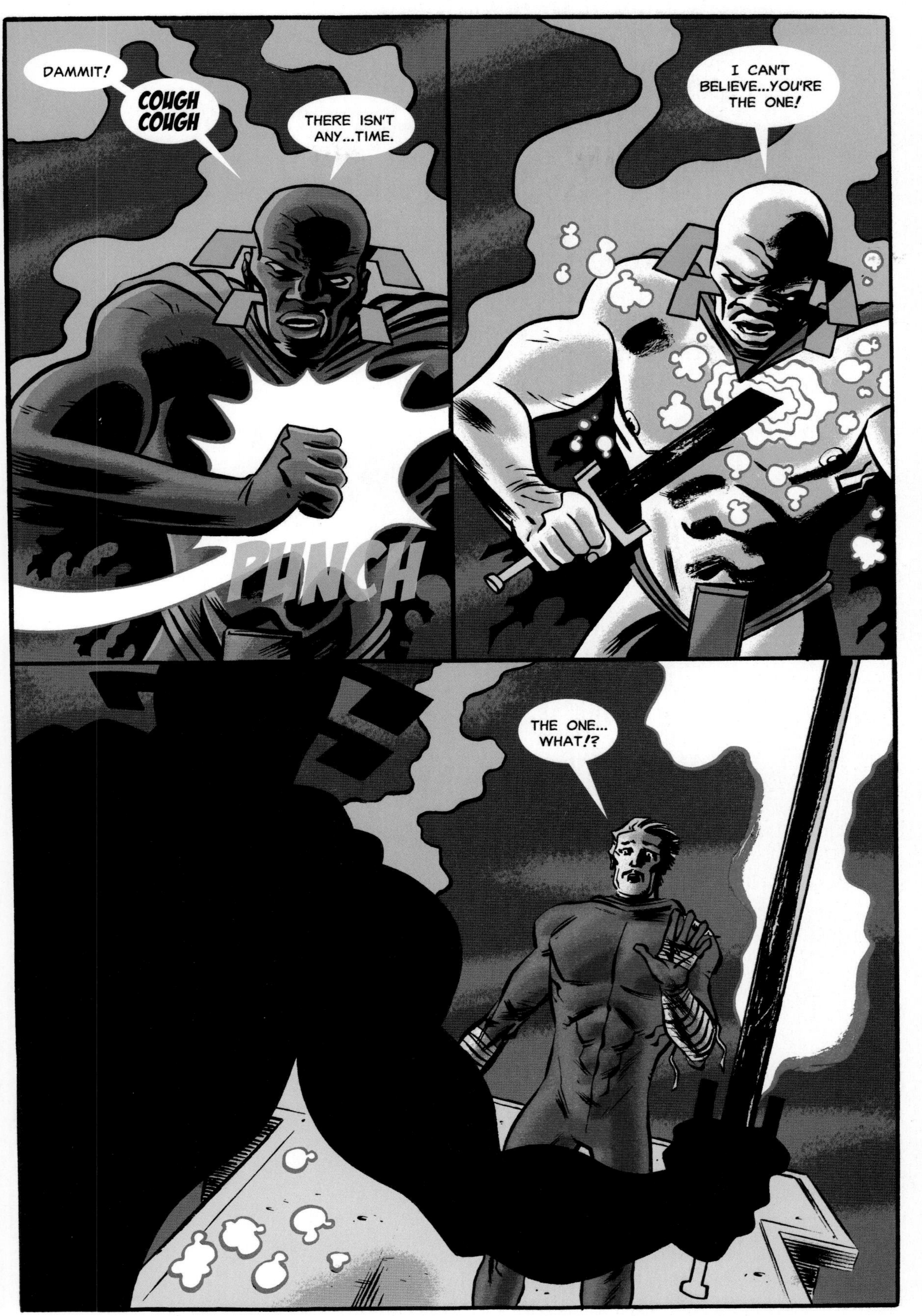
DAMMIT!
COUGH COUGH
THERE ISN'T ANY...TIME.
PUNCH
I CAN'T BELIEVE...YOU'RE THE ONE!
THE ONE... WHAT!?

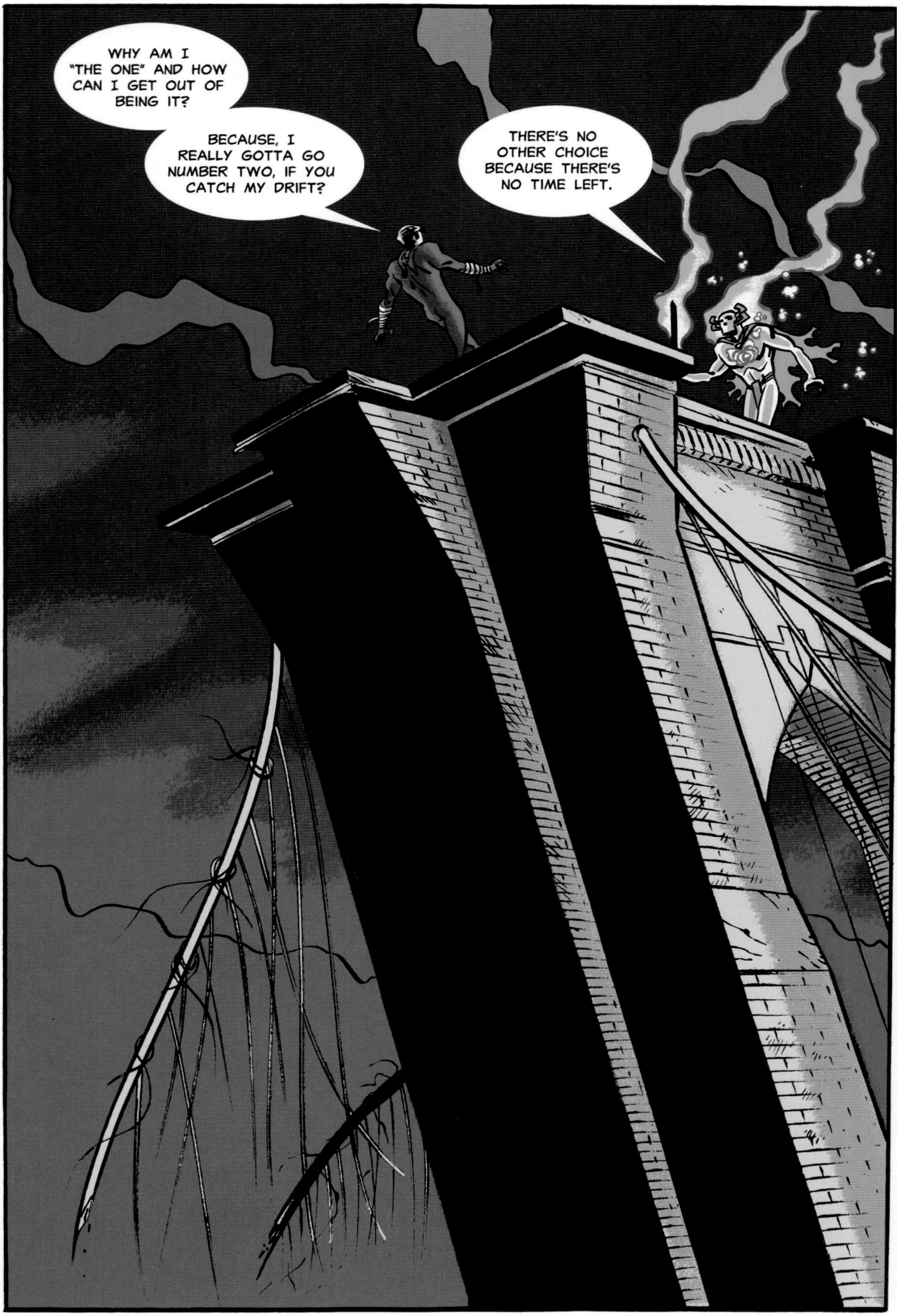
WHY AM I "THE ONE" AND HOW CAN I GET OUT OF BEING IT?
BECAUSE, I REALLY GOTTA GO NUMBER TWO, IF YOU CATCH MY DRIFT?
THERE'S NO OTHER CHOICE BECAUSE THERE'S NO TIME LEFT.

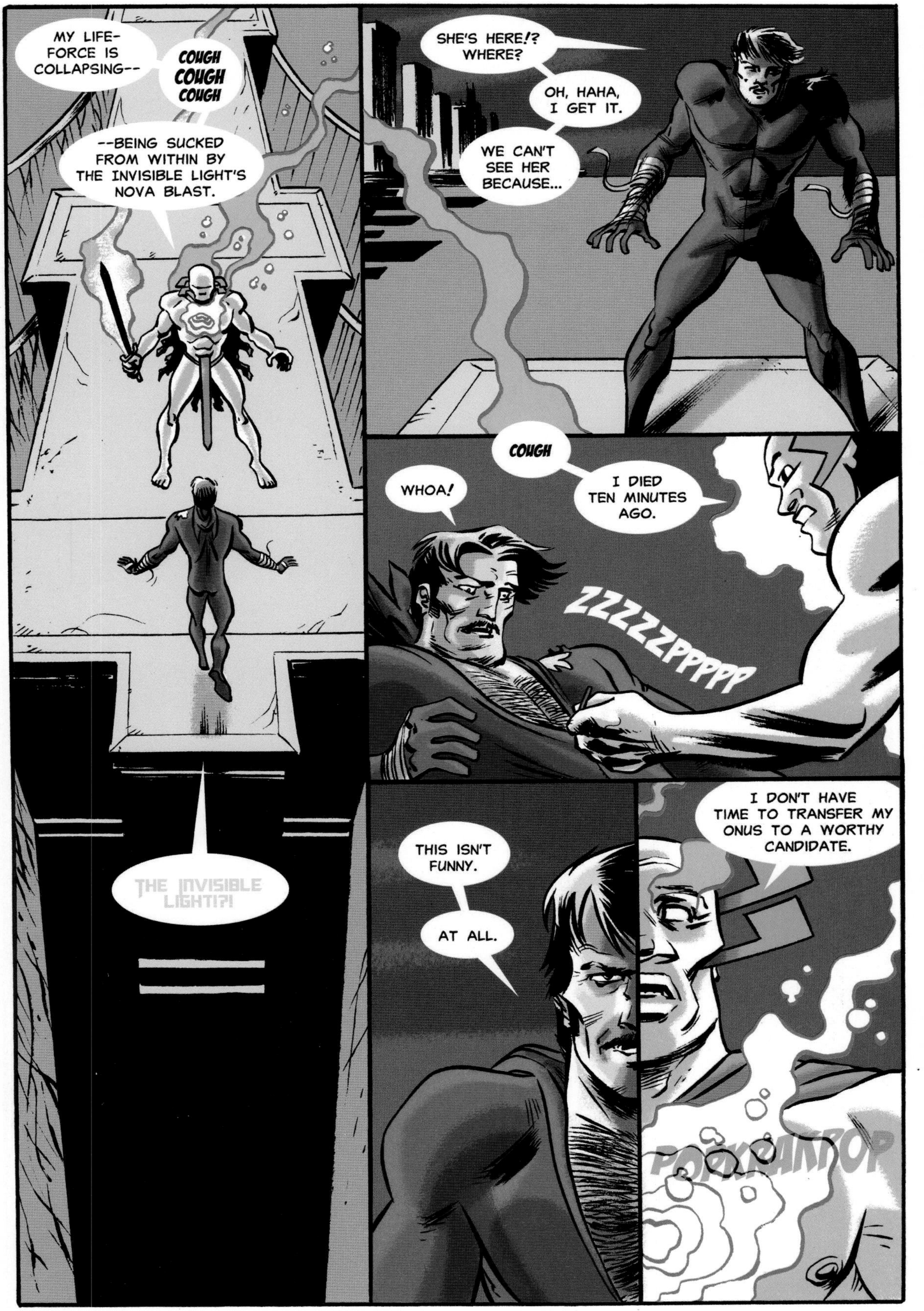
MY LIFE-FORCE IS COLLAPSING--
COUGH COUGH COUGH
--BEING SUCKED FROM WITHIN BY THE INVISIBLE LIGHT'S NOVA BLAST.
THE INVISIBLE LIGHT!?!
SHE'S HERE!? WHERE?
OH, HAHA, I GET IT.
WE CAN'T SEE HER BECAUSE...
COUGH
WHOA!
I DIED TEN MINUTES AGO.
ZZZZZPPPPP
THIS ISN'T FUNNY.
AT ALL.
I DON'T HAVE TIME TO TRANSFER MY ONUS TO A WORTHY CANDIDATE.
POPKRAKPOP

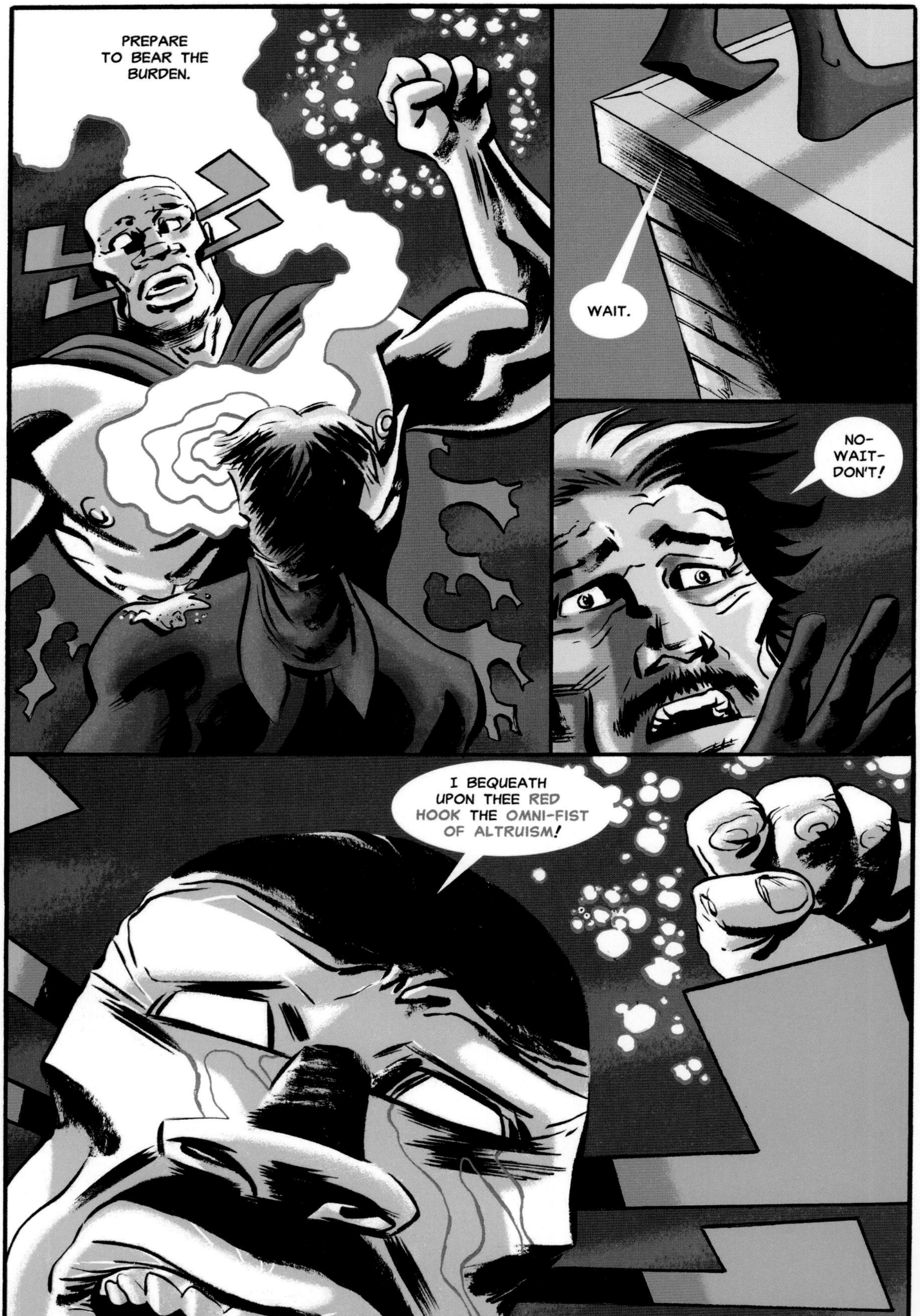
PREPARE TO BEAR THE BURDEN.
WAIT.
NO-WAIT-DON'T!
I BEQUEATH UPON THEE RED HOOK THE OMNI-FIST OF ALTRUISM!

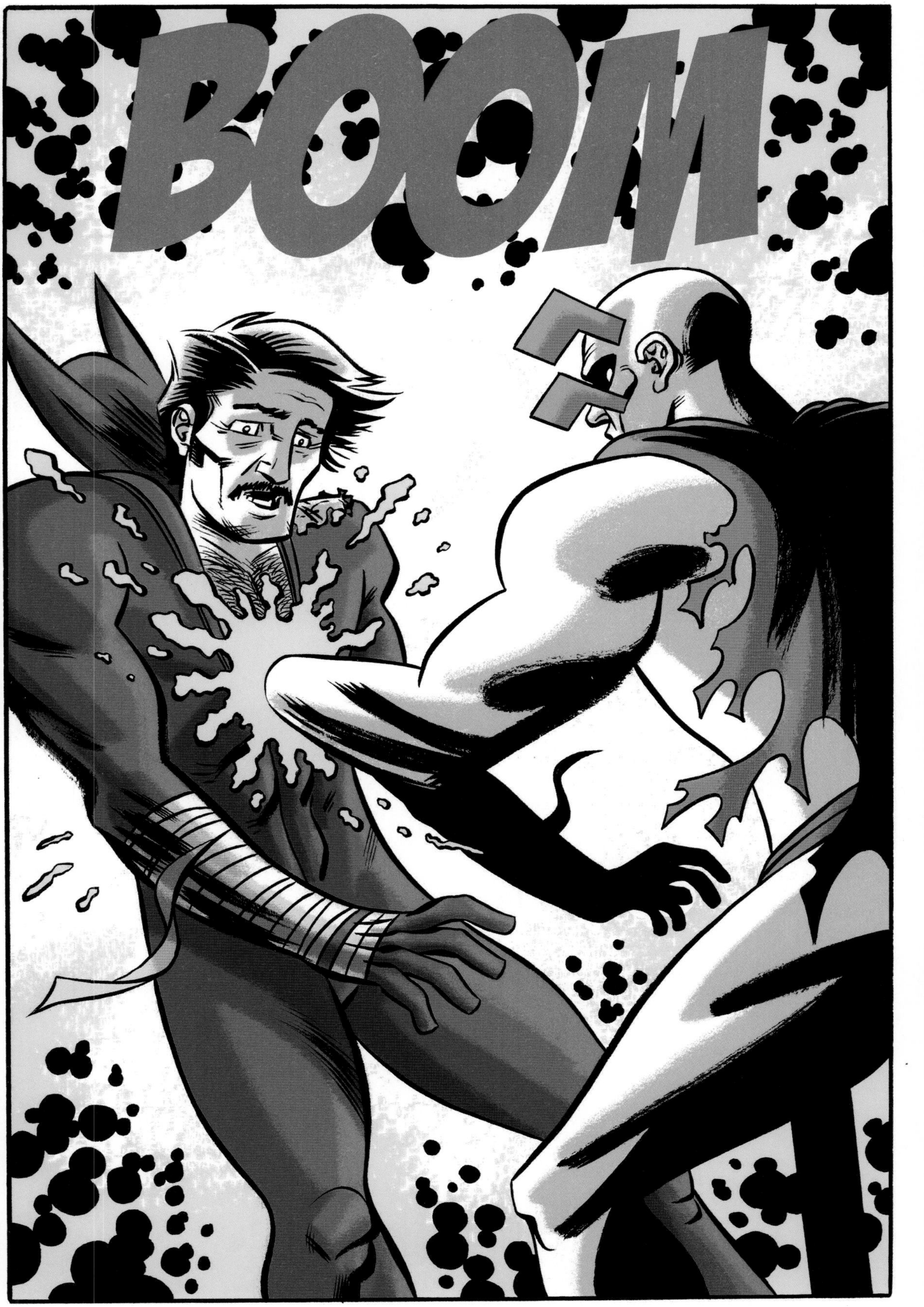
BOOM

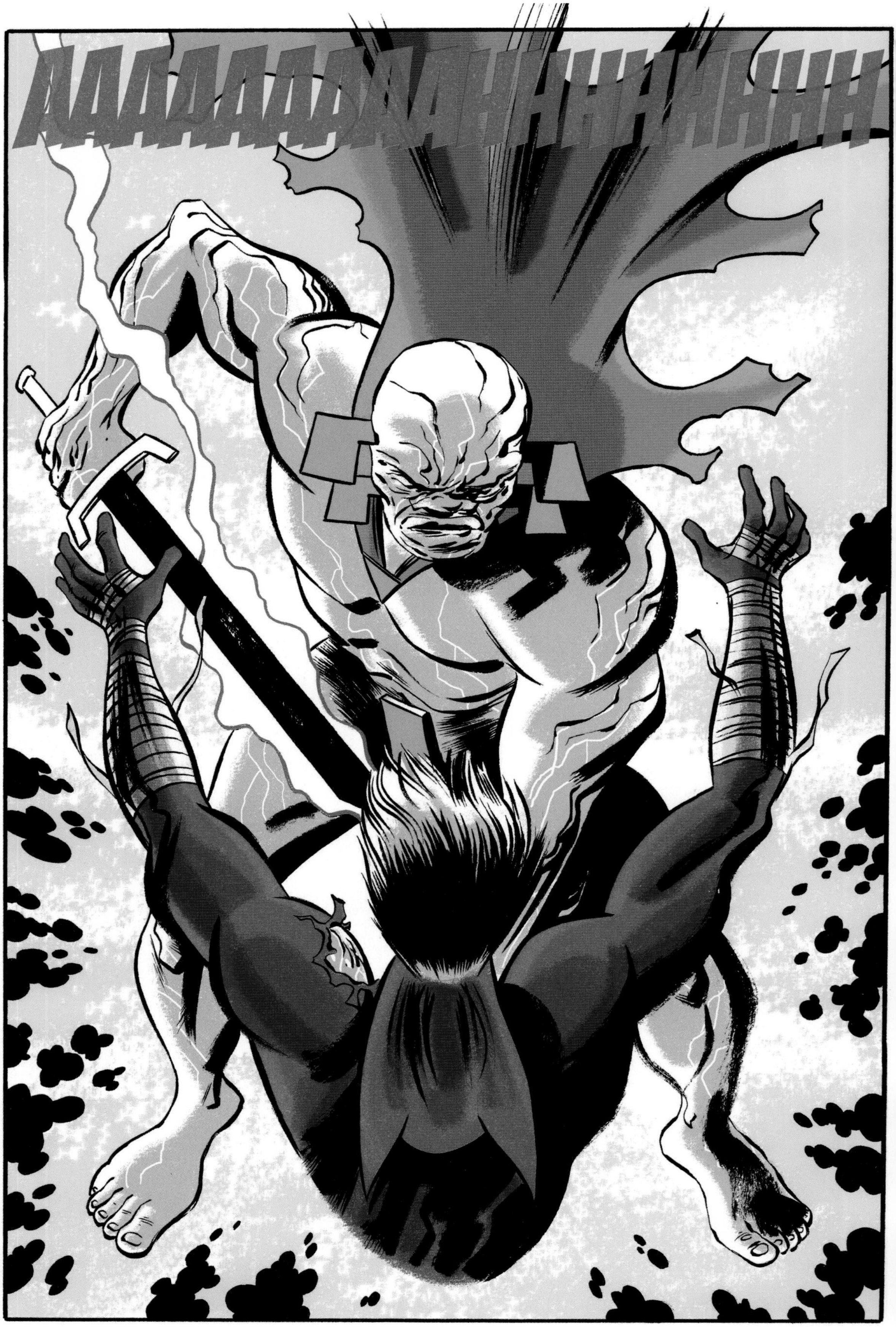
AAAAAAAAAHHHHHHHHH

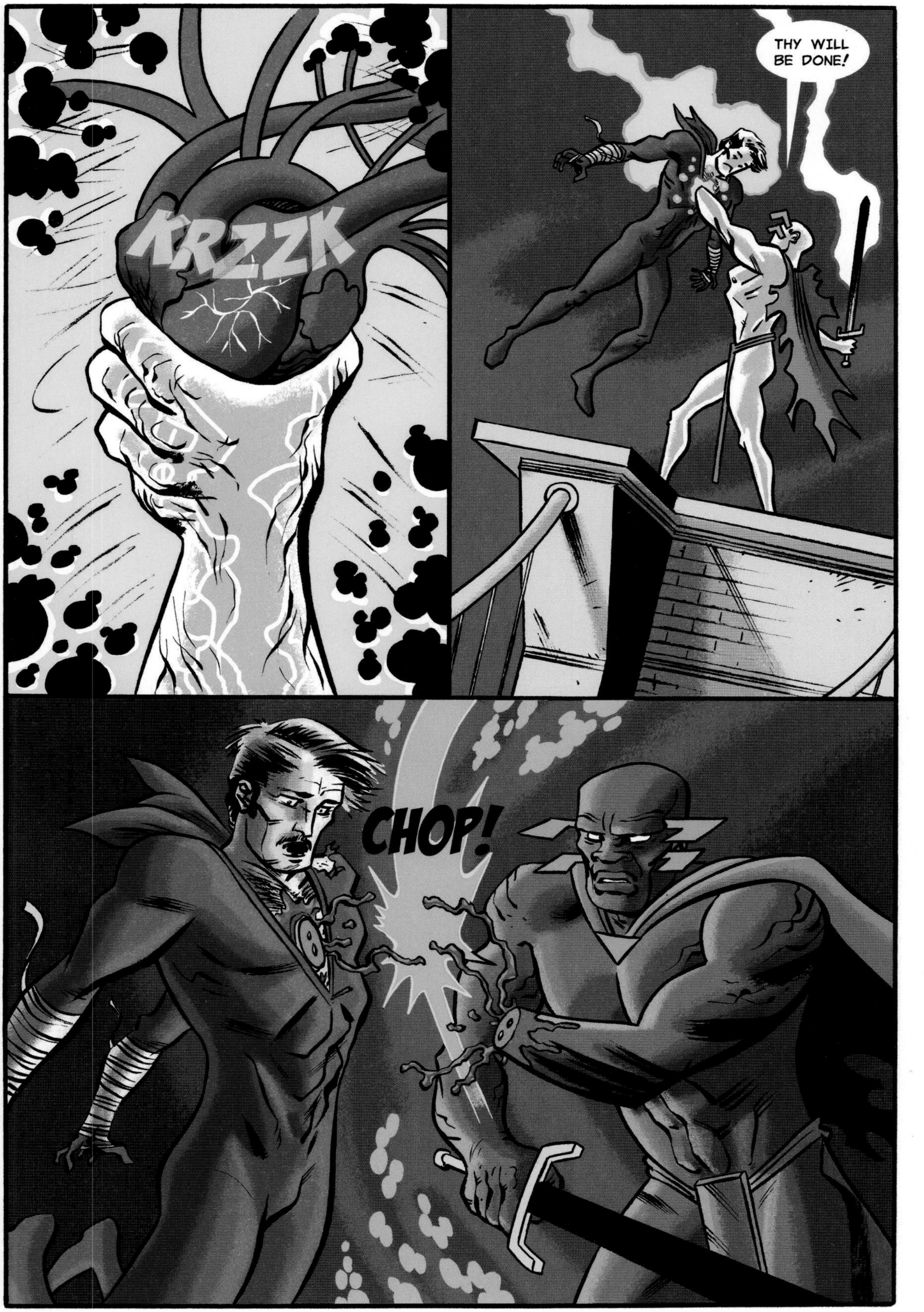
KRZZK
THY WILL BE DONE!
CHOP!

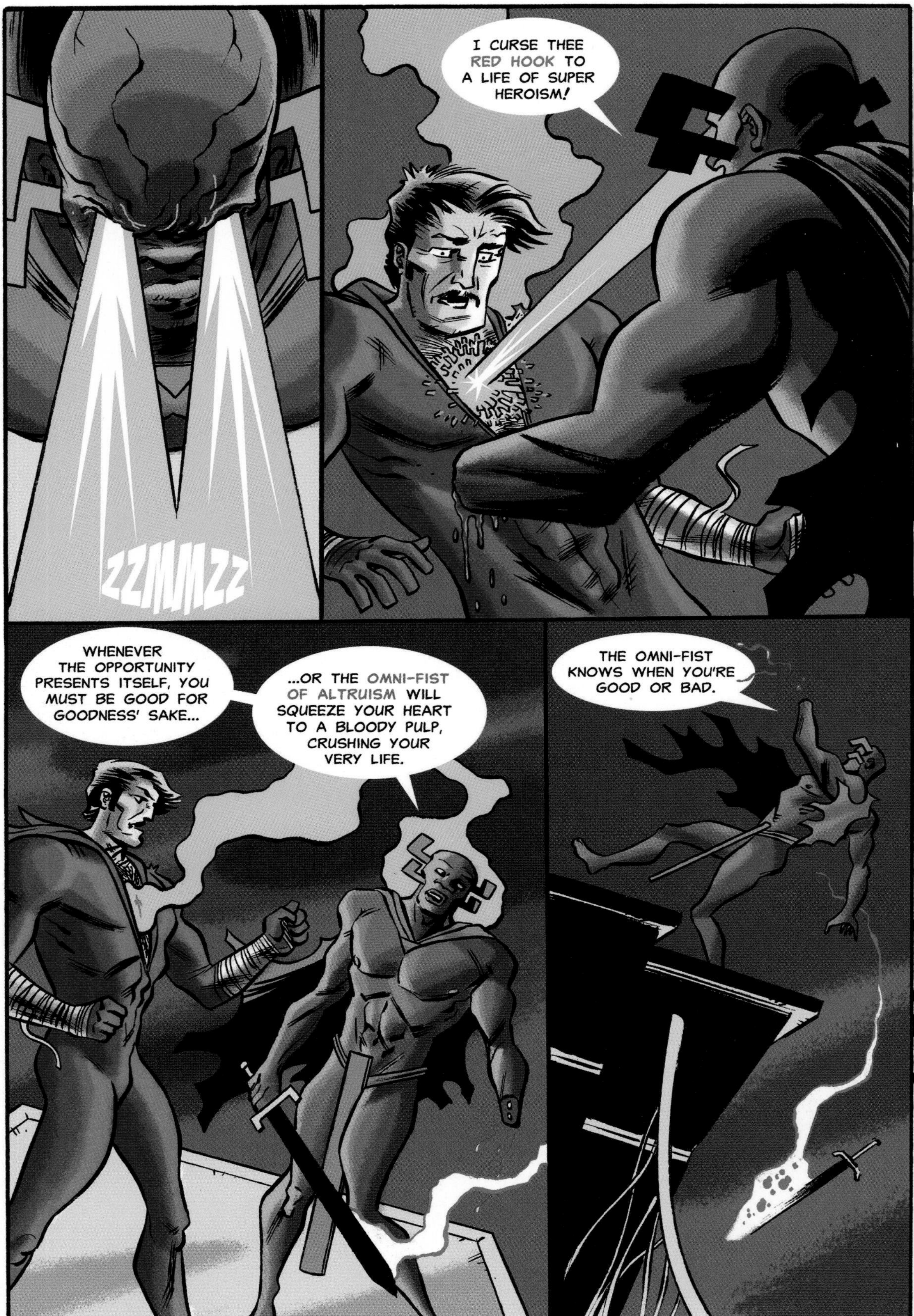
ZZMMMZZ
I CURSE THEE RED HOOK TO A LIFE OF SUPER HEROISM!
WHENEVER THE OPPORTUNITY PRESENTS ITSELF, YOU MUST BE GOOD FOR GOODNESS' SAKE...
...OR THE OMNI-FIST OF ALTRUISM WILL SQUEEZE YOUR HEART TO A BLOODY PULP, CRUSHING YOUR VERY LIFE.
THE OMNI-FIST KNOWS WHEN YOU'RE GOOD OR BAD.

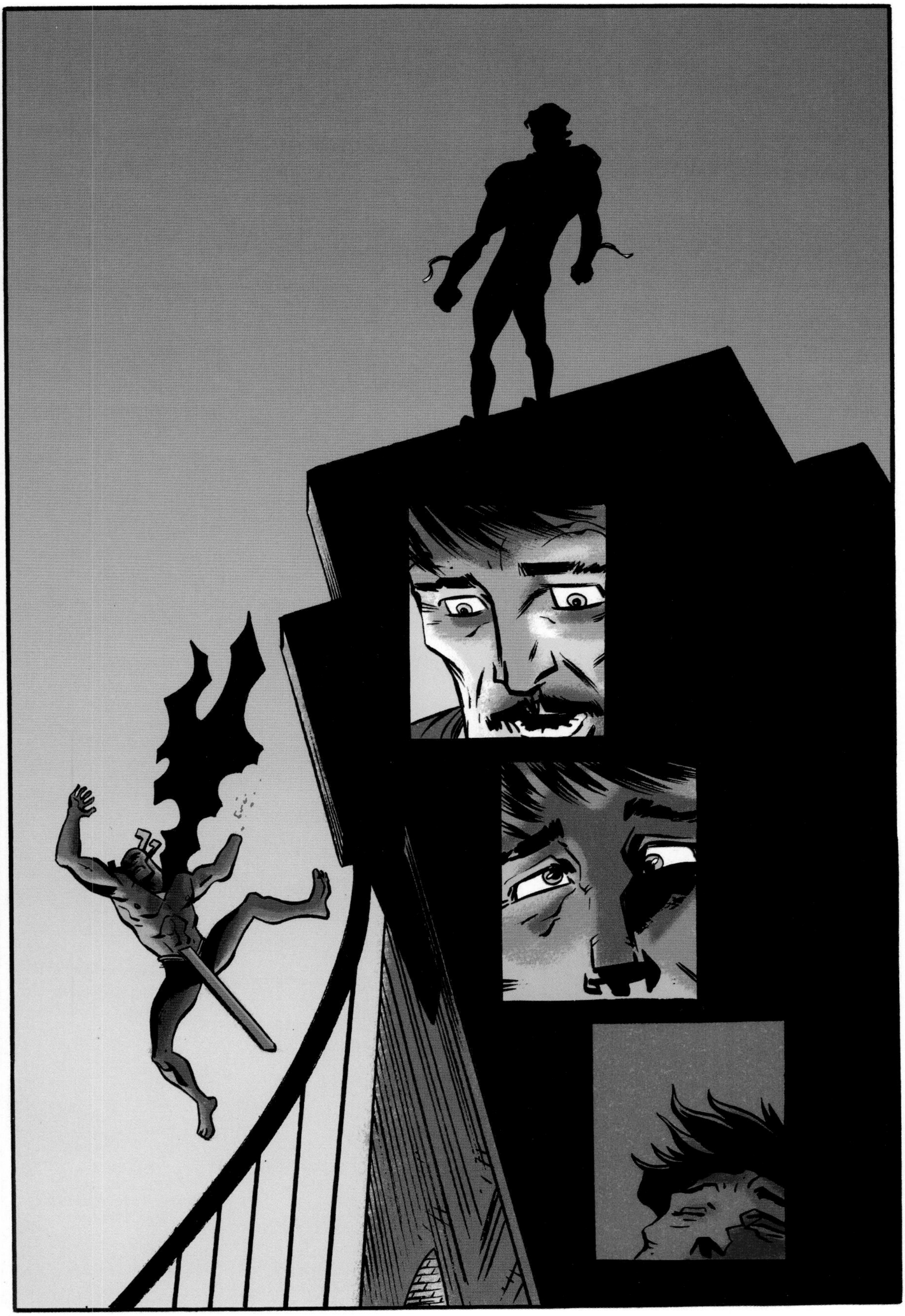

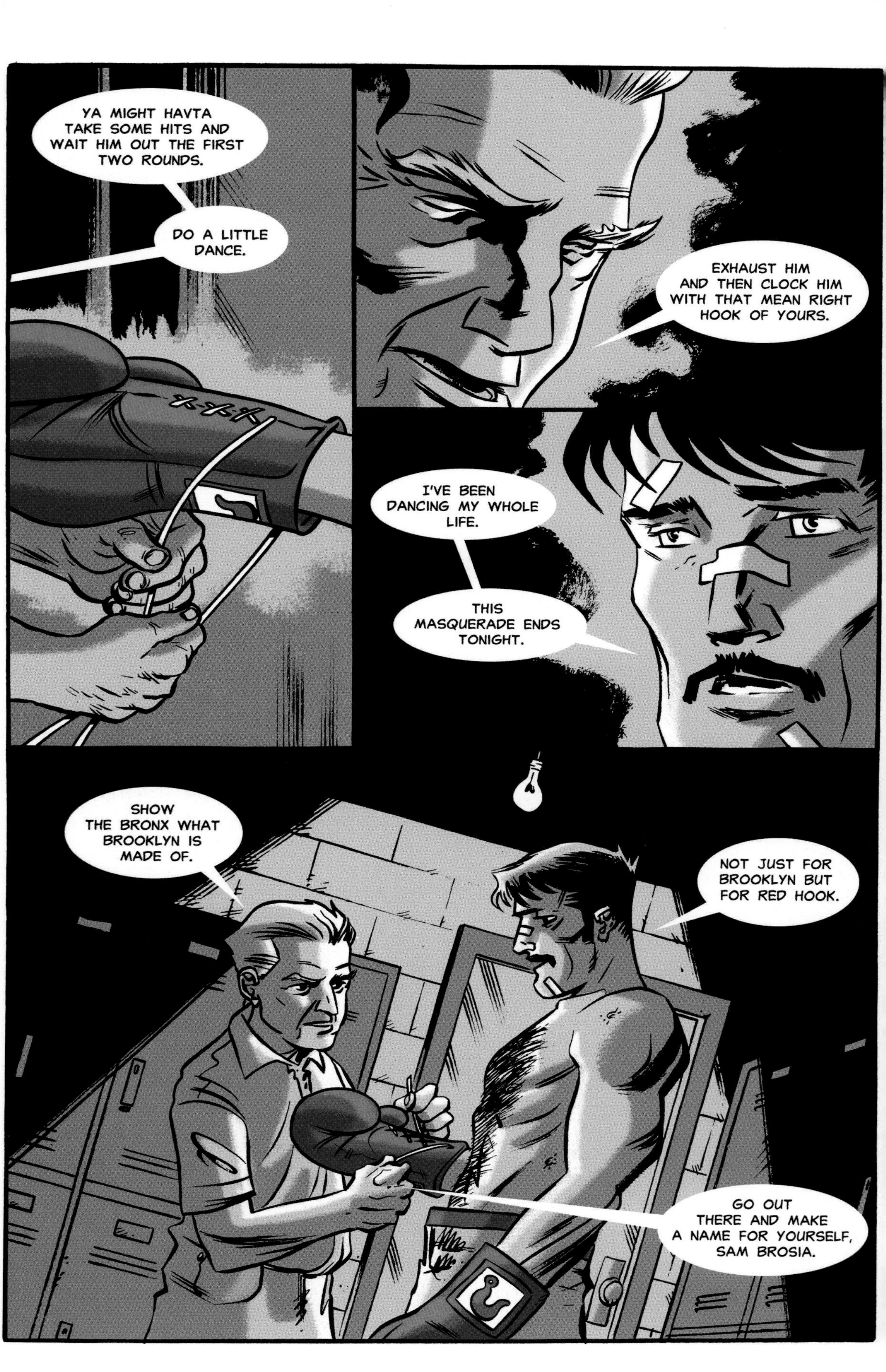
YA MIGHT HAVTA TAKE SOME HITS AND WAIT HIM OUT THE FIRST TWO ROUNDS.
DO A LITTLE DANCE.
EXHAUST HIM AND THEN CLOCK HIM WITH THAT MEAN RIGHT HOOK OF YOURS.
I'VE BEEN DANCING MY WHOLE LIFE.
THIS MASQUERADE ENDS TONIGHT.
SHOW THE BRONX WHAT BROOKLYN IS MADE OF.
NOT JUST FOR BROOKLYN BUT FOR RED HOOK.
GO OUT THERE AND MAKE A NAME FOR YOURSELF, SAM BROSIA.

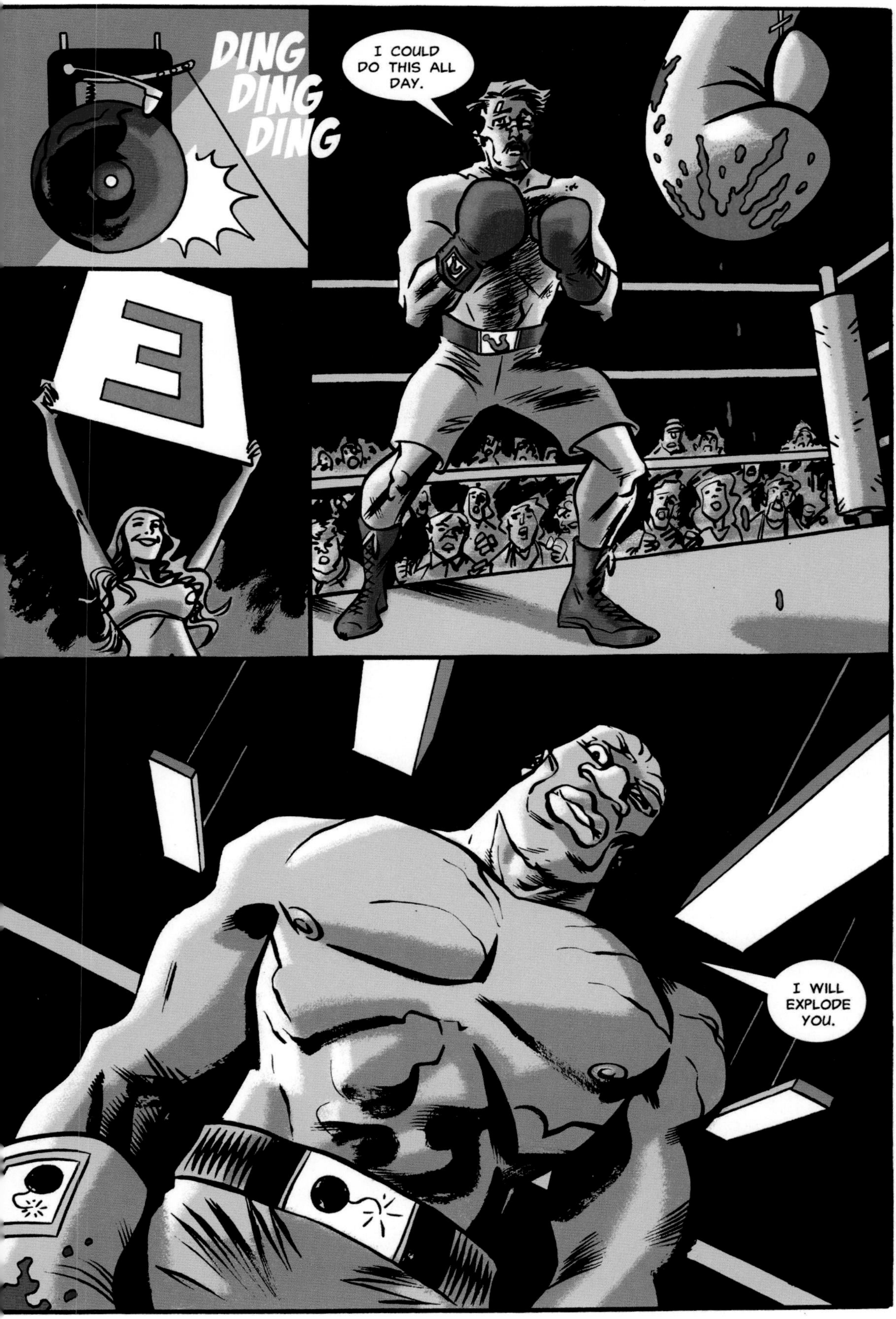
DING DING DING
I COULD DO THIS ALL DAY.
I WILL EXPLODE YOU.

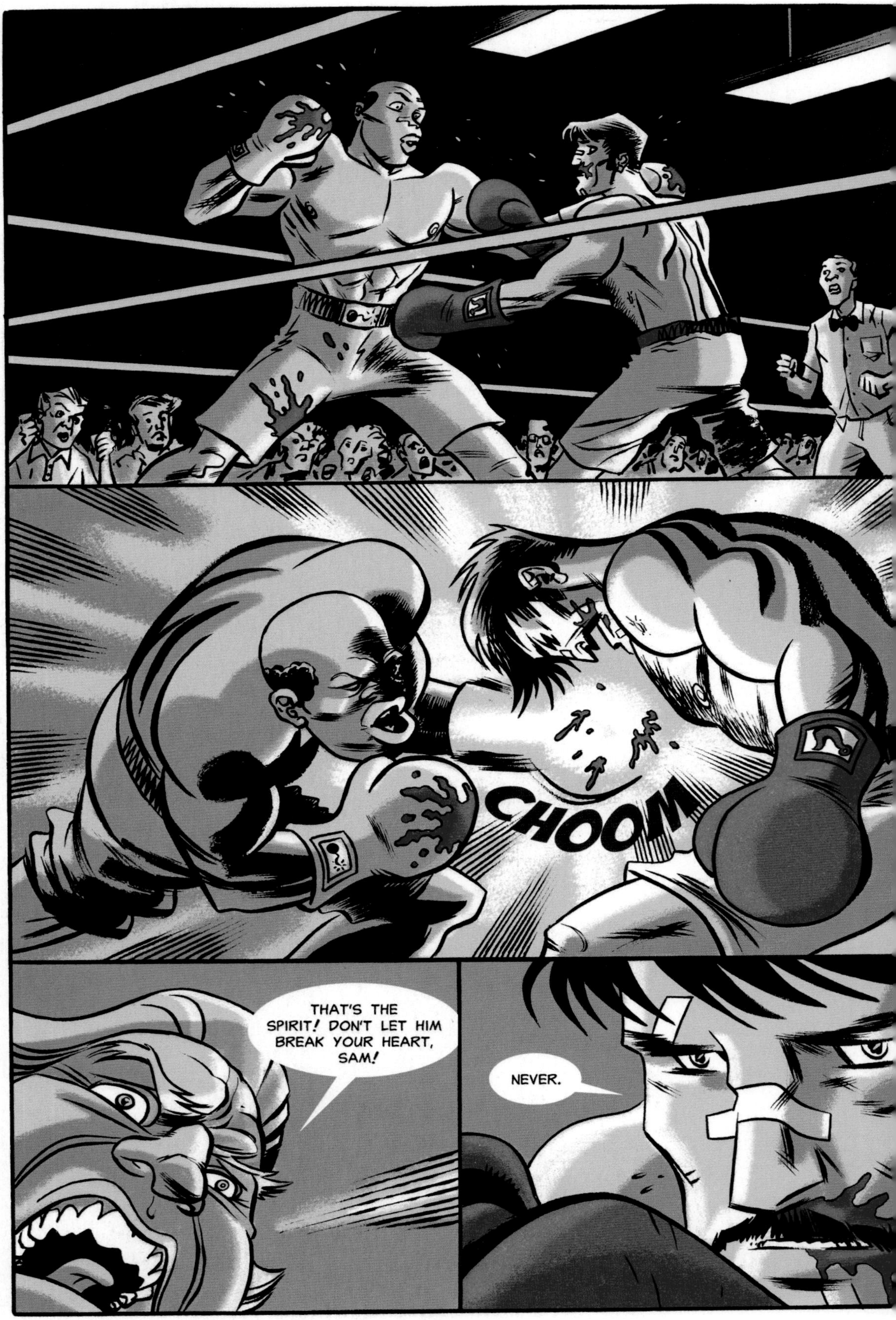
CHOOM
THAT'S THE SPIRIT! DON'T LET HIM BREAK YOUR HEART, SAM!
NEVER.

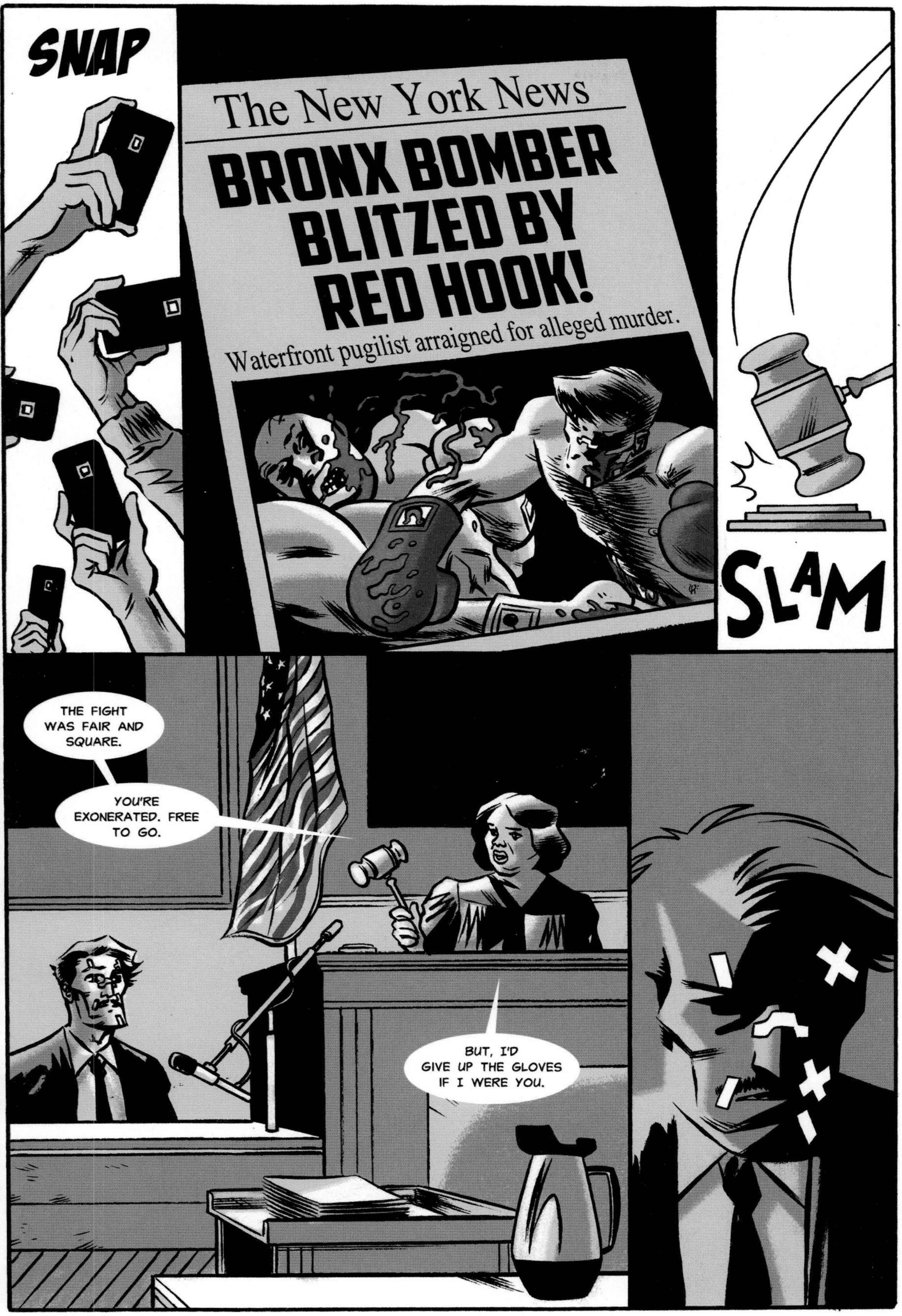
SNAP
The New York News
BRONX BOMBER BLITZED BY RED HOOK!
Waterfront pugilist arraigned for alleged murder.
SLAM
THE FIGHT WAS FAIR AND SQUARE.
YOU'RE EXONERATED. FREE TO GO.
BUT, I'D GIVE UP THE GLOVES IF I WERE YOU.

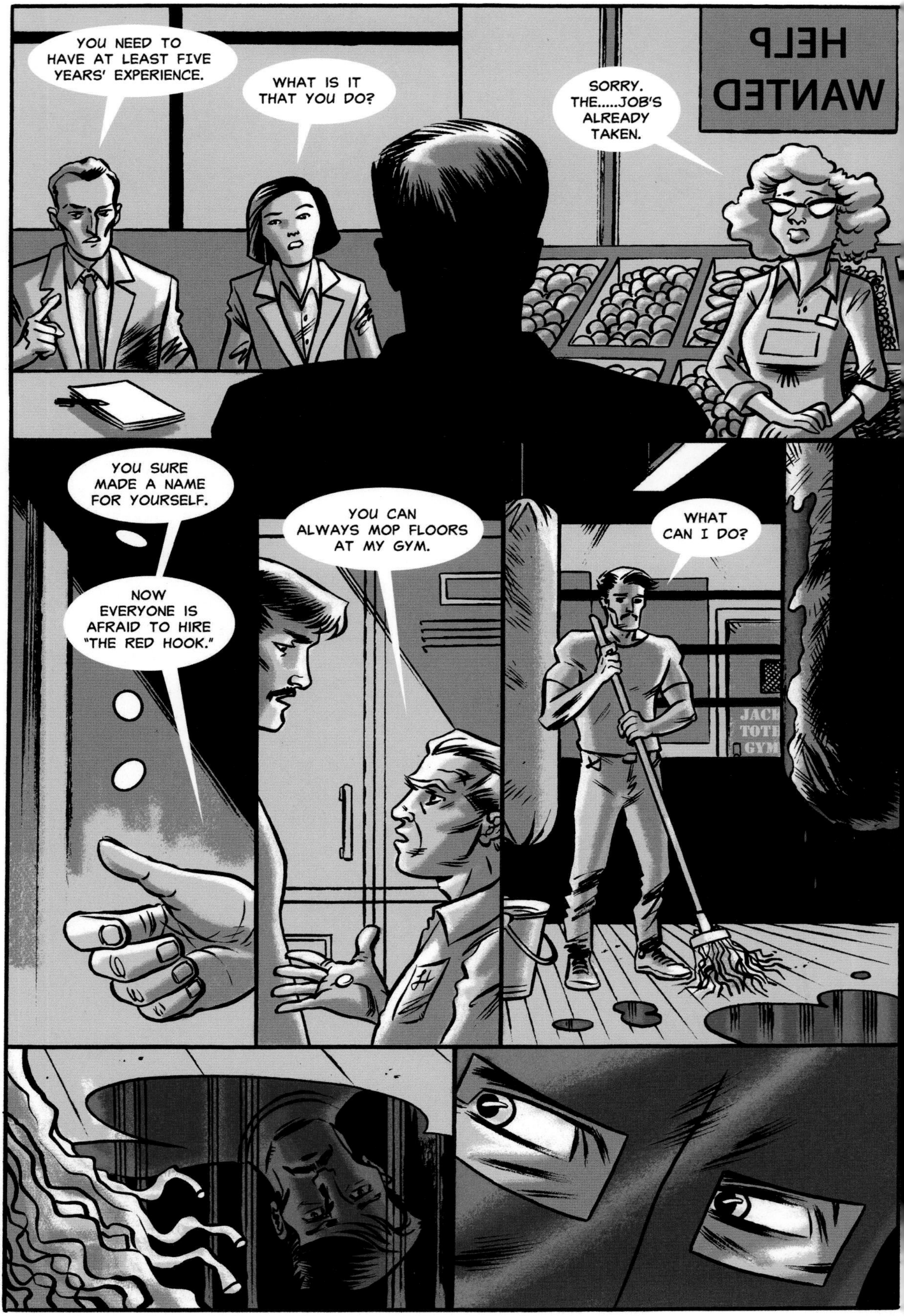
HELP WANTED
YOU NEED TO HAVE AT LEAST FIVE YEARS' EXPERIENCE.
WHAT IS IT THAT YOU DO?
SORRY. THE.....JOB'S ALREADY TAKEN.
YOU SURE MADE A NAME FOR YOURSELF.
NOW EVERYONE IS AFRAID TO HIRE "THE RED HOOK."
YOU CAN ALWAYS MOP FLOORS AT MY GYM.
WHAT CAN I DO?

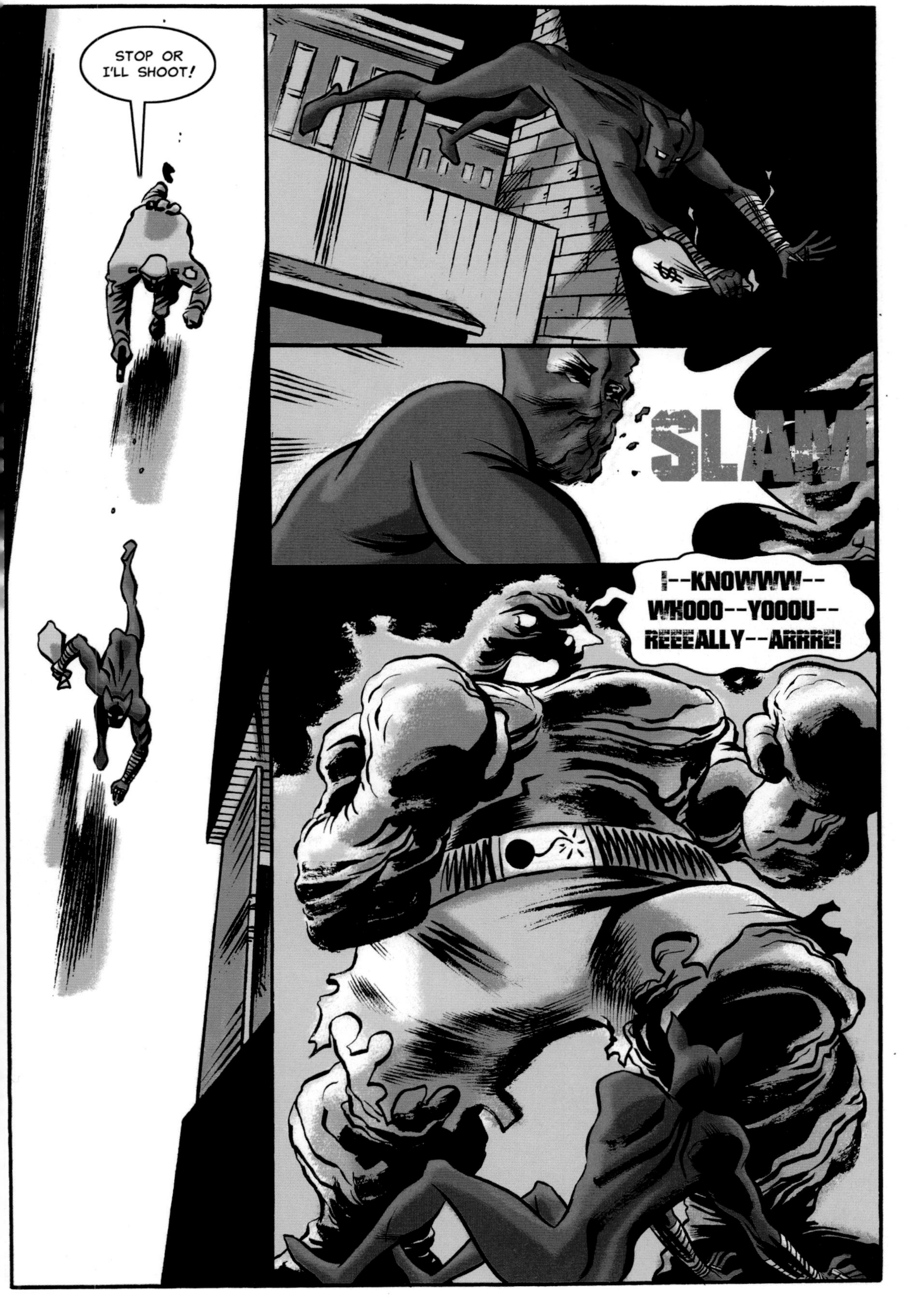
STOP OR I'LL SHOOT!
SLAM
I--KNOWWW--WHOOO--YOOOU--REEEALLY--ARRRE!

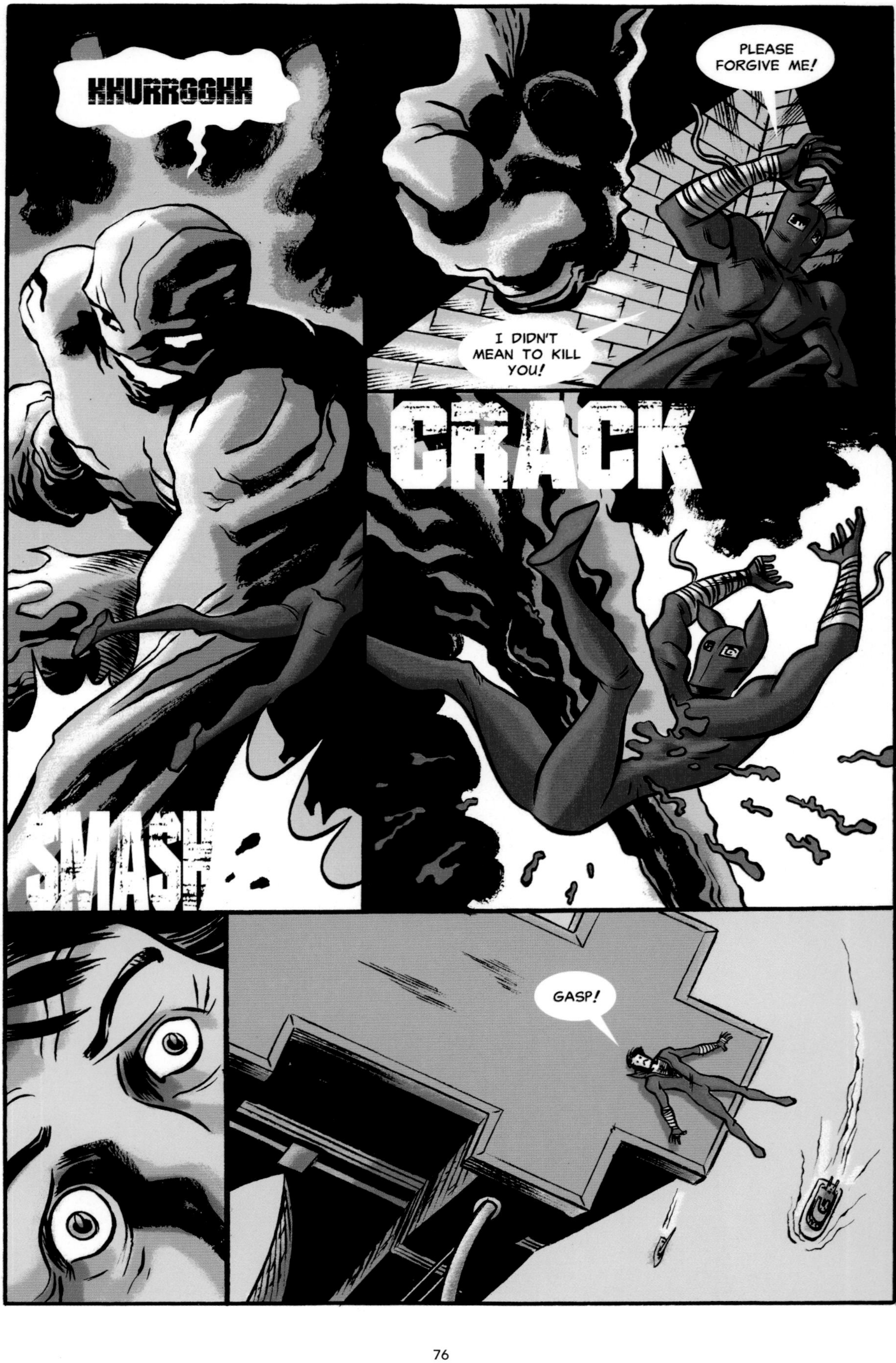

KHURRGGHK
PLEASE FORGIVE ME!
I DIDN'T MEAN TO KILL YOU!
SMASH
CRACK
GASP!

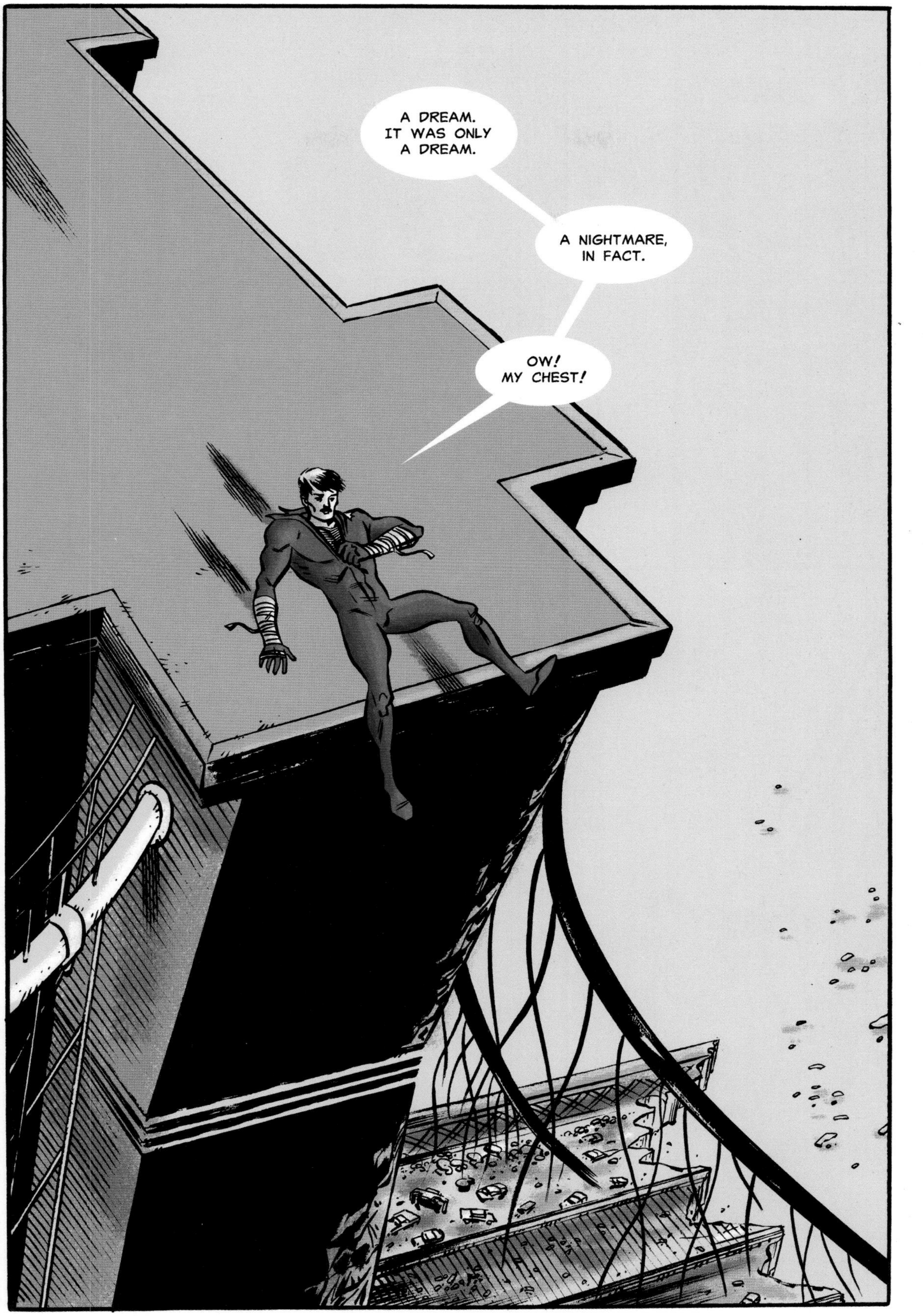
A DREAM. IT WAS ONLY A DREAM.
A NIGHTMARE, IN FACT.
OW! MY CHEST!

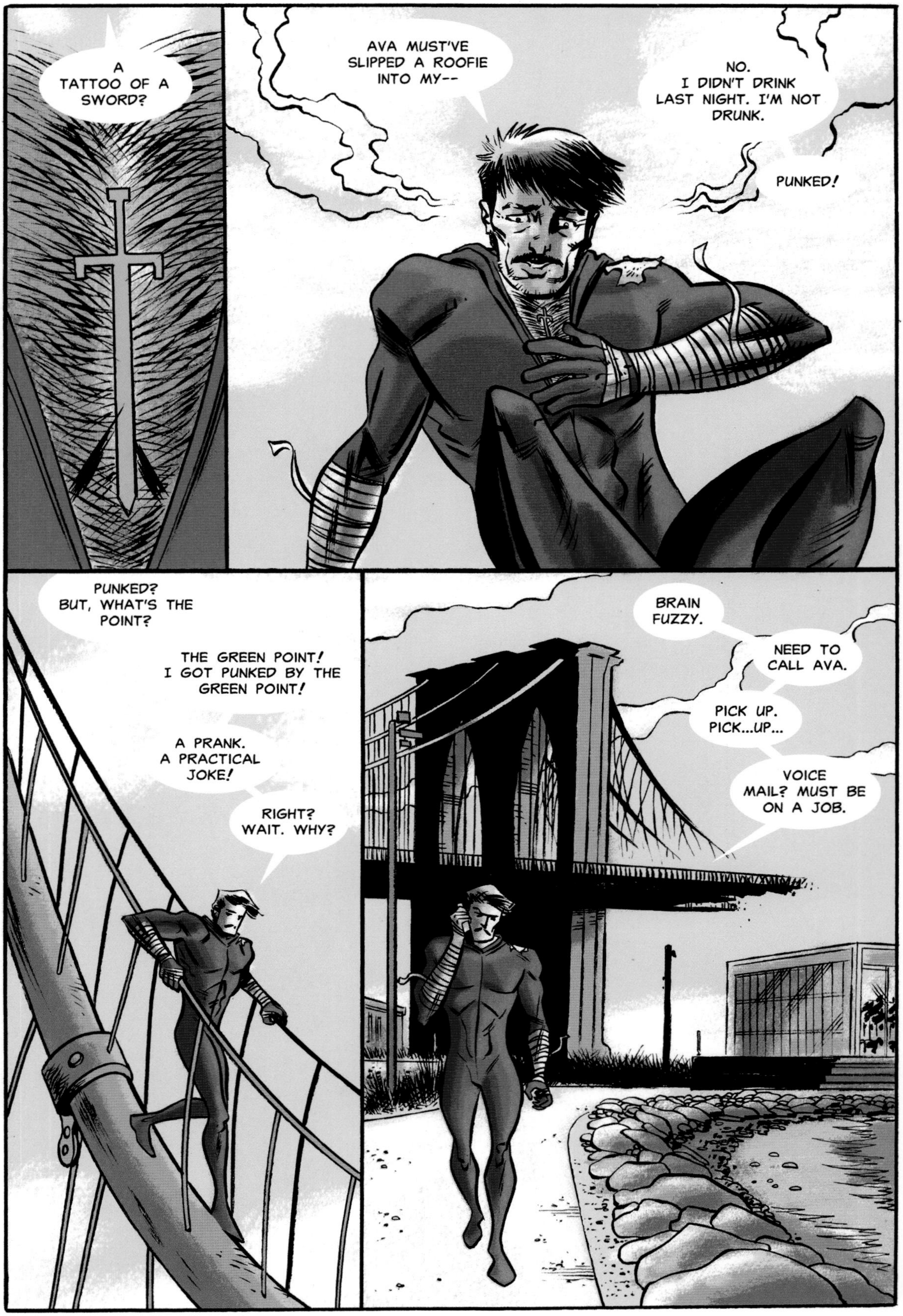
A TATTOO OF A SWORD?
AVA MUST'VE SLIPPED A ROOFIE INTO MY--
NO. I DIDN'T DRINK LAST NIGHT. I'M NOT DRUNK.
PUNKED!
PUNKED? BUT, WHAT'S THE POINT?
THE GREEN POINT! I GOT PUNKED BY THE GREEN POINT!
A PRANK. A PRACTICAL JOKE!
RIGHT? WAIT. WHY?
BRAIN FUZZY.
NEED TO CALL AVA.
PICK UP. PICK...UP...
VOICE MAIL? MUST BE ON A JOB.

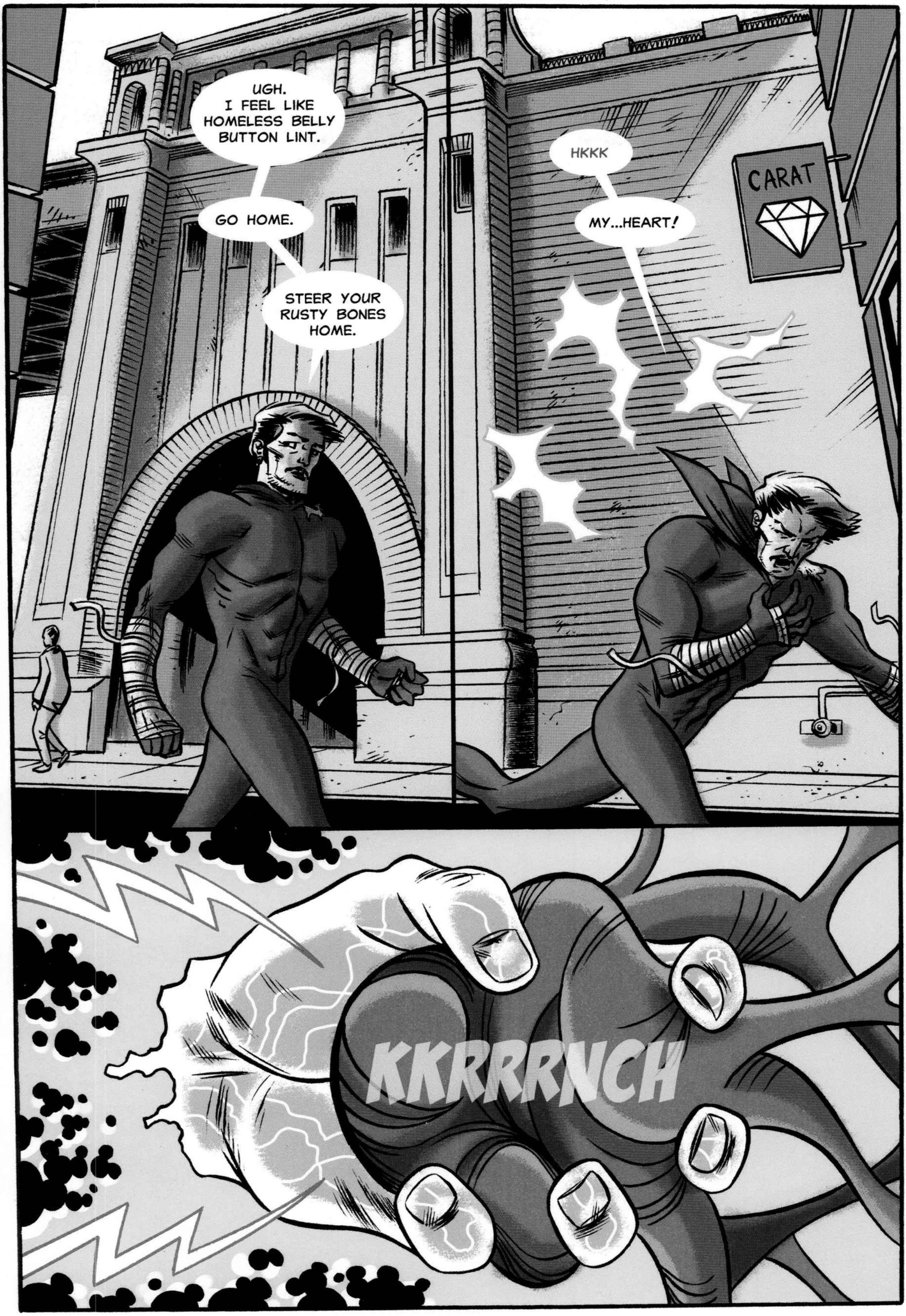
UGH.
I FEEL LIKE
HOMELESS BELLY
BUTTON LINT.
GO HOME.
STEER YOUR
RUSTY BONES
HOME.
HKKK
MY...HEART!
CARAT
KKRRRNCH

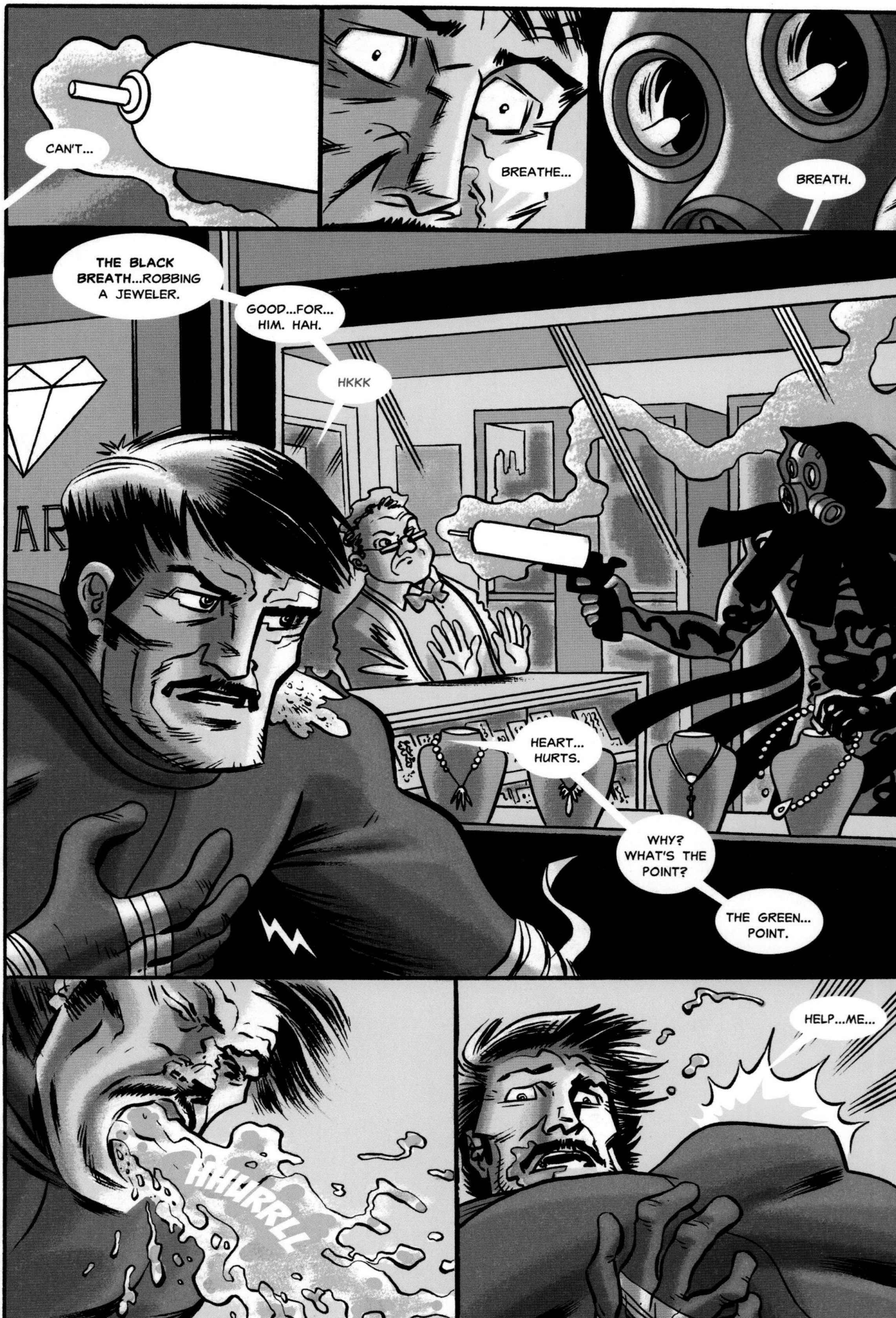
CAN'T...
BREATHE...
BREATH.
THE BLACK BREATH...ROBBING A JEWELER.
GOOD...FOR... HIM. HAH.
HKKK
HEART... HURTS.
WHY? WHAT'S THE POINT?
THE GREEN... POINT.
HHWRRLL
HELP...ME...

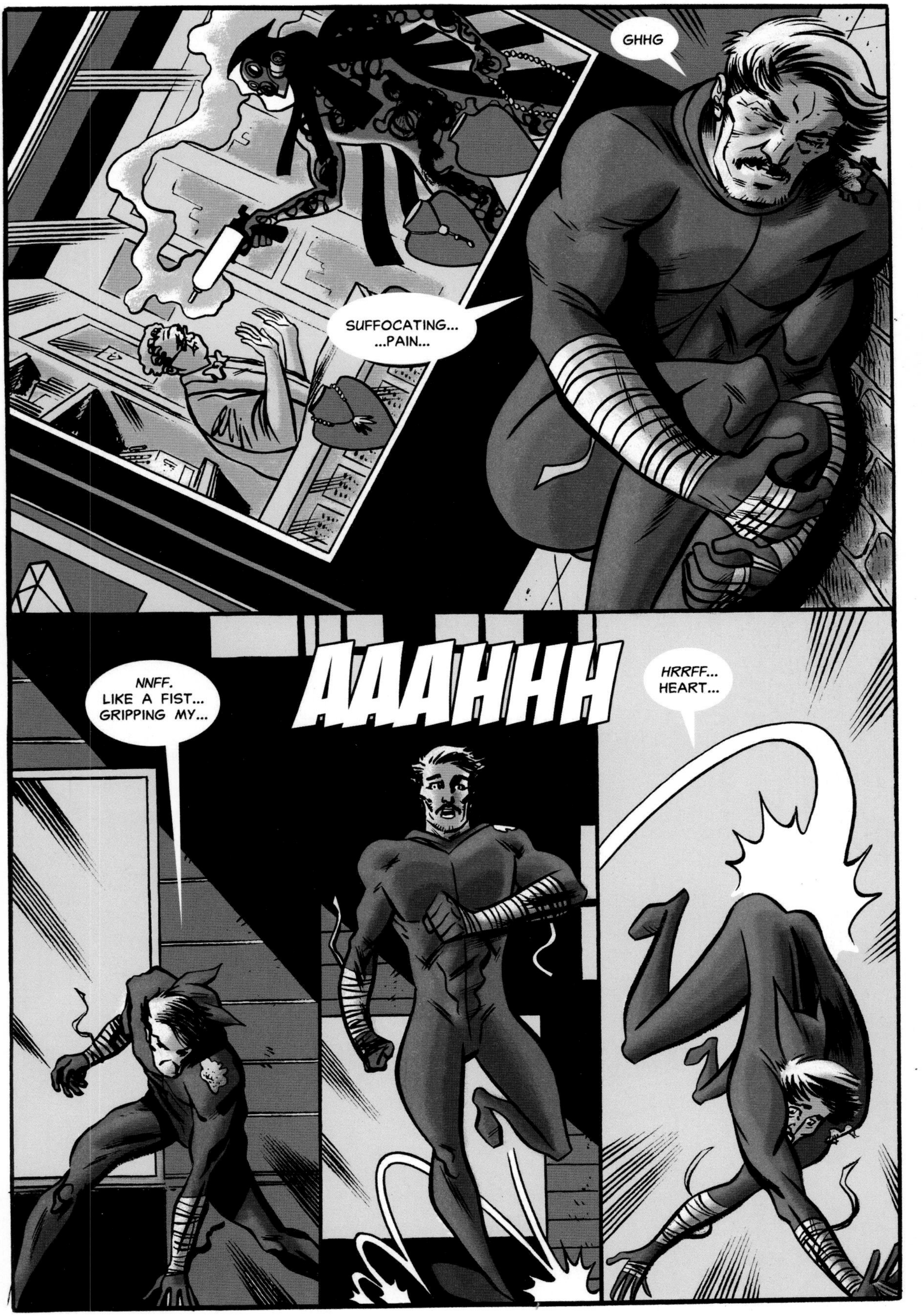
GHHG
SUFFOCATING... ...PAIN...
NNFF. LIKE A FIST... GRIPPING MY...
AAAHHH
HRRFF... HEART...

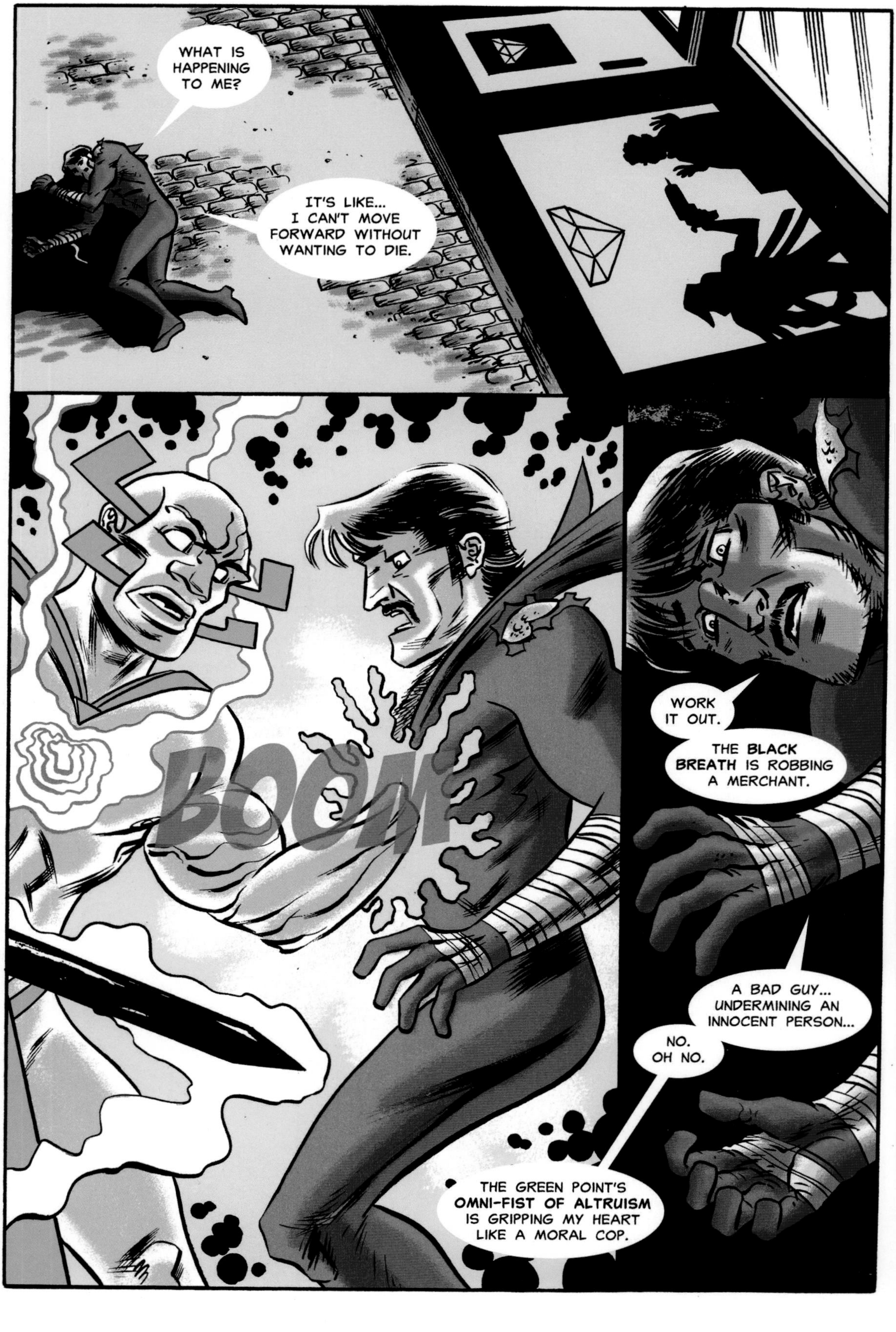
WHAT IS HAPPENING TO ME?
IT'S LIKE... I CAN'T MOVE FORWARD WITHOUT WANTING TO DIE.
BOOM
WORK IT OUT.
THE BLACK BREATH IS ROBBING A MERCHANT.
A BAD GUY... UNDERMINING AN INNOCENT PERSON...
NO. OH NO.
THE GREEN POINT'S OMNI-FIST OF ALTRUISM IS GRIPPING MY HEART LIKE A MORAL COP.

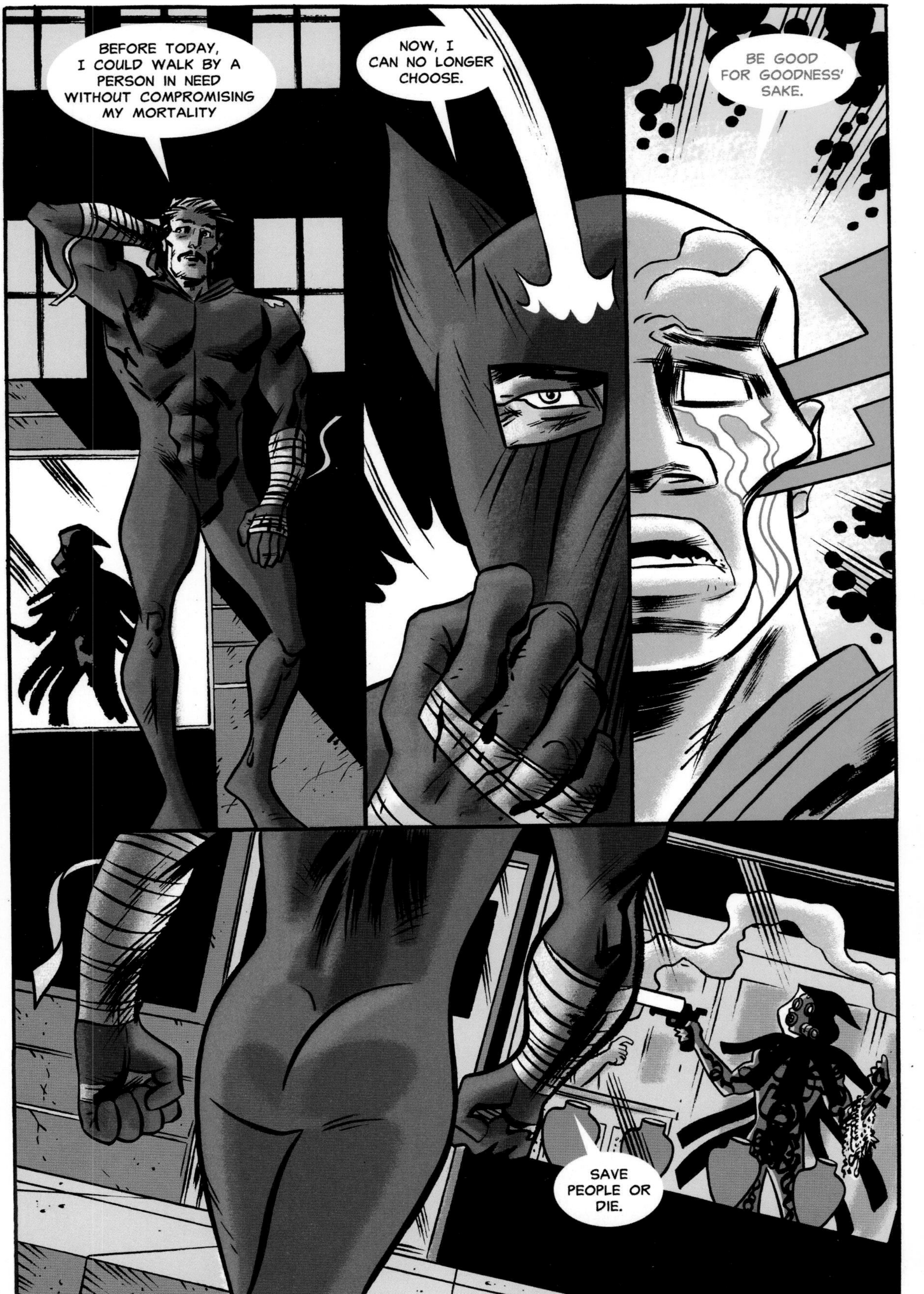
BEFORE TODAY, I COULD WALK BY A PERSON IN NEED WITHOUT COMPROMISING MY MORTALITY
NOW, I CAN NO LONGER CHOOSE.
BE GOOD FOR GOODNESS' SAKE.
SAVE PEOPLE OR DIE.

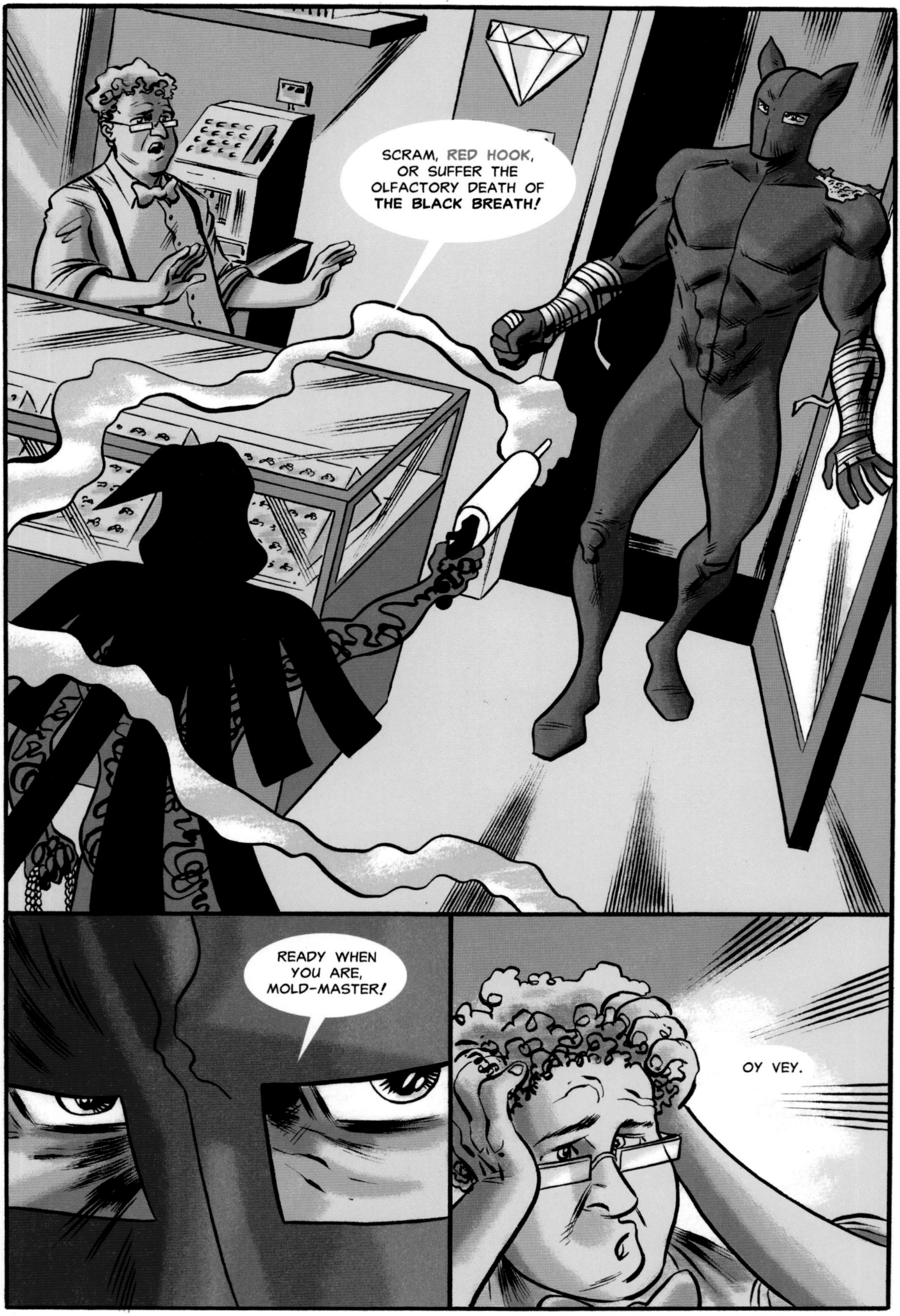
SCRAM, RED HOOK, OR SUFFER THE OLFACTORY DEATH OF THE BLACK BREATH!
READY WHEN YOU ARE, MOLD-MASTER!
OY VEY.

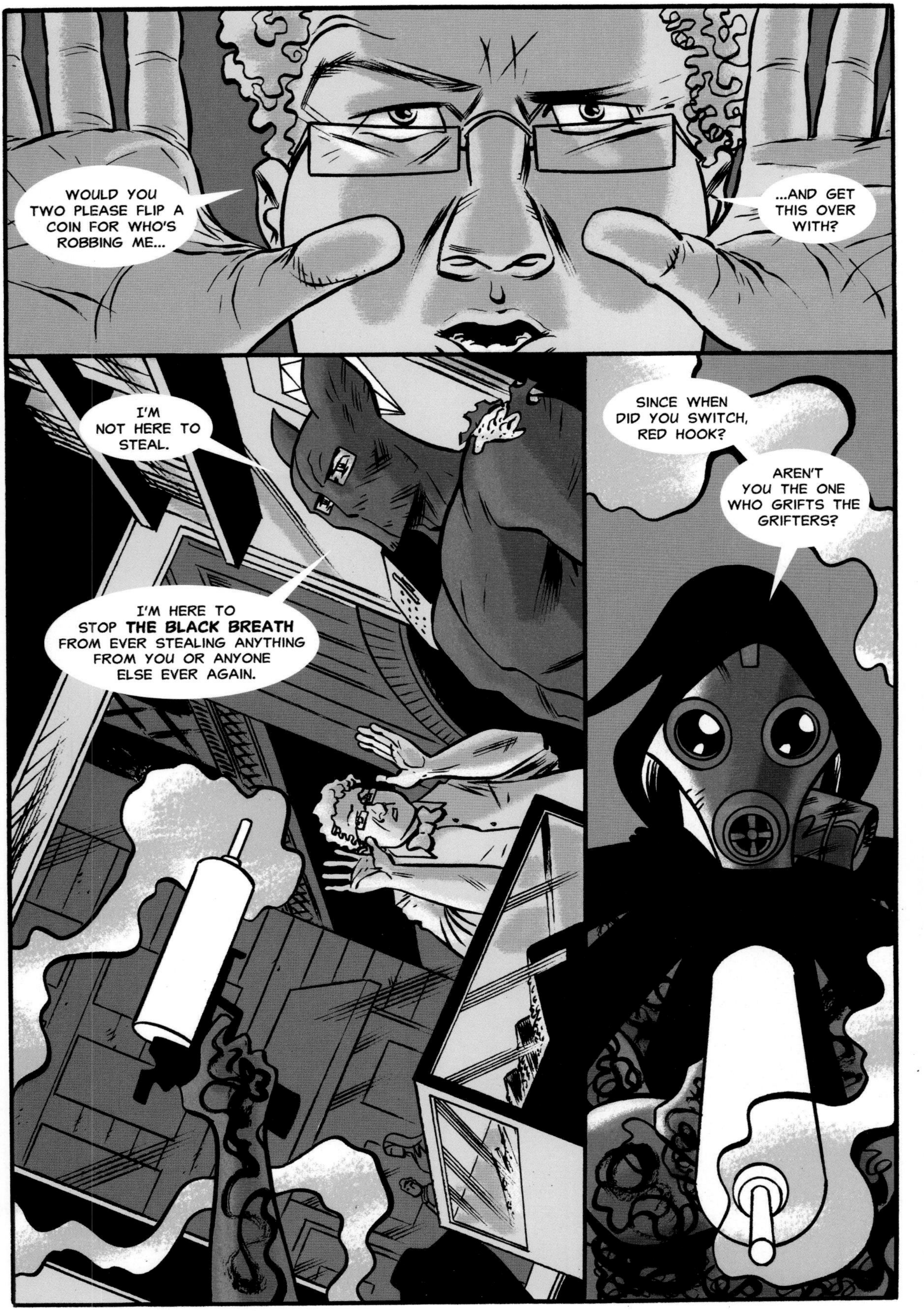
WOULD YOU TWO PLEASE FLIP A COIN FOR WHO'S ROBBING ME...
...AND GET THIS OVER WITH?
I'M NOT HERE TO STEAL.
I'M HERE TO STOP **THE BLACK BREATH** FROM EVER STEALING ANYTHING FROM YOU OR ANYONE ELSE EVER AGAIN.
SINCE WHEN DID YOU SWITCH, RED HOOK?
AREN'T YOU THE ONE WHO GRIFTS THE GRIFTERS?

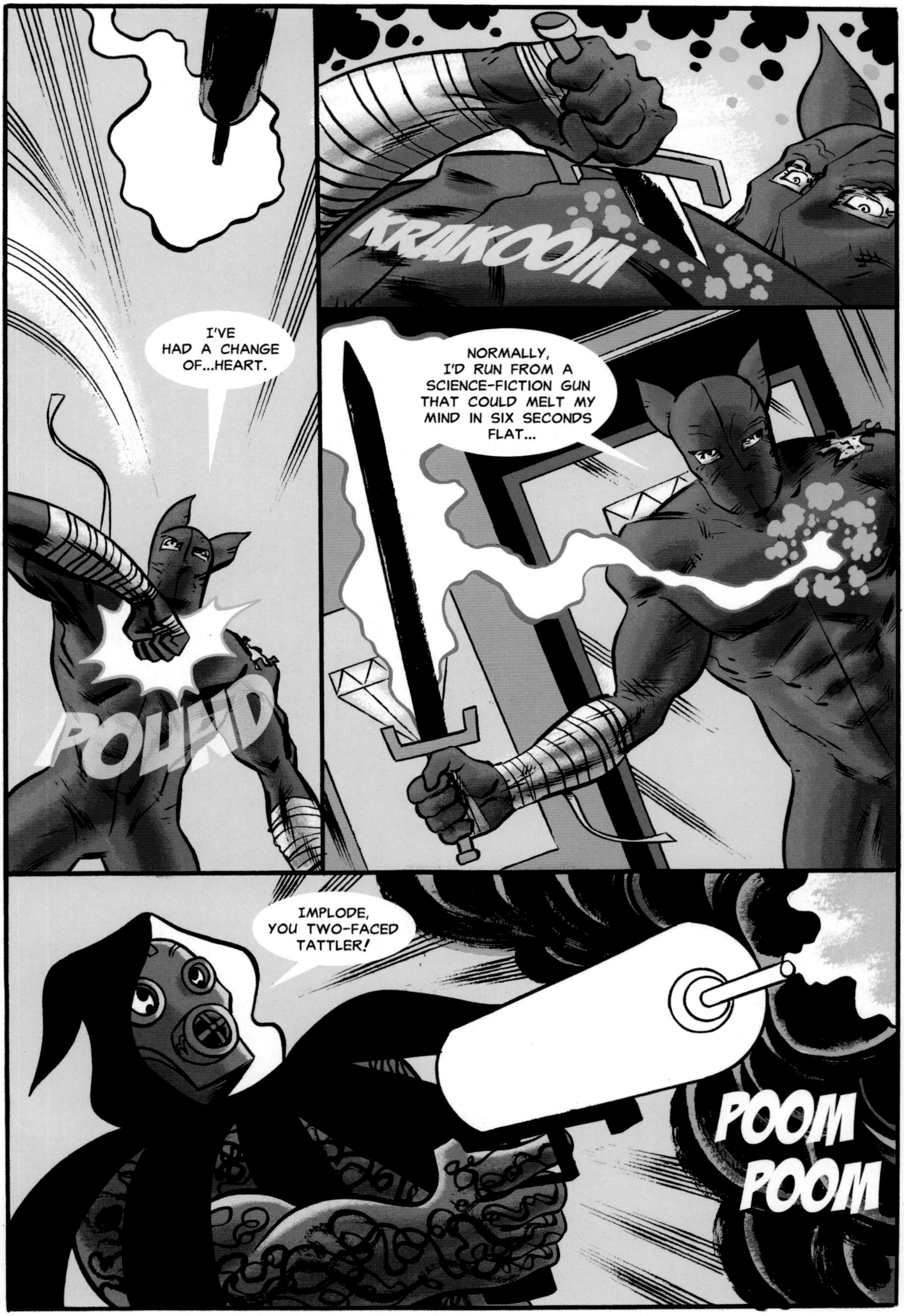
KRAKOOM
I'VE HAD A CHANGE OF...HEART.
POUND
NORMALLY, I'D RUN FROM A SCIENCE-FICTION GUN THAT COULD MELT MY MIND IN SIX SECONDS FLAT...
IMPLODE, YOU TWO-FACED TATTLER!
POOM
POOM

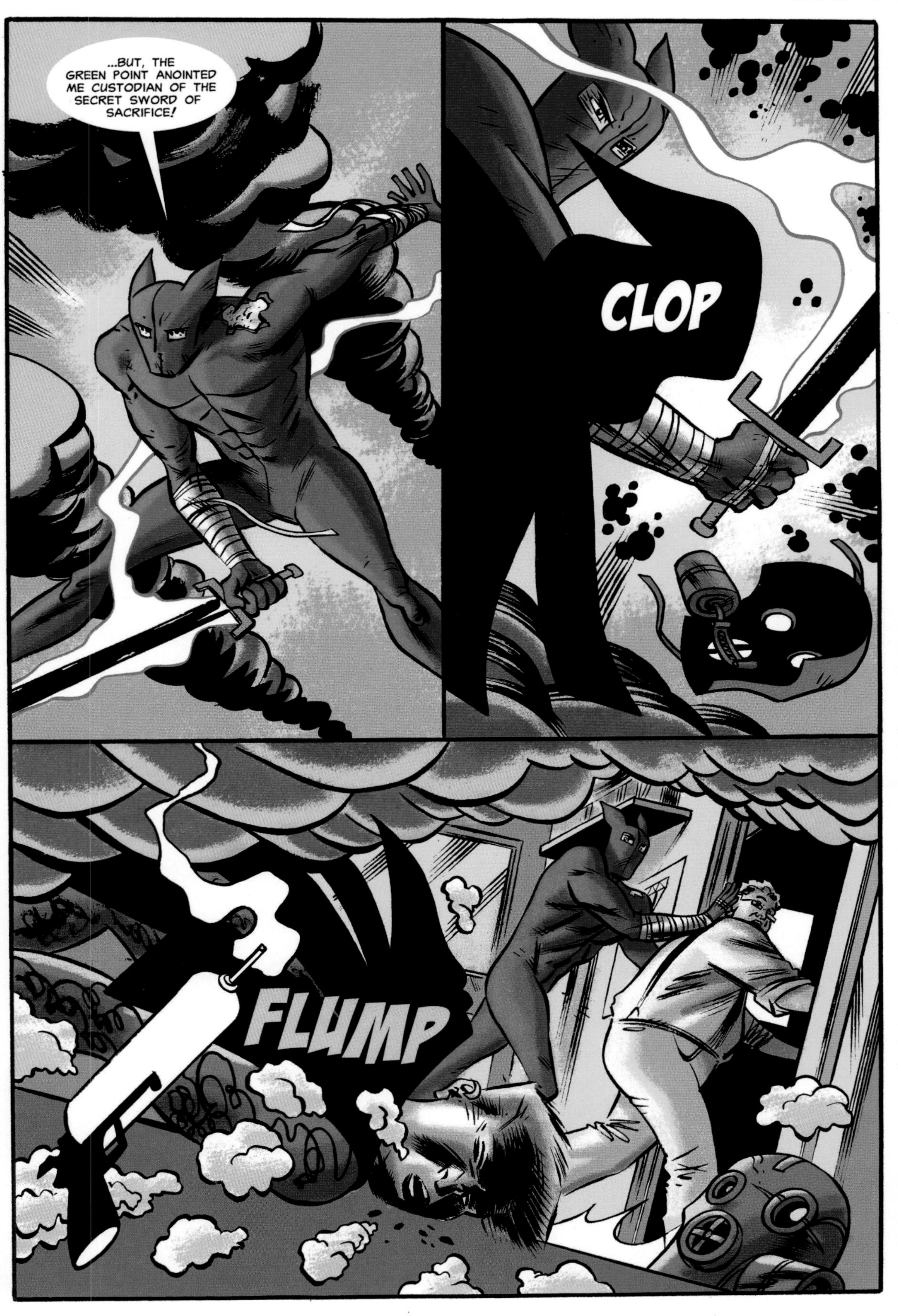
...BUT, THE GREEN POINT ANOINTED ME CUSTODIAN OF THE SECRET SWORD OF SACRIFICE!
CLOP
FLUMP

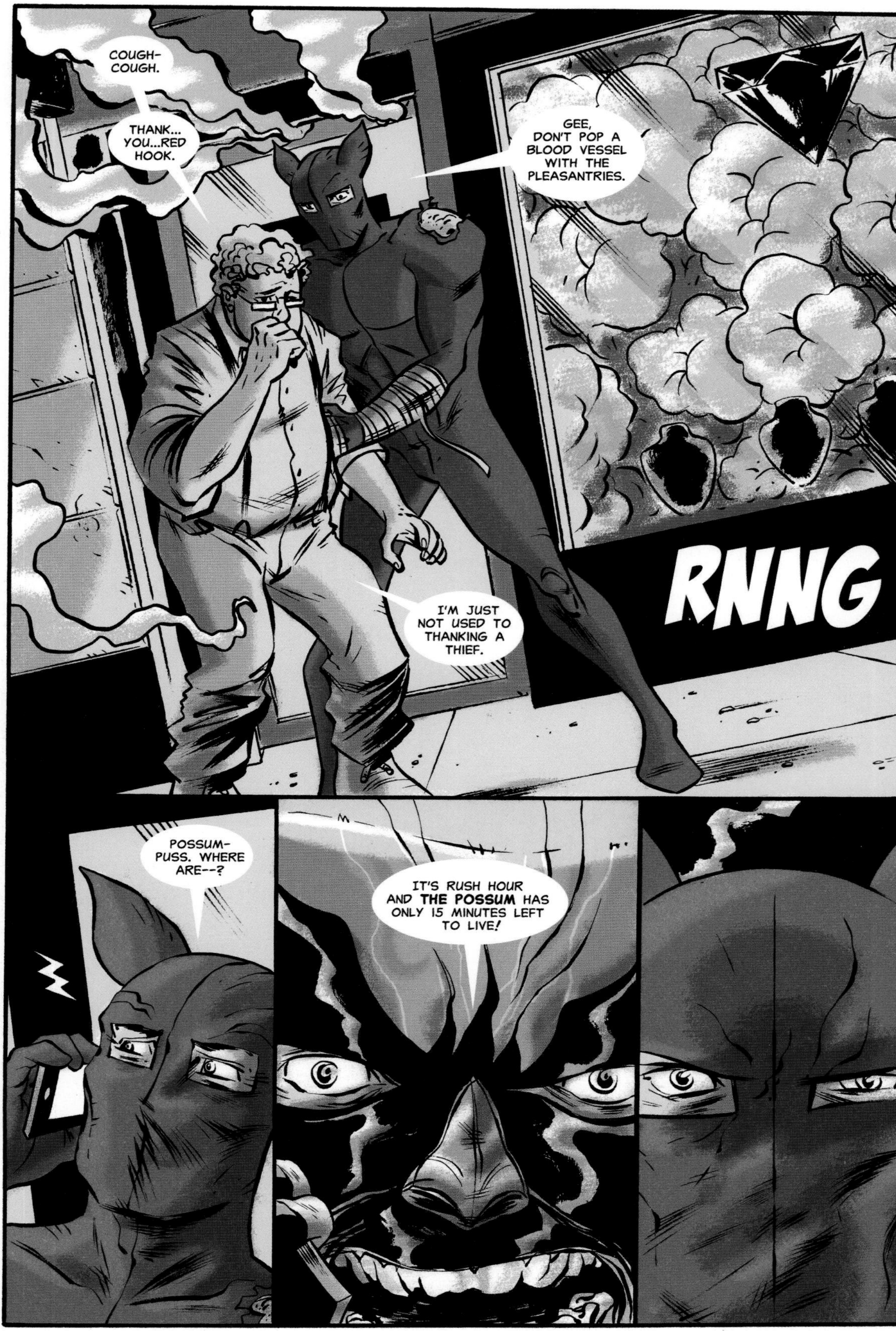
COUGH-COUGH.
THANK... YOU...RED HOOK.
GEE, DON'T POP A BLOOD VESSEL WITH THE PLEASANTRIES.
RNNG
I'M JUST NOT USED TO THANKING A THIEF.
POSSUM-PUSS. WHERE ARE--?
IT'S RUSH HOUR AND **THE POSSUM** HAS ONLY 15 MINUTES LEFT TO LIVE!

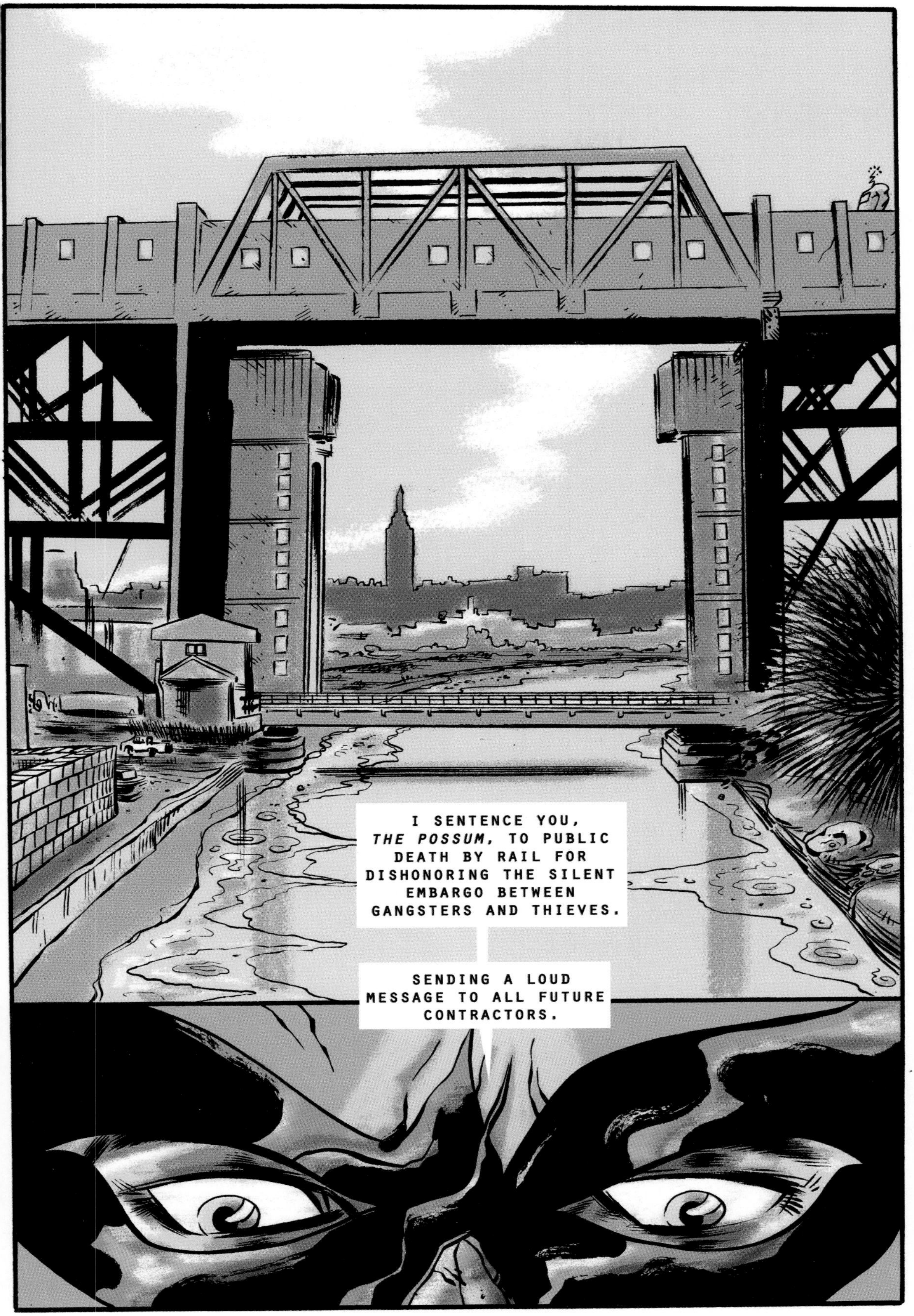
I SENTENCE YOU, *THE POSSUM,* TO PUBLIC DEATH BY RAIL FOR DISHONORING THE SILENT EMBARGO BETWEEN GANGSTERS AND THIEVES.
SENDING A LOUD MESSAGE TO ALL FUTURE CONTRACTORS.

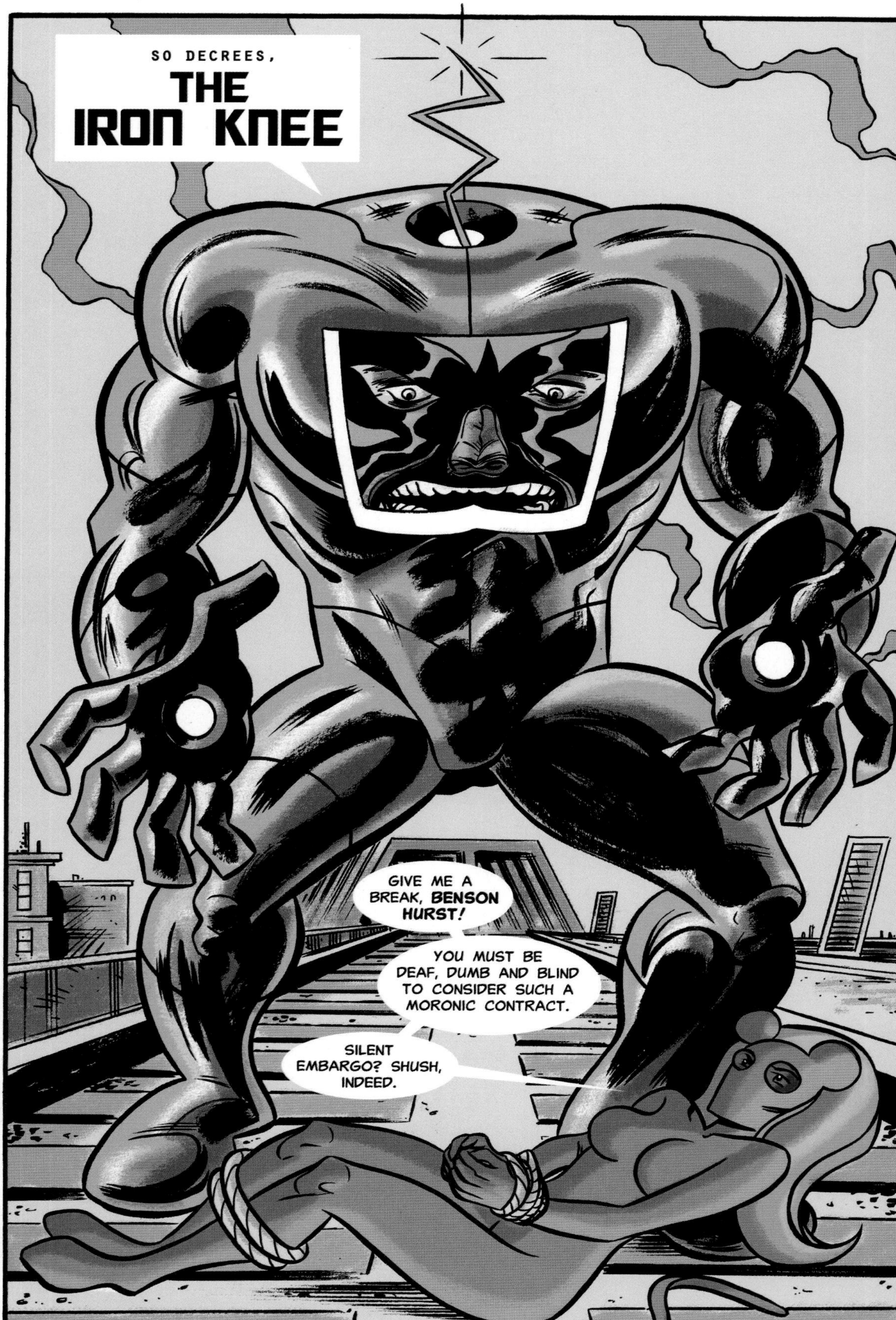
SO DECREES,
THE IRON KNEE
GIVE ME A BREAK, BENSON HURST!
YOU MUST BE DEAF, DUMB AND BLIND TO CONSIDER SUCH A MORONIC CONTRACT.
SILENT EMBARGO? SHUSH, INDEED.

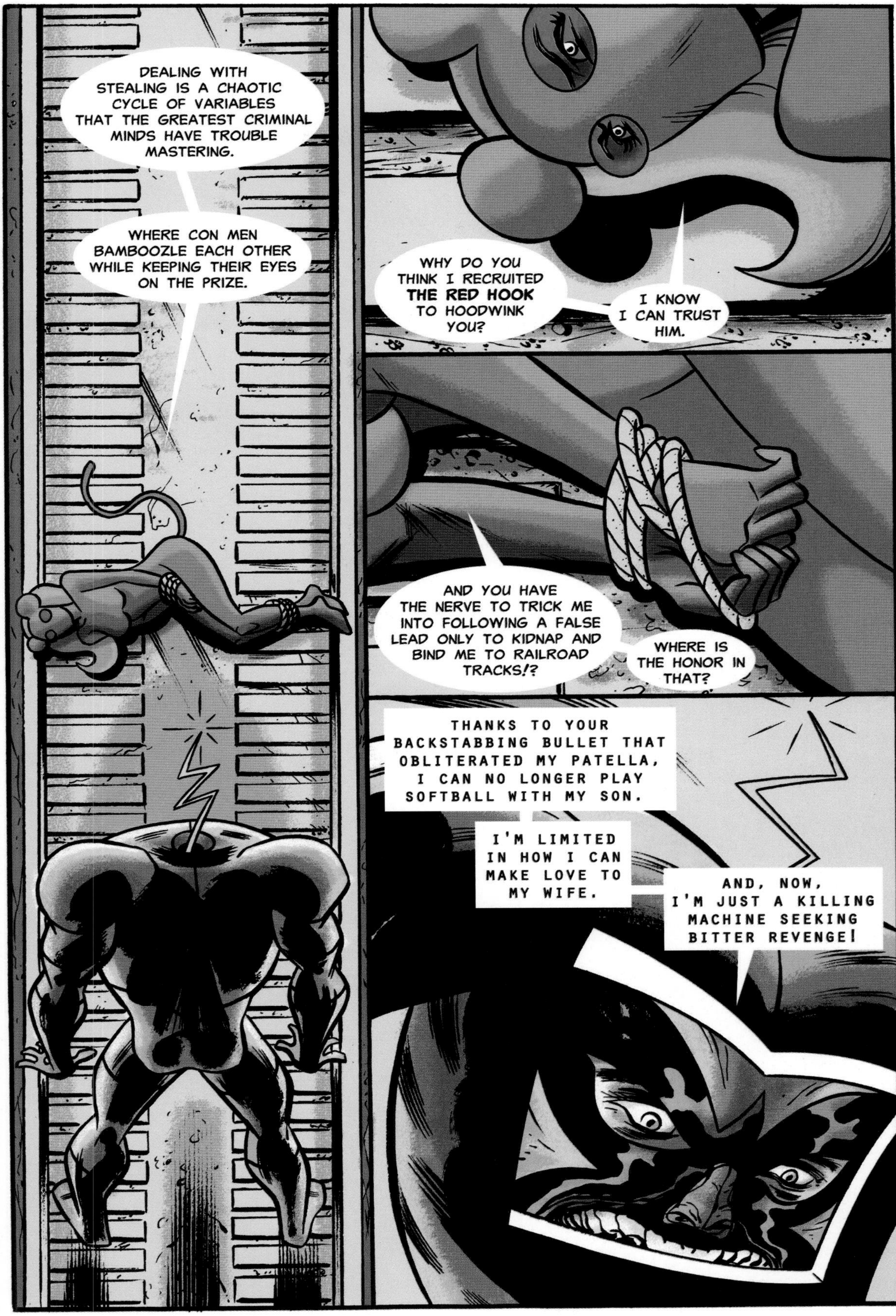
DEALING WITH STEALING IS A CHAOTIC CYCLE OF VARIABLES THAT THE GREATEST CRIMINAL MINDS HAVE TROUBLE MASTERING.
WHERE CON MEN BAMBOOZLE EACH OTHER WHILE KEEPING THEIR EYES ON THE PRIZE.
WHY DO YOU THINK I RECRUITED **THE RED HOOK** TO HOODWINK YOU?
I KNOW I CAN TRUST HIM.
AND YOU HAVE THE NERVE TO TRICK ME INTO FOLLOWING A FALSE LEAD ONLY TO KIDNAP AND BIND ME TO RAILROAD TRACKS!?
WHERE IS THE HONOR IN THAT?
THANKS TO YOUR BACKSTABBING BULLET THAT OBLITERATED MY PATELLA, I CAN NO LONGER PLAY SOFTBALL WITH MY SON.
I'M LIMITED IN HOW I CAN MAKE LOVE TO MY WIFE.
AND, NOW, I'M JUST A KILLING MACHINE SEEKING BITTER REVENGE!

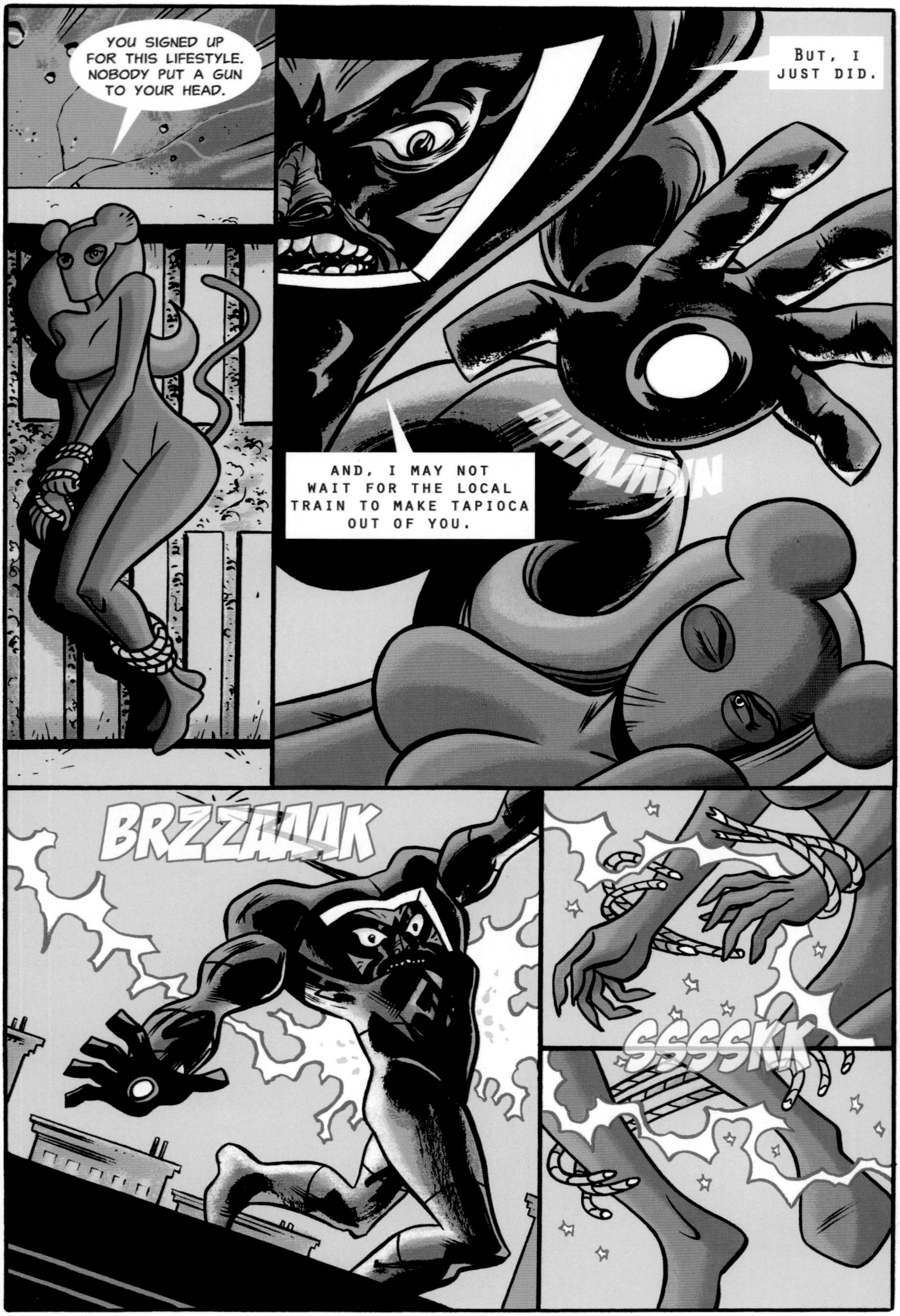
YOU SIGNED UP FOR THIS LIFESTYLE. NOBODY PUT A GUN TO YOUR HEAD.
BUT, I JUST DID.
AND, I MAY NOT WAIT FOR THE LOCAL TRAIN TO MAKE TAPIOCA OUT OF YOU.
BRZZAAAK
SSSSSKK

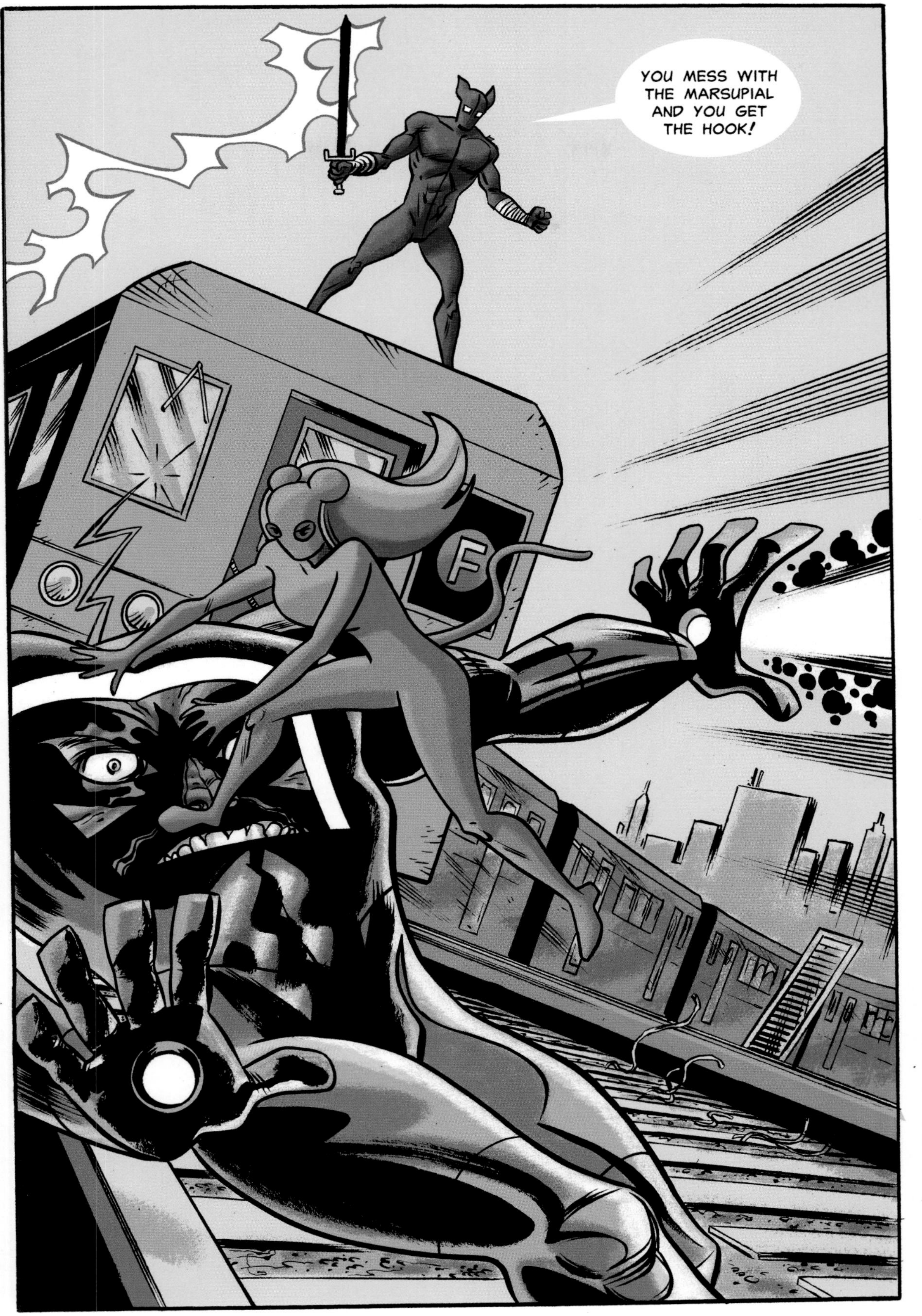
YOU MESS WITH THE MARSUPIAL AND YOU GET THE HOOK!
F

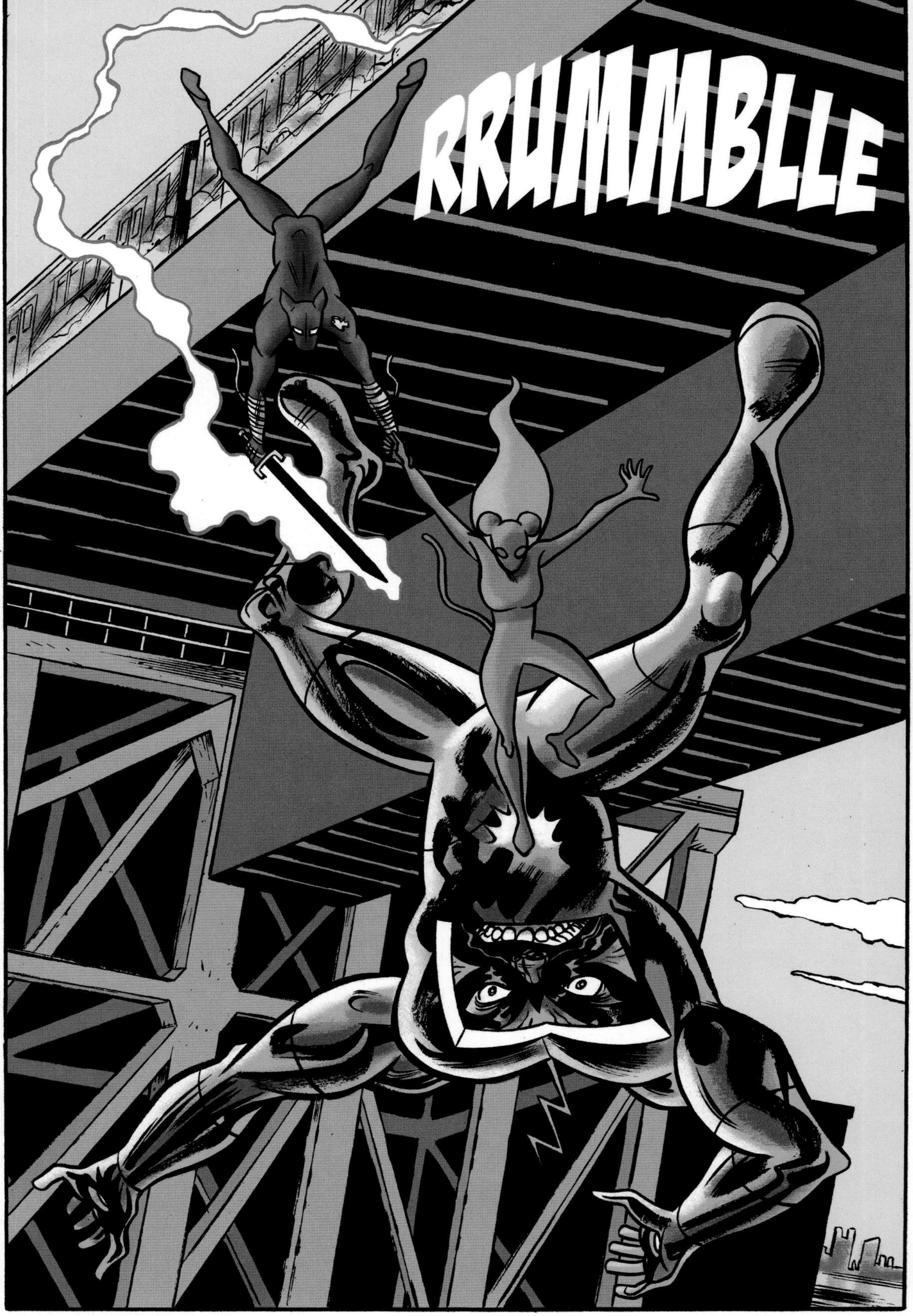
RRUMMBLLE

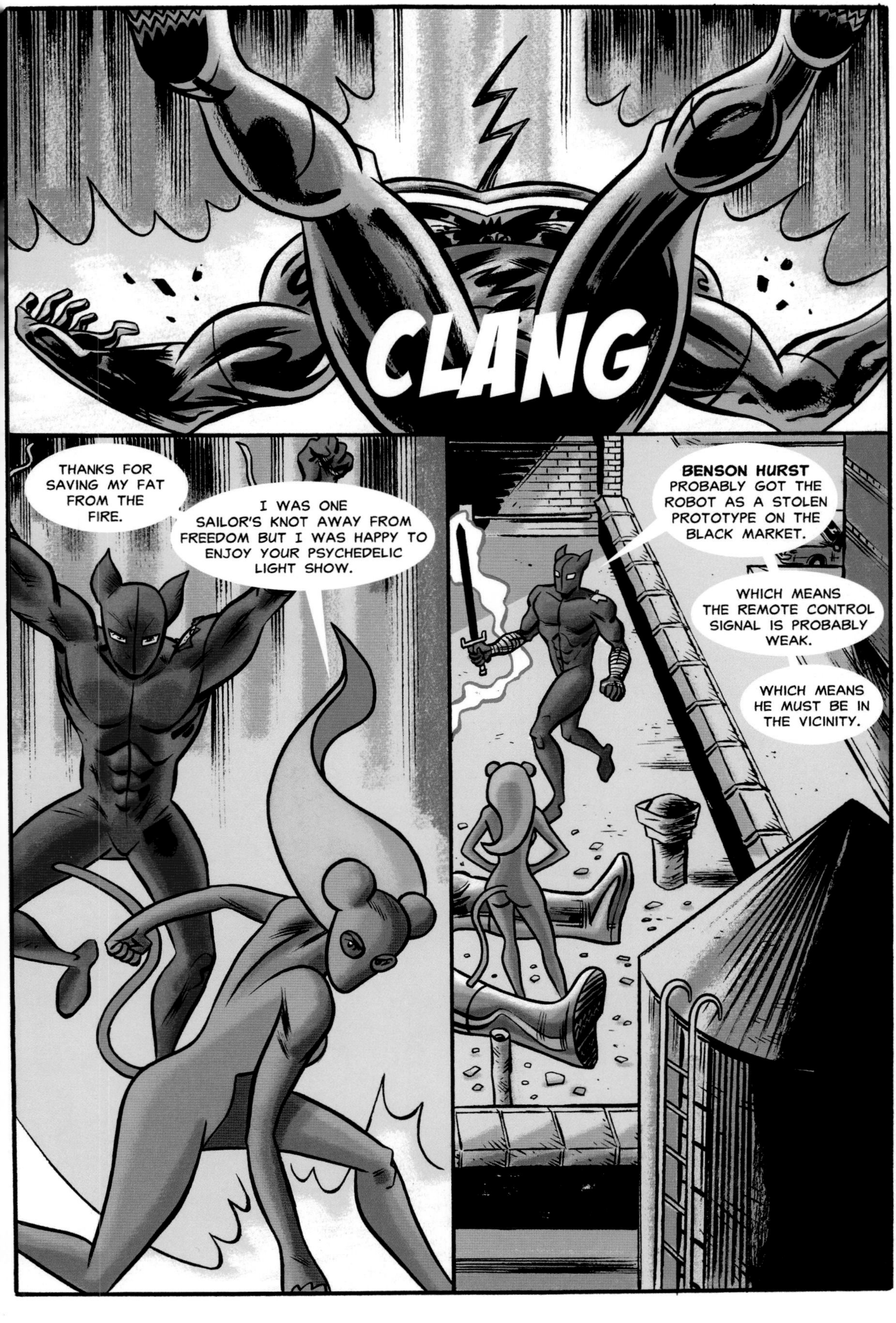
CLANG
THANKS FOR SAVING MY FAT FROM THE FIRE.
I WAS ONE SAILOR'S KNOT AWAY FROM FREEDOM BUT I WAS HAPPY TO ENJOY YOUR PSYCHEDELIC LIGHT SHOW.
BENSON HURST PROBABLY GOT THE ROBOT AS A STOLEN PROTOTYPE ON THE BLACK MARKET.
WHICH MEANS THE REMOTE CONTROL SIGNAL IS PROBABLY WEAK.
WHICH MEANS HE MUST BE IN THE VICINITY.

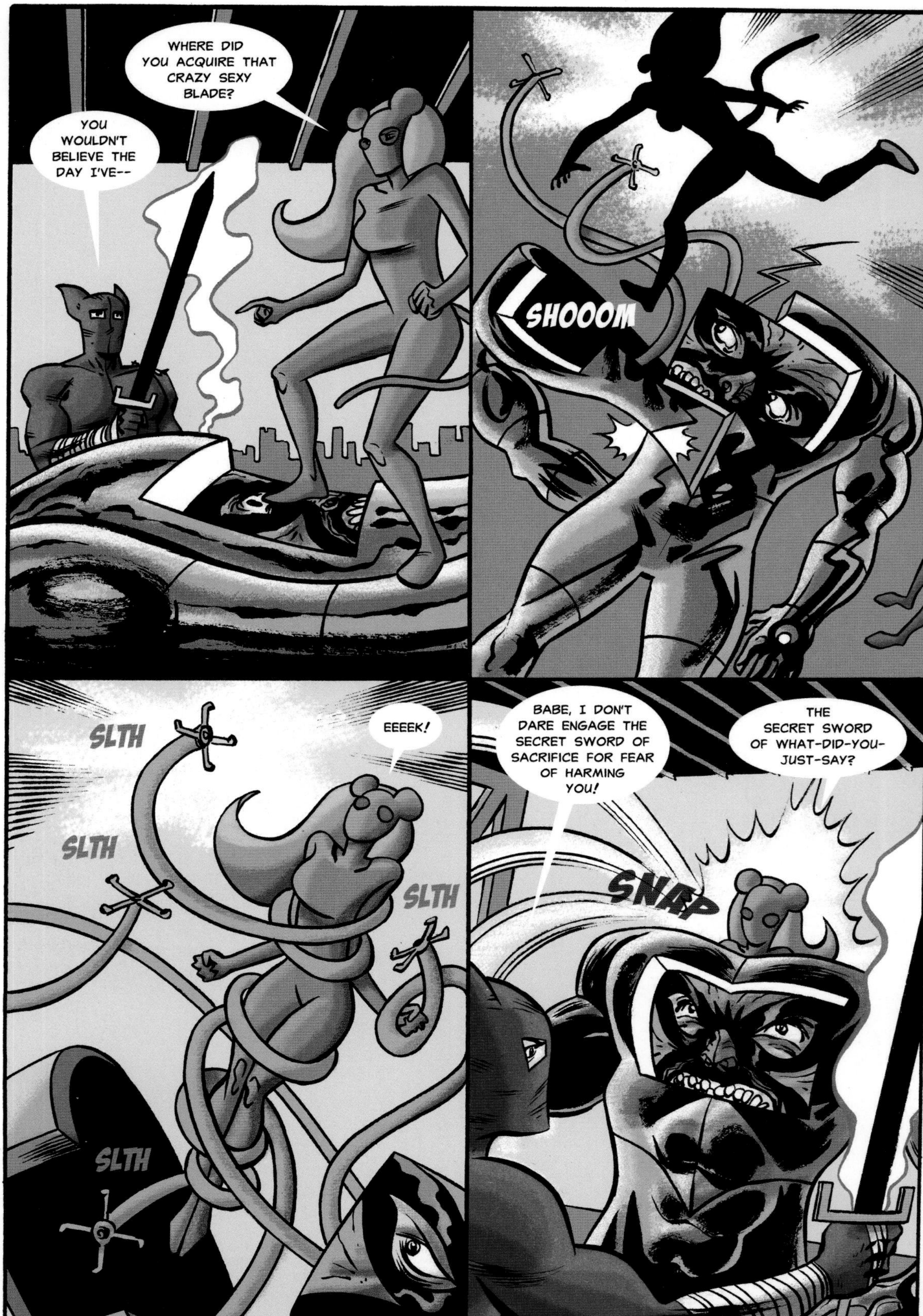
WHERE DID YOU ACQUIRE THAT CRAZY SEXY BLADE?
YOU WOULDN'T BELIEVE THE DAY I'VE--
SHOOOM
SLTH
EEEEK!
SLTH
SLTH
SLTH
BABE, I DON'T DARE ENGAGE THE SECRET SWORD OF SACRIFICE FOR FEAR OF HARMING YOU!
THE SECRET SWORD OF WHAT-DID-YOU-JUST-SAY?
SNAP

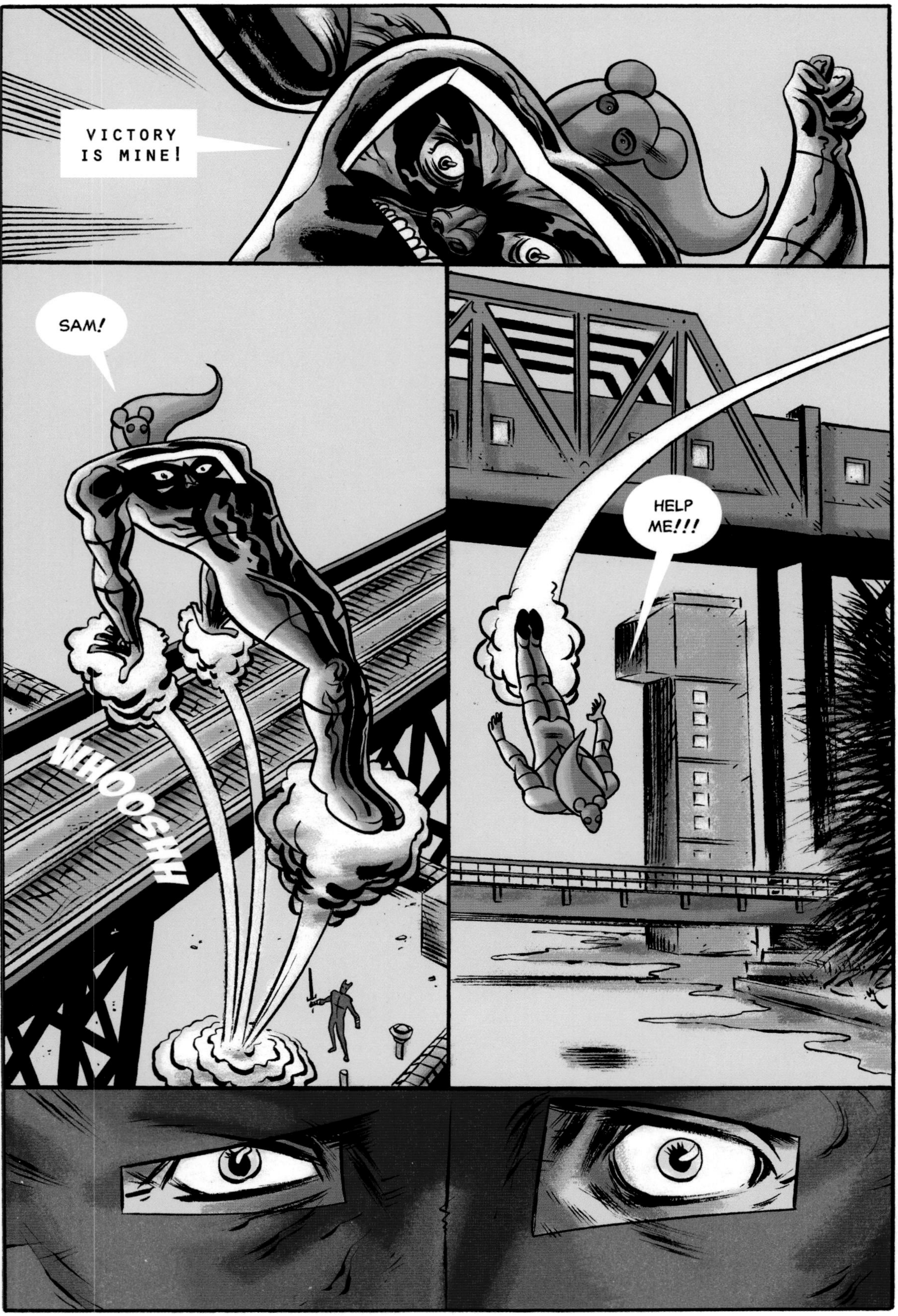
VICTORY IS MINE!
SAM!
WHOOSH!
HELP ME!!!

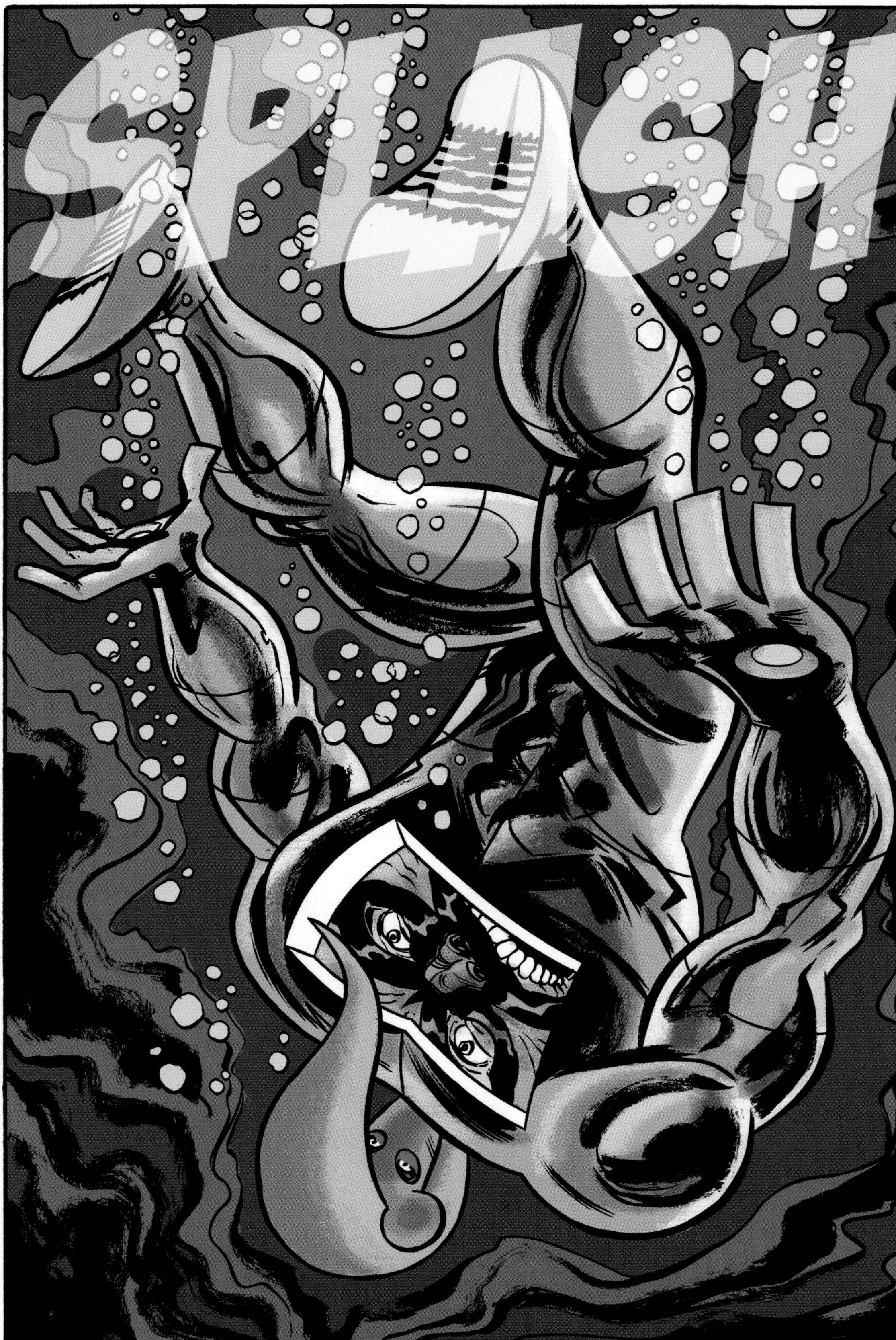
SPLASH

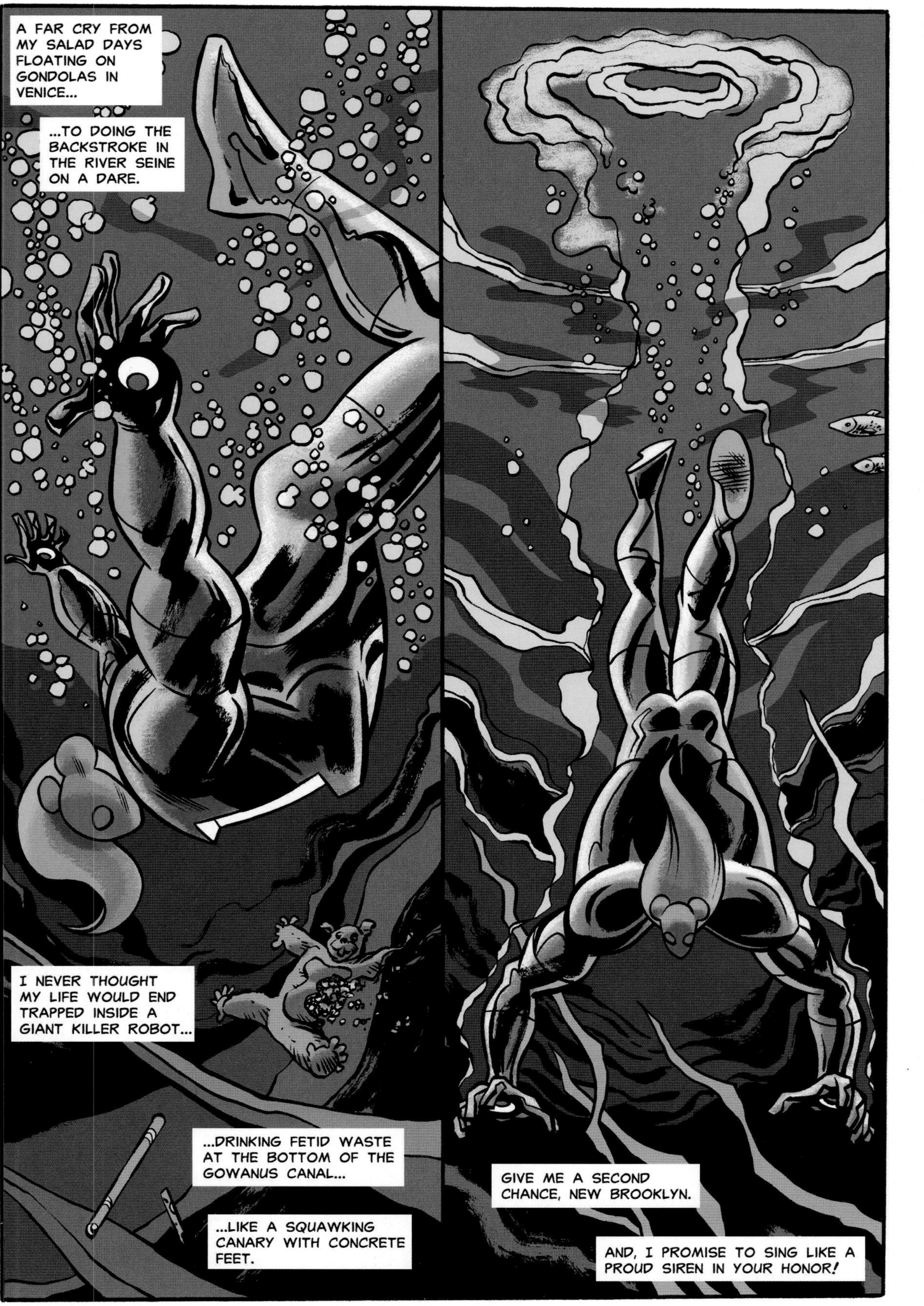
A FAR CRY FROM MY SALAD DAYS FLOATING ON GONDOLAS IN VENICE...
...TO DOING THE BACKSTROKE IN THE RIVER SEINE ON A DARE.
I NEVER THOUGHT MY LIFE WOULD END TRAPPED INSIDE A GIANT KILLER ROBOT...
...DRINKING FETID WASTE AT THE BOTTOM OF THE GOWANUS CANAL...
...LIKE A SQUAWKING CANARY WITH CONCRETE FEET.
GIVE ME A SECOND CHANCE, NEW BROOKLYN.
AND, I PROMISE TO SING LIKE A PROUD SIREN IN YOUR HONOR!

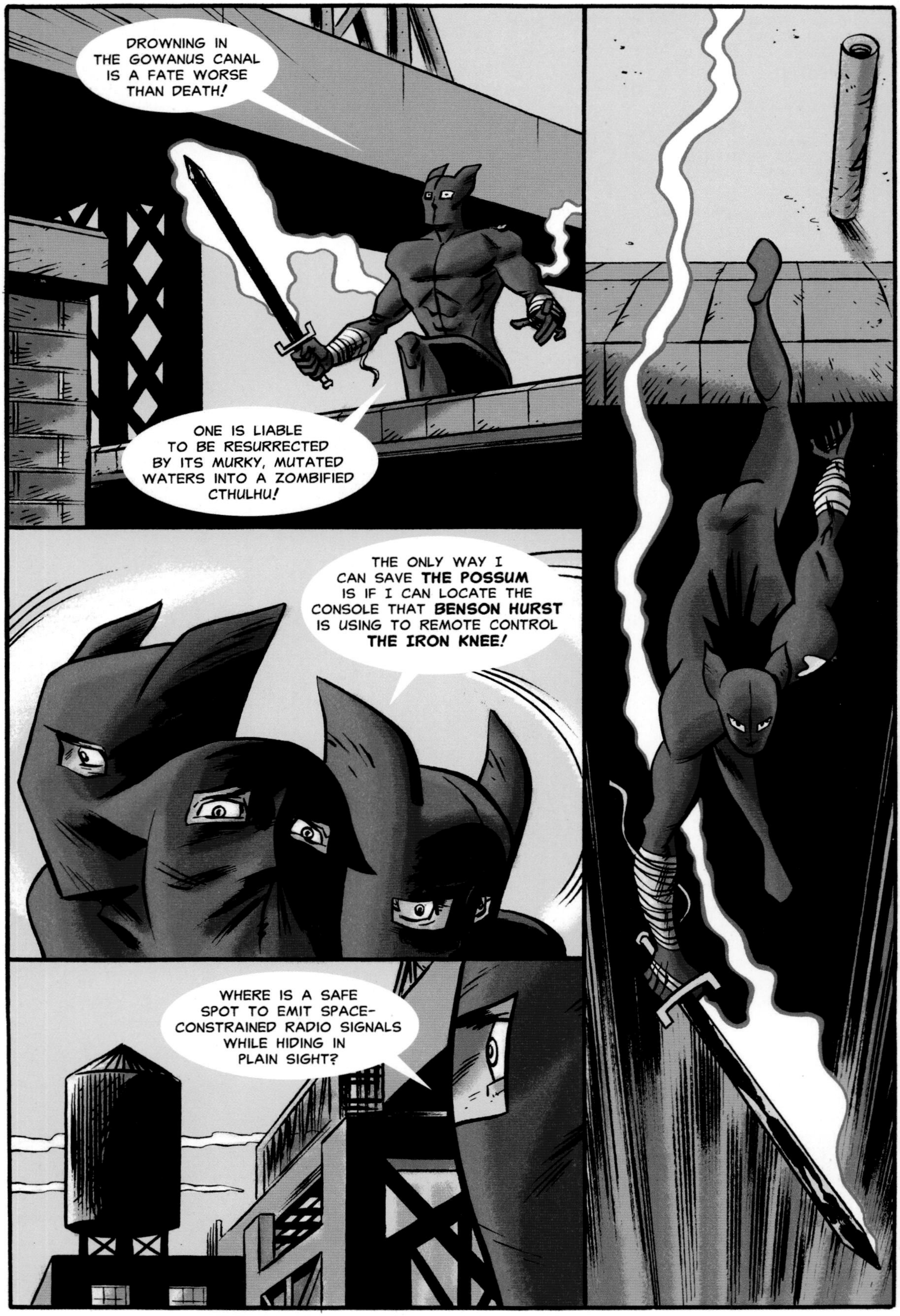
DROWNING IN THE GOWANUS CANAL IS A FATE WORSE THAN DEATH!
ONE IS LIABLE TO BE RESURRECTED BY ITS MURKY, MUTATED WATERS INTO A ZOMBIFIED CTHULHU!
THE ONLY WAY I CAN SAVE **THE POSSUM** IS IF I CAN LOCATE THE CONSOLE THAT **BENSON HURST** IS USING TO REMOTE CONTROL **THE IRON KNEE**!
WHERE IS A SAFE SPOT TO EMIT SPACE-CONSTRAINED RADIO SIGNALS WHILE HIDING IN PLAIN SIGHT?

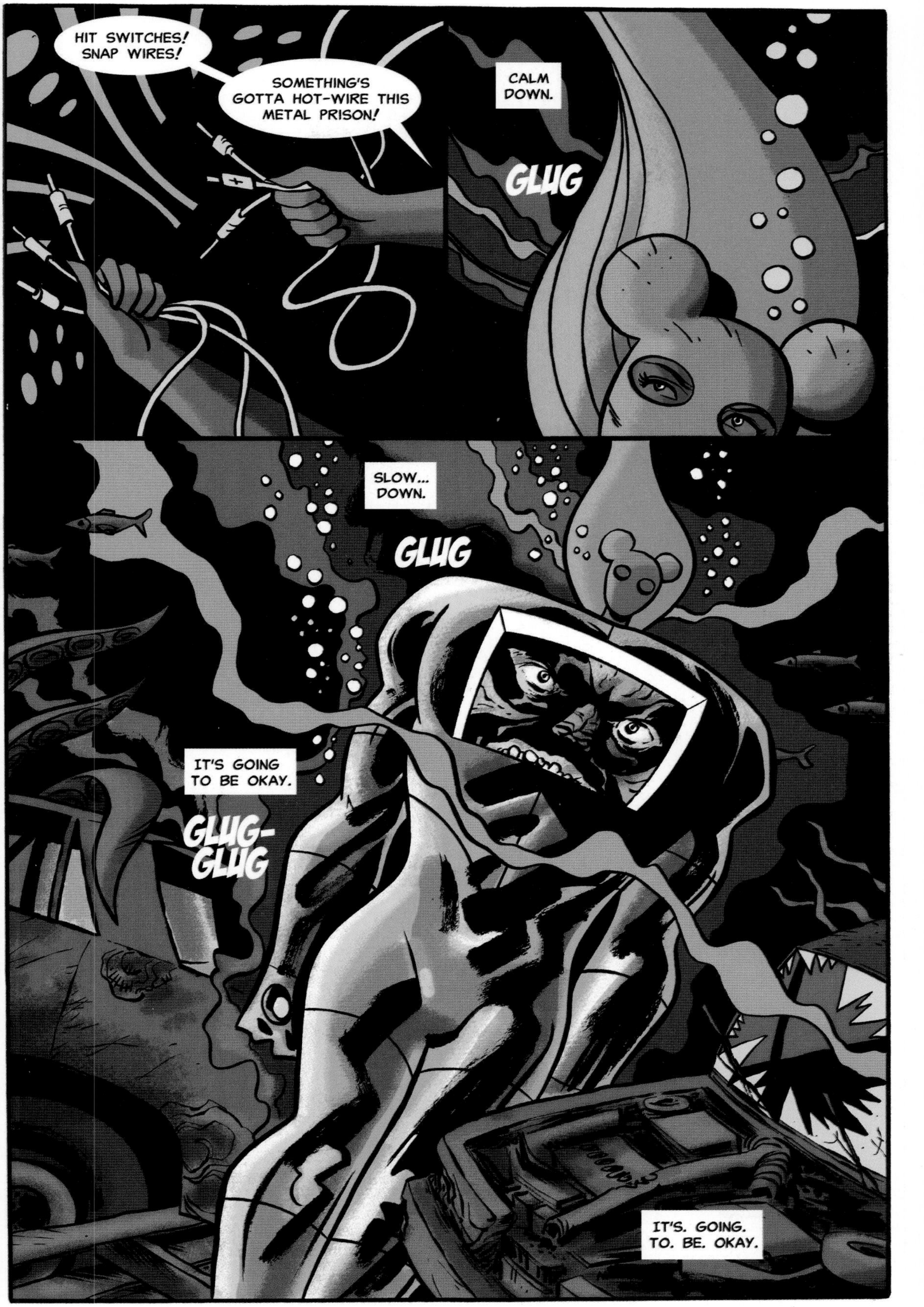

HIT SWITCHES! SNAP WIRES!
SOMETHING'S GOTTA HOT-WIRE THIS METAL PRISON!
CALM DOWN.
GLUG
SLOW... DOWN.
GLUG
IT'S GOING TO BE OKAY.
GLUG-GLUG
IT'S. GOING. TO. BE. OKAY.

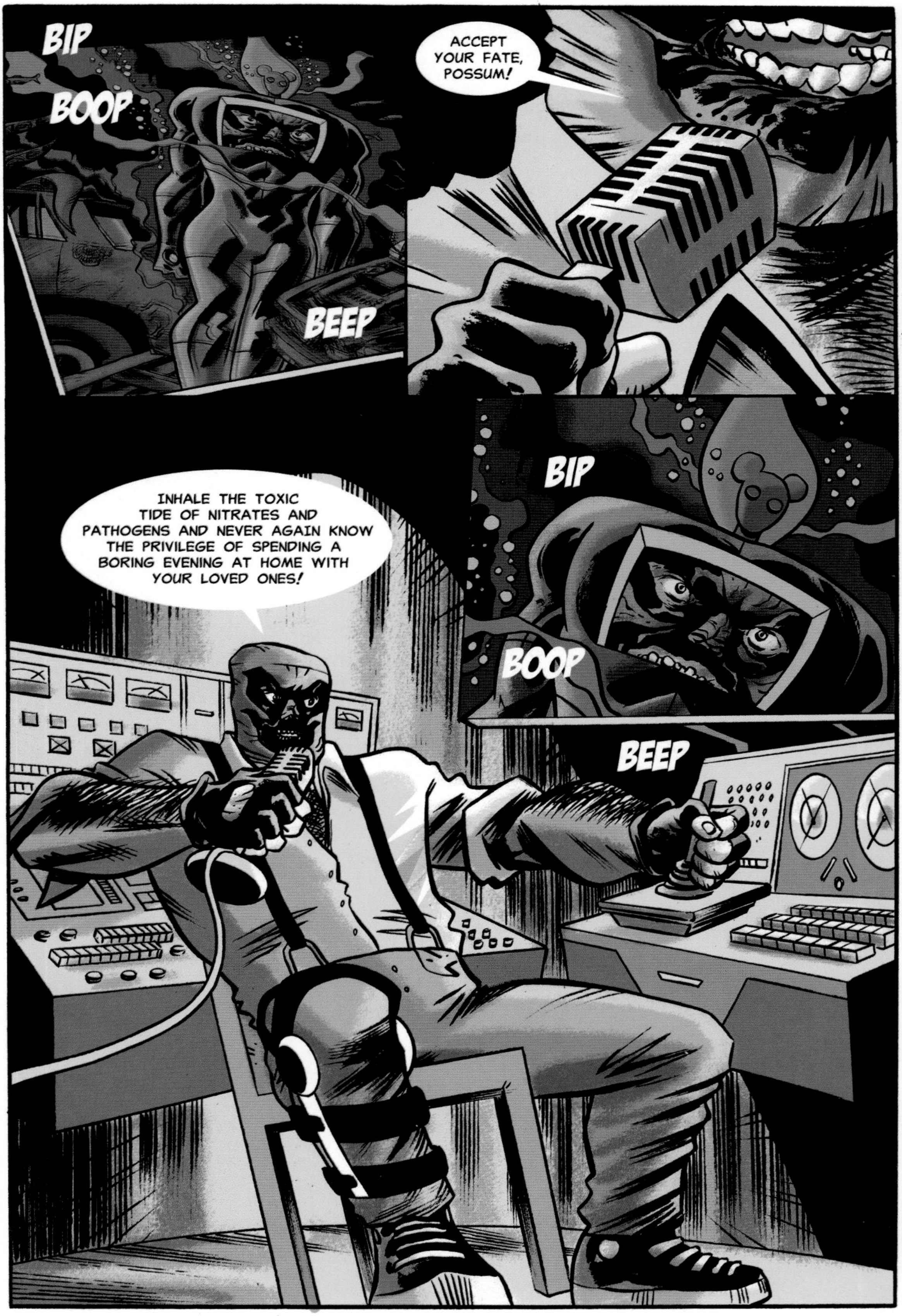
BIP
BOOP
BEEP
ACCEPT YOUR FATE, POSSUM!
BIP
BOOP
BEEP
INHALE THE TOXIC TIDE OF NITRATES AND PATHOGENS AND NEVER AGAIN KNOW THE PRIVILEGE OF SPENDING A BORING EVENING AT HOME WITH YOUR LOVED ONES!

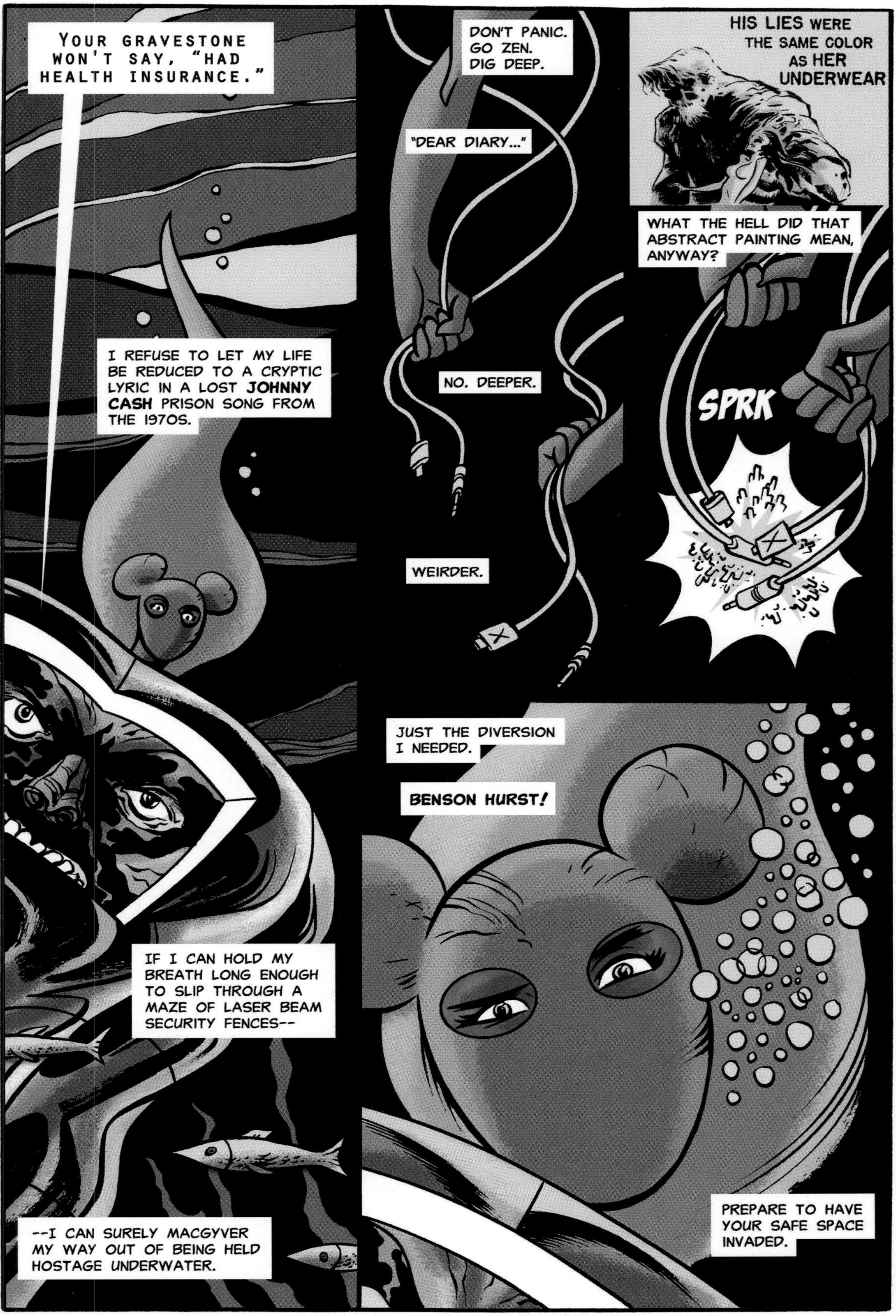
YOUR GRAVESTONE WON'T SAY, "HAD HEALTH INSURANCE."
I REFUSE TO LET MY LIFE BE REDUCED TO A CRYPTIC LYRIC IN A LOST JOHNNY CASH PRISON SONG FROM THE 1970S.
IF I CAN HOLD MY BREATH LONG ENOUGH TO SLIP THROUGH A MAZE OF LASER BEAM SECURITY FENCES--
--I CAN SURELY MACGYVER MY WAY OUT OF BEING HELD HOSTAGE UNDERWATER.
DON'T PANIC. GO ZEN. DIG DEEP.
"DEAR DIARY..."
NO. DEEPER.
WEIRDER.
HIS LIES WERE THE SAME COLOR AS HER UNDERWEAR
WHAT THE HELL DID THAT ABSTRACT PAINTING MEAN, ANYWAY?
SPRK
JUST THE DIVERSION I NEEDED.
BENSON HURST!
PREPARE TO HAVE YOUR SAFE SPACE INVADED.

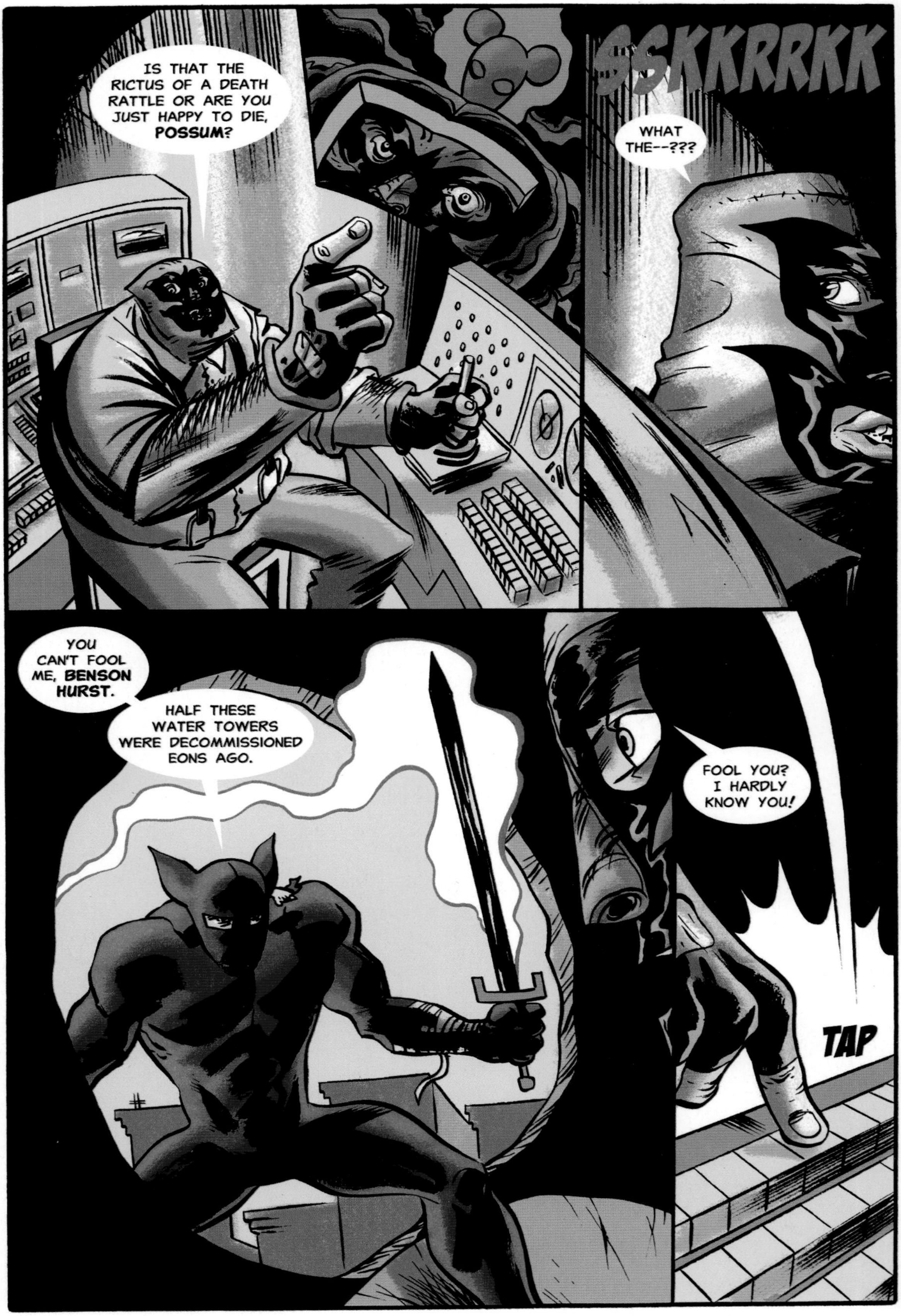
IS THAT THE RICTUS OF A DEATH RATTLE OR ARE YOU JUST HAPPY TO DIE, POSSUM?
SSKKRRRKK
WHAT THE--???
YOU CAN'T FOOL ME, BENSON HURST.
HALF THESE WATER TOWERS WERE DECOMMISSIONED EONS AGO.
FOOL YOU? I HARDLY KNOW YOU!
TAP

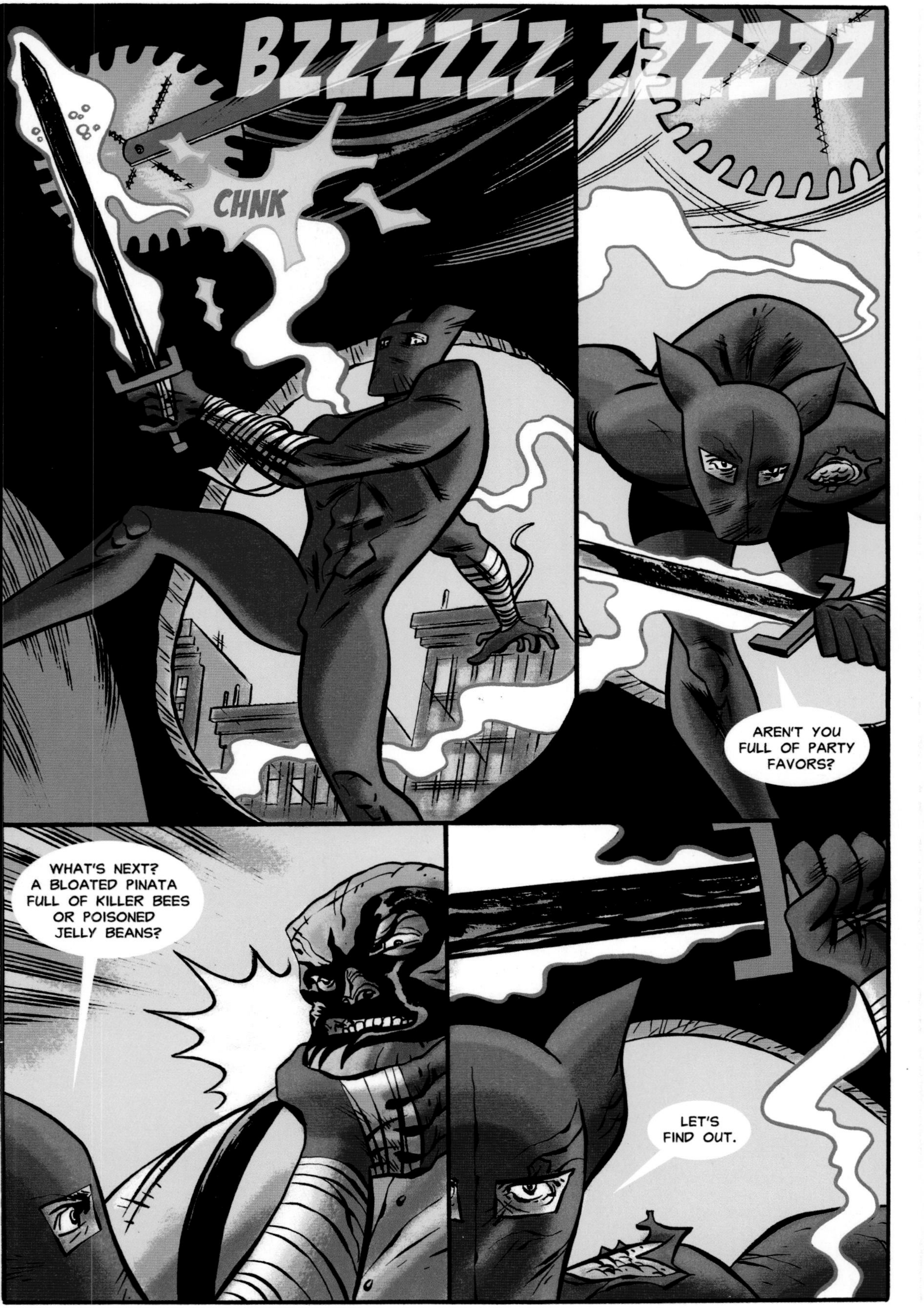
BZZZZZZ ZZZZZZ
CHNK
AREN'T YOU FULL OF PARTY FAVORS?
WHAT'S NEXT? A BLOATED PINATA FULL OF KILLER BEES OR POISONED JELLY BEANS?
LET'S FIND OUT.

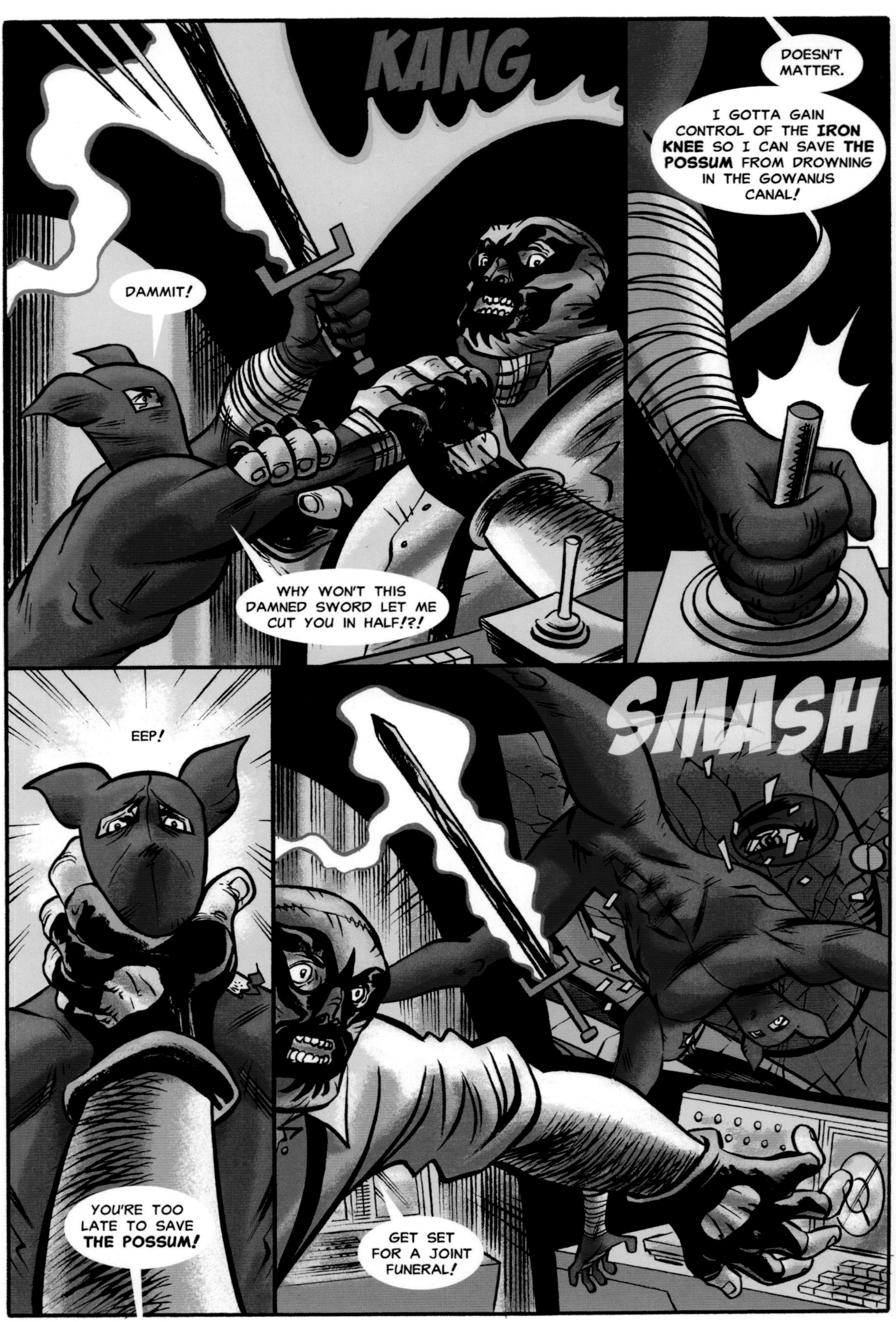
KANG
DAMMIT!
WHY WON'T THIS DAMNED SWORD LET ME CUT YOU IN HALF!?!
DOESN'T MATTER.
I GOTTA GAIN CONTROL OF THE IRON KNEE SO I CAN SAVE THE POSSUM FROM DROWNING IN THE GOWANUS CANAL!
EEP!
YOU'RE TOO LATE TO SAVE THE POSSUM!
SMASH
GET SET FOR A JOINT FUNERAL!

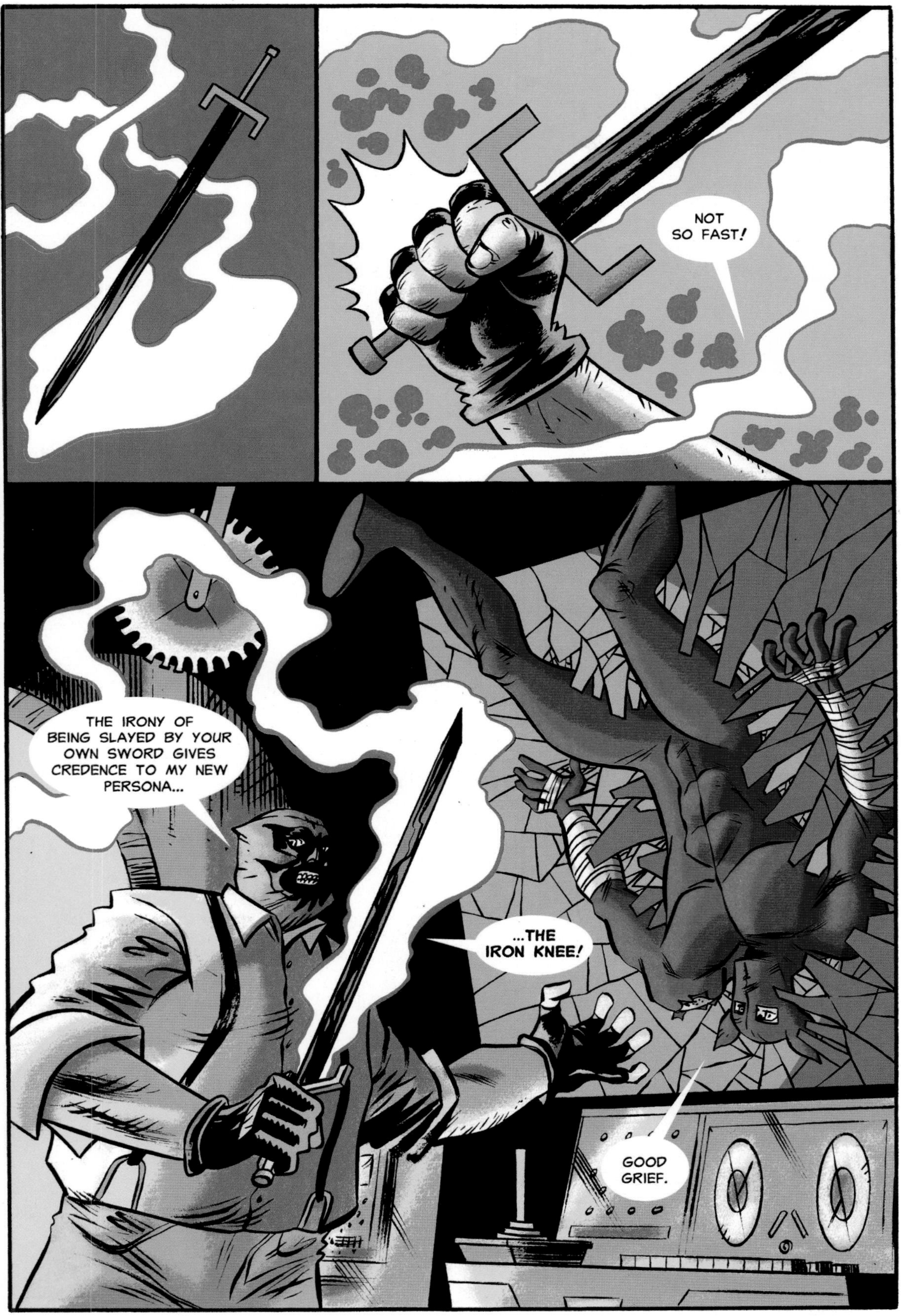
NOT SO FAST!
THE IRONY OF BEING SLAYED BY YOUR OWN SWORD GIVES CREDENCE TO MY NEW PERSONA...
...THE IRON KNEE!
GOOD GRIEF.

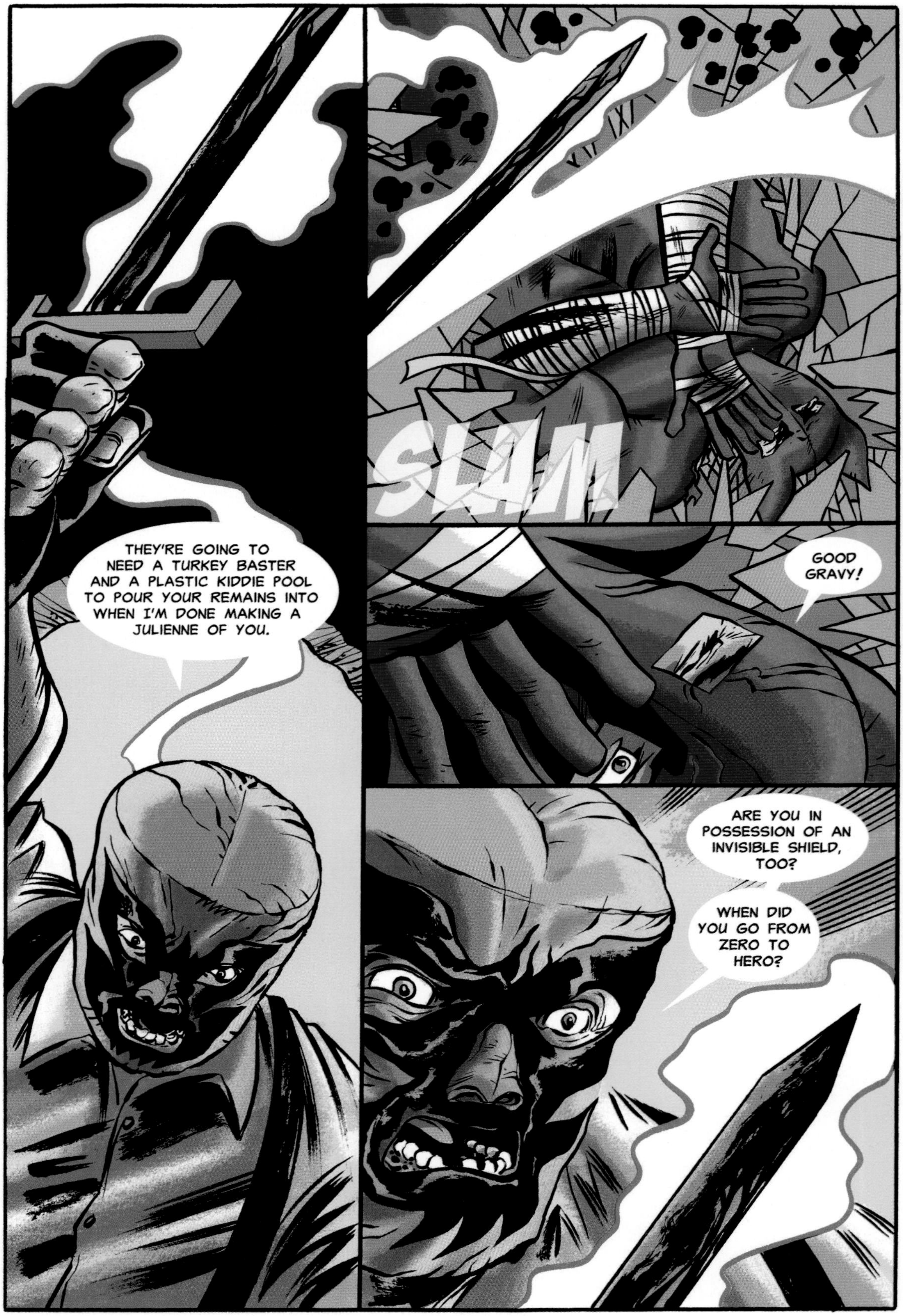
SLAM
THEY'RE GOING TO NEED A TURKEY BASTER AND A PLASTIC KIDDIE POOL TO POUR YOUR REMAINS INTO WHEN I'M DONE MAKING A JULIENNE OF YOU.
GOOD GRAVY!
ARE YOU IN POSSESSION OF AN INVISIBLE SHIELD, TOO?
WHEN DID YOU GO FROM ZERO TO HERO?

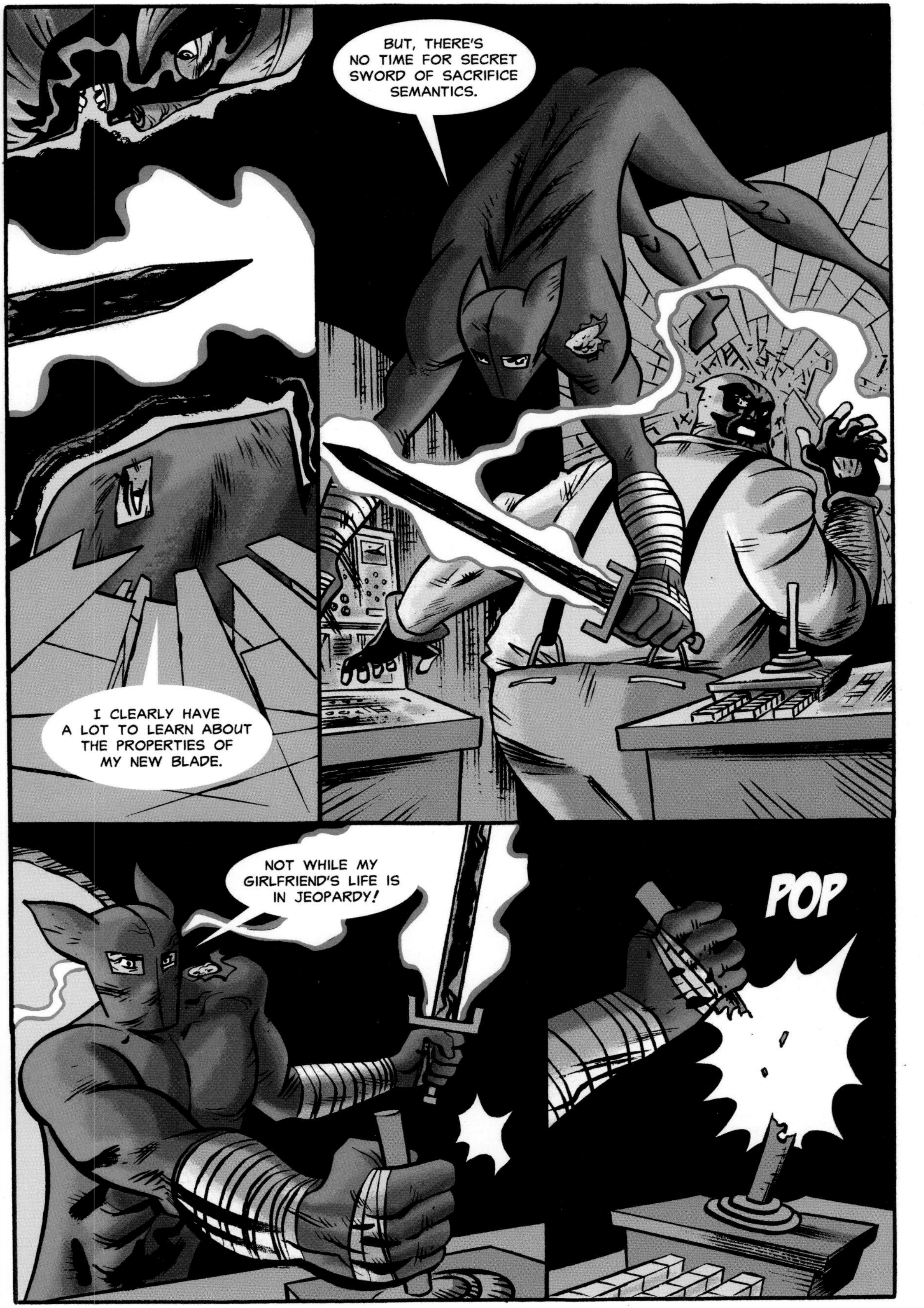
I CLEARLY HAVE A LOT TO LEARN ABOUT THE PROPERTIES OF MY NEW BLADE.
BUT, THERE'S NO TIME FOR SECRET SWORD OF SACRIFICE SEMANTICS.
NOT WHILE MY GIRLFRIEND'S LIFE IS IN JEOPARDY!
POP

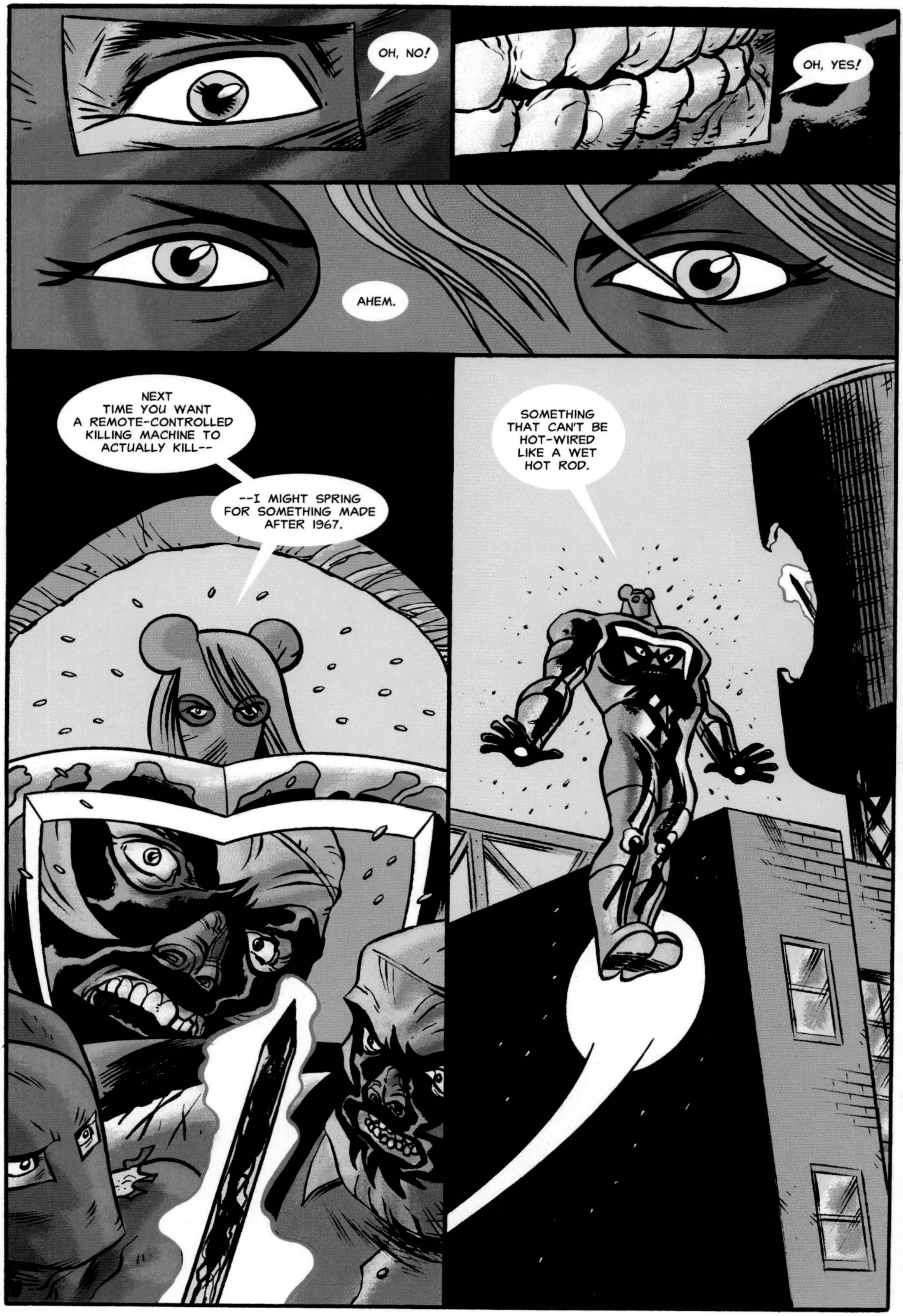

OH, NO!
OH, YES!
AHEM.
NEXT TIME YOU WANT A REMOTE-CONTROLLED KILLING MACHINE TO ACTUALLY KILL--
--I MIGHT SPRING FOR SOMETHING MADE AFTER 1967.
SOMETHING THAT CAN'T BE HOT-WIRED LIKE A WET HOT ROD.

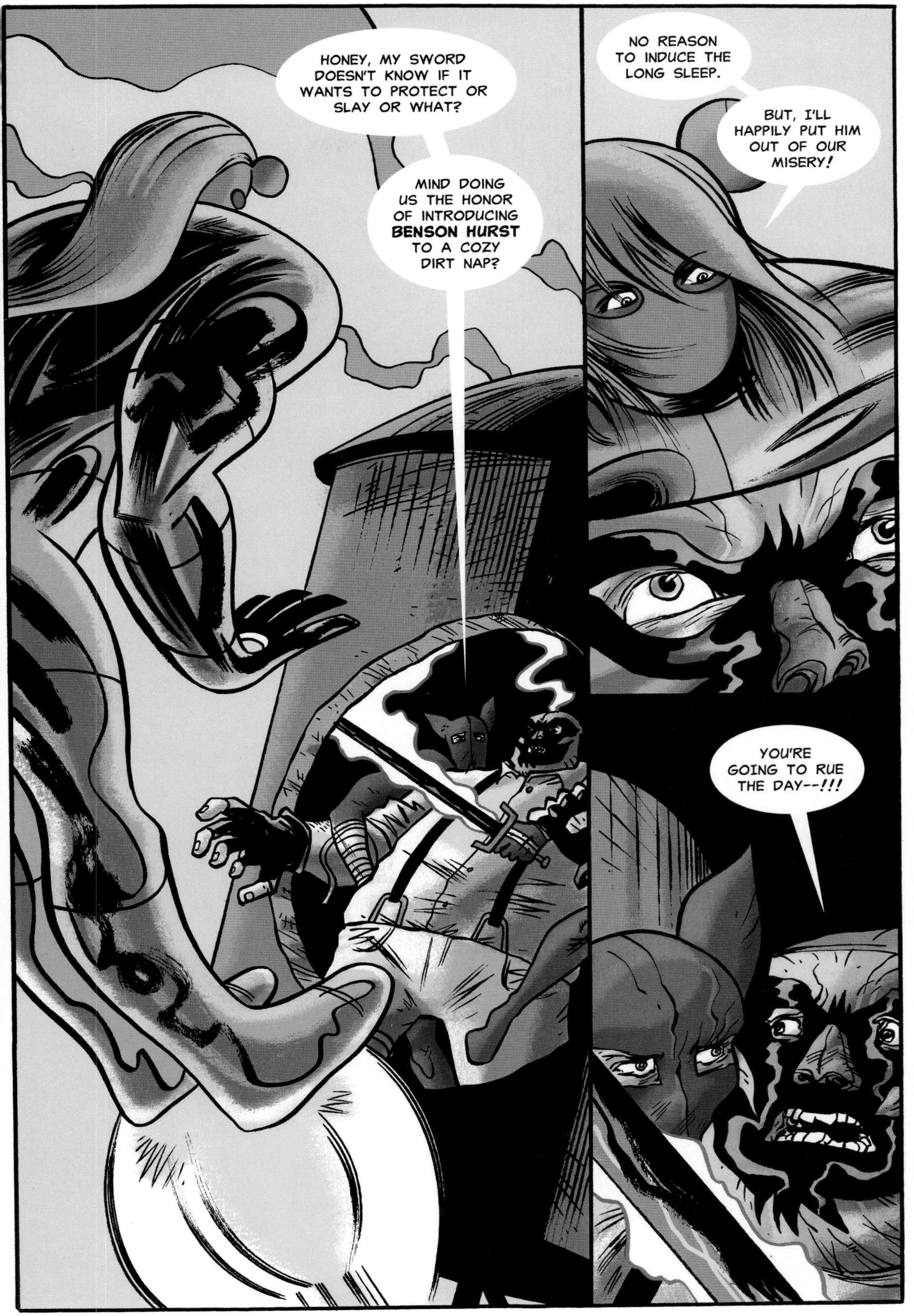
HONEY, MY SWORD DOESN'T KNOW IF IT WANTS TO PROTECT OR SLAY OR WHAT?
MIND DOING US THE HONOR OF INTRODUCING **BENSON HURST** TO A COZY DIRT NAP?
NO REASON TO INDUCE THE LONG SLEEP.
BUT, I'LL HAPPILY PUT HIM OUT OF OUR MISERY!
YOU'RE GOING TO RUE THE DAY--!!!

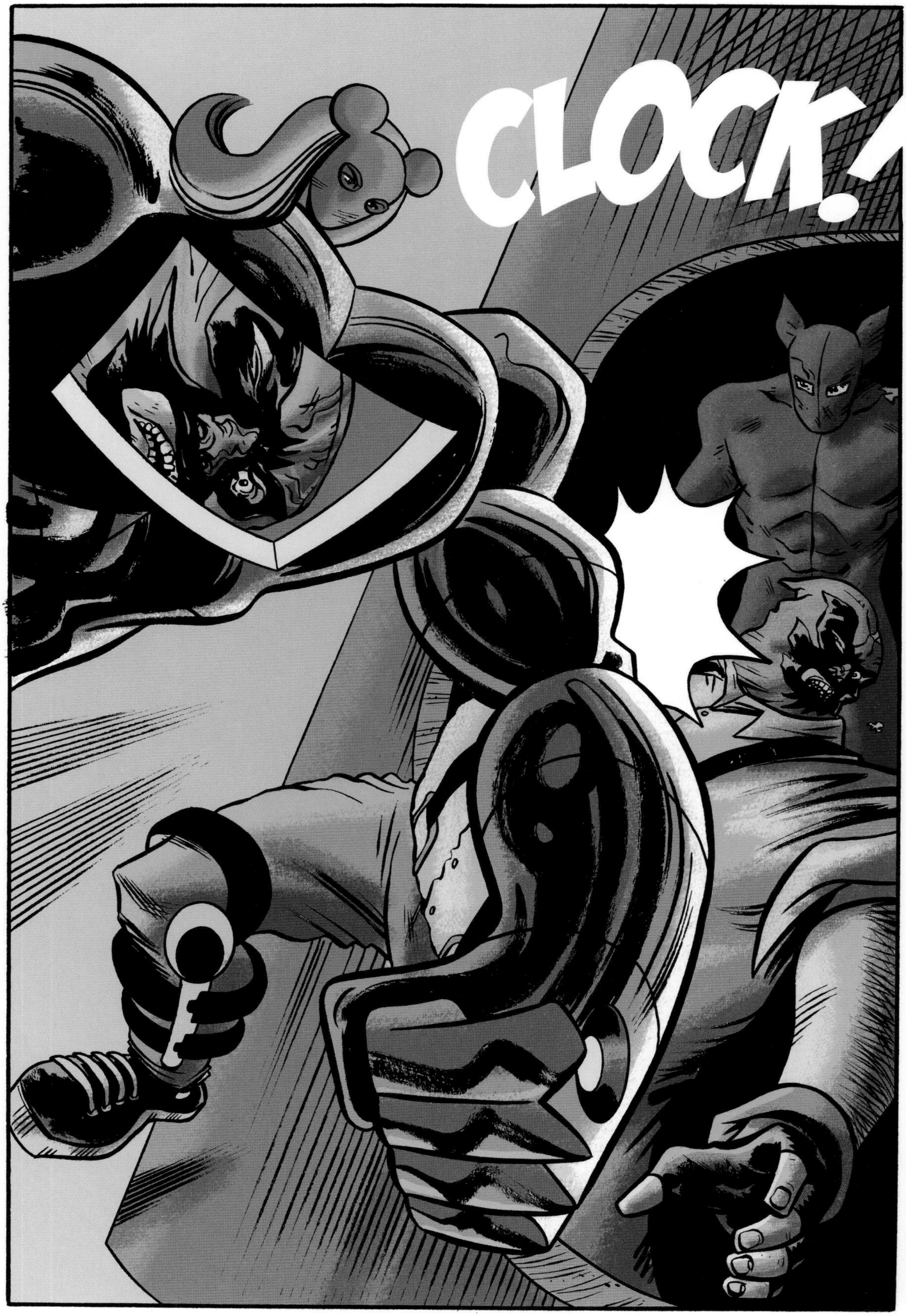
CLOCK!

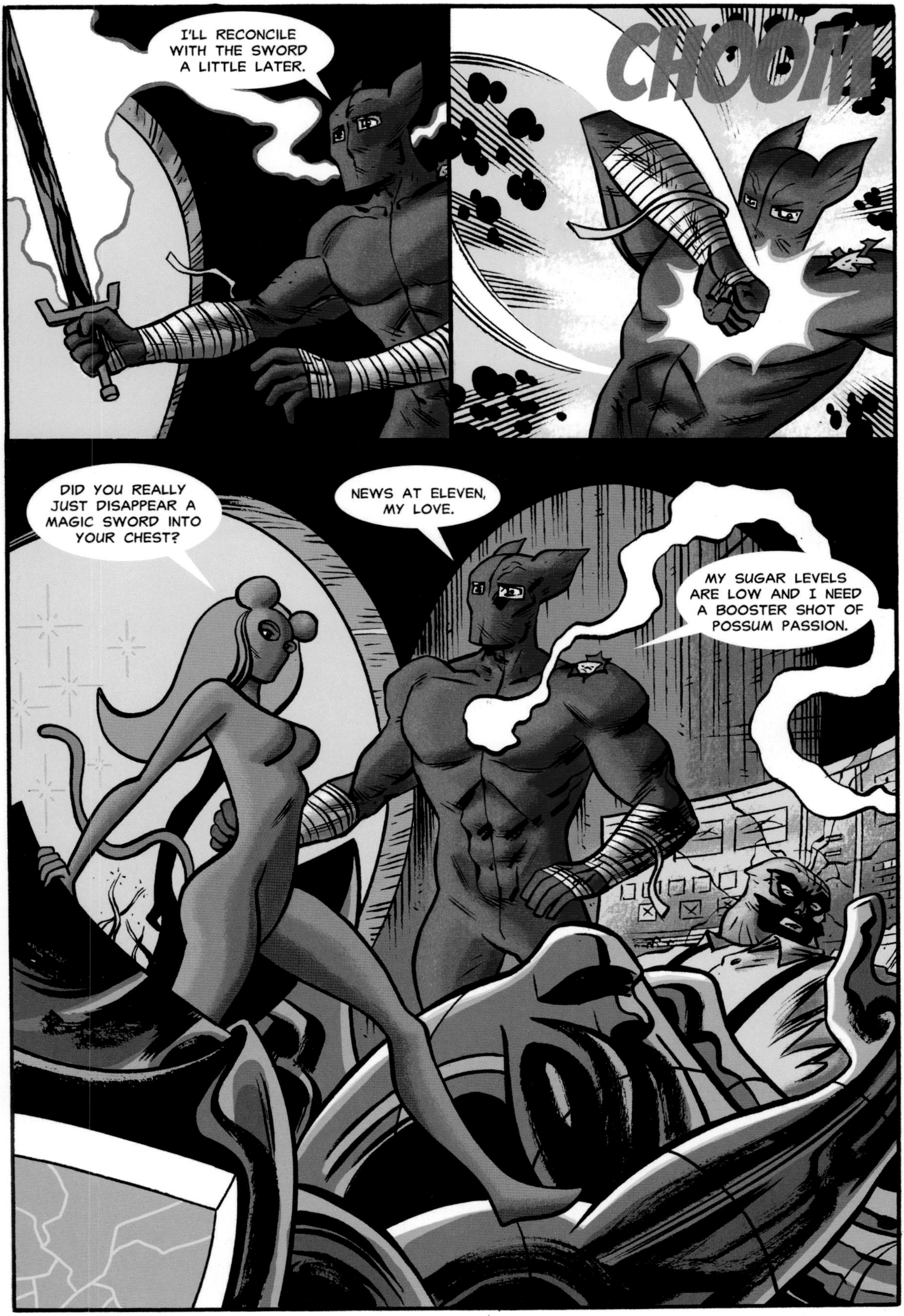
I'LL RECONCILE WITH THE SWORD A LITTLE LATER.
CHOOM
DID YOU REALLY JUST DISAPPEAR A MAGIC SWORD INTO YOUR CHEST?
NEWS AT ELEVEN, MY LOVE.
MY SUGAR LEVELS ARE LOW AND I NEED A BOOSTER SHOT OF POSSUM PASSION.

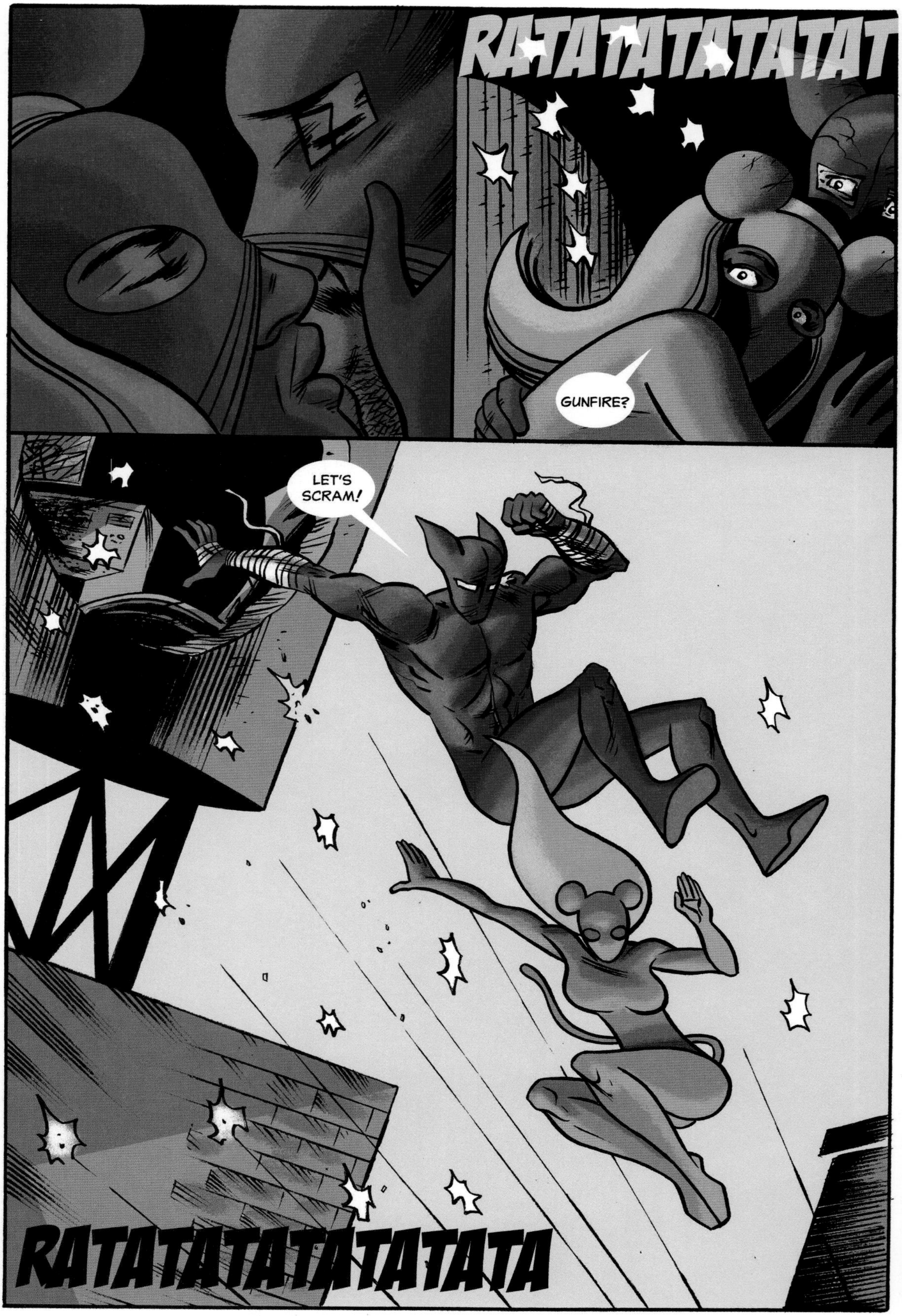
RATATATATATATAT
GUNFIRE?
LET'S SCRAM!
RATATATATATATATATA

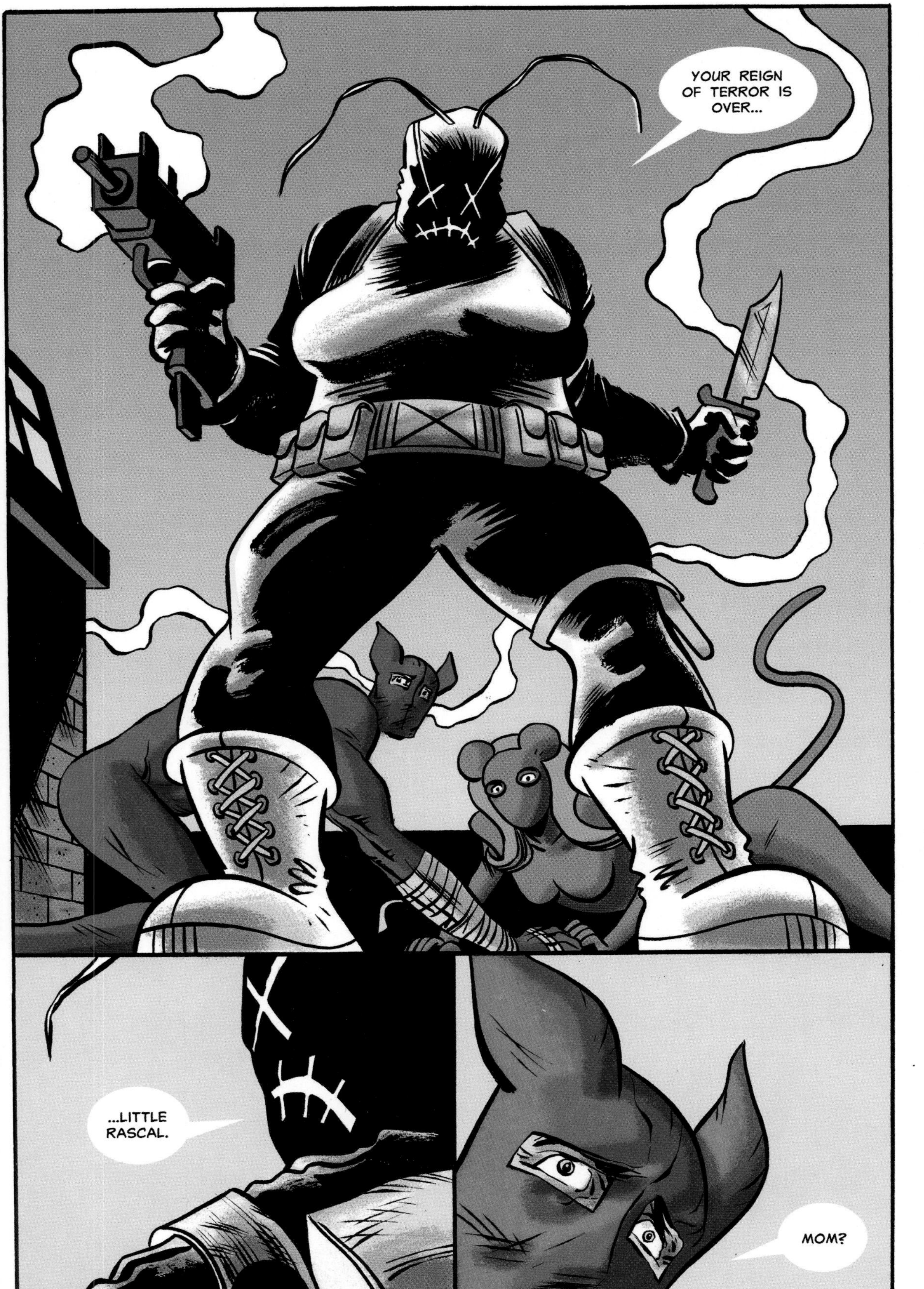
YOUR REIGN OF TERROR IS OVER...
...LITTLE RASCAL.
MOM?

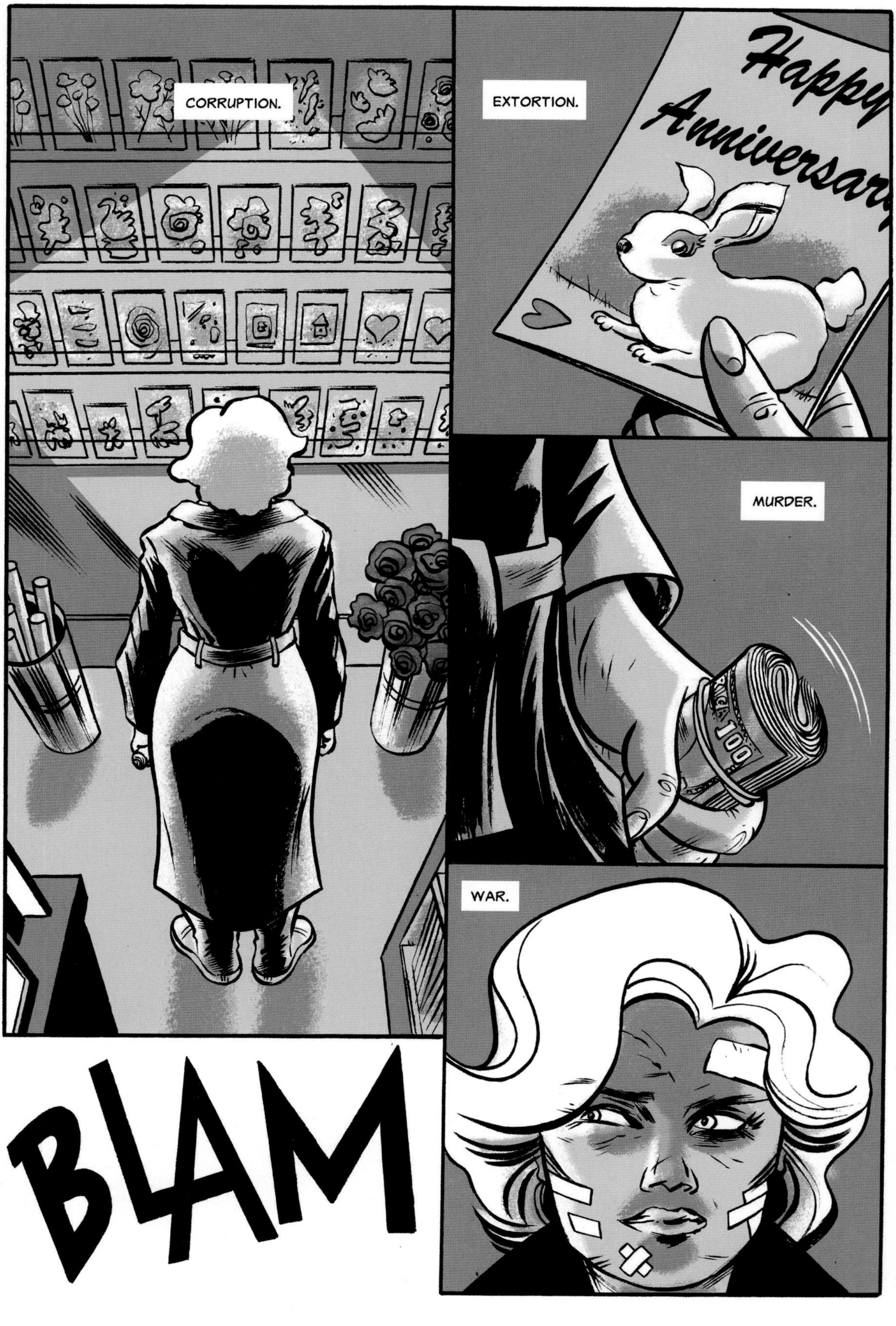
CORRUPTION.
EXTORTION.
Happy Anniversary
MURDER.
100
WAR.
BLAM

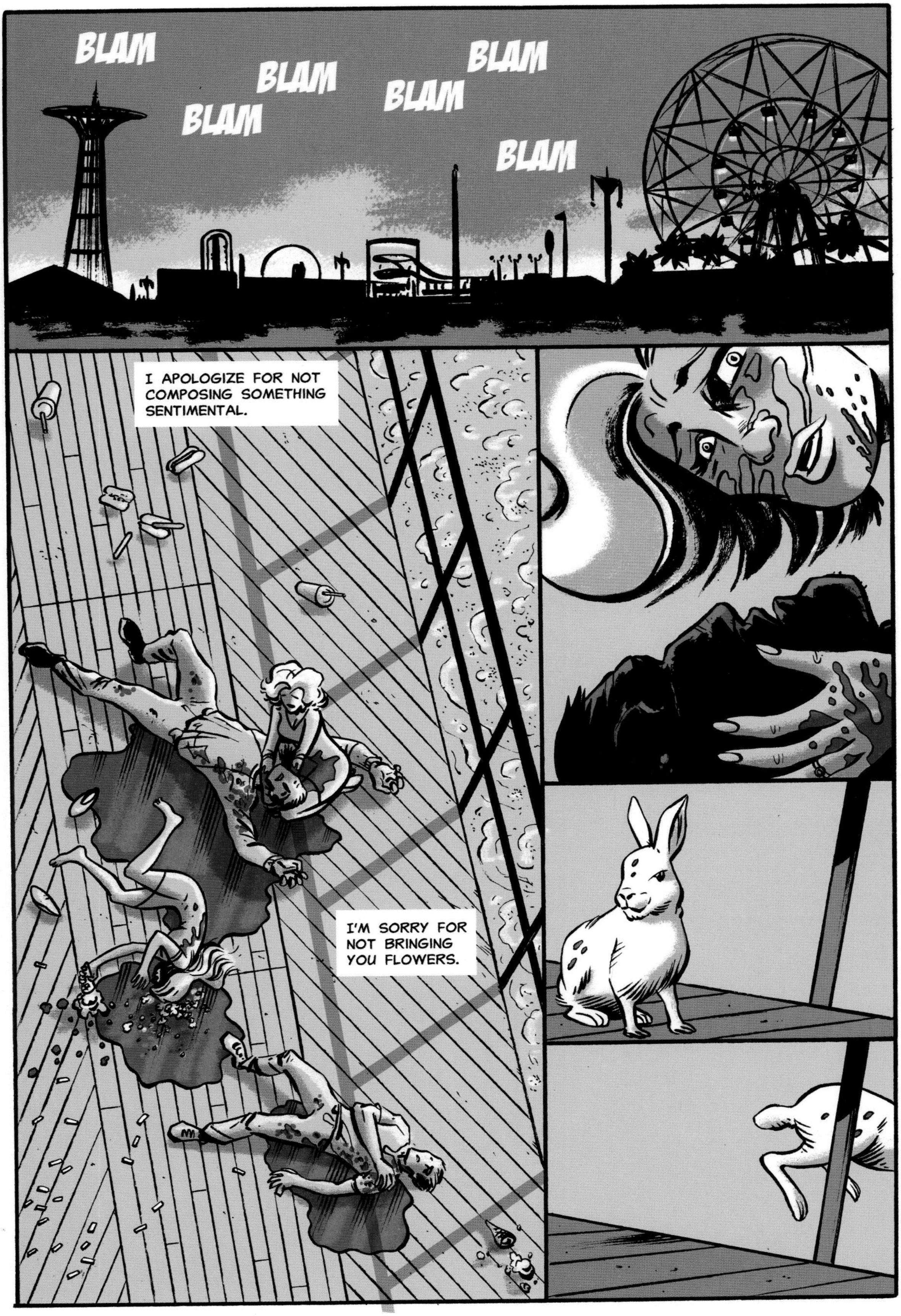
BLAM
BLAM
BLAM
BLAM
BLAM
BLAM
I APOLOGIZE FOR NOT COMPOSING SOMETHING SENTIMENTAL.
I'M SORRY FOR NOT BRINGING YOU FLOWERS.

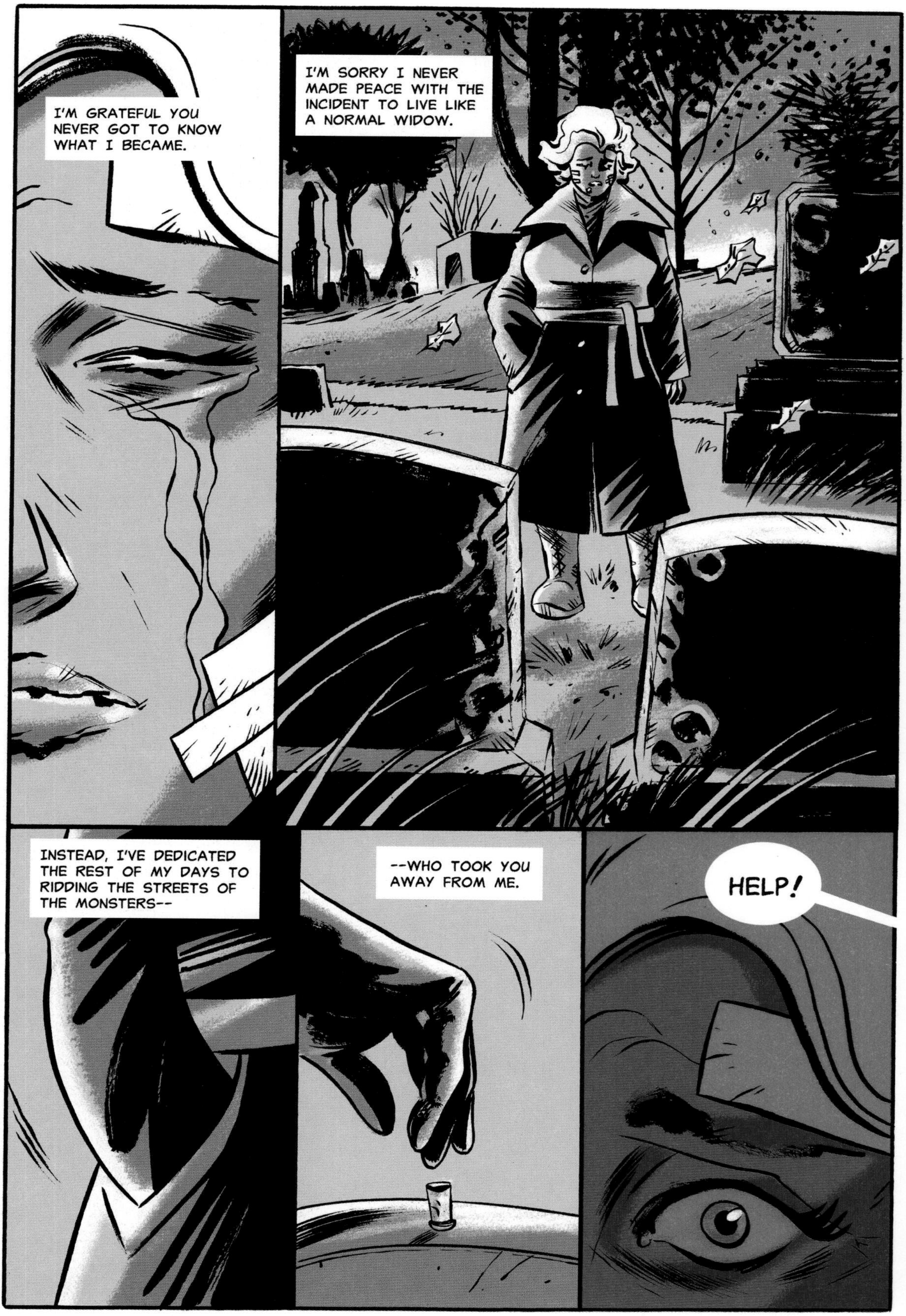
I'M GRATEFUL YOU NEVER GOT TO KNOW WHAT I BECAME.
I'M SORRY I NEVER MADE PEACE WITH THE INCIDENT TO LIVE LIKE A NORMAL WIDOW.
INSTEAD, I'VE DEDICATED THE REST OF MY DAYS TO RIDDING THE STREETS OF THE MONSTERS--
--WHO TOOK YOU AWAY FROM ME.
HELP!

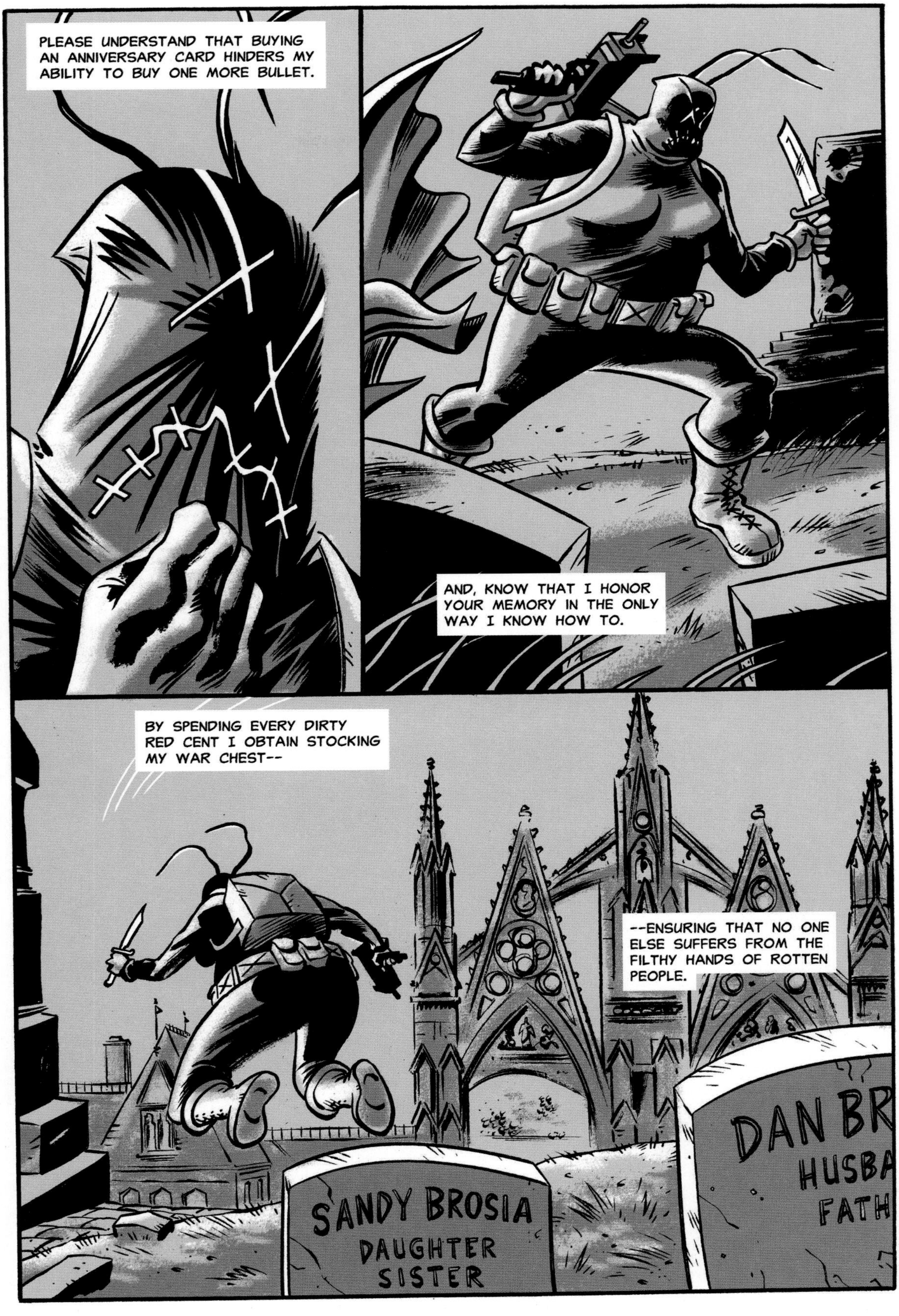
PLEASE UNDERSTAND THAT BUYING AN ANNIVERSARY CARD HINDERS MY ABILITY TO BUY ONE MORE BULLET.
AND, KNOW THAT I HONOR YOUR MEMORY IN THE ONLY WAY I KNOW HOW TO.
BY SPENDING EVERY DIRTY RED CENT I OBTAIN STOCKING MY WAR CHEST--
--ENSURING THAT NO ONE ELSE SUFFERS FROM THE FILTHY HANDS OF ROTTEN PEOPLE.
SANDY BROSIA
DAUGHTER
SISTER
DAN BR
HUSBA
FATH

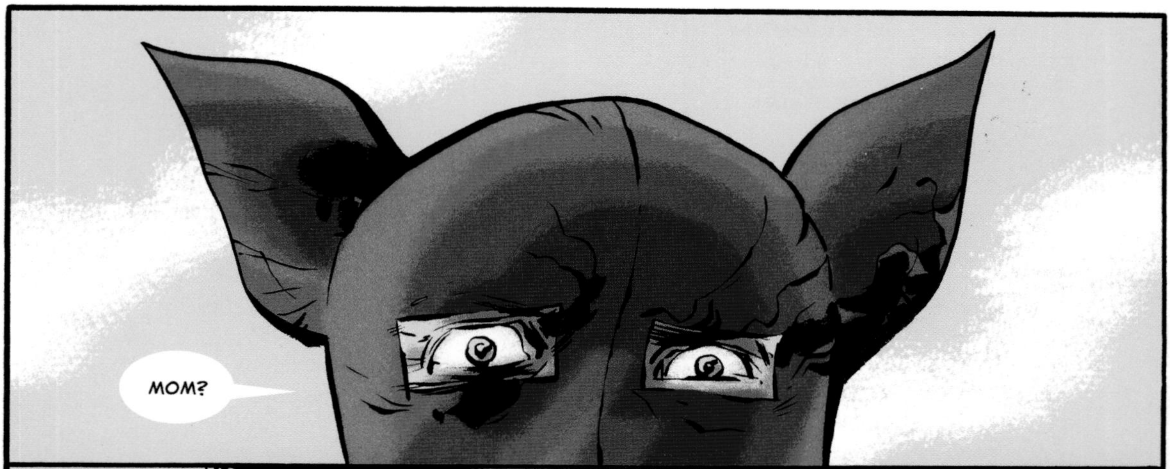
MOM?

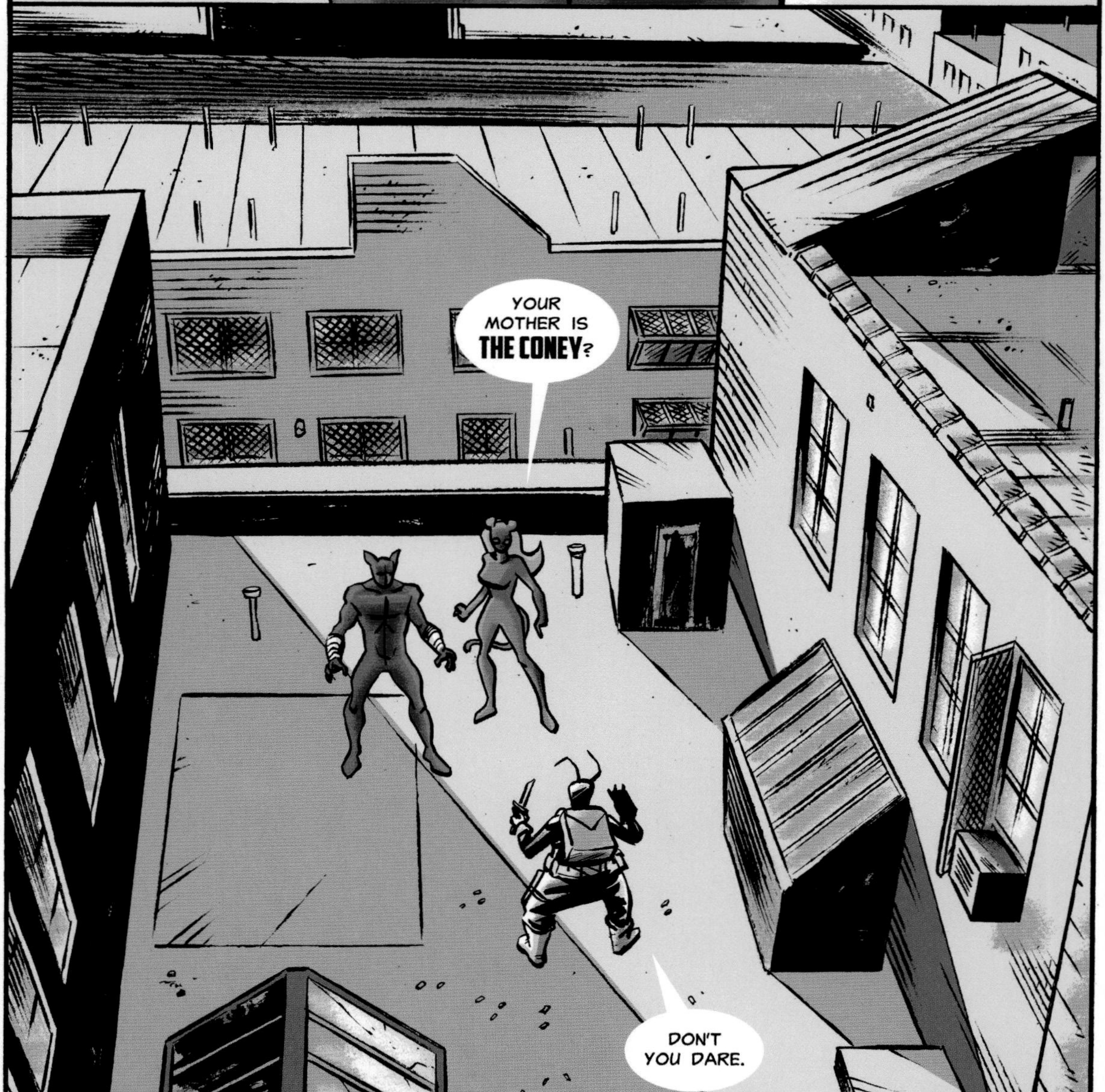
YOUR MOTHER IS THE CONEY?
DON'T YOU DARE.

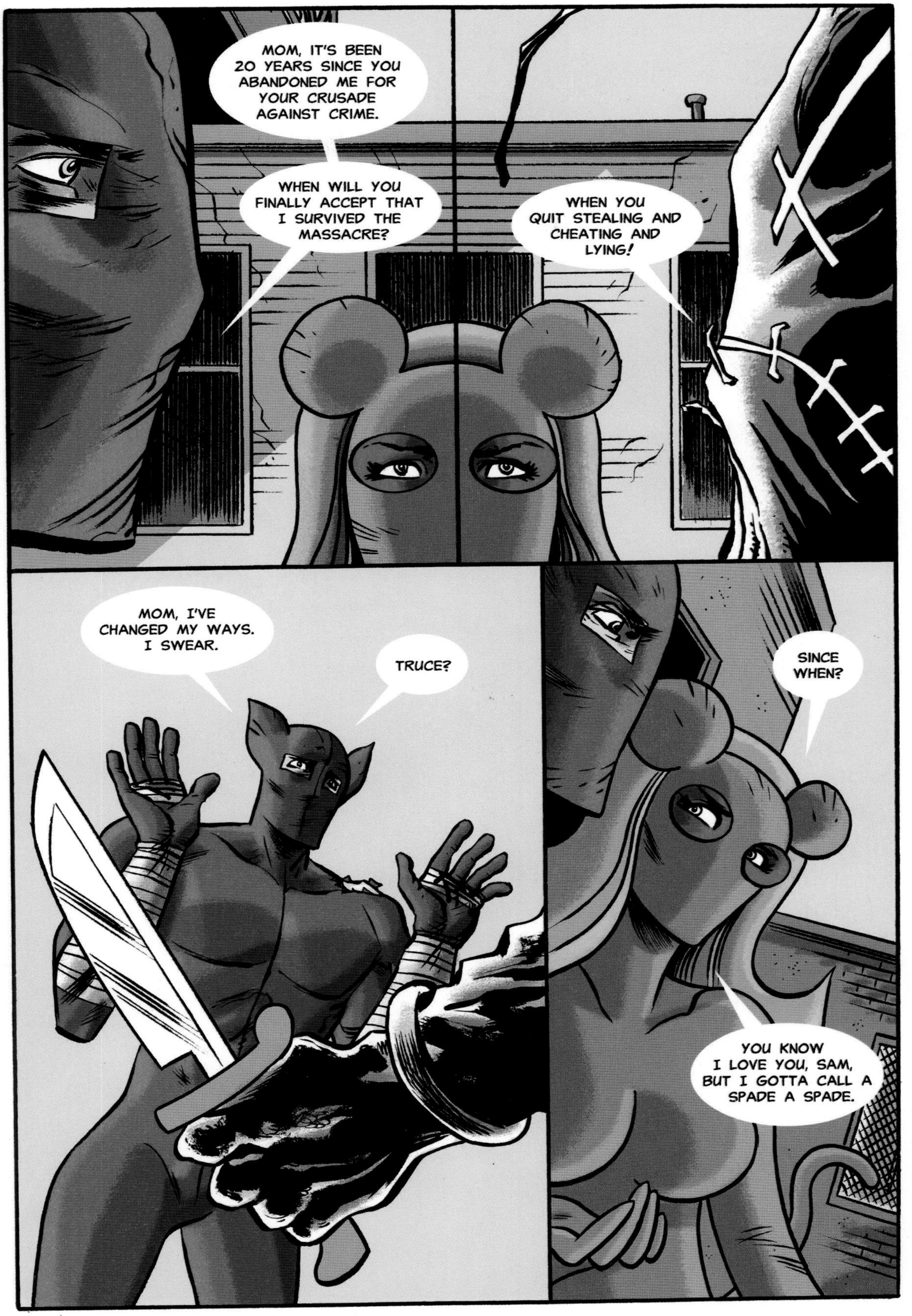
MOM, IT'S BEEN 20 YEARS SINCE YOU ABANDONED ME FOR YOUR CRUSADE AGAINST CRIME.
WHEN WILL YOU FINALLY ACCEPT THAT I SURVIVED THE MASSACRE?
WHEN YOU QUIT STEALING AND CHEATING AND LYING!
MOM, I'VE CHANGED MY WAYS. I SWEAR.
TRUCE?
SINCE WHEN?
YOU KNOW I LOVE YOU, SAM, BUT I GOTTA CALL A SPADE A SPADE.

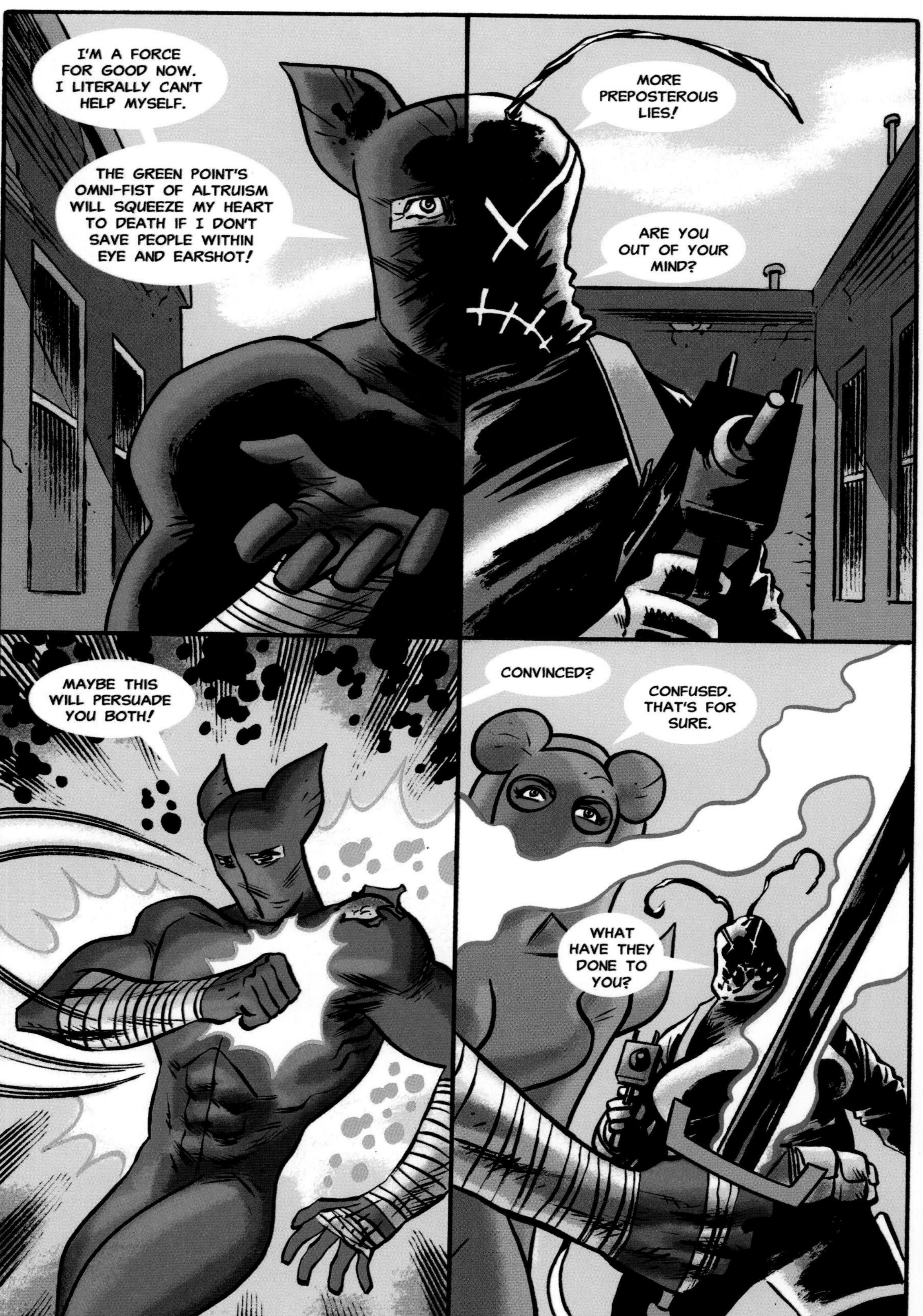
I'M A FORCE FOR GOOD NOW. I LITERALLY CAN'T HELP MYSELF.
THE GREEN POINT'S OMNI-FIST OF ALTRUISM WILL SQUEEZE MY HEART TO DEATH IF I DON'T SAVE PEOPLE WITHIN EYE AND EARSHOT!
MORE PREPOSTEROUS LIES!
ARE YOU OUT OF YOUR MIND?
MAYBE THIS WILL PERSUADE YOU BOTH!
CONVINCED?
CONFUSED. THAT'S FOR SURE.
WHAT HAVE THEY DONE TO YOU?

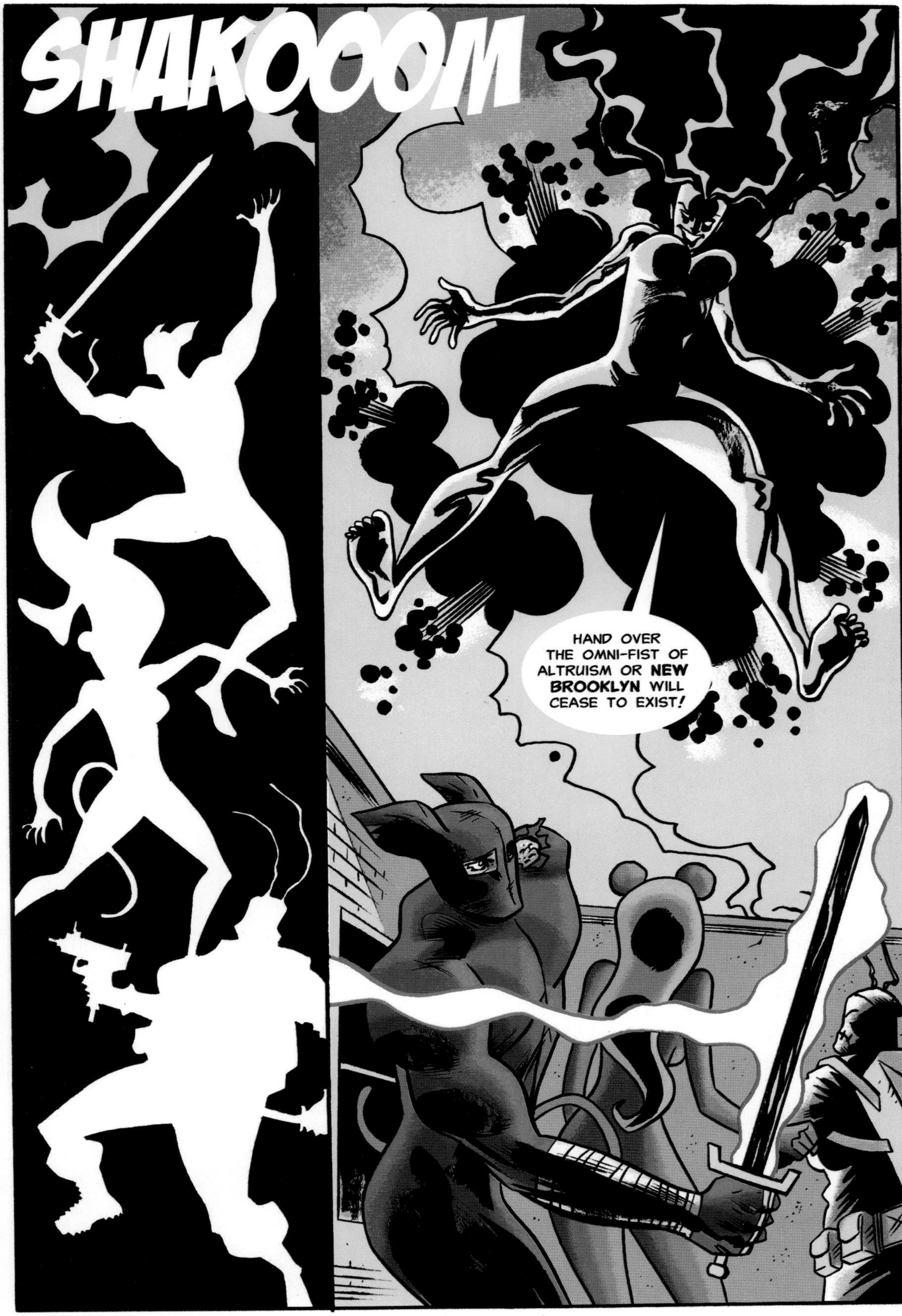
SHAKOOOM
HAND OVER THE OMNI-FIST OF ALTRUISM OR NEW BROOKLYN WILL CEASE TO EXIST!

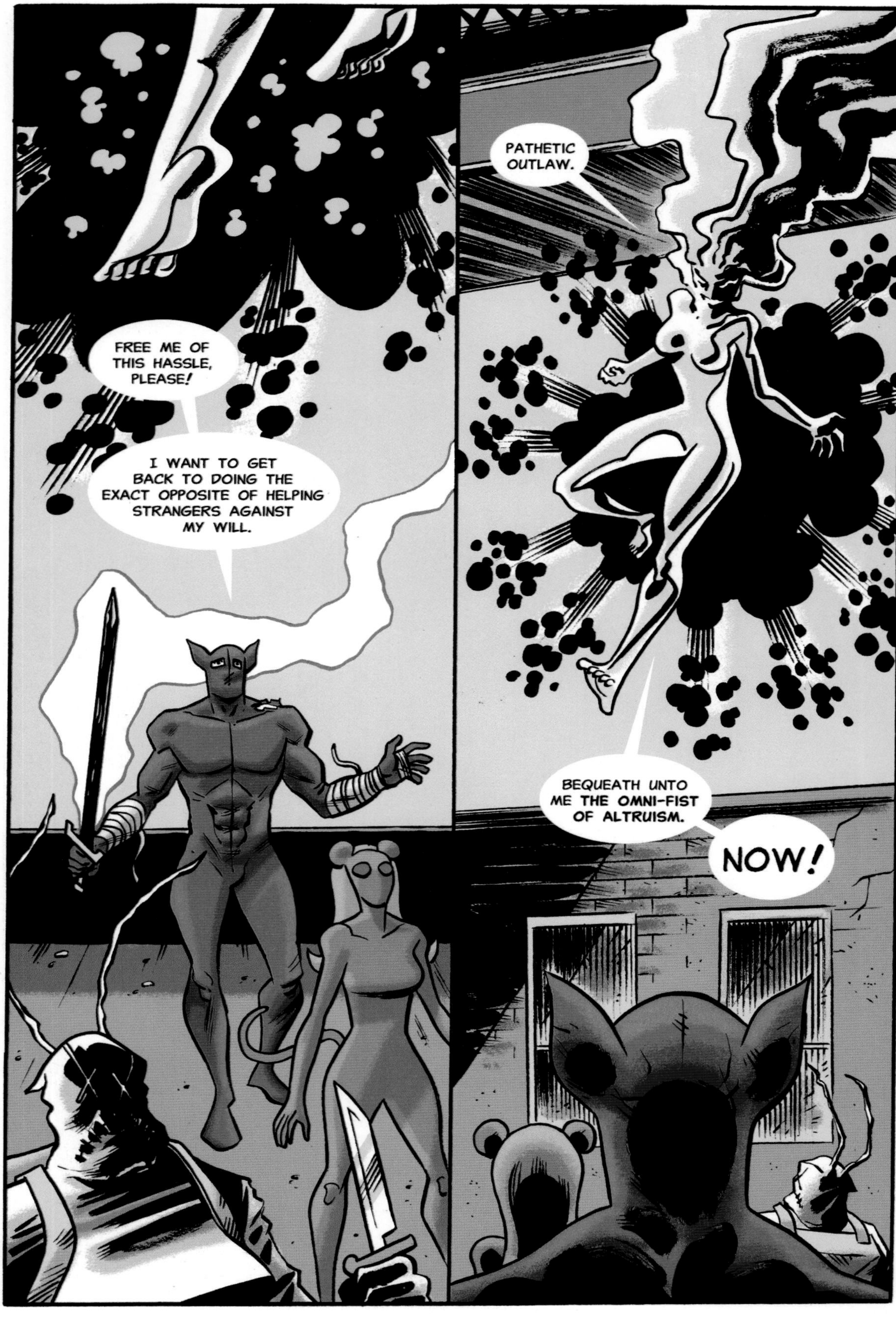
FREE ME OF THIS HASSLE, PLEASE!
I WANT TO GET BACK TO DOING THE EXACT OPPOSITE OF HELPING STRANGERS AGAINST MY WILL.
PATHETIC OUTLAW.
BEQUEATH UNTO ME THE OMNI-FIST OF ALTRUISM.
NOW!

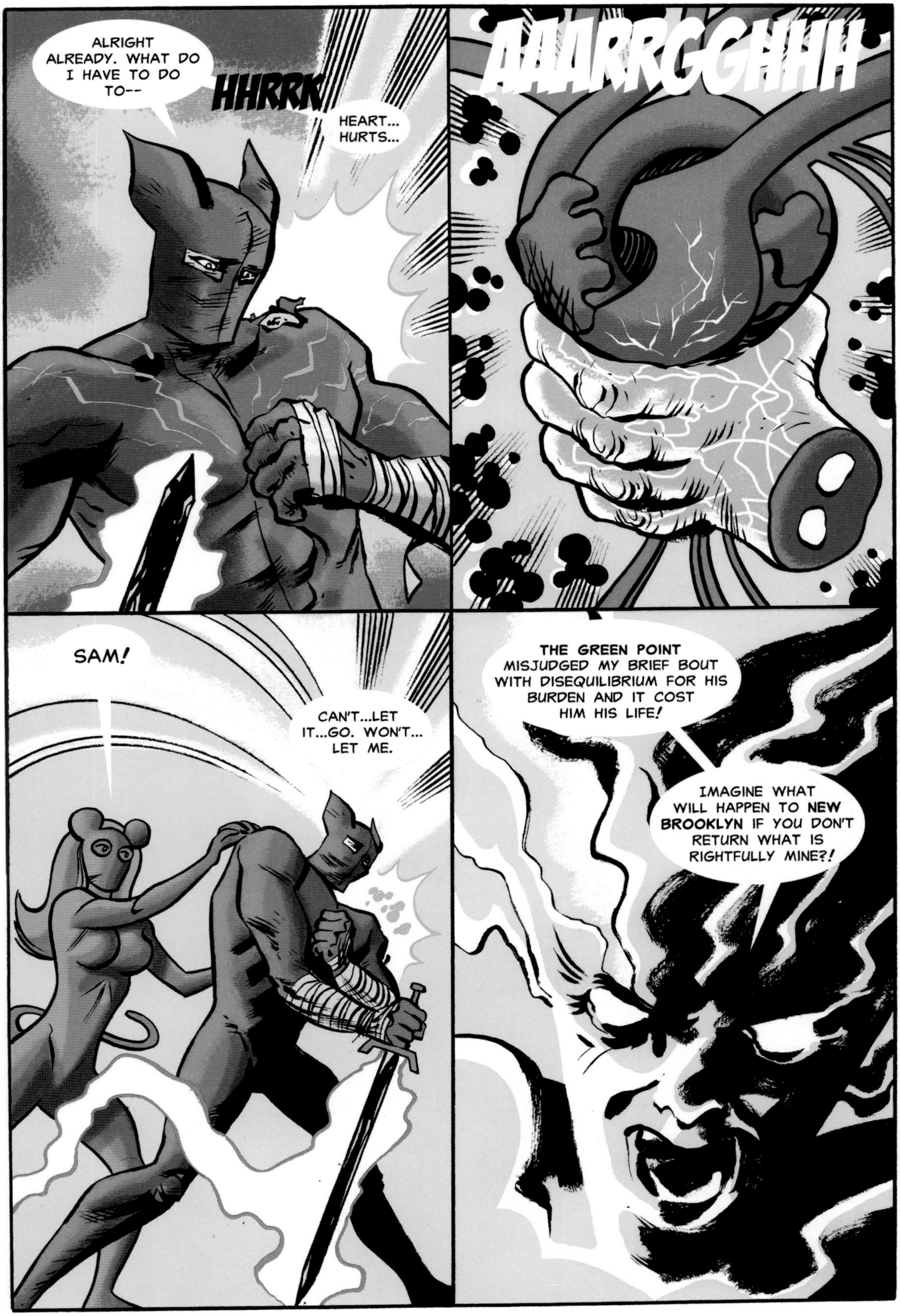
ALRIGHT ALREADY. WHAT DO I HAVE TO DO TO--
HHRRK
HEART... HURTS...
AAARRGGHHH
SAM!
CAN'T...LET IT...GO. WON'T... LET ME.
THE GREEN POINT MISJUDGED MY BRIEF BOUT WITH DISEQUILIBRIUM FOR HIS BURDEN AND IT COST HIM HIS LIFE!
IMAGINE WHAT WILL HAPPEN TO NEW BROOKLYN IF YOU DON'T RETURN WHAT IS RIGHTFULLY MINE?!

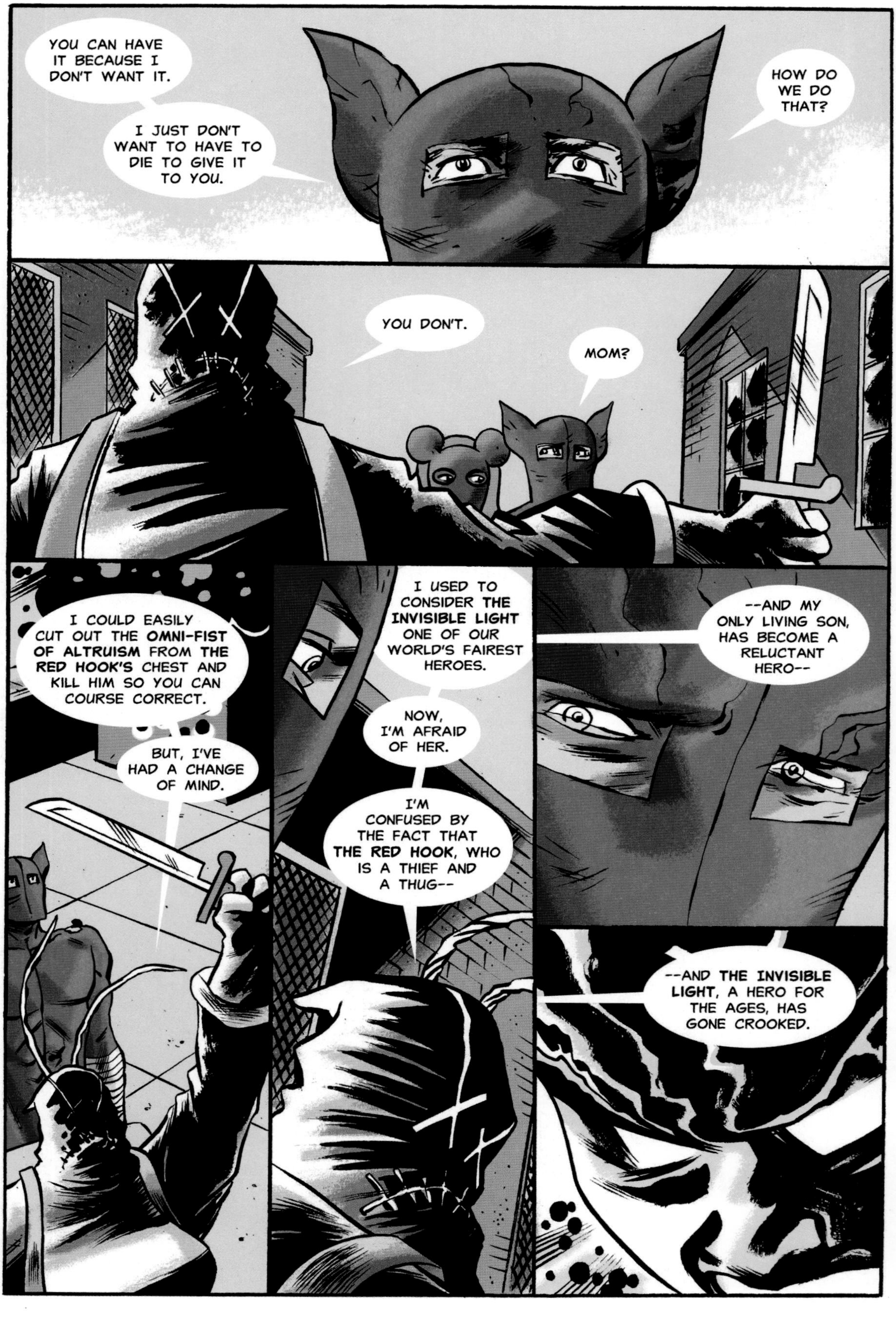

YOU CAN HAVE IT BECAUSE I DON'T WANT IT.
I JUST DON'T WANT TO HAVE TO DIE TO GIVE IT TO YOU.
HOW DO WE DO THAT?
YOU DON'T.
MOM?
I COULD EASILY CUT OUT THE **OMNI-FIST OF ALTRUISM** FROM **THE RED HOOK'S** CHEST AND KILL HIM SO YOU CAN COURSE CORRECT.
BUT, I'VE HAD A CHANGE OF MIND.
I USED TO CONSIDER **THE INVISIBLE LIGHT** ONE OF OUR WORLD'S FAIREST HEROES.
NOW, I'M AFRAID OF HER.
I'M CONFUSED BY THE FACT THAT **THE RED HOOK**, WHO IS A THIEF AND A THUG--
--AND MY ONLY LIVING SON, HAS BECOME A RELUCTANT HERO--
--AND **THE INVISIBLE LIGHT**, A HERO FOR THE AGES, HAS GONE CROOKED.

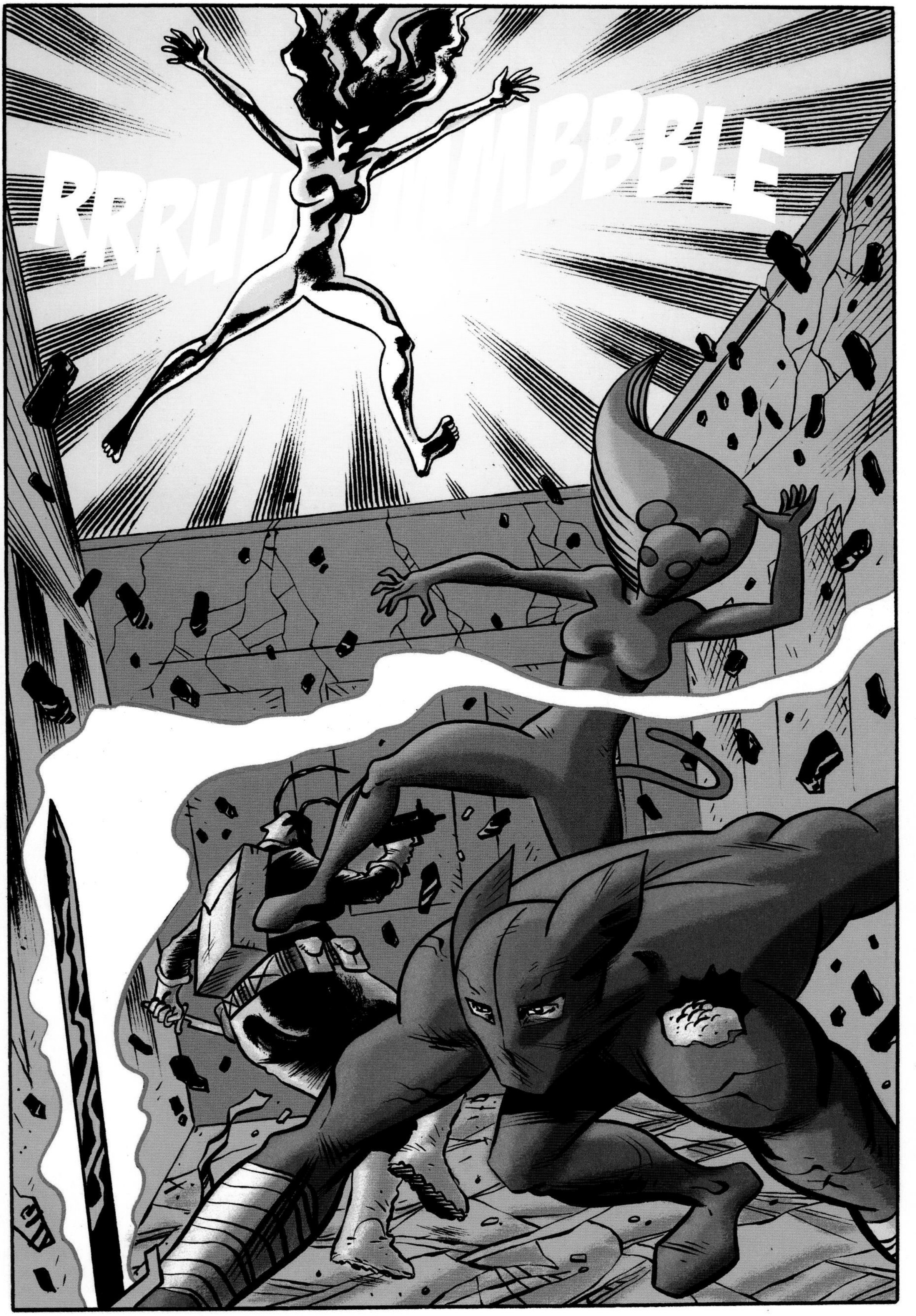
RRRUU MBBBLE

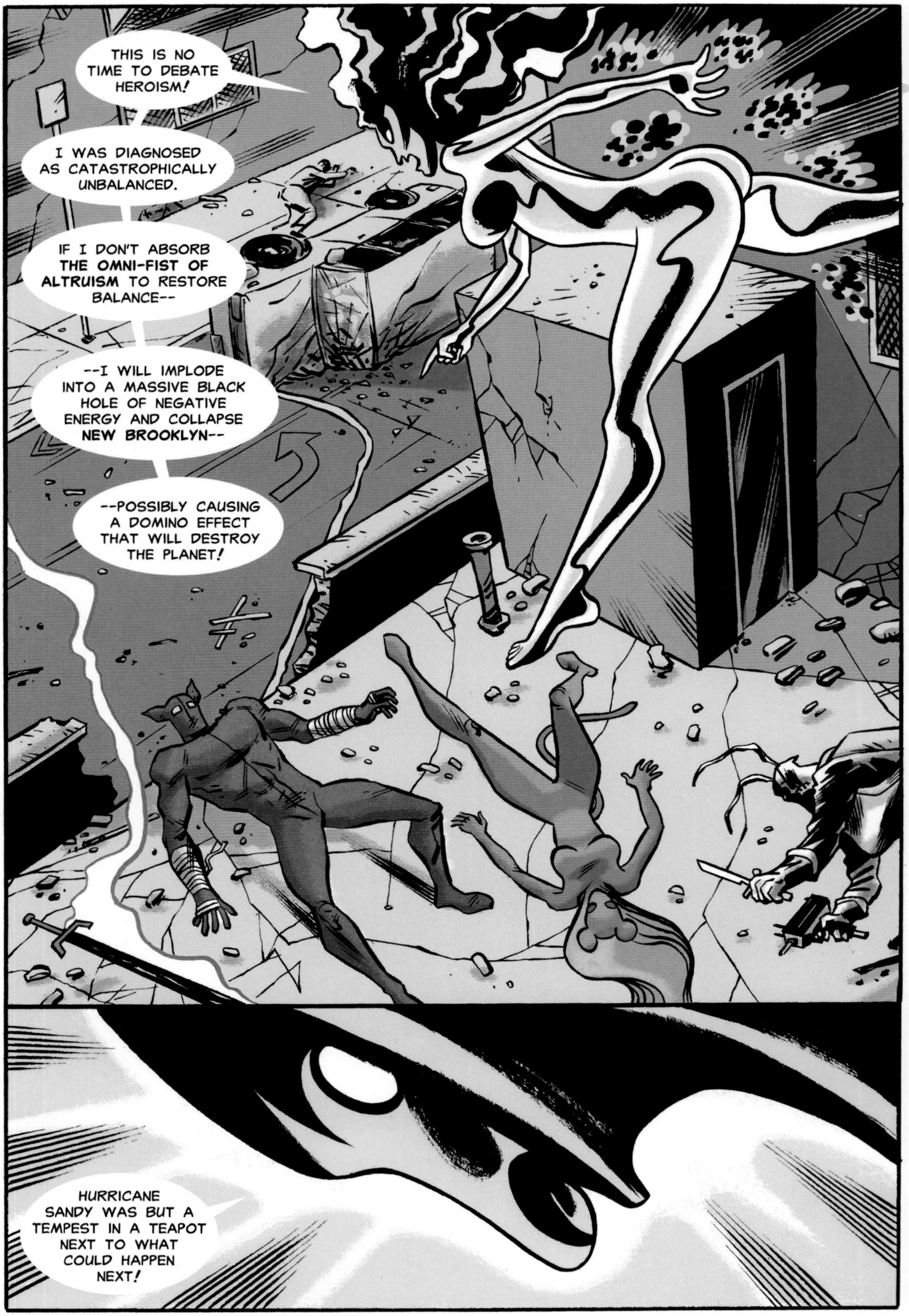
THIS IS NO TIME TO DEBATE HEROISM!
I WAS DIAGNOSED AS CATASTROPHICALLY UNBALANCED.
IF I DON'T ABSORB THE OMNI-FIST OF ALTRUISM TO RESTORE BALANCE--
--I WILL IMPLODE INTO A MASSIVE BLACK HOLE OF NEGATIVE ENERGY AND COLLAPSE NEW BROOKLYN--
--POSSIBLY CAUSING A DOMINO EFFECT THAT WILL DESTROY THE PLANET!
HURRICANE SANDY WAS BUT A TEMPEST IN A TEAPOT NEXT TO WHAT COULD HAPPEN NEXT!

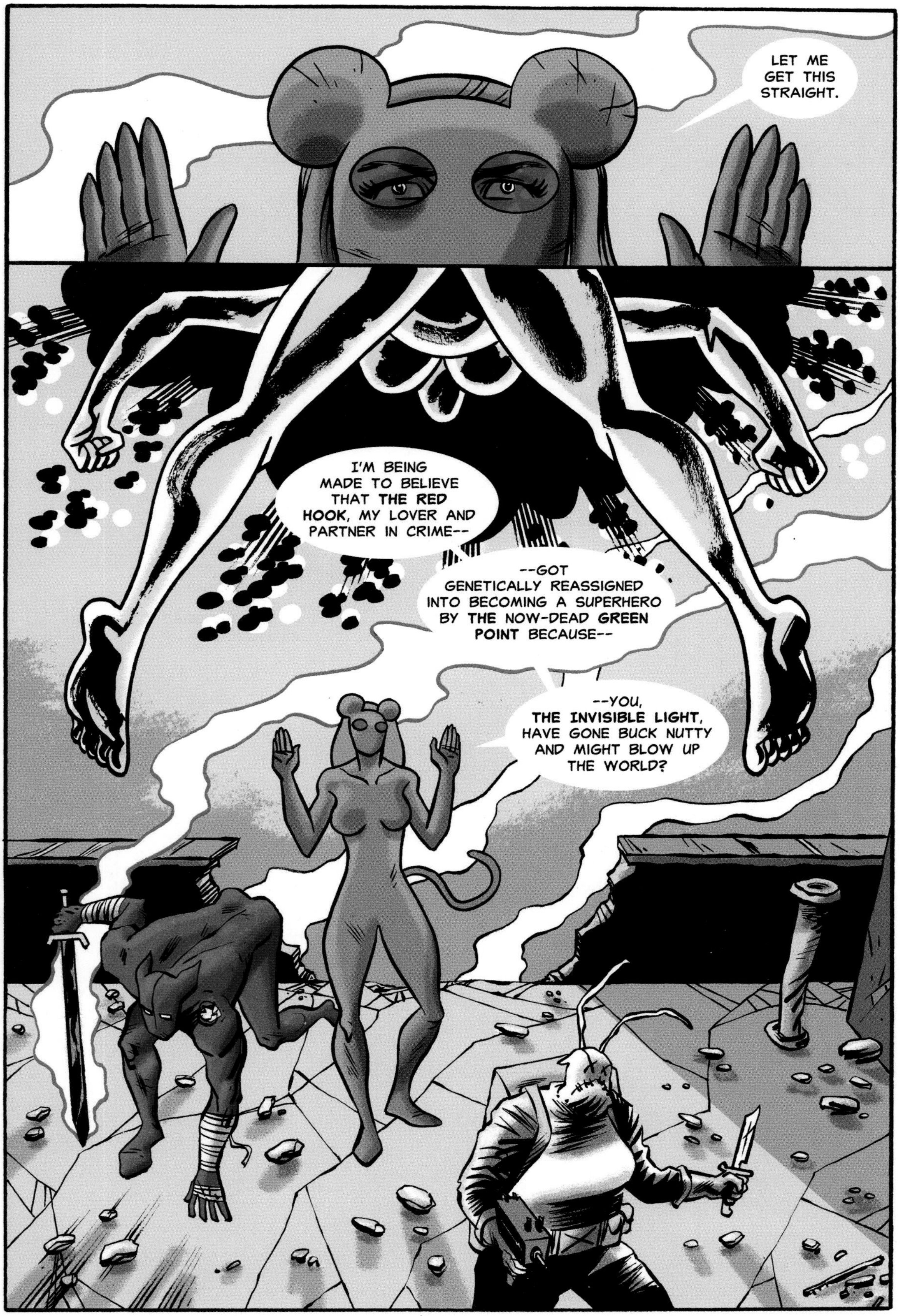
LET ME GET THIS STRAIGHT.
I'M BEING MADE TO BELIEVE THAT THE RED HOOK, MY LOVER AND PARTNER IN CRIME--
--GOT GENETICALLY REASSIGNED INTO BECOMING A SUPERHERO BY THE NOW-DEAD GREEN POINT BECAUSE--
--YOU, THE INVISIBLE LIGHT, HAVE GONE BUCK NUTTY AND MIGHT BLOW UP THE WORLD?

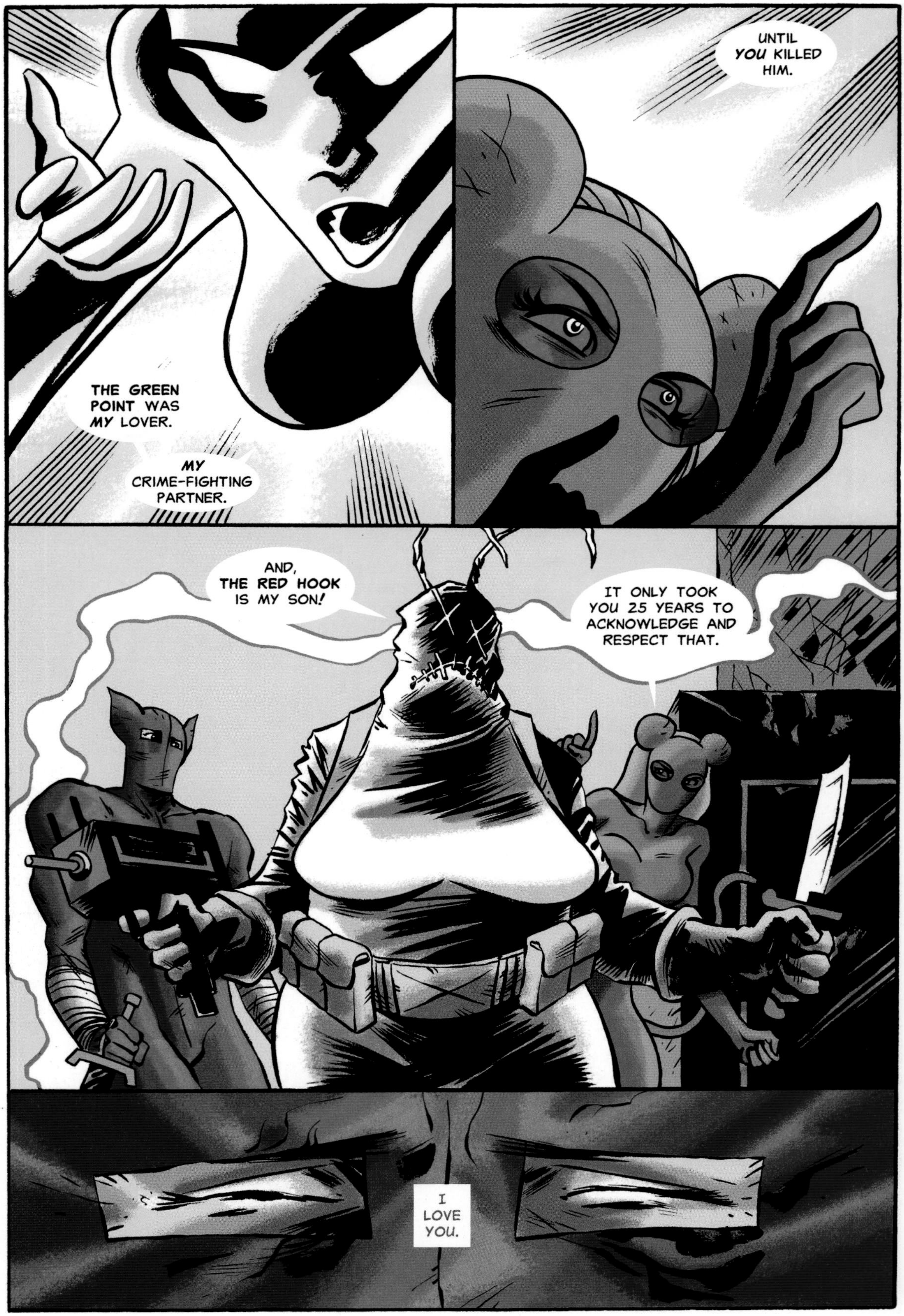
THE GREEN POINT WAS MY LOVER.
MY CRIME-FIGHTING PARTNER.
UNTIL YOU KILLED HIM.
AND, THE RED HOOK IS MY SON!
IT ONLY TOOK YOU 25 YEARS TO ACKNOWLEDGE AND RESPECT THAT.
I LOVE YOU.

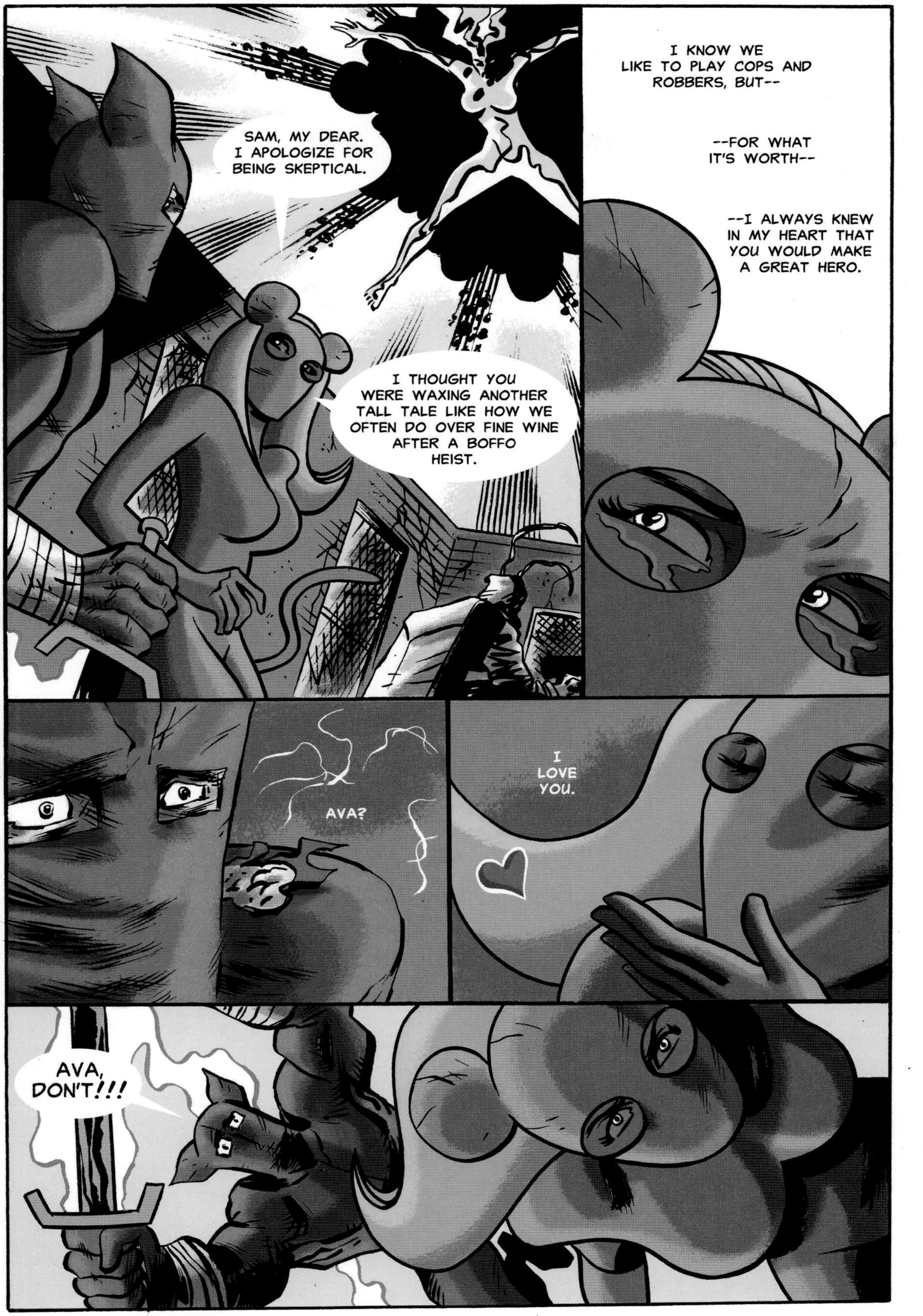
SAM, MY DEAR. I APOLOGIZE FOR BEING SKEPTICAL.
I THOUGHT YOU WERE WAXING ANOTHER TALL TALE LIKE HOW WE OFTEN DO OVER FINE WINE AFTER A BOFFO HEIST.
I KNOW WE LIKE TO PLAY COPS AND ROBBERS, BUT--
--FOR WHAT IT'S WORTH--
--I ALWAYS KNEW IN MY HEART THAT YOU WOULD MAKE A GREAT HERO.
AVA?
I LOVE YOU.
AVA, DON'T!!!

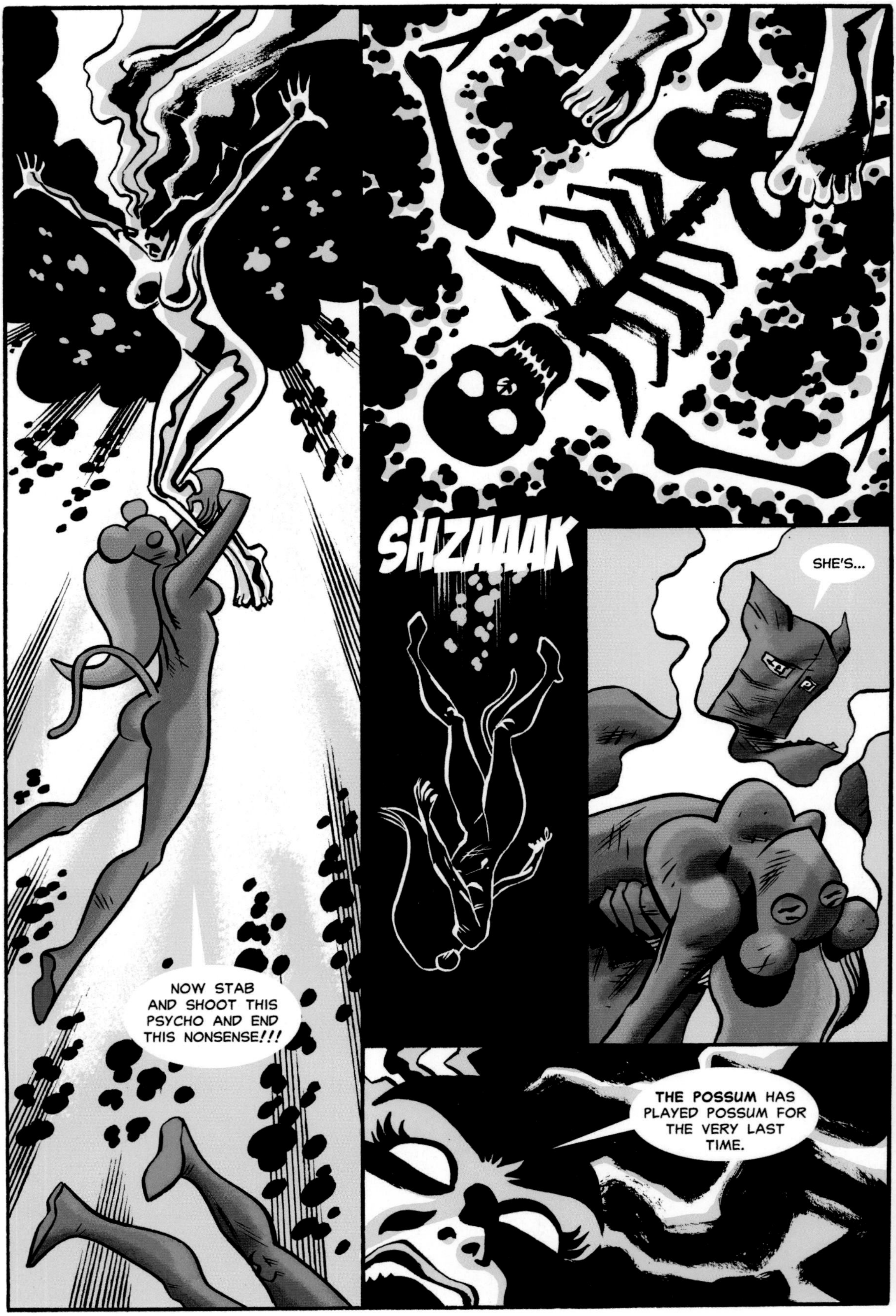
NOW STAB AND SHOOT THIS PSYCHO AND END THIS NONSENSE!!!
SHZAAAK
SHE'S...
THE POSSUM HAS PLAYED POSSUM FOR THE VERY LAST TIME.

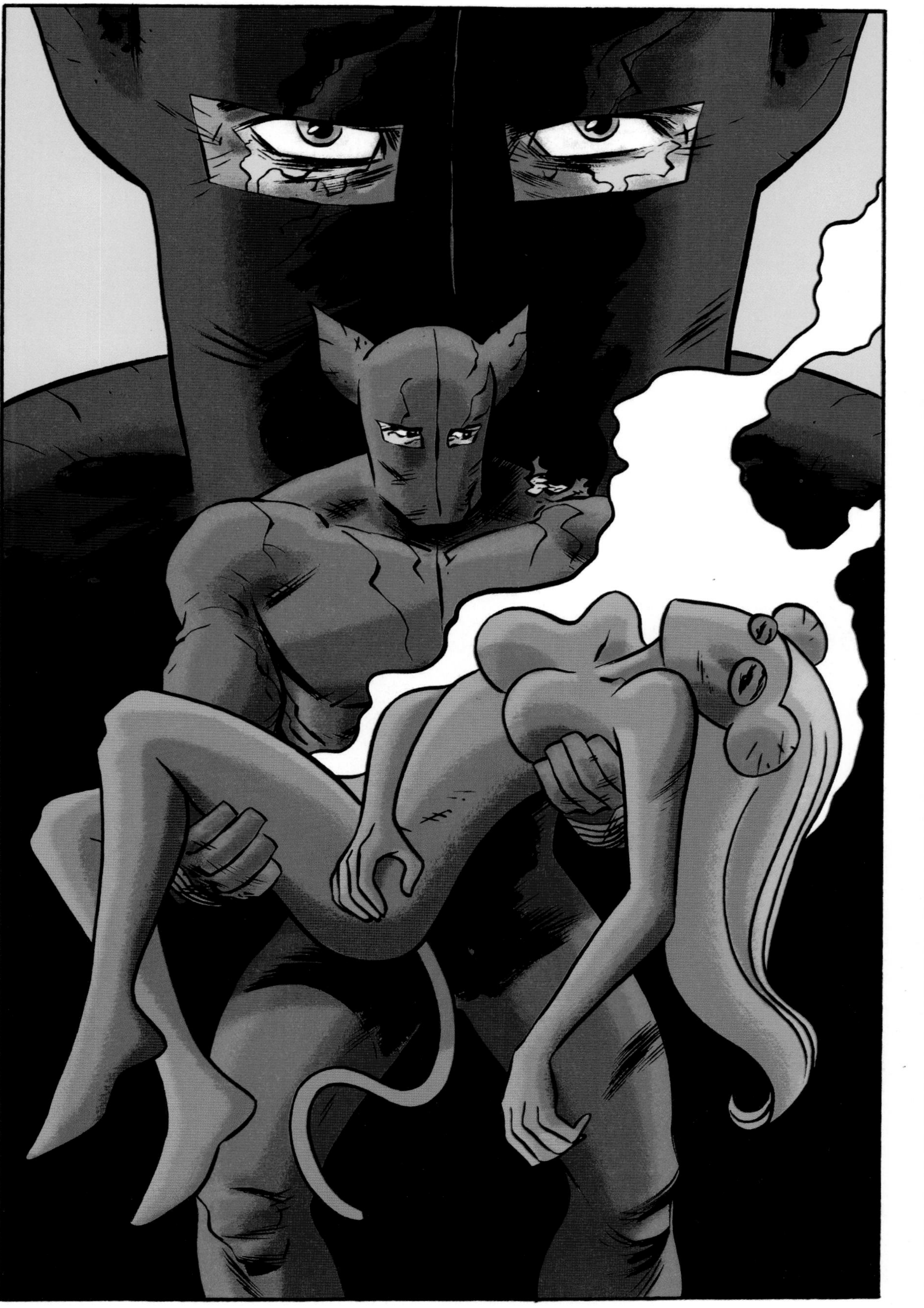

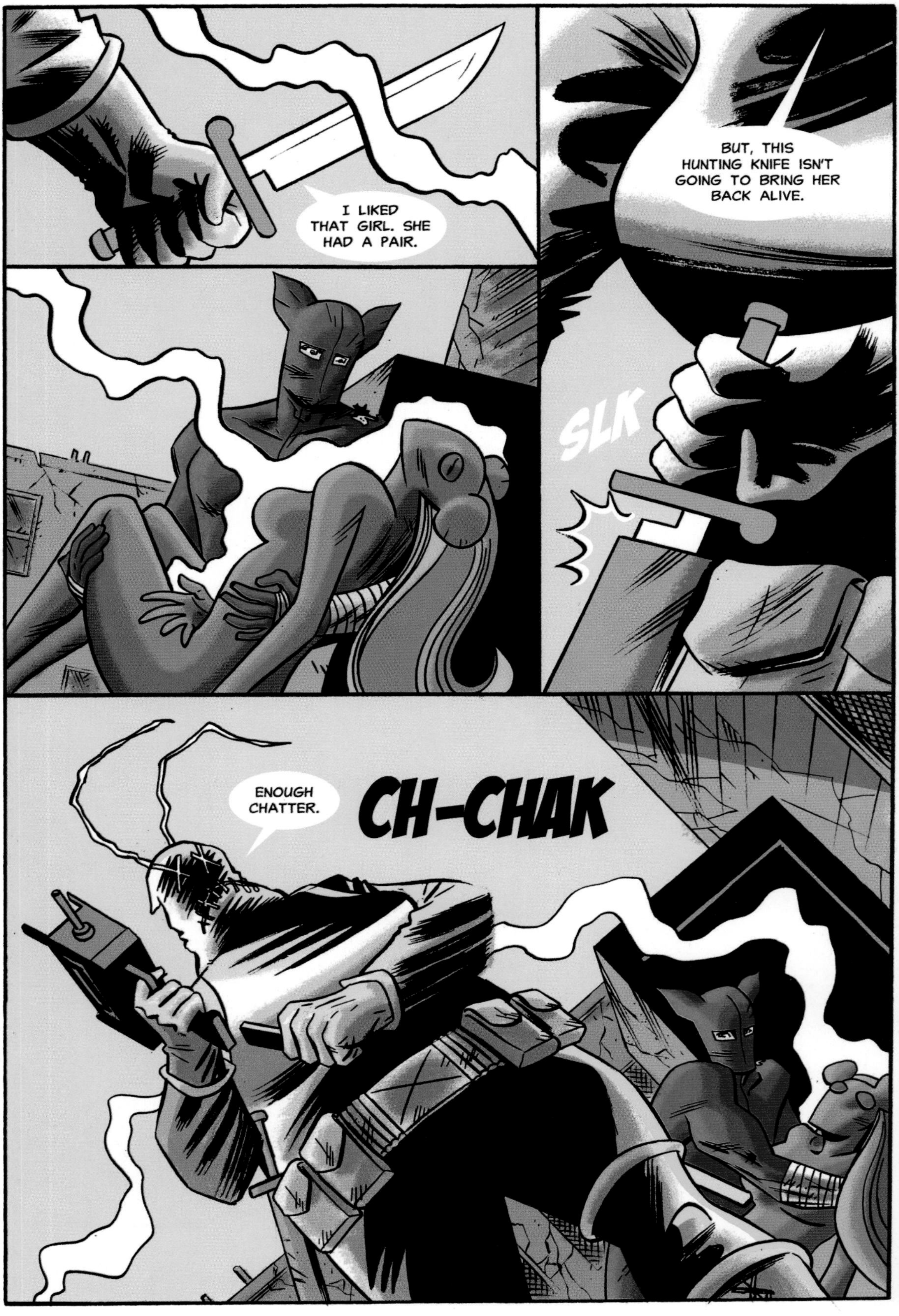
I LIKED THAT GIRL. SHE HAD A PAIR.
BUT, THIS HUNTING KNIFE ISN'T GOING TO BRING HER BACK ALIVE.
SLK
ENOUGH CHATTER.
CH-CHAK

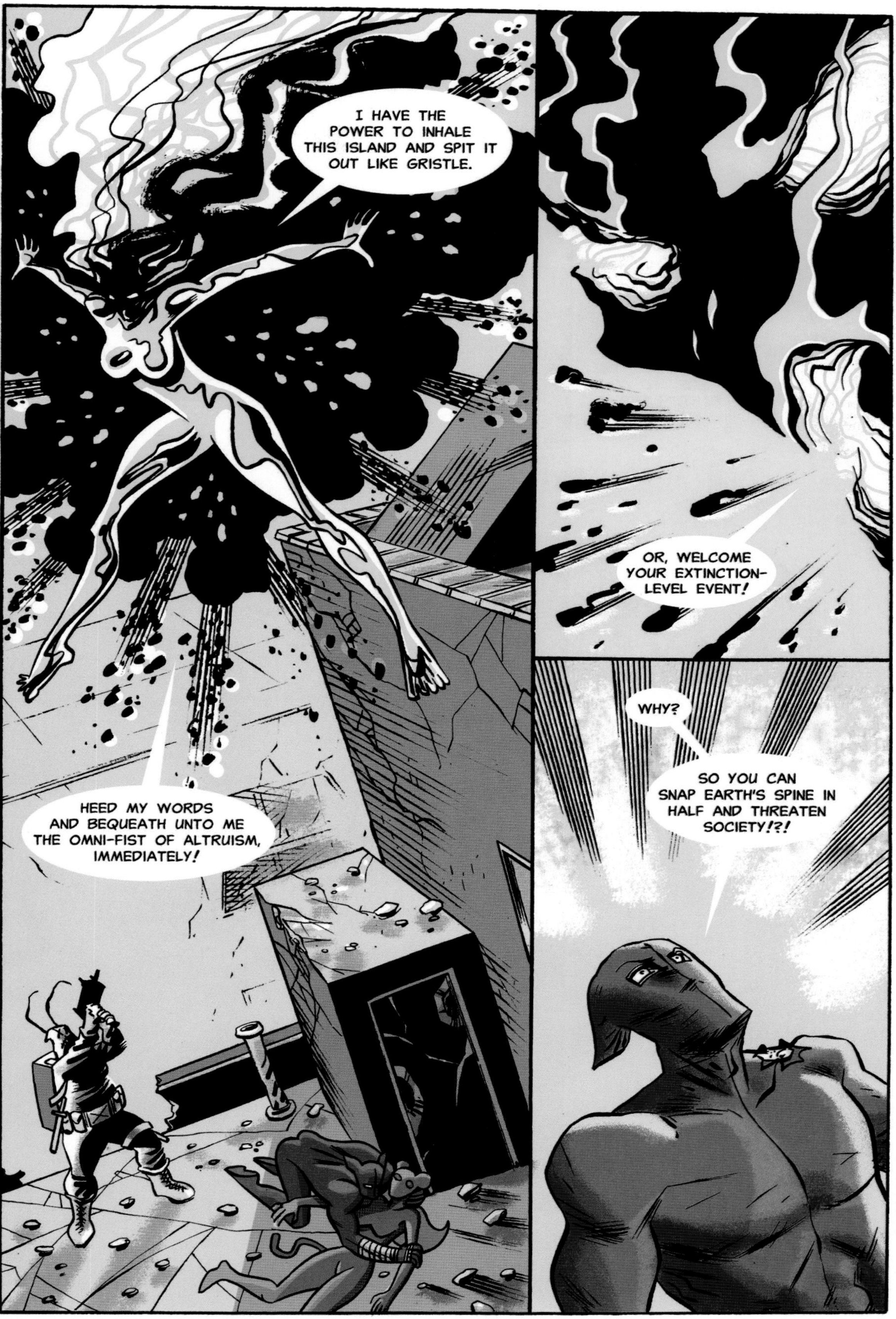
I HAVE THE POWER TO INHALE THIS ISLAND AND SPIT IT OUT LIKE GRISTLE.
HEED MY WORDS AND BEQUEATH UNTO ME THE OMNI-FIST OF ALTRUISM, IMMEDIATELY!
OR, WELCOME YOUR EXTINCTION-LEVEL EVENT!
WHY?
SO YOU CAN SNAP EARTH'S SPINE IN HALF AND THREATEN SOCIETY!?!

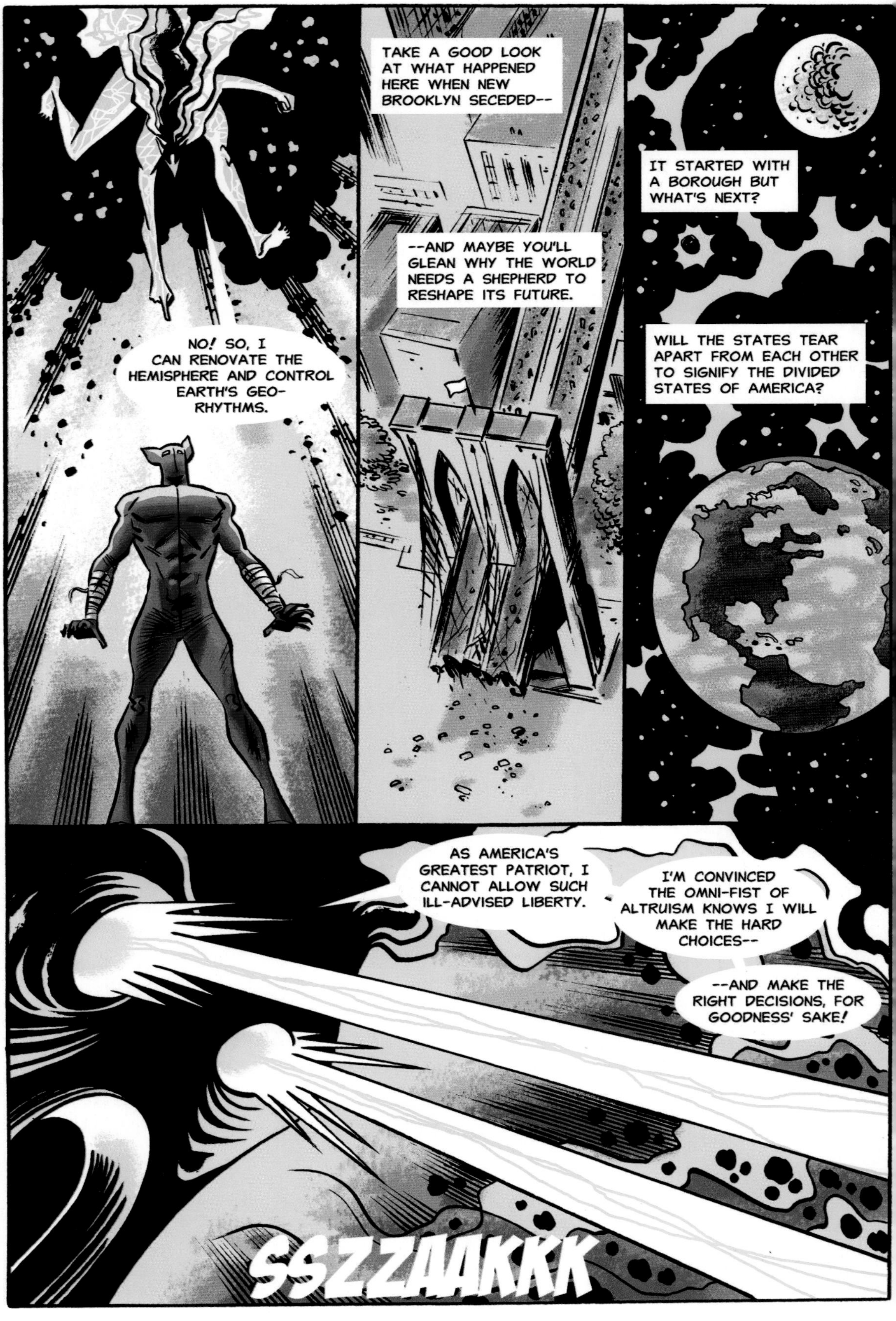
NO! SO, I CAN RENOVATE THE HEMISPHERE AND CONTROL EARTH'S GEO-RHYTHMS.
TAKE A GOOD LOOK AT WHAT HAPPENED HERE WHEN NEW BROOKLYN SECEDED--
--AND MAYBE YOU'LL GLEAN WHY THE WORLD NEEDS A SHEPHERD TO RESHAPE ITS FUTURE.
IT STARTED WITH A BOROUGH BUT WHAT'S NEXT?
WILL THE STATES TEAR APART FROM EACH OTHER TO SIGNIFY THE DIVIDED STATES OF AMERICA?
AS AMERICA'S GREATEST PATRIOT, I CANNOT ALLOW SUCH ILL-ADVISED LIBERTY.
I'M CONVINCED THE OMNI-FIST OF ALTRUISM KNOWS I WILL MAKE THE HARD CHOICES--
--AND MAKE THE RIGHT DECISIONS, FOR GOODNESS' SAKE!
SSZZAAKKK

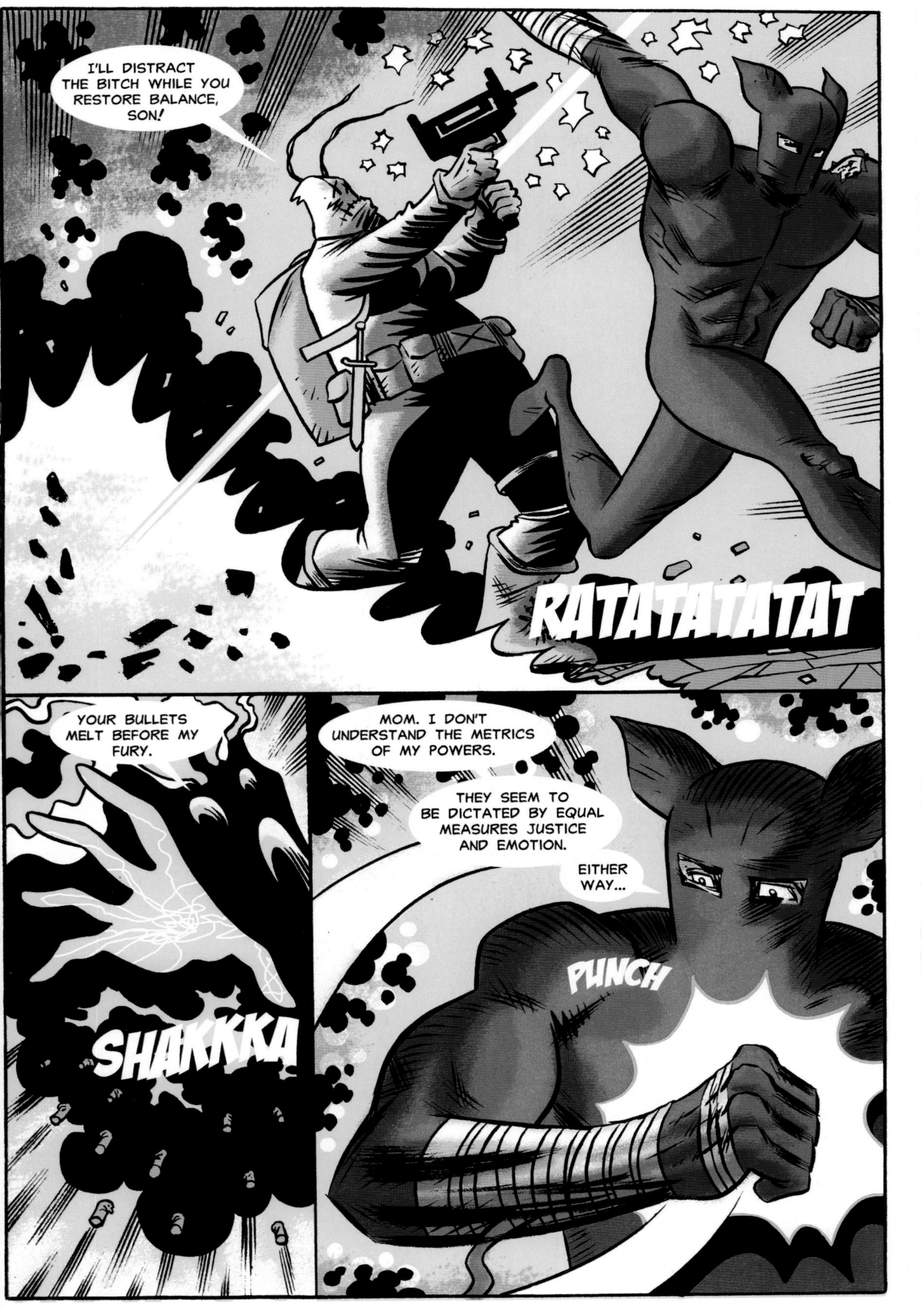

I'LL DISTRACT THE BITCH WHILE YOU RESTORE BALANCE, SON!
RATATATATAT
YOUR BULLETS MELT BEFORE MY FURY.
SHAKKKA
MOM. I DON'T UNDERSTAND THE METRICS OF MY POWERS.
THEY SEEM TO BE DICTATED BY EQUAL MEASURES JUSTICE AND EMOTION.
EITHER WAY...
PUNCH

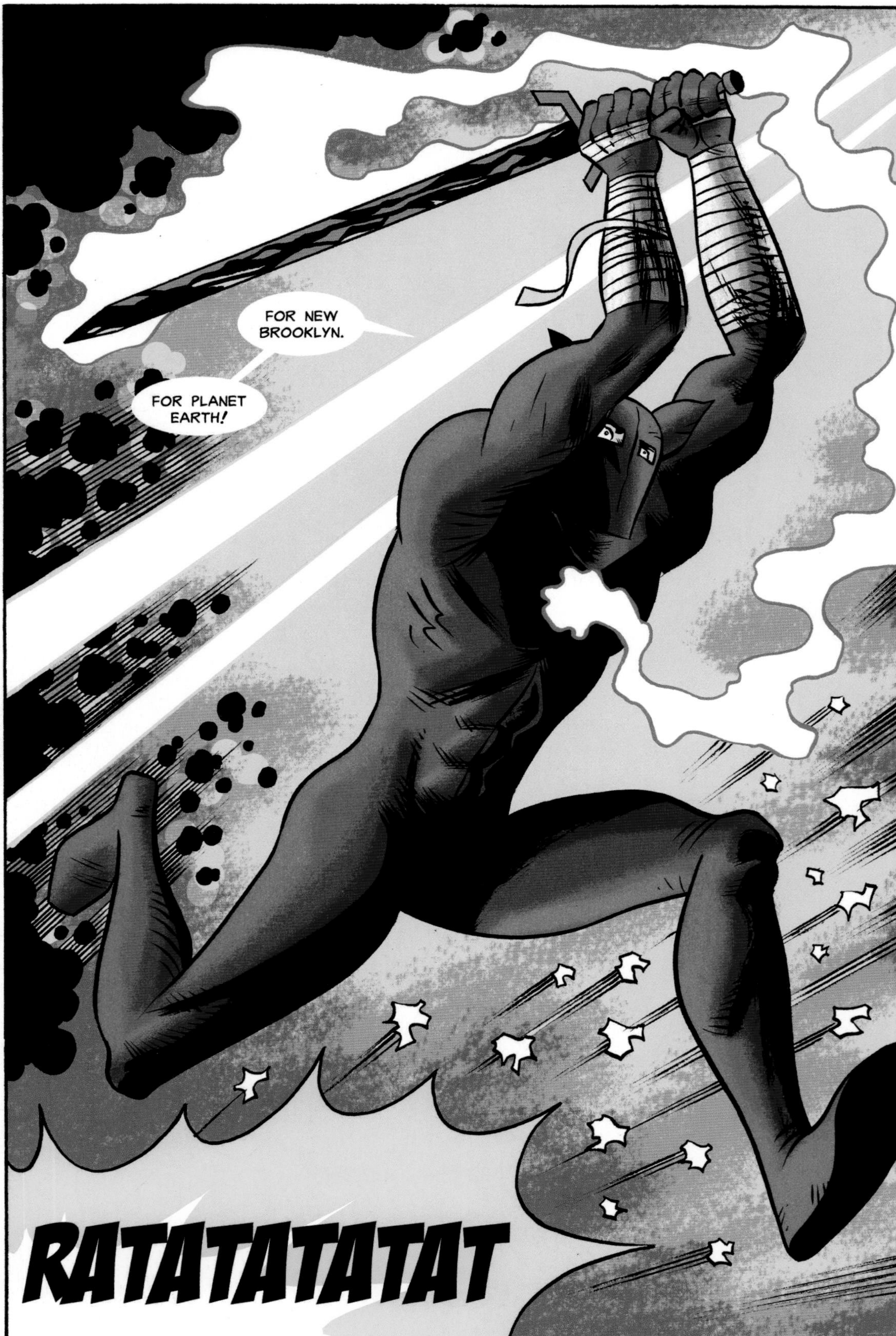
FOR NEW BROOKLYN.
FOR PLANET EARTH!
RATATATATATAT

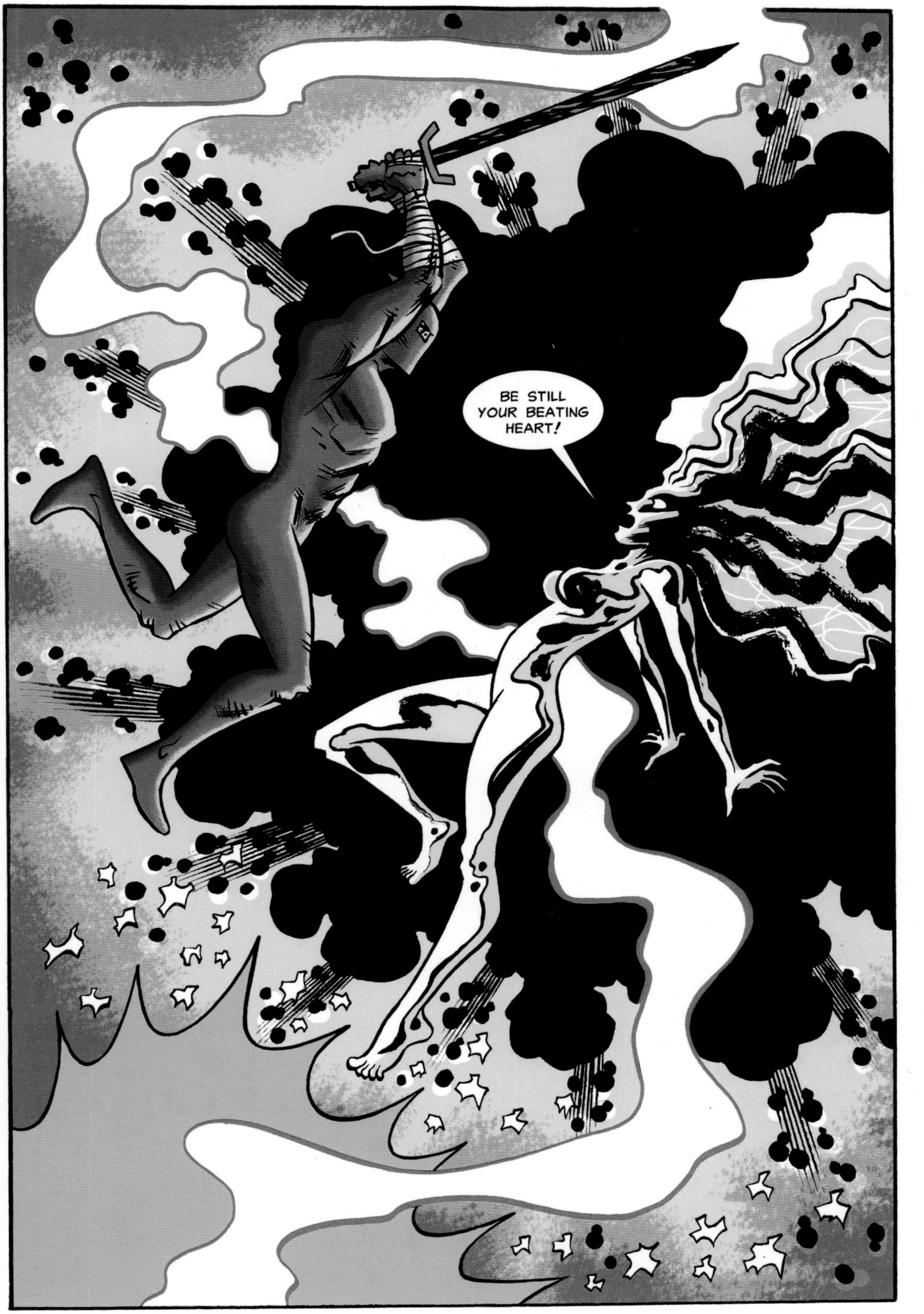
BE STILL YOUR BEATING HEART!

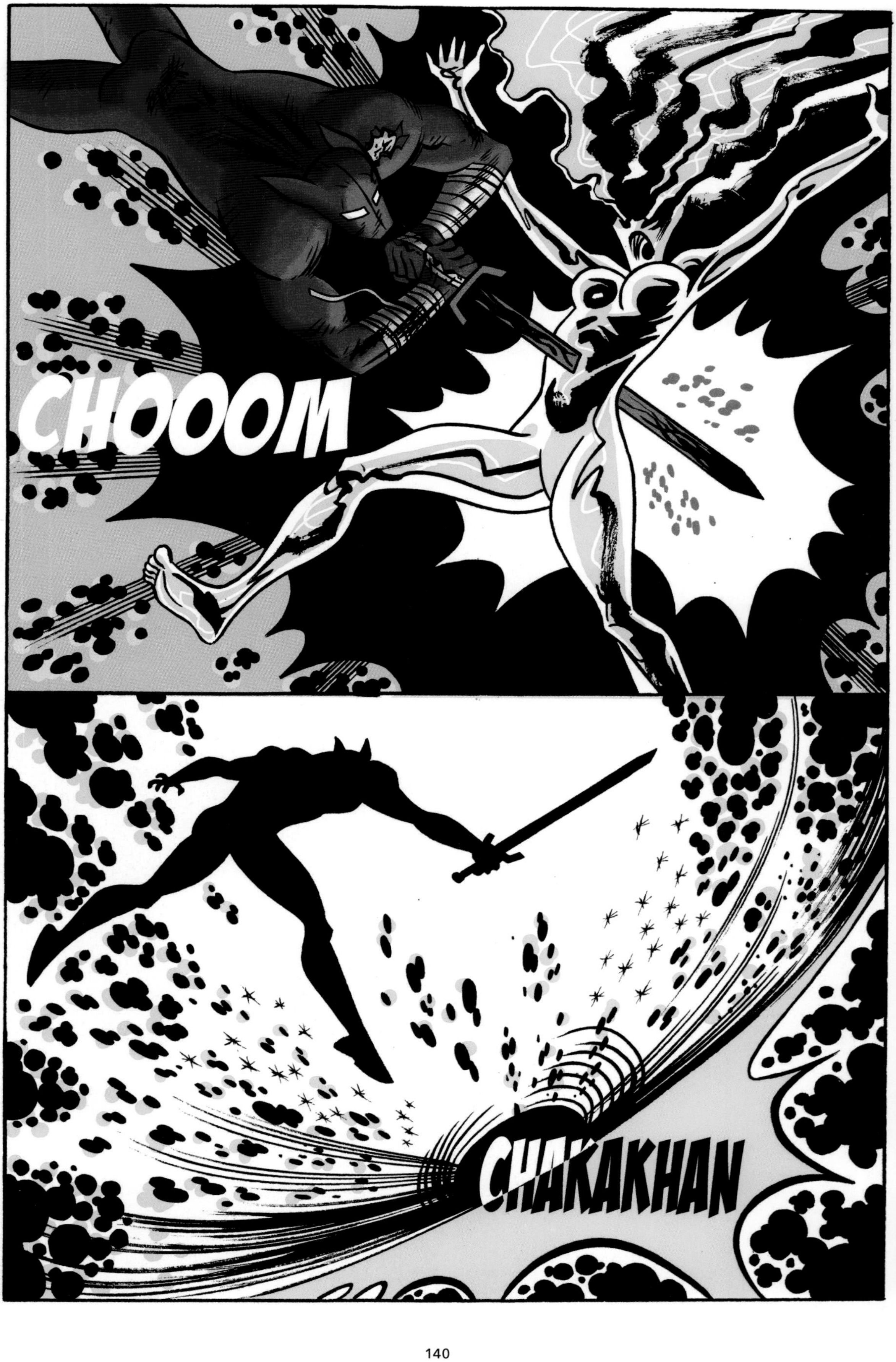
CHOOOM
CHAKAKHAN

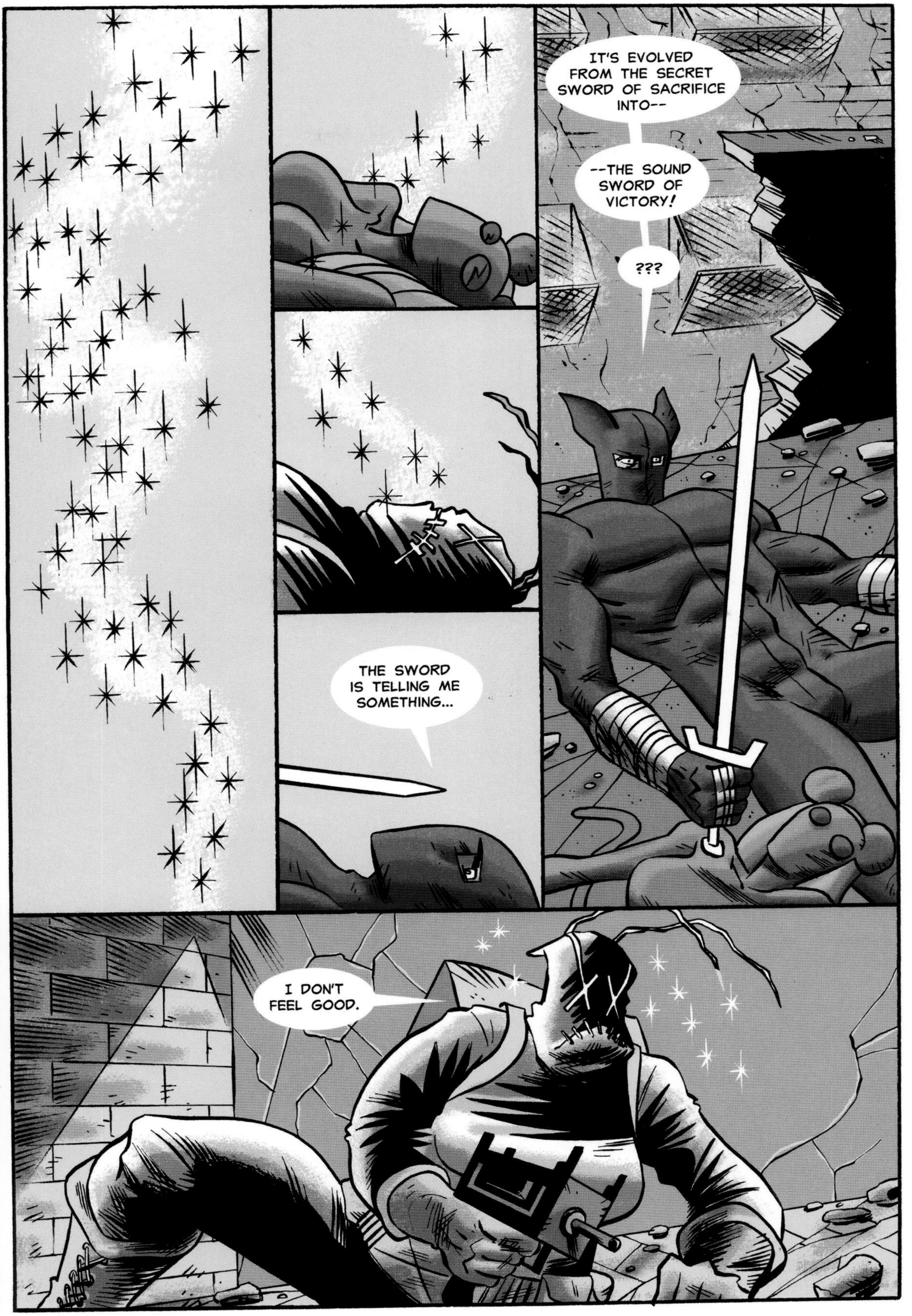
IT'S EVOLVED FROM THE SECRET SWORD OF SACRIFICE INTO--
--THE SOUND SWORD OF VICTORY!
???
THE SWORD IS TELLING ME SOMETHING...
I DON'T FEEL GOOD.

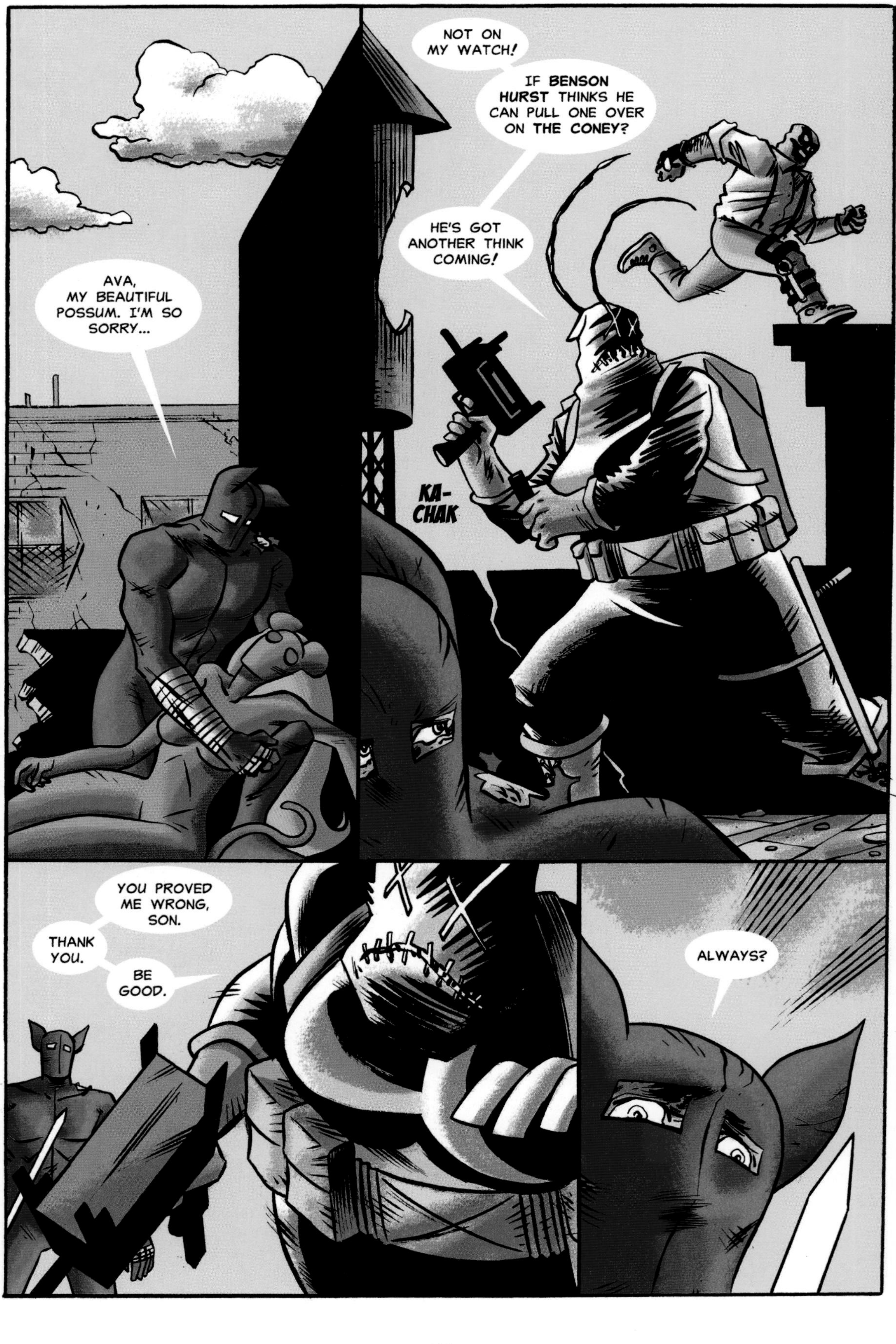
AVA, MY BEAUTIFUL POSSUM. I'M SO SORRY...
NOT ON MY WATCH!
IF BENSON HURST THINKS HE CAN PULL ONE OVER ON THE CONEY?
HE'S GOT ANOTHER THINK COMING!
KA-CHAK
YOU PROVED ME WRONG, SON.
THANK YOU.
BE GOOD.
ALWAYS?

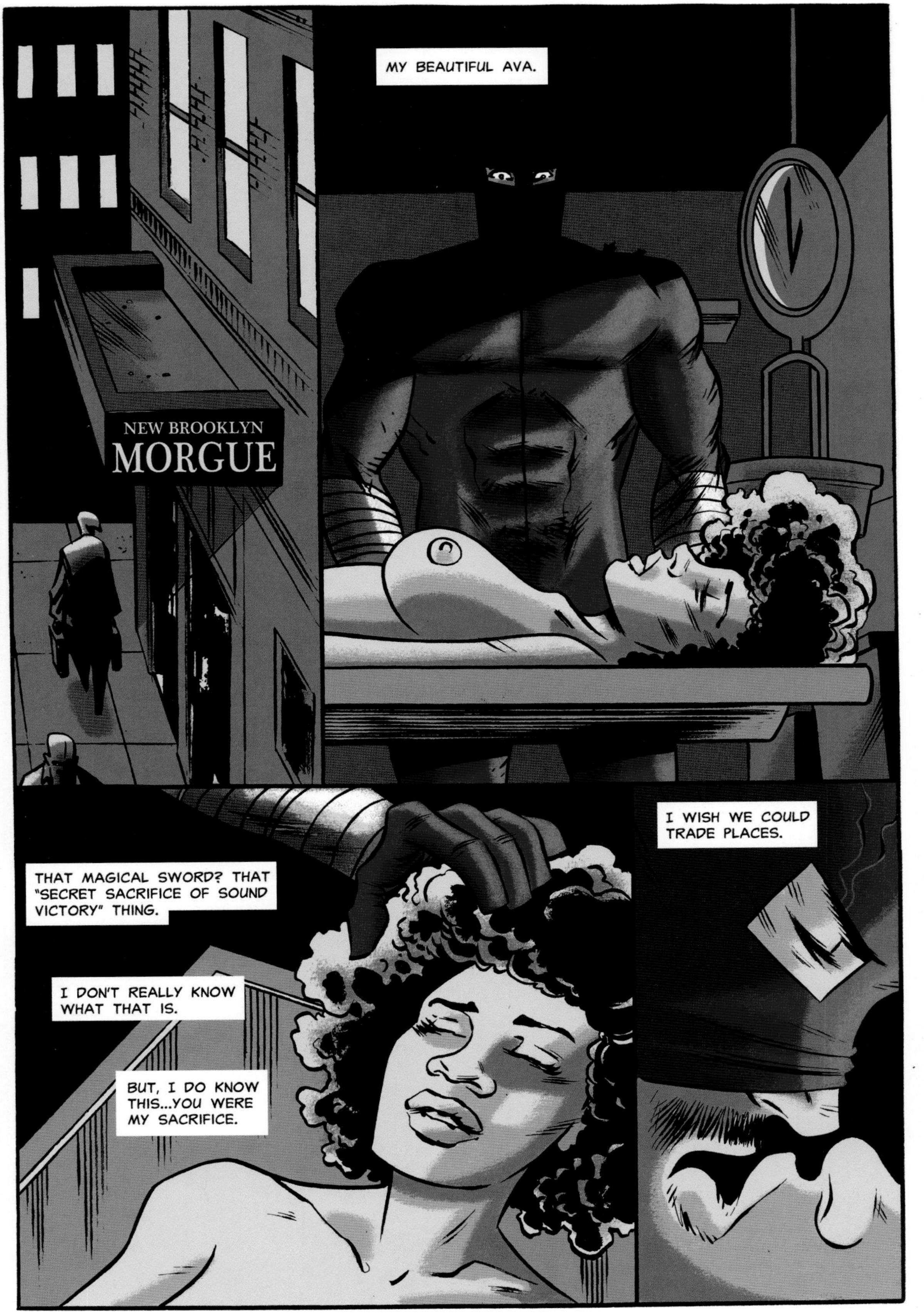
NEW BROOKLYN
MORGUE
MY BEAUTIFUL AVA.
THAT MAGICAL SWORD? THAT "SECRET SACRIFICE OF SOUND VICTORY" THING.
I DON'T REALLY KNOW WHAT THAT IS.
BUT, I DO KNOW THIS...YOU WERE MY SACRIFICE.
I WISH WE COULD TRADE PLACES.

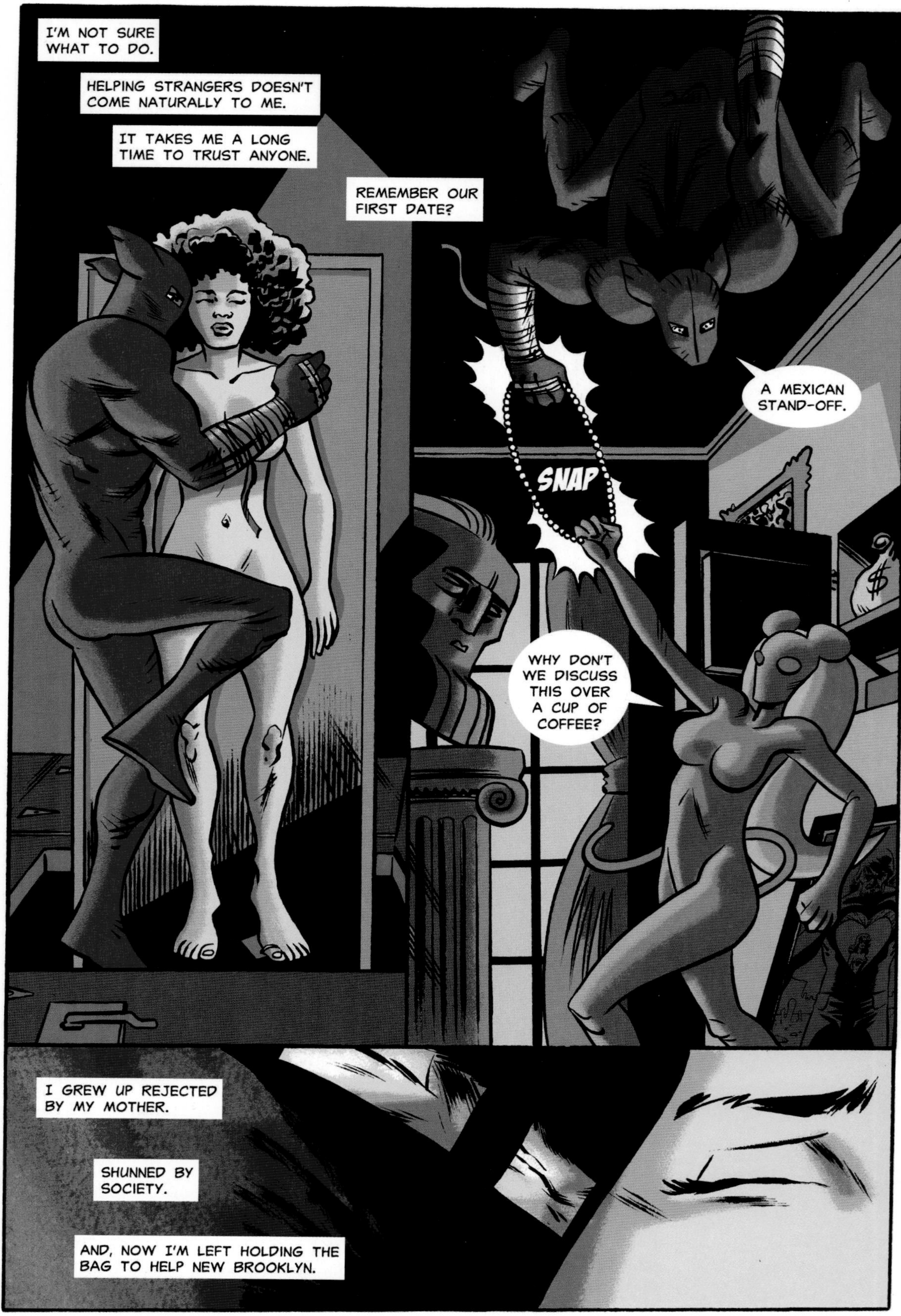
I'M NOT SURE WHAT TO DO.
HELPING STRANGERS DOESN'T COME NATURALLY TO ME.
IT TAKES ME A LONG TIME TO TRUST ANYONE.
REMEMBER OUR FIRST DATE?
A MEXICAN STAND-OFF.
SNAP
WHY DON'T WE DISCUSS THIS OVER A CUP OF COFFEE?
I GREW UP REJECTED BY MY MOTHER.
SHUNNED BY SOCIETY.
AND, NOW I'M LEFT HOLDING THE BAG TO HELP NEW BROOKLYN.

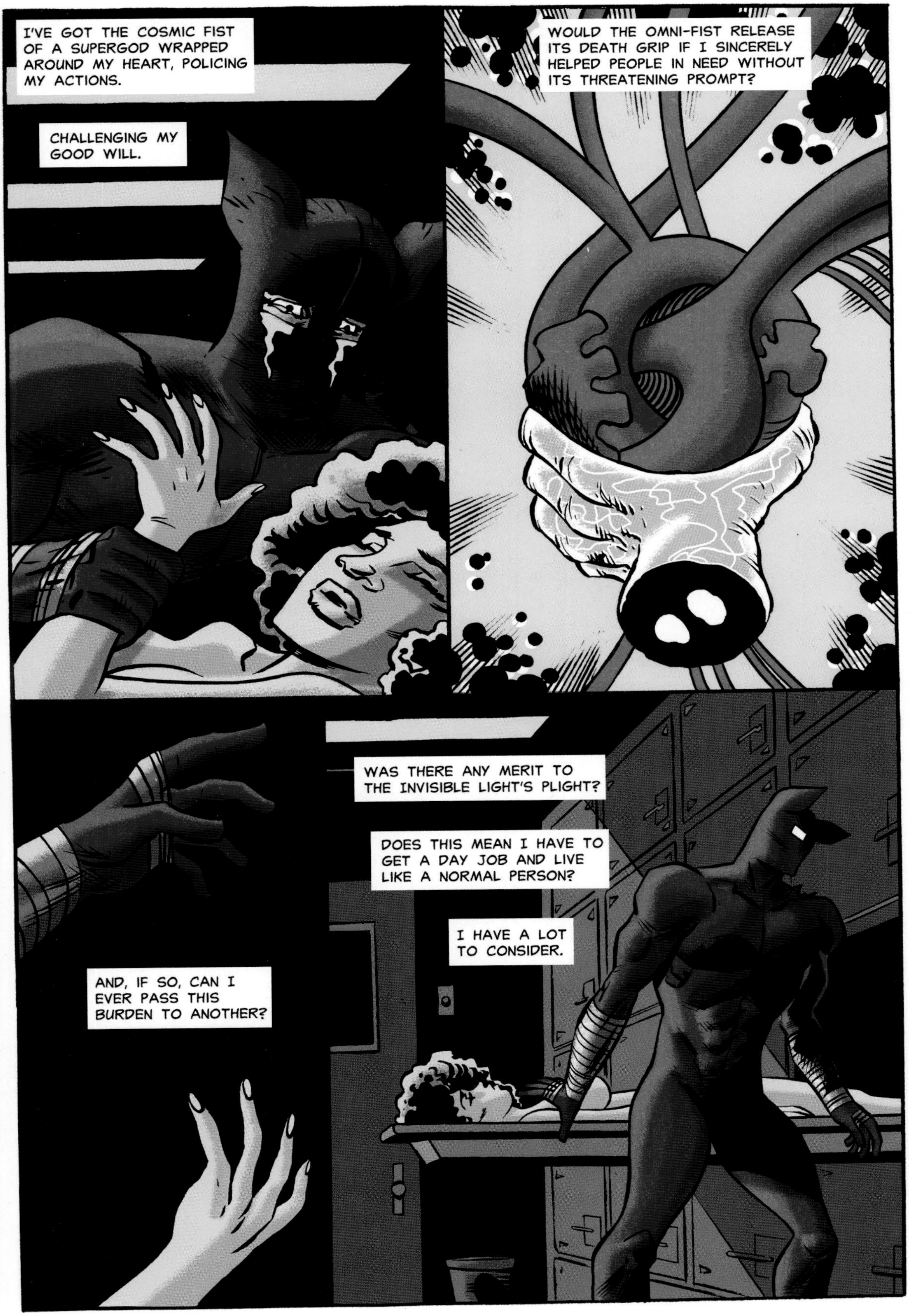
I'VE GOT THE COSMIC FIST OF A SUPERGOD WRAPPED AROUND MY HEART, POLICING MY ACTIONS.
CHALLENGING MY GOOD WILL.
WOULD THE OMNI-FIST RELEASE ITS DEATH GRIP IF I SINCERELY HELPED PEOPLE IN NEED WITHOUT ITS THREATENING PROMPT?
WAS THERE ANY MERIT TO THE INVISIBLE LIGHT'S PLIGHT?
DOES THIS MEAN I HAVE TO GET A DAY JOB AND LIVE LIKE A NORMAL PERSON?
I HAVE A LOT TO CONSIDER.
AND, IF SO, CAN I EVER PASS THIS BURDEN TO ANOTHER?

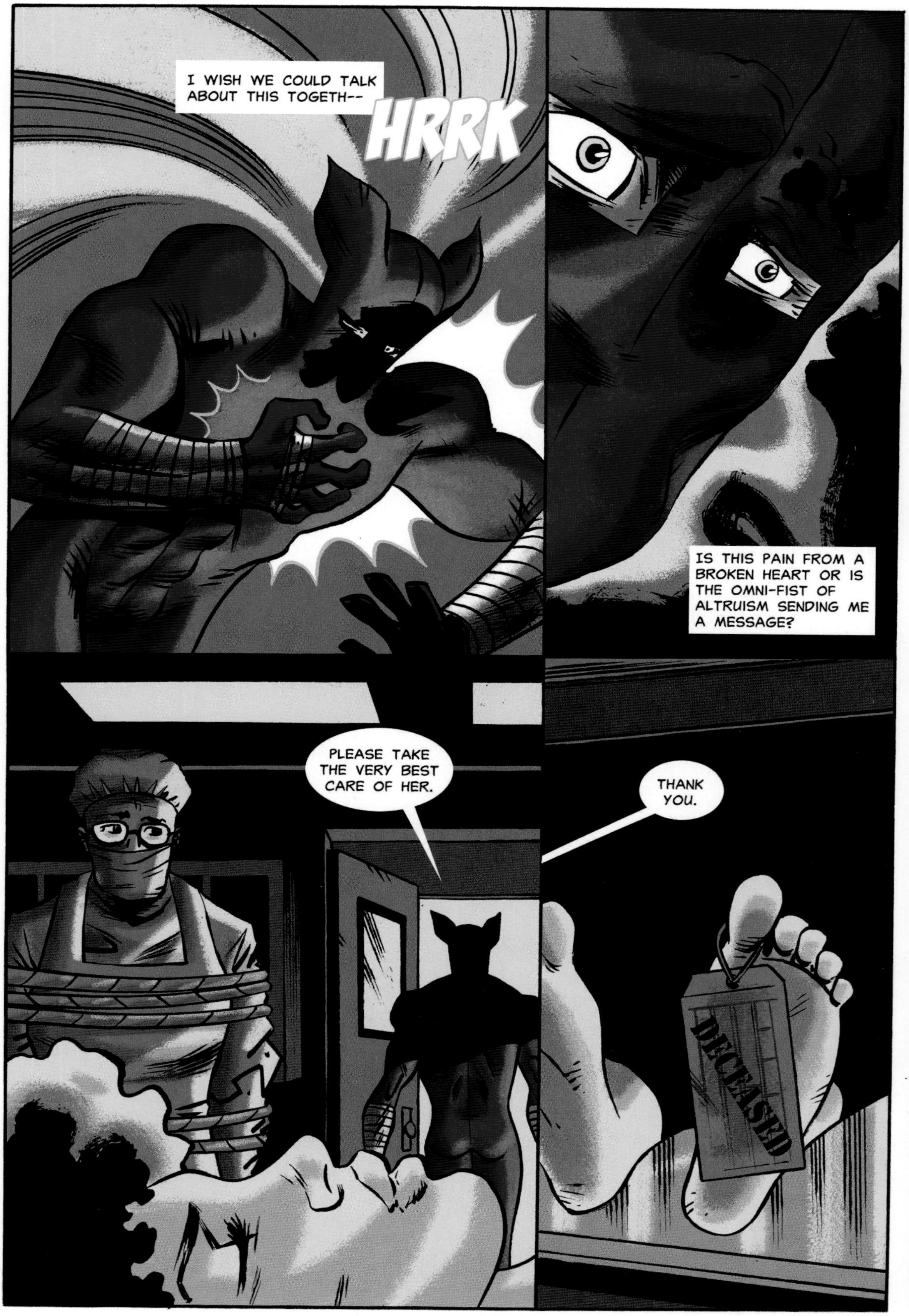
I WISH WE COULD TALK ABOUT THIS TOGETH--
HRRK
IS THIS PAIN FROM A BROKEN HEART OR IS THE OMNI-FIST OF ALTRUISM SENDING ME A MESSAGE?
PLEASE TAKE THE VERY BEST CARE OF HER.
THANK YOU.
DECEASED

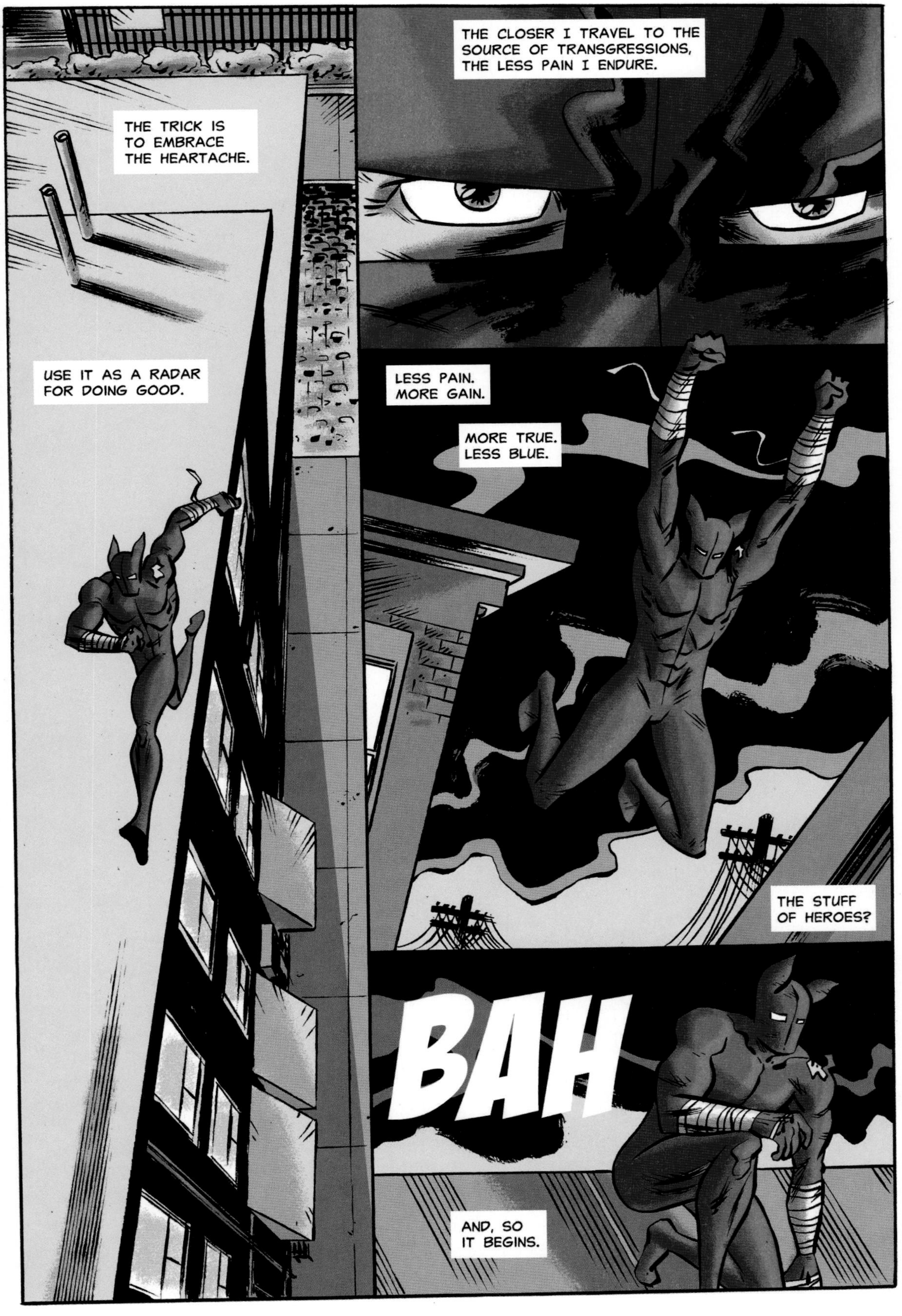
THE TRICK IS TO EMBRACE THE HEARTACHE.
USE IT AS A RADAR FOR DOING GOOD.
THE CLOSER I TRAVEL TO THE SOURCE OF TRANSGRESSIONS, THE LESS PAIN I ENDURE.
LESS PAIN. MORE GAIN.
MORE TRUE. LESS BLUE.
THE STUFF OF HEROES?
BAH
AND, SO IT BEGINS.

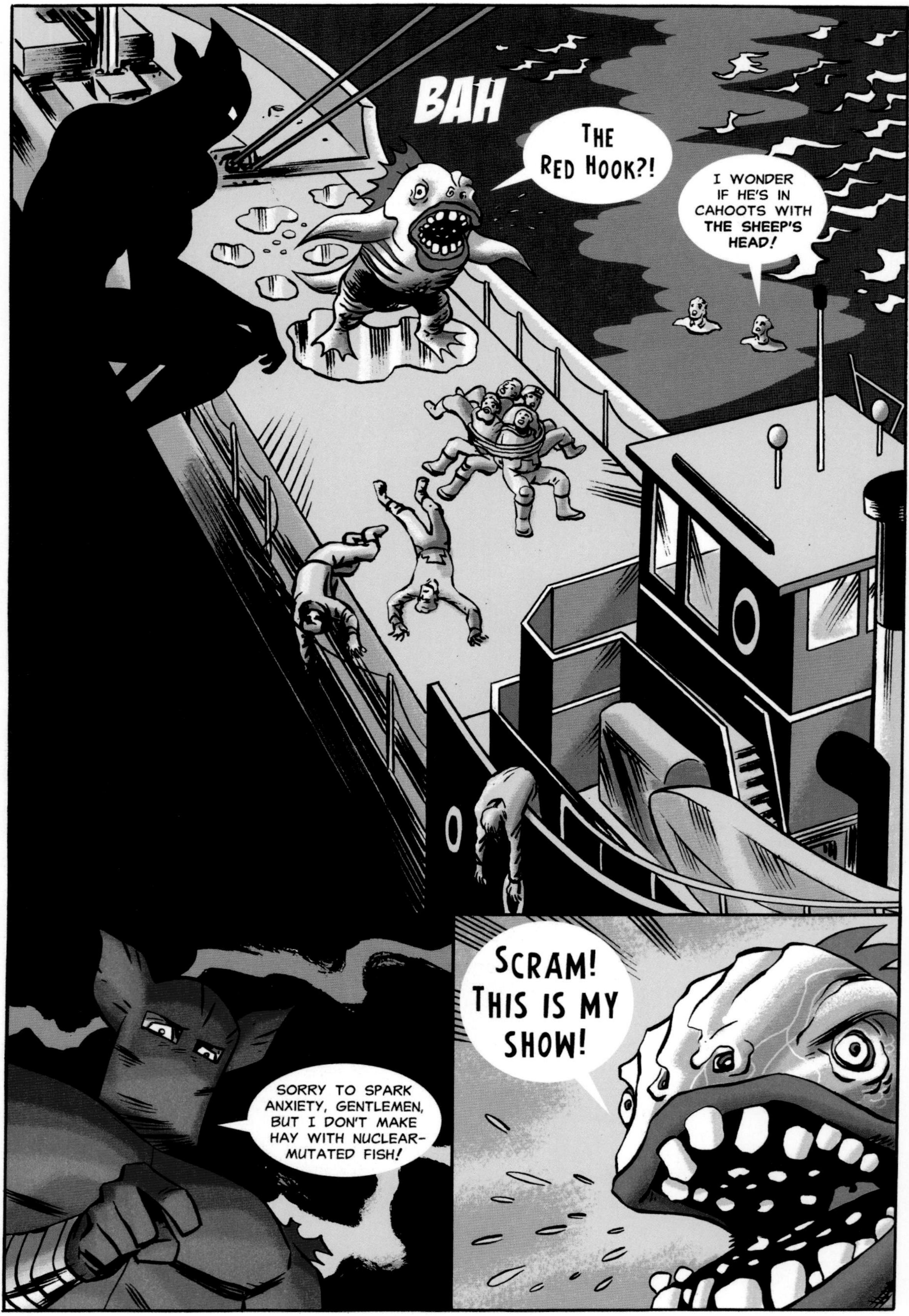
BAH
THE RED HOOK?!
I WONDER IF HE'S IN CAHOOTS WITH THE SHEEP'S HEAD!
SORRY TO SPARK ANXIETY, GENTLEMEN, BUT I DON'T MAKE HAY WITH NUCLEAR-MUTATED FISH!
SCRAM! THIS IS MY SHOW!

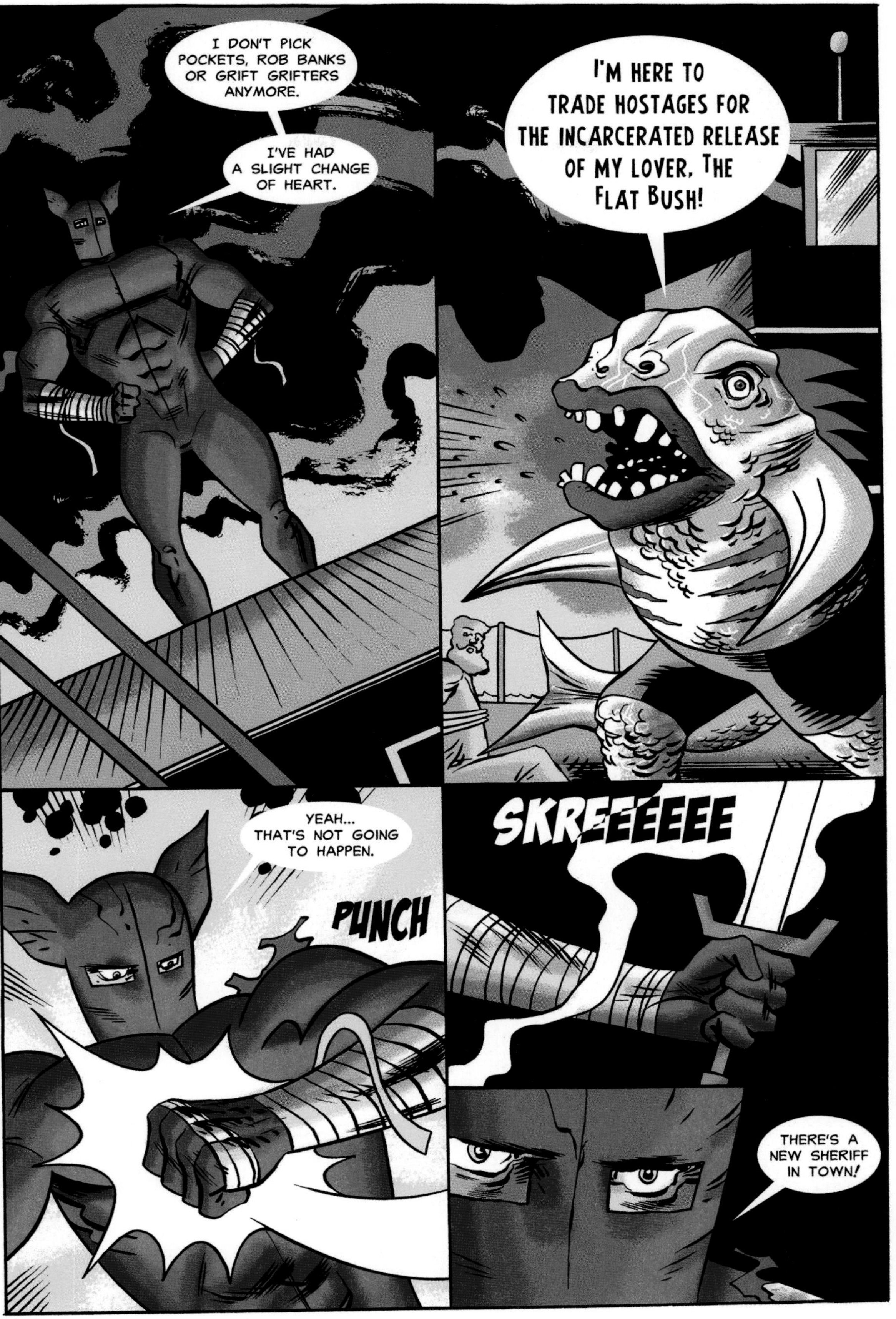
I DON'T PICK POCKETS, ROB BANKS OR GRIFT GRIFTERS ANYMORE.
I'VE HAD A SLIGHT CHANGE OF HEART.
I'M HERE TO TRADE HOSTAGES FOR THE INCARCERATED RELEASE OF MY LOVER, THE FLAT BUSH!
YEAH... THAT'S NOT GOING TO HAPPEN.
PUNCH
SKREEEEEEE
THERE'S A NEW SHERIFF IN TOWN!

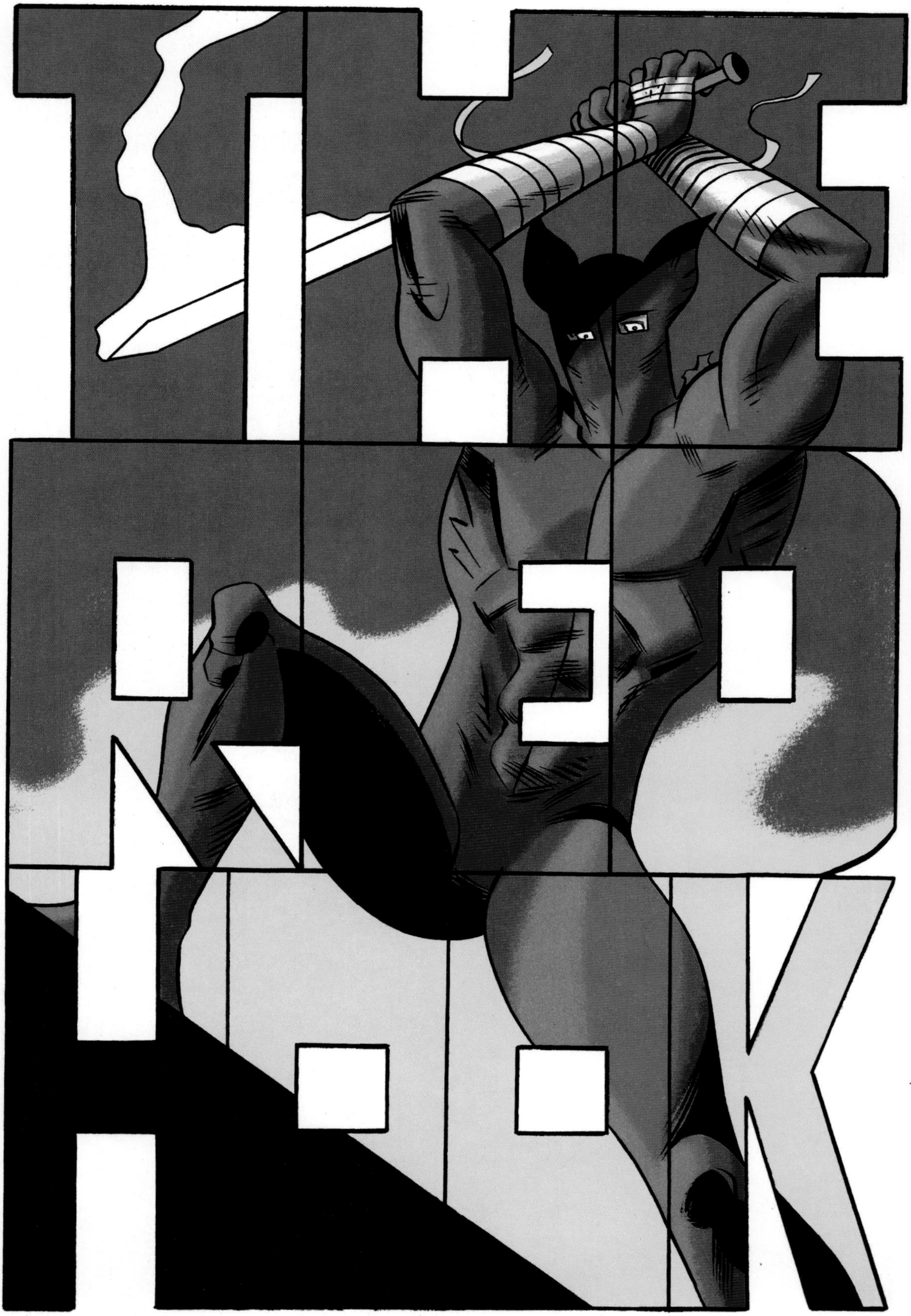
THE
ROOK

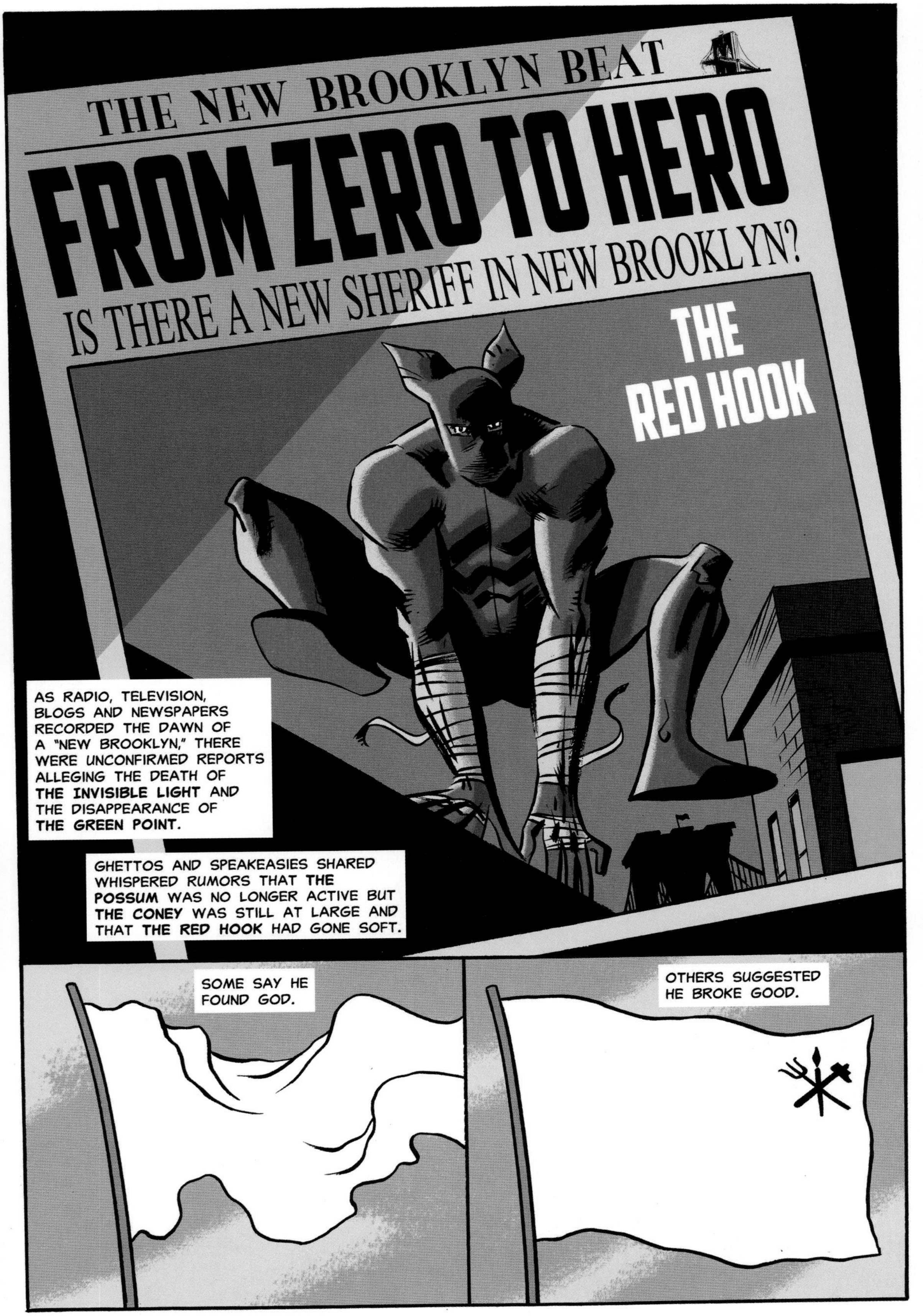
THE NEW BROOKLYN BEAT
FROM ZERO TO HERO
IS THERE A NEW SHERIFF IN NEW BROOKLYN?
THE RED HOOK
AS RADIO, TELEVISION, BLOGS AND NEWSPAPERS RECORDED THE DAWN OF A "NEW BROOKLYN," THERE WERE UNCONFIRMED REPORTS ALLEGING THE DEATH OF THE INVISIBLE LIGHT AND THE DISAPPEARANCE OF THE GREEN POINT.
GHETTOS AND SPEAKEASIES SHARED WHISPERED RUMORS THAT THE POSSUM WAS NO LONGER ACTIVE BUT THE CONEY WAS STILL AT LARGE AND THAT THE RED HOOK HAD GONE SOFT.
SOME SAY HE FOUND GOD.
OTHERS SUGGESTED HE BROKE GOOD.

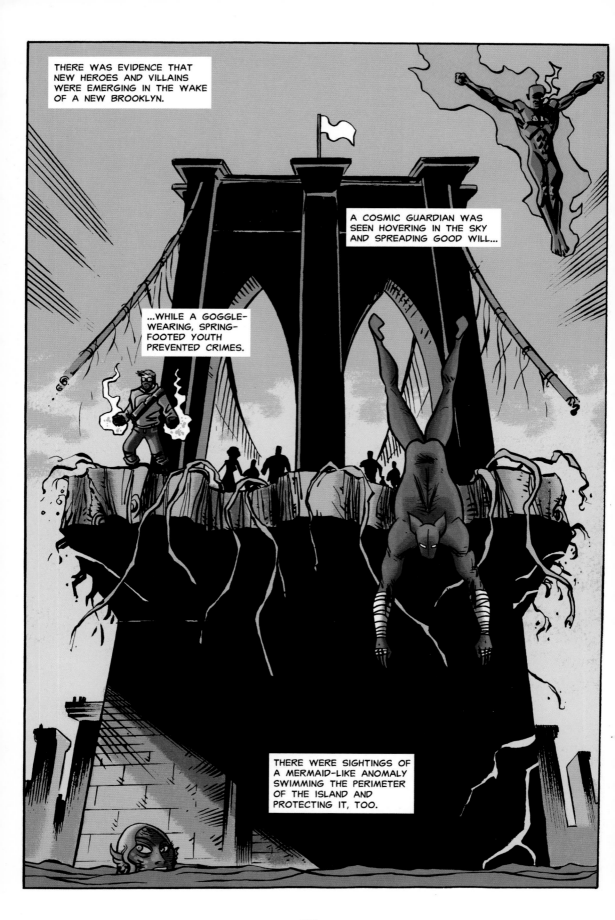

THERE WAS EVIDENCE THAT NEW HEROES AND VILLAINS WERE EMERGING IN THE WAKE OF A NEW BROOKLYN.

A COSMIC GUARDIAN WAS SEEN HOVERING IN THE SKY AND SPREADING GOOD WILL...

...WHILE A GOGGLE-WEARING, SPRING-FOOTED YOUTH PREVENTED CRIMES.

THERE WERE SIGHTINGS OF A MERMAID-LIKE ANOMALY SWIMMING THE PERIMETER OF THE ISLAND AND PROTECTING IT, TOO.

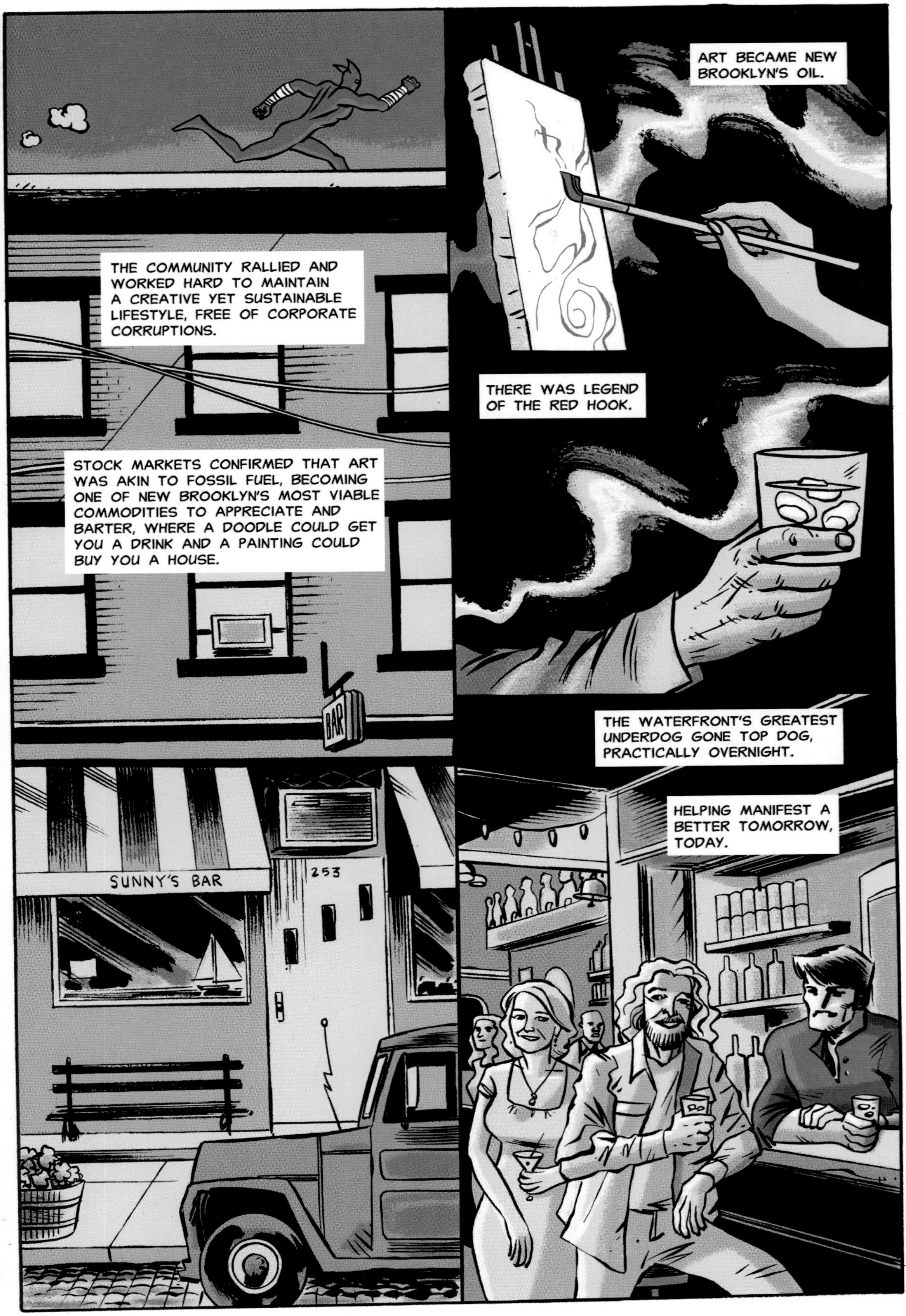
THE COMMUNITY RALLIED AND WORKED HARD TO MAINTAIN A CREATIVE YET SUSTAINABLE LIFESTYLE, FREE OF CORPORATE CORRUPTIONS.
STOCK MARKETS CONFIRMED THAT ART WAS AKIN TO FOSSIL FUEL, BECOMING ONE OF NEW BROOKLYN'S MOST VIABLE COMMODITIES TO APPRECIATE AND BARTER, WHERE A DOODLE COULD GET YOU A DRINK AND A PAINTING COULD BUY YOU A HOUSE.
BAR
ART BECAME NEW BROOKLYN'S OIL.
THERE WAS LEGEND OF THE RED HOOK.
SUNNY'S BAR
253
THE WATERFRONT'S GREATEST UNDERDOG GONE TOP DOG, PRACTICALLY OVERNIGHT.
HELPING MANIFEST A BETTER TOMORROW, TODAY.

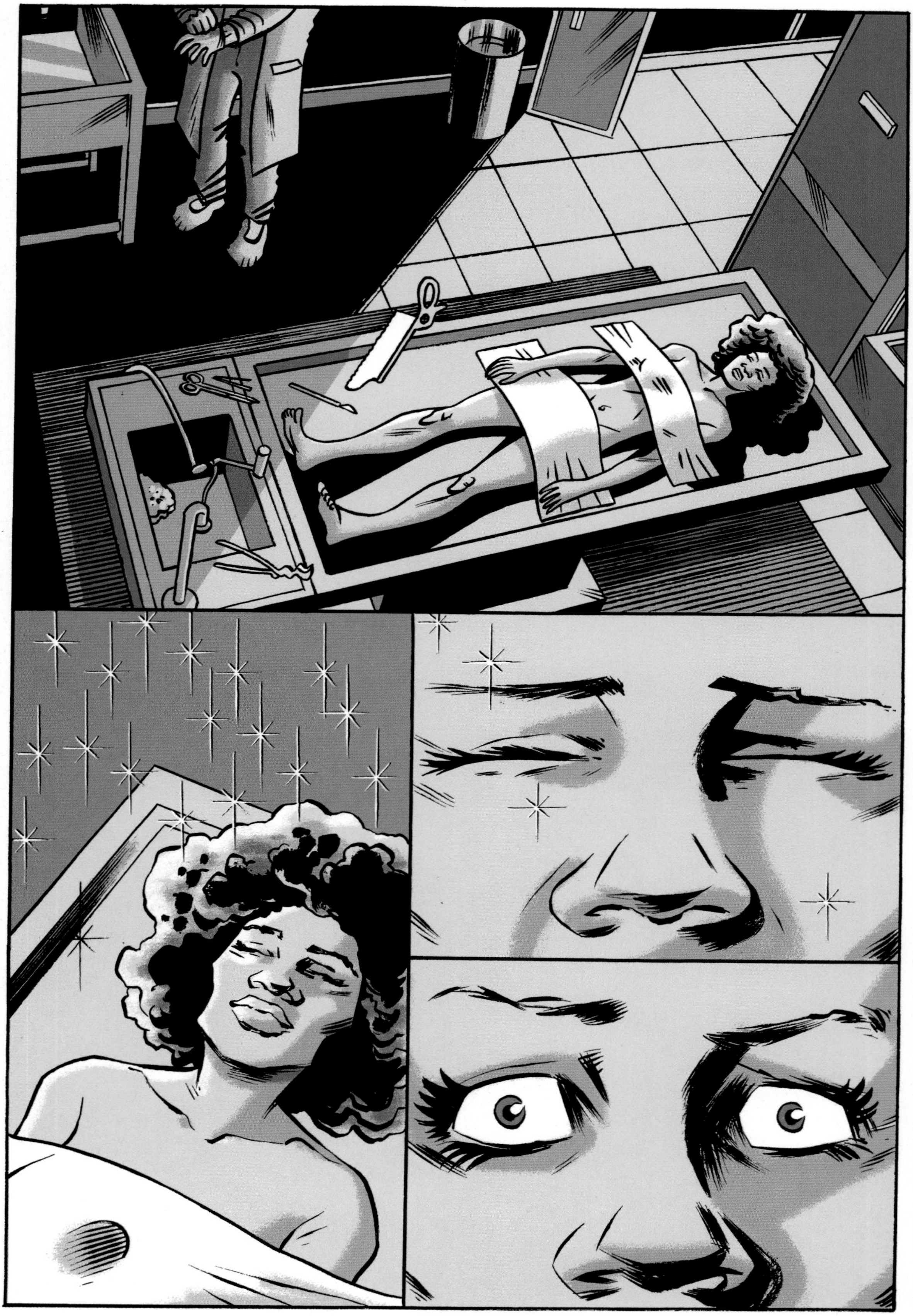

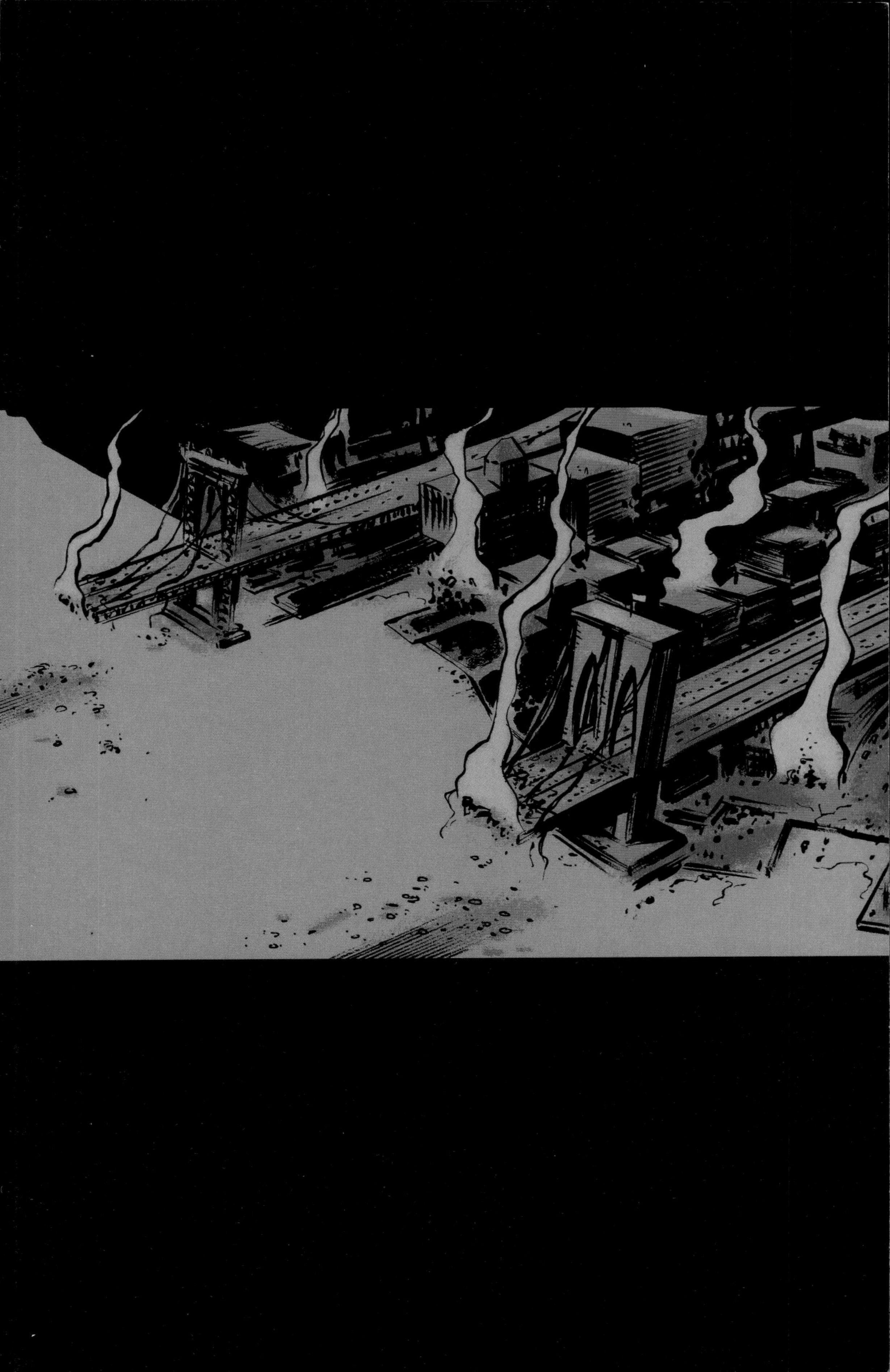

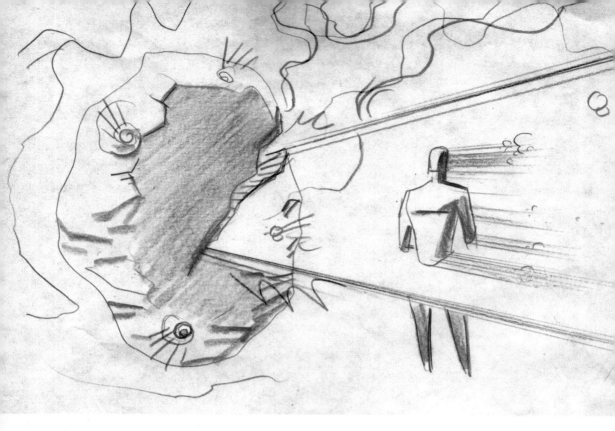

AFTERWORD BY VITO DELSANTE

Where were you when the white flags were raised?

Within the context of the New Brooklyn Universe, it's a very important question. One of those moments that is etched into your mind. One that never leaves and makes you a part of history in a very personal way. "Where were you when John F. Kennedy was shot?" Or, Martin Luther King, Jr., or John Lennon? "Where were you when man landed on the moon?" I was in class when The Challenger exploded. I was sleeping on my friend's couch when the first World Trade Center tower went down.

When the white flags were raised on the Brooklyn Bridge in 2014, I wasn't anywhere of note. In fact, I didn't even register the event until the next day when I saw it in the newspaper. A few days later, I was at Hang Dai Studios in Gowanus, Brooklyn. The comix studio had a really good view of the neighborhood and this is where New Brooklyn was born.

The Red Hook was not conceived in this studio, though. For a good while, Dean Haspiel was messing around with designs in his head for a "What if Alex Toth and Jack Kirby combined efforts and created a new character" idea. This would be roughly around summer of 2012. In 2013, I was given a wonderful opportunity to write *The Black Hood* for the Archie Comics Red Circle line. Dean asked if I would recommend him. So, I hooked him up with my editor, Paul Kaminski, and thus was born Dean's zany run on *The Fox* with co-writer Mark Waid. But, it's important to note that Sam Brosia aka The Red Hook, came first for Dean. And like all children, The Red Hook was waiting for his moment. Waiting for a sign.

The white flags.

That summer day in 2014, it was just Dean and me in the studio. Normally, Seth would be there, but Seth had just found out that his flu was actually leukemia and he was at home. I sat at Seth's work desk, a blue glass table that stood in front of a "Lion as Superman" painting. Dean asked me if I knew about the white flags. I affirmed that I did and then he asked a question that all good and great creators ask themselves. But, in asking out loud, he invited me into a very special world. He asked…

"What if Brooklyn gave up?"

On the surface, that is a very simple, almost childlike, question. It's blunt and to the point, but as you mull the answer in your head, you realize that it has multiple layers. The two of us bandied about scenarios. Dean came up with the idea of a borough-sized broken heart and a literal secession. As the excitement of seeing these ideas catch fire took hold, Dean called Seth and put him on speakerphone. Seth had this pet project that was semi-inspired by his photo-essay book, *The Brooklynite*. See, Seth, was a born and bred Brooklyn boy. Dino? He's a native Manhattanite, but his soul is pure Brooklyn. Me? I'm a Staten Islander that crossed the Verrazano. Seth, in a lot of ways, embodied the spirit of what we were trying to accomplish; the idea of a shared yet autonomous universe, a truly cosmic land that existed purely for the glorification of art. Seth co-created Jake Jeffries with artist Shamus Beyale, the protagonist of *The Brooklynite*, as a sort of...well, schmuck by day/hero by night. Then Dean asked me what I was going to bring to the table and I quickly weighed in with "Oh snap, that's how we can use The Purple Heart!" A character Dean and I concocted years earlier but never went anywhere until now. Dean suggested that we tell more about Brooklyn's broken heart in the Purple Heart story. Something Dean wasn't planning on addressing too much in *Red Hook*. When we found our artist in Ricardo Venâncio, we had our mission. We had our *New Brooklyn* trinity.

What you've just read in the first volume of *The Red Hook* is a love letter to Silver Age superhero comics. But, it's also a "Dear John" letter to the world we currently live in. It's the idea that we can be better than our carnal desires and technological dependence if we start putting our heart where our mouth is. Art, the ultimate expression of oneself, has value. As Dean was creating this comic, the studio where the *New Brooklyn Universe* was born started to slip away. The owner decided to sell the property, forcing dozens of artists and artisans to find a new home. Capitalism, am I right? The archenemy of art. See, beauty is in the eye of the beholder, but still lines its pockets with green, dig? For Dean (and Sam Brosia) to exist in Brooklyn, both had to put value into soul. Which is why the Red Hook, a super-thief, gets his heart compromised by pure altruism to find his way in this NEW Brooklyn. Because Dean, torn between his heart (or home, in this case) and reality (the rising prices of New York real estate), is trying to find HIS way in a new Brooklyn.

We put a lot of ourselves in the *New Brooklyn Trinity* (*The Red Hook*, *The Brooklynite*, and *The Purple Heart*). For me, Zeke (the hero of *The Purple Heart*) has a simple wish that I can boil down into a very basic concept; he just wants to sleep in his own bed. Nature, however, conspires against him. He's got a lot to learn before he can go "home" again. We can all understand that, right?

Go back. Reread this book. Look across the bridge. See the white flags?

SURRENDER.

Vito Delsante
April 2018

Vito Delsante is a comic book writer, graphic novelist, editor, letterer, and the co-creator/writer of *Stray*, and *The Purple Heart* with Dean Haspiel and artist Ricardo Venâncio. He's written for DC Comics, Marvel Comics, Image Comics, AdHouse Books, and Simon & Schuster among others, and his stories have been reprinted in other countries. He lives in Pittsburgh, PA with his wife Michelle, his daughter Sadie, his son James, and his pitbull Kirby.

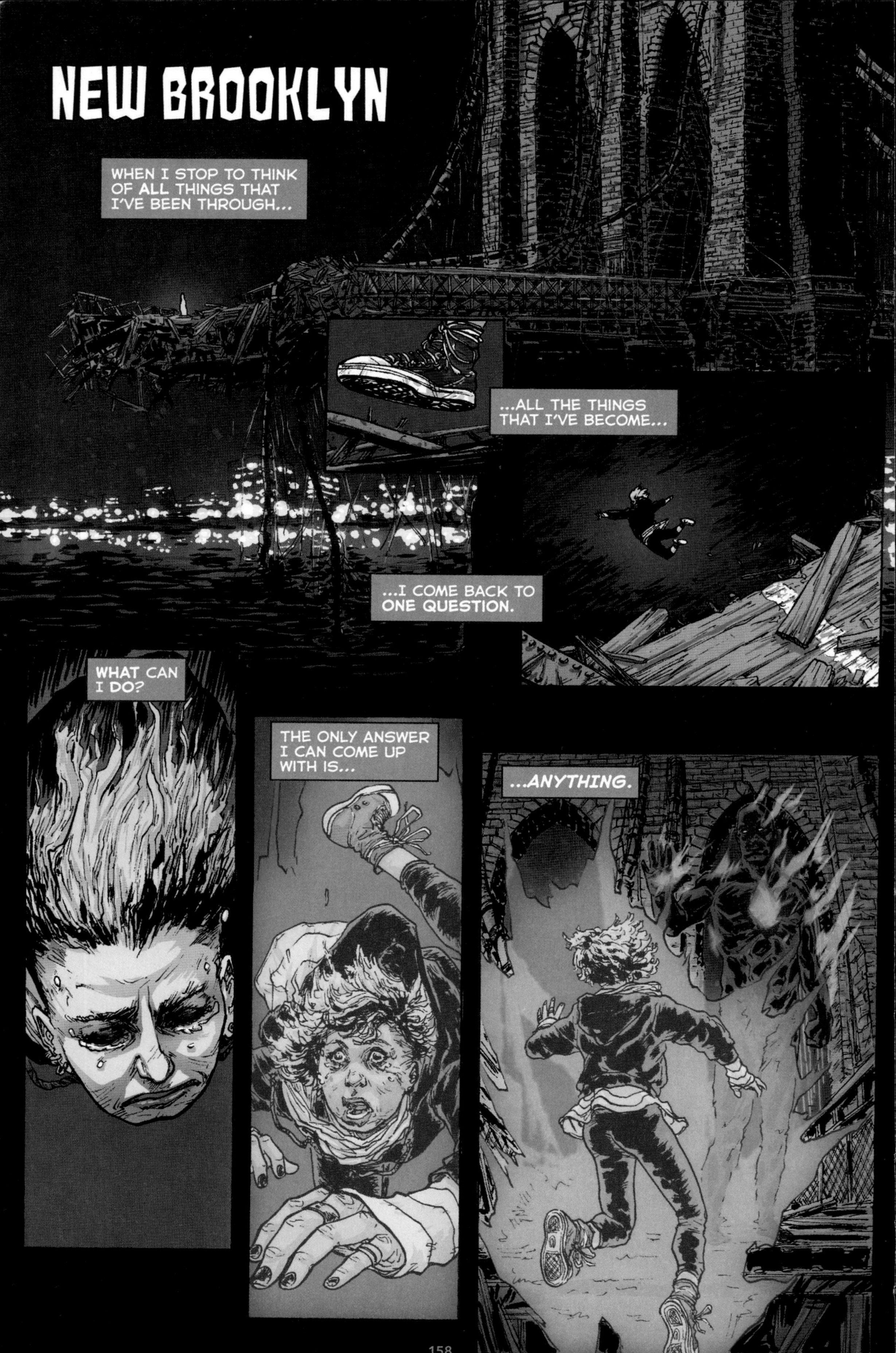
NEW BROOKLYN
WHEN I STOP TO THINK OF ALL THINGS THAT I'VE BEEN THROUGH...
...ALL THE THINGS THAT I'VE BECOME...
...I COME BACK TO ONE QUESTION.
WHAT CAN I DO?
THE ONLY ANSWER I CAN COME UP WITH IS...
...ANYTHING.

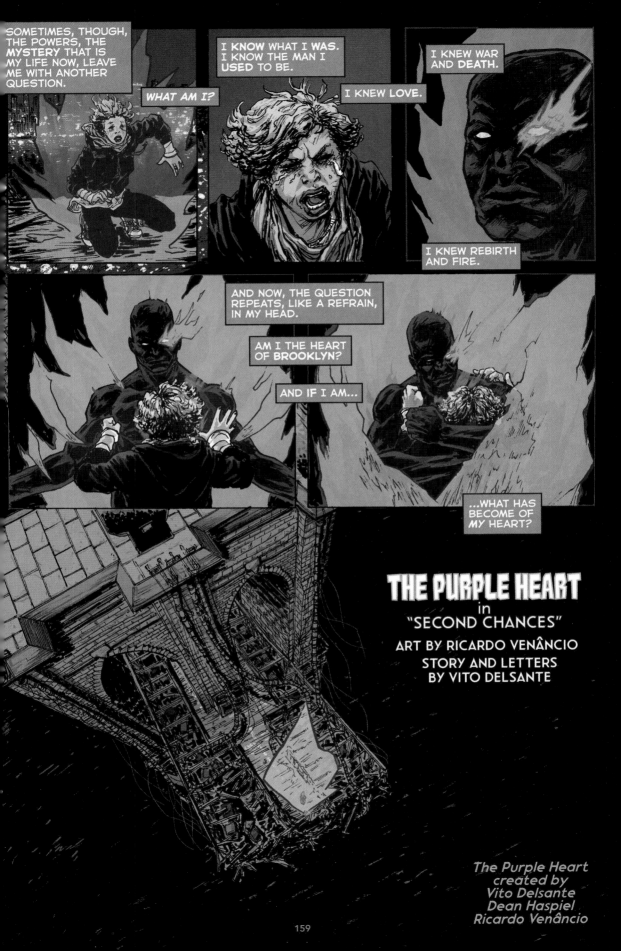

SOMETIMES, THOUGH, THE POWERS, THE **MYSTERY** THAT IS MY LIFE NOW, LEAVE ME WITH ANOTHER QUESTION.

WHAT AM I?

I KNOW WHAT I WAS. I KNOW THE MAN I USED TO BE.

I KNEW LOVE.

I KNEW WAR AND **DEATH.**

I KNEW REBIRTH AND FIRE.

AND NOW, THE QUESTION REPEATS, LIKE A REFRAIN, IN MY HEAD.

AM I THE HEART OF **BROOKLYN?**

AND IF I AM...

...WHAT HAS BECOME OF **MY** HEART?

THE PURPLE HEART
in
"SECOND CHANCES"
ART BY RICARDO VENÂNCIO
STORY AND LETTERS BY VITO DELSANTE

The Purple Heart created by Vito Delsante Dean Haspiel Ricardo Venâncio

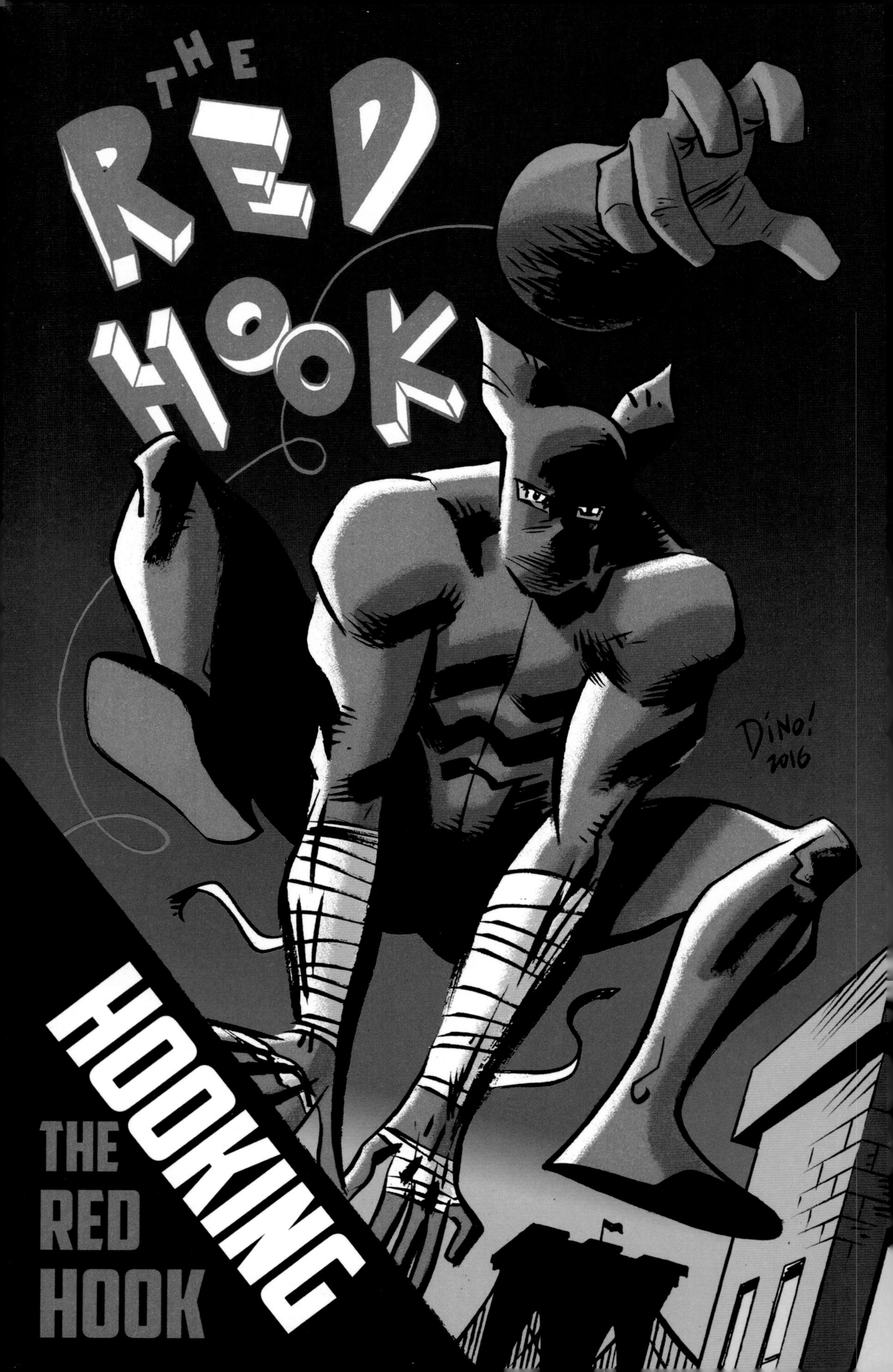
THE RED HOOK
DINO! 2016
HOOKING
THE RED HOOK

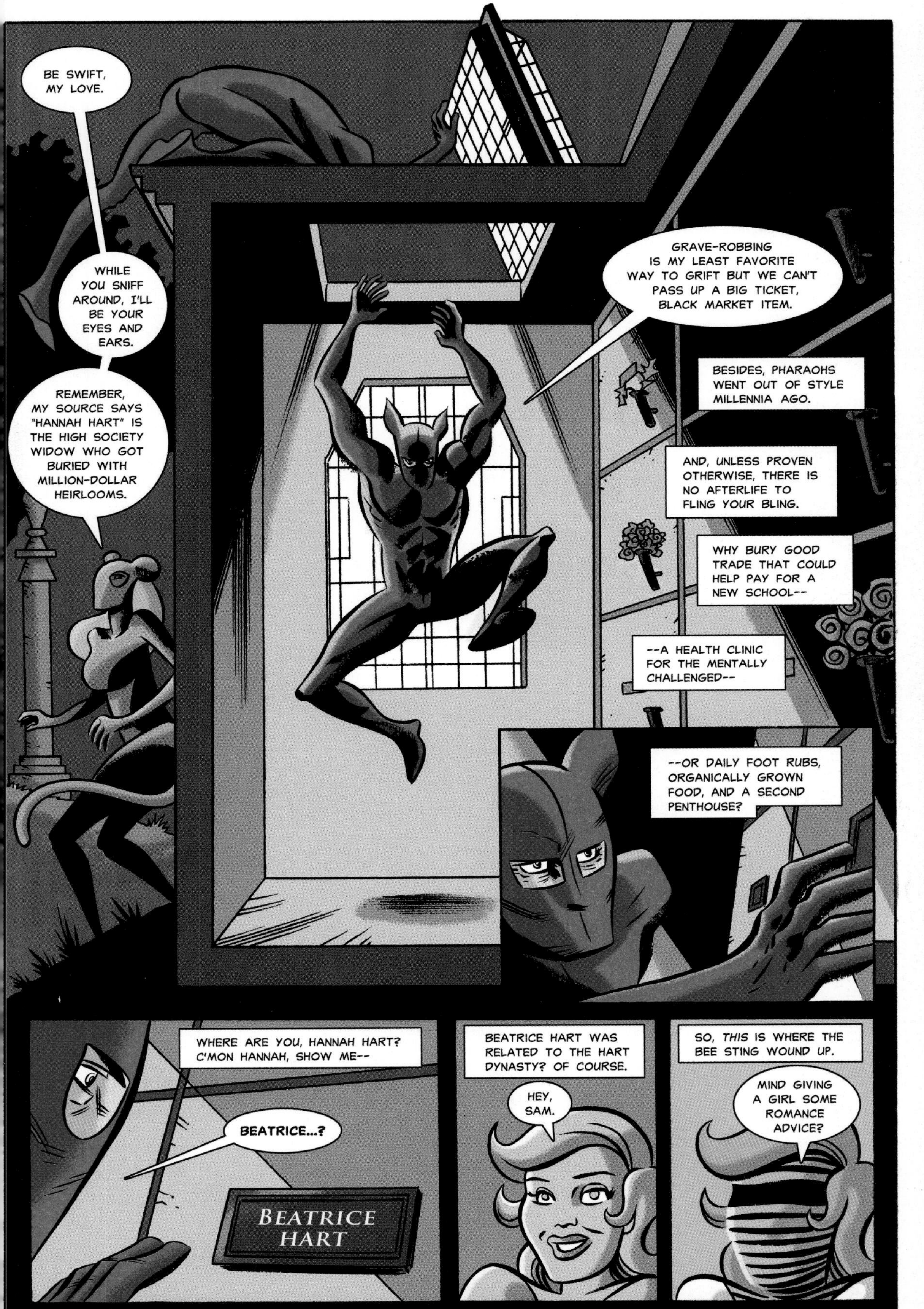
BE SWIFT, MY LOVE.
WHILE YOU SNIFF AROUND, I'LL BE YOUR EYES AND EARS.
REMEMBER, MY SOURCE SAYS "HANNAH HART" IS THE HIGH SOCIETY WIDOW WHO GOT BURIED WITH MILLION-DOLLAR HEIRLOOMS.
GRAVE-ROBBING IS MY LEAST FAVORITE WAY TO GRIFT BUT WE CAN'T PASS UP A BIG TICKET, BLACK MARKET ITEM.
BESIDES, PHARAOHS WENT OUT OF STYLE MILLENNIA AGO.
AND, UNLESS PROVEN OTHERWISE, THERE IS NO AFTERLIFE TO FLING YOUR BLING.
WHY BURY GOOD TRADE THAT COULD HELP PAY FOR A NEW SCHOOL--
--A HEALTH CLINIC FOR THE MENTALLY CHALLENGED--
--OR DAILY FOOT RUBS, ORGANICALLY GROWN FOOD, AND A SECOND PENTHOUSE?
WHERE ARE *YOU*, HANNAH HART? C'MON HANNAH, SHOW ME--
BEATRICE...?
BEATRICE HART
BEATRICE HART WAS RELATED TO THE HART DYNASTY? OF COURSE.
HEY, SAM.
SO, *THIS* IS WHERE THE BEE STING WOUND UP.
MIND GIVING A GIRL SOME ROMANCE ADVICE?

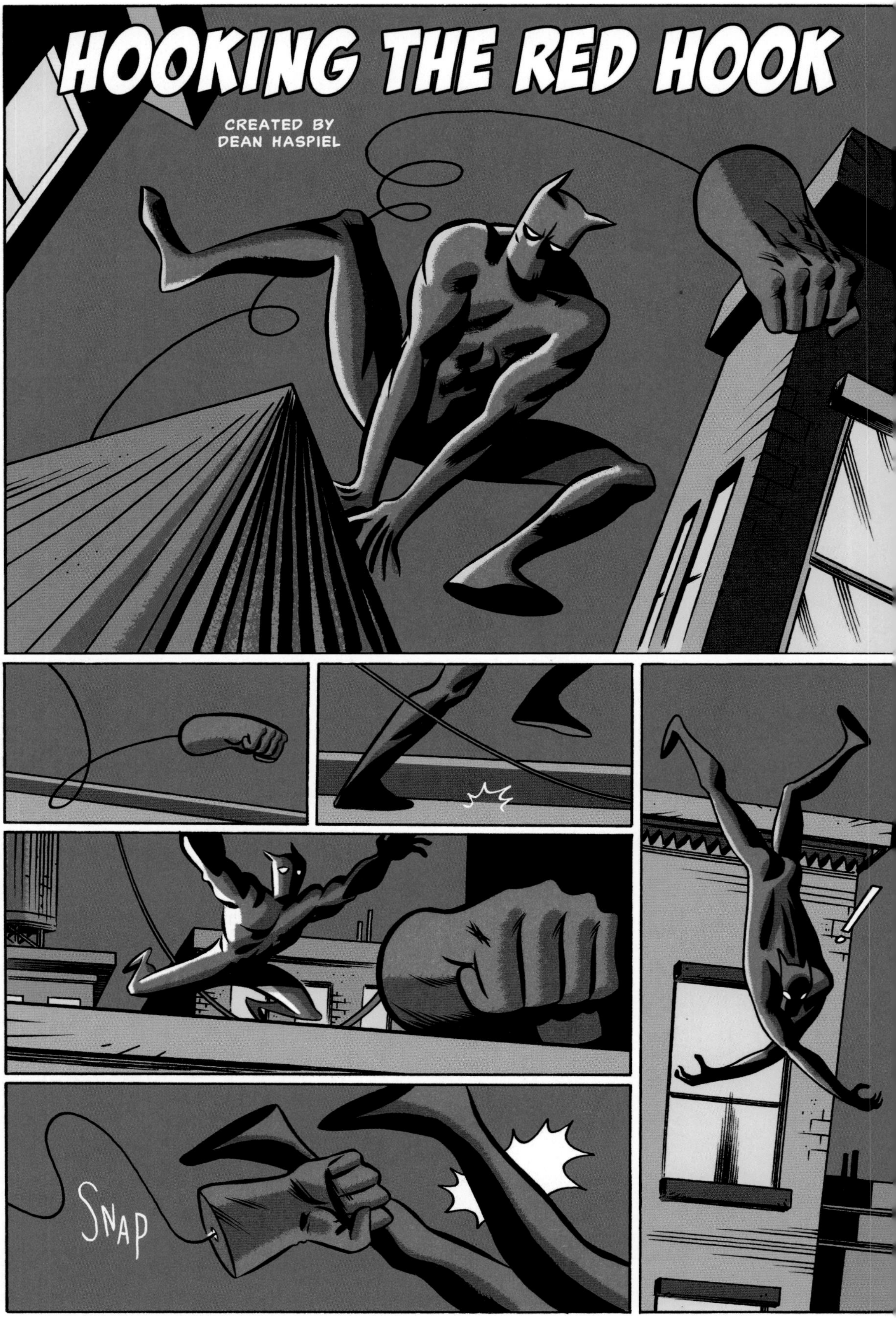
HOOKING THE RED HOOK
CREATED BY
DEAN HASPIEL
SNAP

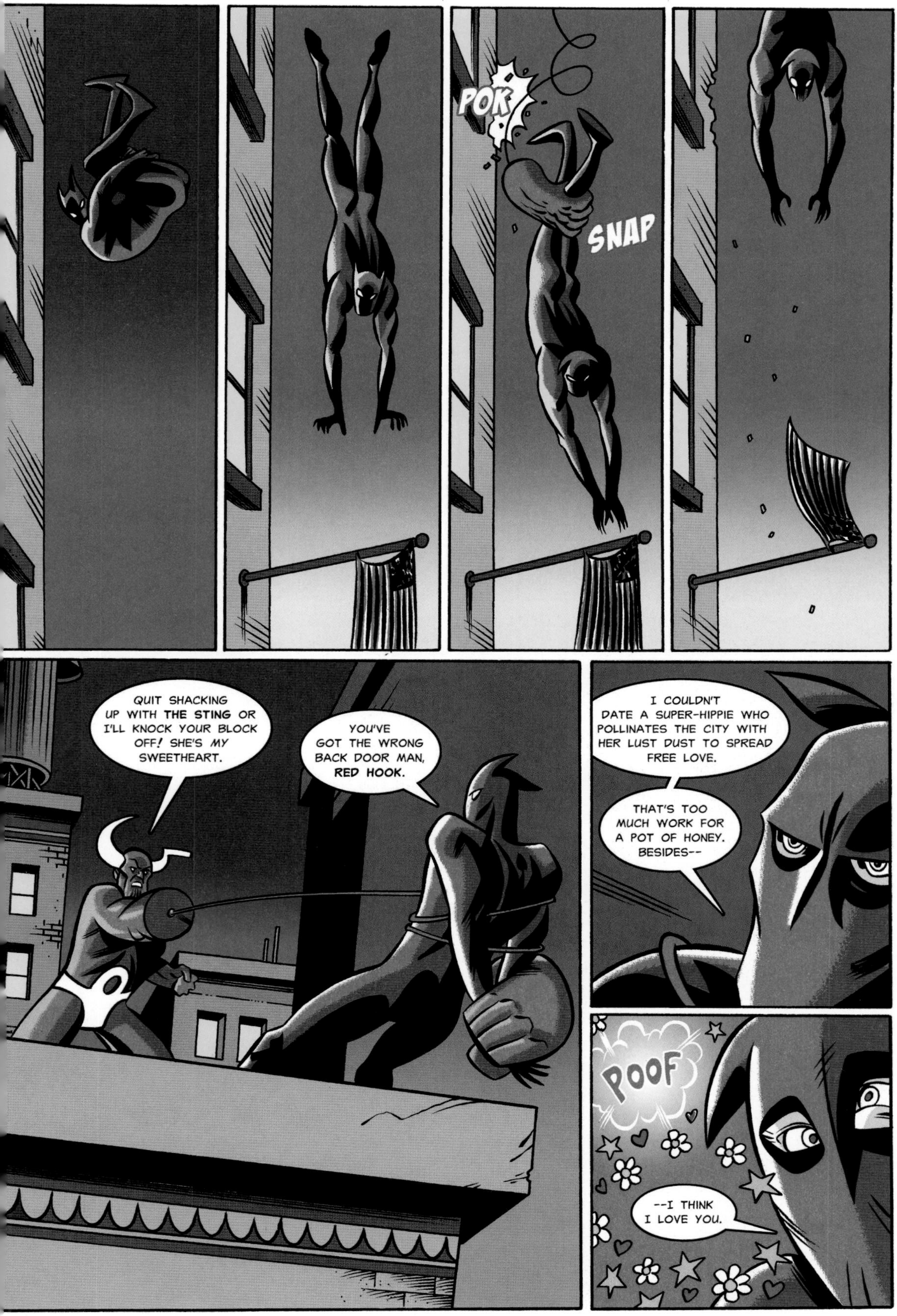
POK
SNAP
QUIT SHACKING UP WITH THE STING OR I'LL KNOCK YOUR BLOCK OFF! SHE'S MY SWEETHEART.
YOU'VE GOT THE WRONG BACK DOOR MAN, RED HOOK.
I COULDN'T DATE A SUPER-HIPPIE WHO POLLINATES THE CITY WITH HER LUST DUST TO SPREAD FREE LOVE.
THAT'S TOO MUCH WORK FOR A POT OF HONEY. BESIDES--
POOF
--I THINK I LOVE YOU.

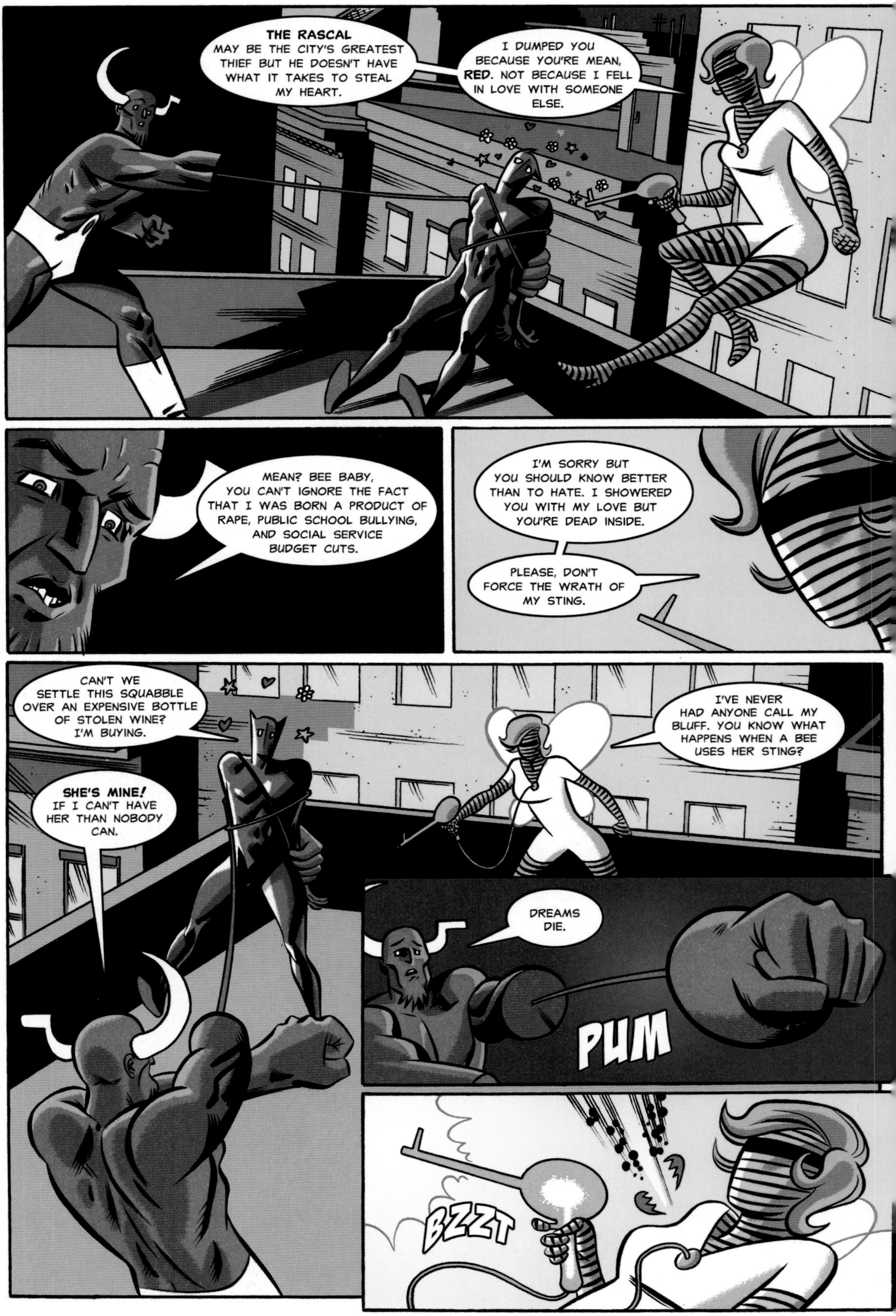
THE RASCAL MAY BE THE CITY'S GREATEST THIEF BUT HE DOESN'T HAVE WHAT IT TAKES TO STEAL MY HEART.
I DUMPED YOU BECAUSE YOU'RE MEAN, RED. NOT BECAUSE I FELL IN LOVE WITH SOMEONE ELSE.
MEAN? BEE BABY, YOU CAN'T IGNORE THE FACT THAT I WAS BORN A PRODUCT OF RAPE, PUBLIC SCHOOL BULLYING, AND SOCIAL SERVICE BUDGET CUTS.
I'M SORRY BUT YOU SHOULD KNOW BETTER THAN TO HATE. I SHOWERED YOU WITH MY LOVE BUT YOU'RE DEAD INSIDE.
PLEASE, DON'T FORCE THE WRATH OF MY STING.
CAN'T WE SETTLE THIS SQUABBLE OVER AN EXPENSIVE BOTTLE OF STOLEN WINE? I'M BUYING.
SHE'S MINE! IF I CAN'T HAVE HER THAN NOBODY CAN.
I'VE NEVER HAD ANYONE CALL MY BLUFF. YOU KNOW WHAT HAPPENS WHEN A BEE USES HER STING?
DREAMS DIE.
PUM
BZZT

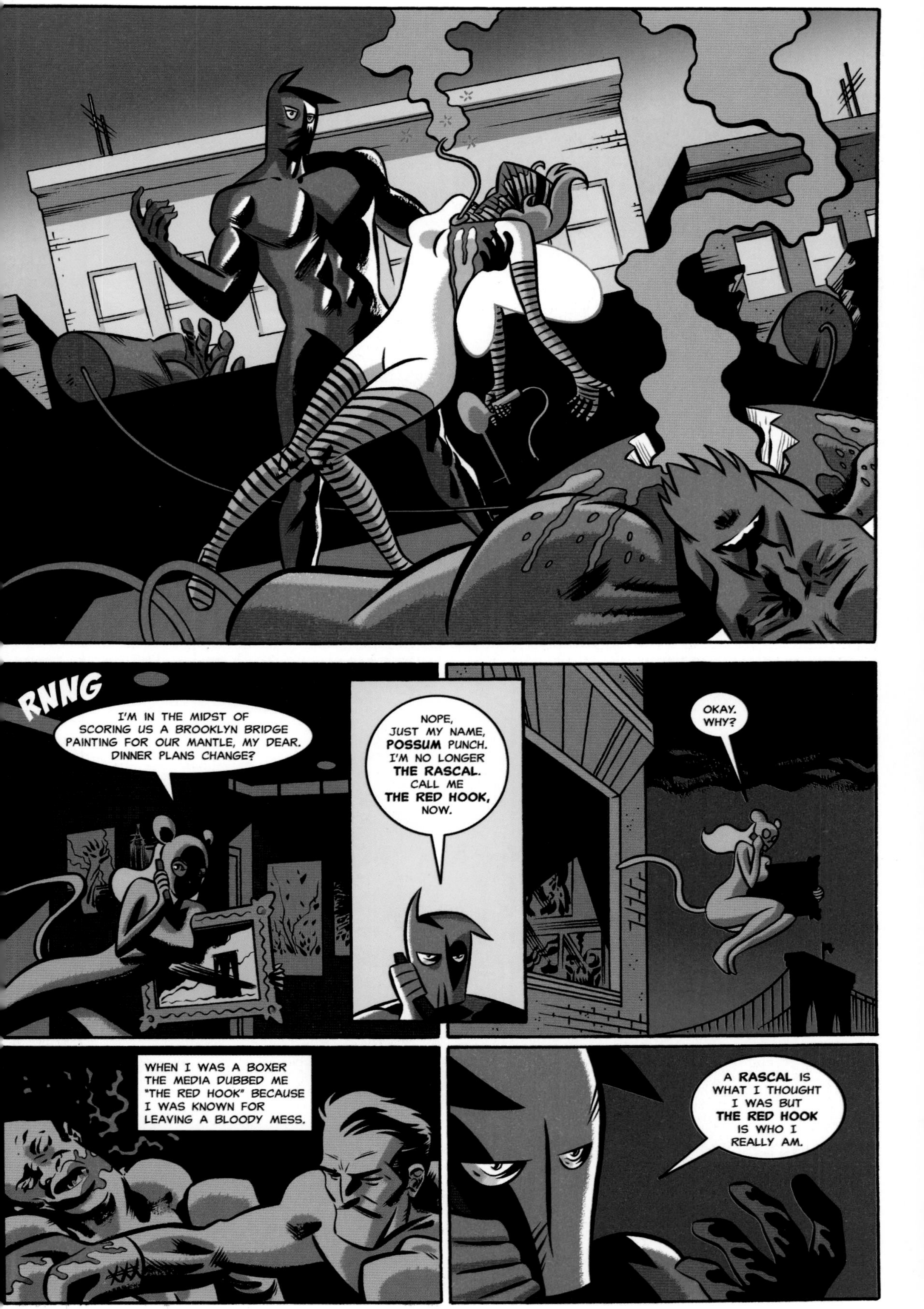

RNNG
I'M IN THE MIDST OF SCORING US A BROOKLYN BRIDGE PAINTING FOR OUR MANTLE, MY DEAR. DINNER PLANS CHANGE?
NOPE, JUST MY NAME, POSSUM PUNCH. I'M NO LONGER THE RASCAL. CALL ME THE RED HOOK, NOW.
OKAY. WHY?
WHEN I WAS A BOXER THE MEDIA DUBBED ME "THE RED HOOK" BECAUSE I WAS KNOWN FOR LEAVING A BLOODY MESS.
A RASCAL IS WHAT I THOUGHT I WAS BUT THE RED HOOK IS WHO I REALLY AM.

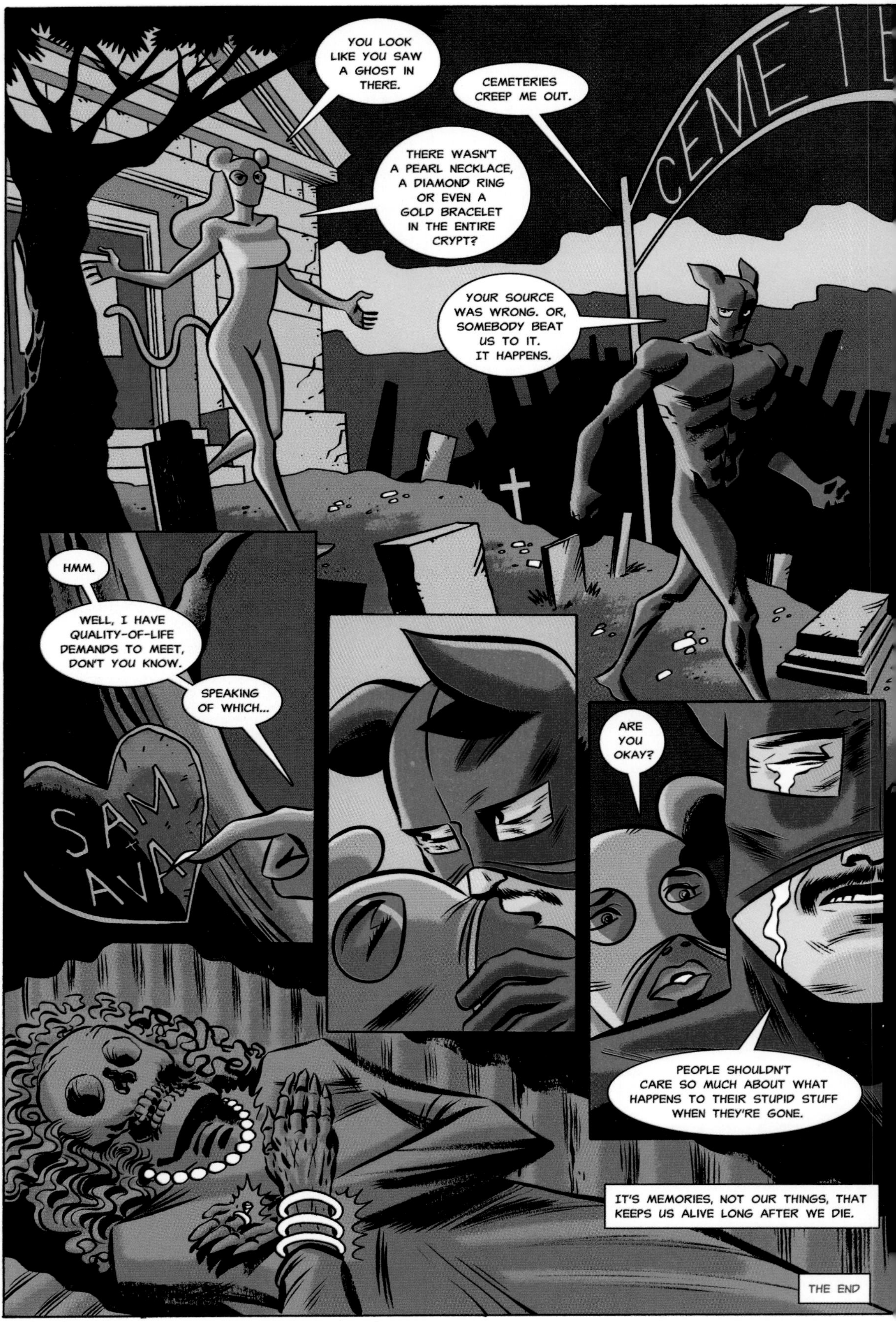
CEME TE
YOU LOOK LIKE YOU SAW A GHOST IN THERE.
CEMETERIES CREEP ME OUT.
THERE WASN'T A PEARL NECKLACE, A DIAMOND RING OR EVEN A GOLD BRACELET IN THE ENTIRE CRYPT?
YOUR SOURCE WAS WRONG. OR, SOMEBODY BEAT US TO IT. IT HAPPENS.
HMM.
WELL, I HAVE QUALITY-OF-LIFE DEMANDS TO MEET, DON'T YOU KNOW.
SPEAKING OF WHICH...
SAM + AVA
ARE YOU OKAY?
PEOPLE SHOULDN'T CARE SO MUCH ABOUT WHAT HAPPENS TO THEIR STUPID STUFF WHEN THEY'RE GONE.
IT'S MEMORIES, NOT OUR THINGS, THAT KEEPS US ALIVE LONG AFTER WE DIE.
THE END

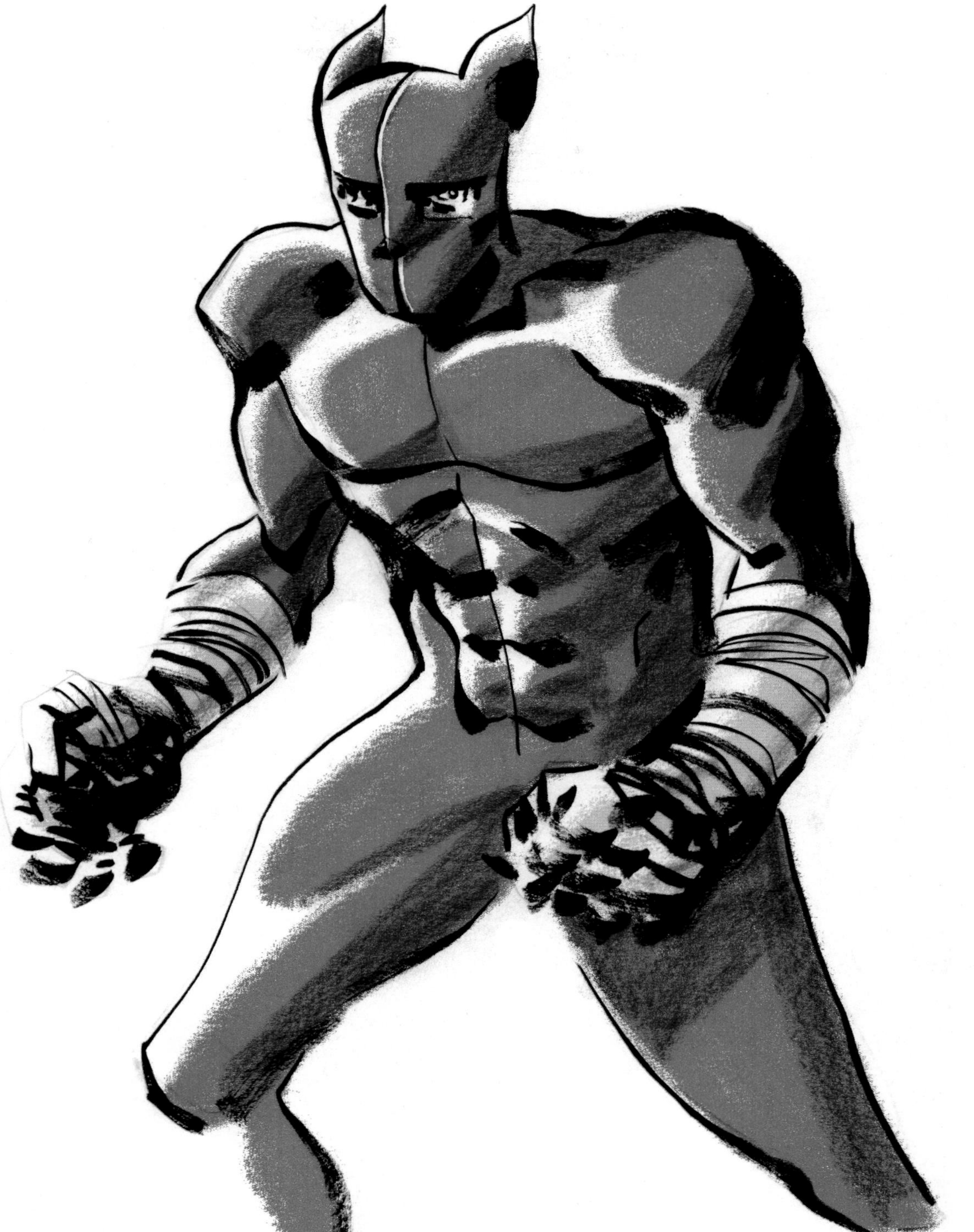

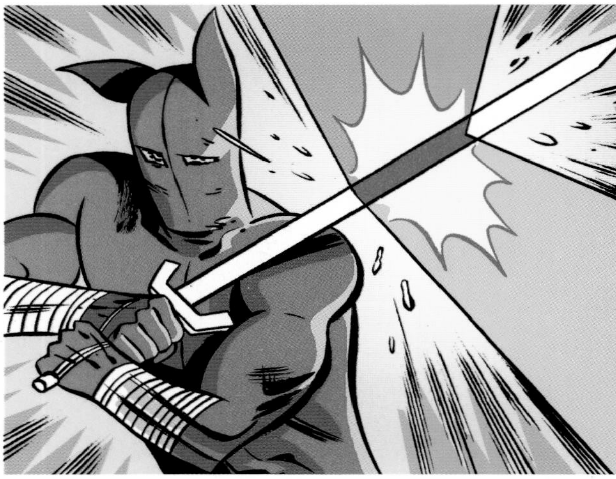

THE NEW BROOKLYN UNIVERSE CONTINUES WHEN THE RED HOOK'S DEAD GIRLFRIEND IS RESURRECTED INTO WAR CRY, A HUMAN OF MASS DESTRUCTION HOSTED BY A TEENAGE BOY NAMED RAJAK ALLAH. WHEN A DEMIGOD FROM THEIR PAST COMES TO HAUNT THEM TO DEATH, THEY MUST RESOLVE THEIR LOST LOVE.

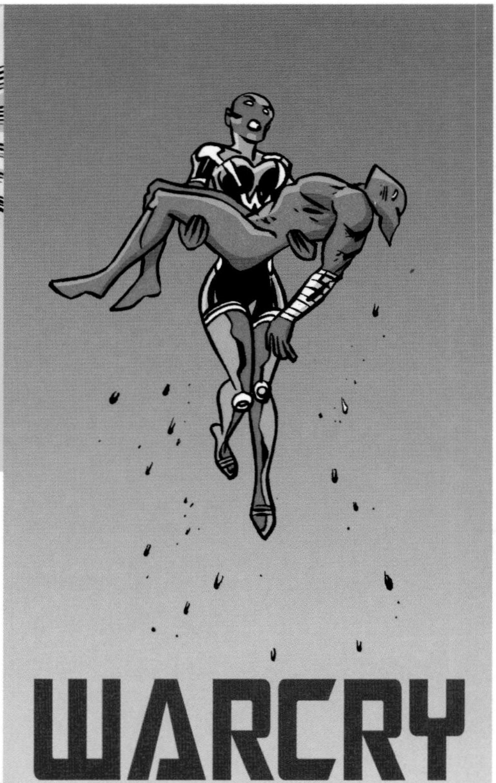
WARCRY

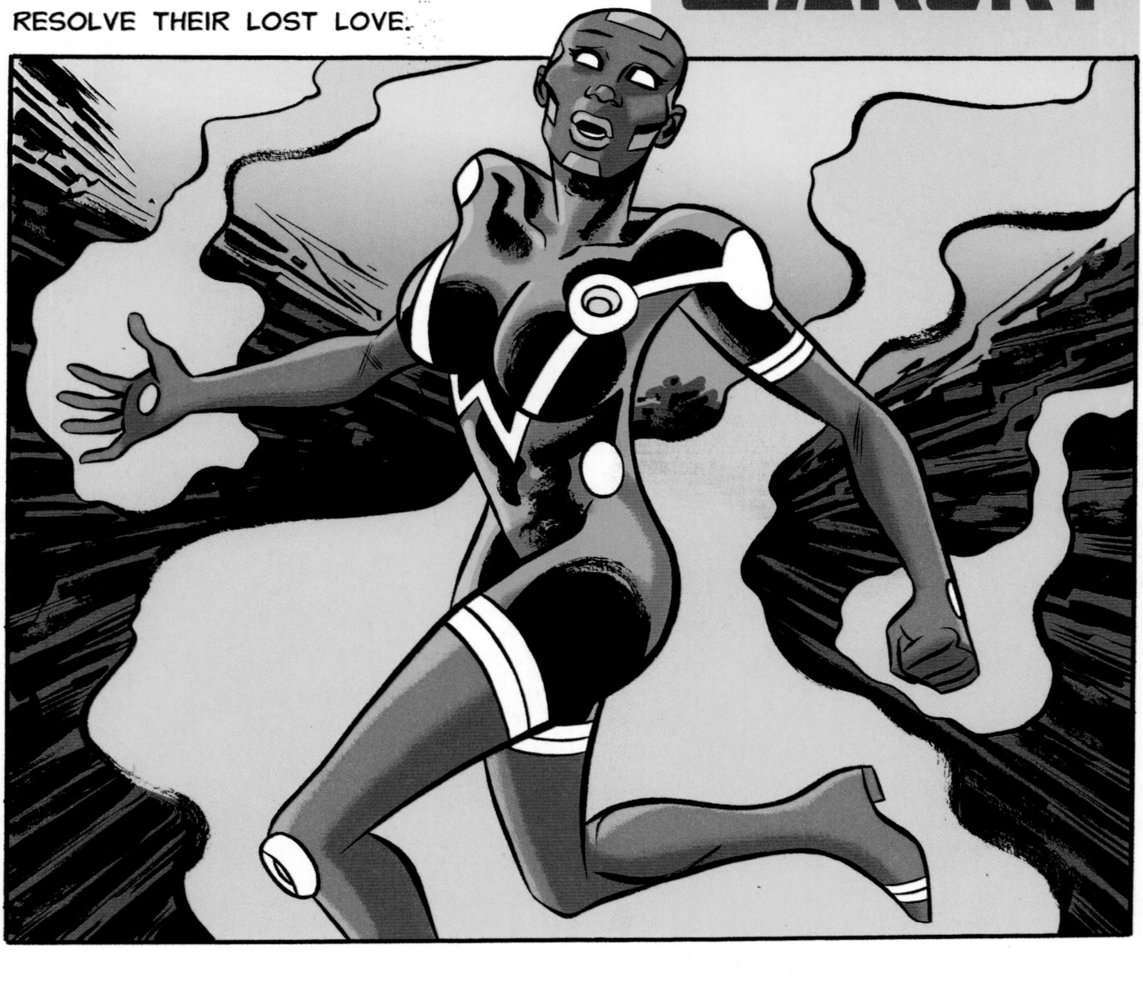